Praise for

Janice Kaplan and Lynn Schnurnberger

MINE ARE SPECTACULAR!

"A novel so delicious readers might feel compelled to diet after devouring it . . . a hilarious hit."　　—*People* (four-star review)

"[The authors] are deservedly renowned for their ability to document the social habits and favorite trends of wealthy women."
　　　　　　　　　　　　　　　　　　　　—*Chicago Sun-Times*

"Makes Wisteria Lane look like Sesame Street."　—*New Jersey Life*

THE BOTOX DIARIES

"This summer's must-have beach read!"　　　　—ABC's *The View*

"[A] midlife-crisis bonbon, which should be sold with fuzzy slippers and a tube of cucumber eye gel."
　　　　　　　　　　　　　　　　—*The New York Times Book Review*

"Fast-paced and with zingers on every page."
　　　　　　　　　　　　　　　　　　　—*The Washington Post*

"A sexy . . . . ly back to
the basi . . . . —*Elle*

Also by Janice Kaplan and Lynn Shnurnberger

MINE ARE SPECTACULAR!
THE BOTOX DIARIES

THE
MEN
I DIDN'T
MARRY

THE
MEN
I DIDN'T
MARRY

A Novel

Janice Kaplan
&
Lynn Schnurnberger

 BALLANTINE BOOKS · NEW YORK

2007 Ballantine Books Trade Paperback Edition

Copyright © 2006 by Janice Kaplan & Lynn Schnurnberger

Published in the United States by Ballantine Books, an imprint of The Random House Publishing Group, a division of Random House, Inc., New York.

BALLANTINE and colophon are registered trademarks of Random House, Inc.

Originally published in hardcover in the United States by Ballantine Books, an imprint of The Random House Publishing Group, a division of Random House, Inc., in 2006.

Library of Congress Cataloging-in-Publication Data

Kaplan, Janice.
The men I didn't marry : a novel / Janice Kaplan & Lynn Schnurnberger.—1st ed.
p. cm.
ISBN 978-0-345-49118-3
1. Divorced mothers—Fiction. 2. Middle-aged women—Fiction. 3. Upper class—Fiction. 4. New York (N.Y.)—Fiction. 5. Suburban life—Fiction. I. Schnurnberger, Lynn Edelman. II. Title.
PS3561.A5593M46 2006
813'.54—dc22
2005057089

Printed in the United States of America

www.ballantinebooks.com

2 4 6 8 9 7 5 3

To the man I married, Ron, my one and only, with love.
—Janice

With love to my mom, Marian Rosenthal Edelman, and my husband,
Martin.
—Lynn

ACKNOWLEDGMENTS

Our warmest thanks to three wonderful people whose talent, commitment, and enthusiasm keep us on track: Remarkable agent Jane Gelfman, savvy editor Allison Dickens, and the indomitable Kim Hovey, Ballantine's associate publisher and director of marketing. We're also grateful to Gina Centrello for her early and continued support of our books. Our thanks also to Sally Willcox and the team at CAA, and to our hardworking international agents who've made sure our books are read everywhere from Madrid to Moscow. Most of all, to our husbands, children, family, and friends, endless gratitude for your loyalty, love, and good humor.

THE
MEN
I DIDN'T
MARRY

Chapter ONE

MY HUSBAND DOESN'T EVEN WAIT until we're in the car to drop his bombshell.

We've just brought our daughter—the brilliant, beautiful, and beloved Emily—to her first day at Yale. I've met her roommate, unpacked her duffels, and made the bed with the soft sheets we got during our four-hour precollege shopping marathon at Bed Bath & Beyond. Okay, I didn't really use the sheets Emily and I bought together. I picked up a better set at the exclusive Frette store on Madison Avenue to surprise her. The girl got into Yale, darn it; she shouldn't sleep on anything less than 600-count sateen.

Bill, the ever-doting father, jokes around with Emily while he sets up her computer and assembles a bookshelf next to her desk. As long as we're both puttering at our little tasks, we can put off the emotional breakdown, sure to come the second we leave Emily behind and head back to our now very quiet house. Emily kisses her dad to thank him for his help, gives me a big hug, and then promises us she'll be okay. Our cue to leave. With less surety, I say we'll be okay, too. Now that our second child has officially become a college student, just like her big brother, Adam, our empty nest couldn't get any emptier.

On the way out of the dorm, we pass the freshman counselor's

"Welcome" table, stacked high with campus maps, orientation bulletins, and two bowls, one filled with Tootsie Roll pops and the other with condoms. Bad idea to offer all that candy—too easy to gain the freshman fifteen. And, oh my god, that other bowl, brimming with ribbed, rainbow-colored, and glow-in-the-dark protection. Should I warn Emily to steer clear of any boy who reaches for the Star Wars condoms?

Bill and I step outside and I grab onto his arm and take a deep breath. I've been dreading this day since the first morning I left Emily off at preschool, but we seem to have made it through.

"I think we did fine, honey," I say, proud that I haven't cried once.

"We sure did. We raised a great kid," he says, distractedly patting my hand.

He's right. Both of us were young when we started our family, but we raised two terrific kids and had fun being parents. But now's the time for Bill and me to have new adventures together. I've planned a wine-tasting weekend, a romantic getaway to a four-star Vermont inn, and I've even snagged season tickets to the Knicks. Knowing this day would come, I'd been on the waiting list to get them for six years.

I look over at my successful stockbroker husband. He's always been handsome, but I realize he's in better shape than ever. The love handles are gone, and so are the muffin tops—the new bakery euphemism for that extra roll of flesh that hangs over the elastic band of your briefs. His abs could make the cover of *Men's Health*—well, an inside page, anyway. And wait a minute, what happened to the wisps of gray hair that were appearing at his temples? I reach over, gently rub his now very dark brown sideburns and giggle to myself. I can't really imagine Bill using Grecian Formula, but he's done something. Maybe after all these years, my honey does have a secret or two.

"So, darling, our first night, just us," I say squeezing his strong arm even tighter. "What's your pleasure? The little Ethiopian restaurant in New Haven, or should we get home right away and I'll slip into something comfortable?" I lean over to kiss his cheek, but Bill has picked up his pace, and I just miss.

"Hallie, I have something to tell you," Bill says. He keeps walking, looking straight ahead.

Uh-oh. Bad opening line. I stumble, my heel catching on the pavement. "I have something to tell you" never comes before "I love you passionately," or even, "I've always liked your pot roast." No, "I've something to tell you" usually precedes bad news like, "The cat died," or "The house just burned down." Or in this case?

"I'm leaving," Bill says without breaking stride.

He's what? I mull the words in my head for a moment. Surely if "leaving" meant leaving for good, my husband, my mate, my partner of two decades, the man who made love to me just three nights ago—or was it four?—would have sat me down before breaking the news. My Bill, my sweet Bill, would even have bought me a cup of coffee first.

Unless he's no longer my sweet Bill.

Leaving.

Time stops and I stand frozen. For a moment, the whole world goes silent and the only sound I hear is a bird off in the distance, with a persistent, mournful call: *You'll be alone you'll be alone you'll be alone.*

But I can't even think about that possibility. Anyway, what does a bird know? I pull my attention back and try to misunderstand Bill's comment the best I can. "Fine, we'll leave New Haven and go home for dinner," I say. Then, prattling on, I add, "I can defrost some lasagna or whip up an omelet. I have some brie. You like a brie omelet, don't you, honey?"

Bill finally stops walking and turns toward me. "What I mean is I'm leaving you." He pauses and looks at me with what I'm sure he thinks is a kind smile. "We've had a good run. A darn good twenty-one years together in a happy marriage. You're a great gal, Hallie. I have no complaints. But it's time for my second act."

What is he talking about? His second act? Even Mike Nichols couldn't get away with that. This sounds like a speech he's been practicing in front of the mirror for days. But the show's not over. It can't be. *He's not leaving.* I take a deep breath. I bet I even know what's going on. Just like me, Bill's upset about Emily's going off to college and he doesn't know how to react. In fact, he's a guy. He doesn't even know that he is reacting. It's my job to reassure him.

"Listen, honey, we're going to be okay," I say gently. "I love you. You love me. I got season tickets to the Knicks—just like you always wanted. We don't need the kids at home to keep us together."

He doesn't reply, so to fill in the space, I keep talking. "I'm thinking of taking a pottery class."

Bill looks at me oddly for a moment, and then he nods. "That's great, Hallie. I'm glad you've got plans. I've made some plans, too."

We get to the car and I slide into my usual seat on the passenger's side. I start to put in the CD of the St. Lawrence Quartet playing Hayden that's always been one of Bill's favorites, but he takes it out immediately and replaces Hayden with something loud and blaring.

"What the heck is that?" I ask.

"Black Eyed Peas," he says, proudly. "My new favorite. They're very hot, way up on the charts."

I turn down the volume, but my head continues pounding. Who's this rap-music-listening Grecian Formula–using man sitting next to me? All these years, I thought I knew every detail about my husband but something changed while I was busy working, raising the kids, and buying him shirts at Brooks Brothers. I suddenly feel like a fool. What else have I missed?

The next hour and a half passes in a haze as we speed down the narrow Merritt Parkway toward the suburbs of New York. Given all the twisty turns, I don't know how anybody survives on this road and, right now, I'm not sure I want to. With the kids gone and Bill leaving, what's left? I stare out the window, seeing only my dismal future, and barely notice that we've missed the exit for our small town, Chaddick, until we pass over the bridge into Manhattan.

"Where are we going?" I ask.

Bill doesn't answer, but his mouth is set and his brow is clenched so tightly that his two eyebrows join in a solid line. One thing I do still know about my husband—the caterpillar brow means something's up. Moments later Bill pulls over in front of a brownstone on a residential block in the West Nineties and stops the car, double-parked. He leans over and gives me a nervous peck on the cheek, then hands me the car keys.

"You know how to get home, sweetheart," he says, feigning nonchalance. And as if nothing has changed, he adds, "Drive carefully. It looked like there was a backup north on the Henry Hudson, so you might want to take Riverside Drive."

My mouth opens but nothing comes out. "You're not coming home?" I finally manage to sputter. "Where are we?"

"My new apartment," Bill says, gesturing toward the limestone stoop. Anxious to make a getaway, he gets out of the car and retrieves a duffel bag I hadn't noticed from the backseat.

"You have an apartment?" I ask, dumbfounded.

"Actually, it's not just mine" he says. He bolts up the steps to his new front door, and when he gets there, he turns and adds, "It's Ashlee's apartment. Ashlee, with two E's."

Ashlee. Ashlee. Ashlee. Ashlee. Ashleeeee. Say it enough times while you're lying under a fluffy duvet and it starts to sound like a primal scream. And screaming is therapeutic. As is banging your head against the wall, gouging your betraying husband's face out of every photo in the house, eating twelve superlarge packages of Oreos—the double stuff kind—in a record two days (without any milk), and reading the entire stack of *U.S. News & World Report* magazines that had been gathering dust in the basement. I might as well live in the past since I have no future. I go through every issue from 1989 to 1994 cover-to-cover and read in a 1990 copy that Vanilla Ice's album is selling like crazy and that he'll last forever. Hah! Where's Vanilla Ice now? His career melted faster than sorbet in the summertime. Like me, he's been replaced.

I haven't watched daytime television since I was home on maternity leave with Emily, but now QVC is my constant companion. It's been a comfort these last four days to know I can order an Italian domed Byzantine necklace or a marquise tanzanite pinwheel brooch any time of the day or night. And I've ordered both—and more. The UPS guy has made so many deliveries he must figure I'm a compulsively early

Christmas shopper. On the other hand, he probably wonders why I haven't bothered to bring any of my bounty inside. Unfortunately that would require my actually getting out of bed and going down the stairs, and right now I'm reserving all my energy for essentials—like replenishing my supply of Oreos.

I made Bill promise that he wouldn't tell Adam and Emily what's happened. I explained I didn't want to ruin the start of their school year, but the truth is I just don't want to talk about it. I figure it's like the tree falling in the forest. If a man leaves his wife and nobody knows, has he really left? But I should have realized that my husband's not that good at keeping promises. Adam has taken to calling twice a day from school and asking solicitously, "How are you, mom?" From the grave tone of Adam's voice, I'm worried that Bill has told him something even more tragic than our news—like maybe, on top of everything else, I have dengue fever.

Whatever's wrong with me, I've called in sick to my office for the first time in my fifteen years as a lawyer for Rosen, O'Grady, and Riccardi—New York's first and probably still only Jewish-Irish-Italian law firm. It's also the only law firm that could hire me, a WASP, on the basis of affirmative action. We specialize in antidiscrimination cases and, given the company dinners of kugel, corned beef and cabbage, and cannoli, we often specialize in indigestion. Still, I like the firm and they like me. I've always been able to keep my workweek down to four days, and the job comes with a good pension plan and a regular supply of Tums.

It's been years since I've had a whole day to fill without work and kids, never mind this many days, but trying to do anything useful right now would be impossible. I'm furious at Bill, and I'm even more furious at myself. How could he do this to me? How could I let him do this to me? You don't just walk out on someone after two kids and twenty-one years and say *Adios*, have a good life. Who the hell does he think he is, leaving without even a single discussion? For chrissakes, when we were renovating the kitchen, we spent six weeks talking about which color tile to pick. He wanted dark green and I wanted white and we settled on a sea foam with cream trim. That's called compromise, Bill, and it's what you do in marriage. The fucker. I don't know if I want to get him back, or just get him.

I sink back into the pillows, exhausted from playing the same rant over and over in my head. I need to do something else—anything. I stretch my hand in front of my face. A little bit of light is coming in through the closed blinds, just enough so I can make a shadow animal on the wall. Look, it's a bunny.

The ringing phone jars me back to reality, the one place I don't want to be. I've barely spoken to anyone in a week, except for the kids and my best friend Bellini. But from the caller ID, I see it's the firm's senior partner, Arthur Rosen—a man who's always been a fair boss. I roll over to answer it and cradle the receiver in the crook of my neck.

Arthur makes small talk for a couple of minutes, then says, "I hate to bother you when you're sick, Hallie, but I had a question on the Tyler case."

Since we're going to talk business, I reluctantly reach under the blankets for the remote so I can turn down the volume on Victoria Principal's pitch for her line of skin-care products. Though, as soon as I get off the call, I'm going to order some of her Prime Secret Reclaim Eye-Mazing Refirming Eye Cream. Never mind whether the stuff works, I just want to see how they fit all those words on a tiny two-ounce tube.

Focus. Focus. Focus. I listen to what Arthur has to say about the case. Our client Charles Tyler is being sued for sexual harassment—with an unusual twist. The defendant claims Mr. Tyler passed her over for a promotion and gave it to another woman in the office—who he was sleeping with. In other words, she's suing him for screwing someone else. I try to make an intelligent comment or two, but mostly I try not to burst into uncontrollable sobs and spill every detail of my now-horrible life to Arthur. But he clearly picks up that something's wrong.

"So Hallie," he says hesitantly, "I don't mean to pry, but you've been out for almost a week. Should I be worried about you?"

Worried about me? Why would anyone worry about me? I've lost my husband to someone named Ashlee, I've been lying here so long I'm probably getting bedsores, and my only source of nutrition comes from Nabisco.

But I'm still not ready to talk about it, and certainly not to my boss, a man so professional that I didn't know he'd become a father until I was invited to his son's third birthday party.

"No, Arthur, I just had . . ." What did I have? I don't like to lie, so I'll tell some version of the truth. "I just had something removed." And I did. I just don't mention it was my husband.

"A little minor surgery?" he asks.

"Yup, that was it." Minor surgery. Bill just cut out my heart.

We hang up and I collect my strength to start on my next activity of the day. I thought I wanted to cry again, but my tear ducts seem to have dried up. Instead, I wrap my arms around my knees and curl into a fetal position. "Ashlee, Ashlee, Ashlee," I moan, rocking back and forth. "ASHLEEEE," I wail with more emotion than Marlon Brando ever mustered for "STELLAAA."

Ashlee. Ashlee, with her two fucking Es. How old could someone named Ashlee be, anyway? I'm betting she's twentysomething and blonde, an ovo-lactarian massage therapist. In the one call I was willing to take from Bill, he told me that this isn't about me—it's about living life to the fullest and following his heart. Give me a break. It's not his heart he's following to goddamn 93rd Street. The man isn't even having an original midlife crisis. No man ever does. To which the makers of Porsche say Thank God.

Still I think I'm having a very original response. I haven't eaten a single pint of Ben & Jerry's or watched even one Meg Ryan movie. Instead, I roll onto my back again and this time stretch out both arms into the spot of light. I'm discovering new talents. Now the shadow bunny is jumping over a fence.

Emily snaps me out of it.

"Mom, I just called your office and they said you're still out," she says when she calls the next morning. "What's going on?"

I take a deep breath. "Emily, I have something to tell you." That phrase again. Is she old enough to know that it means bad news?

Apparently she's old enough to know a lot more than that because

Emily quickly says, "You don't have to tell me anything. I know Daddy left you. Adam told me. Daddy told him. And told him not to tell, but he told."

Hmm. So Emily not only knows the situation, I think she even got all the tenses right. But then it occurs to me to wonder why she doesn't sound upset. I'd expect Emily at least to shed a tear about our wonderful little family breaking apart.

But before I can ask her how she's really feeling about all this, Emily charges on. "I'm still not clear on why you're lying around moping. Dad's just a guy. Your life's not over."

"Emily, are you nuts? This is your father. What are you saying?"

"I'm saying exactly what you said when Paco dumped me. Life goes on. A lot of fish in the sea."

Sure, but I'm not such great bait anymore. And that's beside the point. Comparing Bill to Paco, that tattooed, earring-wearing, no-good creep who dumped Emily a week before the junior prom and never should have been allowed within fifty feet of my perfect, precious daughter anyway?

"I know what you're thinking," says Emily, who seems to know everything—unlike most teenagers who only think they do. "Paco was a three-week boyfriend and you've been married forever. It sucks. I agree. But you've always been my role model, Mom. You make things happen. You can get on with your life without Bill."

"Bill?" I ask quizzically, wondering when her darling daddy became "Bill."

"I think it'll be helpful if we both think of him as just another guy," says Emily efficiently. "Perhaps it would be even better if we called him William. More detached."

I have a feeling Emily signed up for that post-modern feminism class after all. But I have to admit she makes a lot of sense. William. I roll the name around on my tongue. William. William and Ashlee. ASHLEEEEE. Emily's right, this has to stop.

I'm admiring my daughter's insight and maturity when I suddenly hear muffled sobs.

"Hang on a sec, Mom," she says, her voice cracking.

"Em, are you okay?" I ask.

All I hear is the loud honking of Emily blowing her nose, and I know she's in tears. So that's it. She does realize the gravity of the situation and even though she's trying to be tough, she's hurting. I wish I could throw my arms around her and make her feel better. A hug would make me feel better, too.

"Sorry, Mom," Emily says shakily when she gets back on the phone. "I want to be an adult about you and daddy, but I hate what's happening. And I don't get it. You two never even fight."

"Honey, you're right. Who knows why this happened? But don't for one minute think you have to act like an adult. Even the grown-ups aren't acting like adults."

"Then who's coming up for Parents' Day?" Emily asks in a small voice. She's worried about what this will do to her life and I don't blame her.

"You'll always have two parents who love you. We'll both always be there for you," I say, giving the by-the-book answer. Then drifting from the page, I add, "Even though your father's acting like an asshole."

Emily laughs. "You're not supposed to say that to me," she says, recovering a little of her previous bravado. "But it's okay. I know how miserable you must be feeling."

"It hasn't been so bad. My appendectomy two years ago was more painful." Though at least they gave me Vicodin for the surgery.

"Good for you, Mom," says Emily, a little too upbeat herself. In fact, she sounds suspiciously like the cheerleaders she scorned in high school. "And you know what you should do? What will really make you feel better?"

"What?"

"Take a hike."

"A hike?"

"Get out of bed. Get your blood moving. You're not a wimp. You are woman," says Emily.

* * *

Yes, I am woman. A woman all by herself. A woman whose husband has just left her. A woman who can't find her goddamn Timberlands. I rummage through the closet a second time. Wait a minute. I'm a woman who doesn't even have goddamn Timberlands. Maybe that's why Bill left me. I burst into tears again.

But, no, I can make do. That's what my life is about now—making do. I have running shoes, tennis sneakers, cross-trainers, boots, slippers, slip-ons, high-heeled pumps for the office, low-heeled pumps for court, and stilettos that I wore exactly twice. I should be able to get up a hill in one of these.

I lace on my sturdiest pair of Nikes and throw some snacks and water bottles into a backpack, grateful to have a plan. But where am I going? Ah, yes—a metaphor for my life. I can go anywhere I want. I just don't know where that is or how to get there.

"You're out of bed!" says a voice behind me.

I yelp in surprise and spin around, my hand over my chest. Then I see my best friend, Bellini Baxter, standing in my bedroom doorway.

"You almost gave me a heart attack," I say.

"That's progress," says Bellini. "Heart attack's better than heartache."

"It is?"

She plops down on my bed and nods definitively. "For heartache, you get only me in your bedroom. Heart attack, all those cute paramedics come in, strip you down, and massage your chest." She reaches for the phone. "Want me to call them?"

I shake my head and laugh. That's Bellini. Always thinking. She's the only friend I've told about Bill—because, unlike my sanctimonious married pals, she's single and has a profound understanding of men. From her vast experience, she's convinced that they're untrustworthy, unreliable, devious, and deviant. But the only game in town.

"I brought you something to make you feel better," says Bellini, opening a shopping bag she's dragged in from the Bendel's store on Fifth Avenue, where she's the head accessories buyer.

I met Bellini when she first came to New York from Ohio, fresh from being a salesgirl at the Cincinnati Kmart, and landed a job as a temp in our law office. Back then, she was still Mary Jane Baxter, but determined to give up her small-town ways and seem more sophisticated, she changed her name. Going for a *Sex and the City* vibe, she thought about calling herself "Cosmopolitan," after the show's chic cocktail. But she worried that's what mothers everywhere would be christening their babies, so she went for her own favorite drink, Bellini—the nouveau mix of pureed peach and sparkling wine. How the world changes. It used to be that parents named their children after the month they were conceived—April or May. Then it was *where* they were conceived—hello, Paris Hilton. Now it's what they were drinking that fateful night in bed.

In the office, answering phones and filing weren't Bellini's strengths, but she showed an early flair for accessories. She supplied our office with colorful paper clips, and we were the first law office in Manhattan to replace our black Swingline staplers with pastel rubber designs from the Museum of Modern Art. When she quit to take the coveted Bendel's job, we remained good friends, and the office thankfully abandoned the Bellini-selected pale purple legal pads and reverted to standard yellow.

"What have you got in there?" I ask.

"A Judith Lieber minaudière to make you feel better," she says proudly, pulling out a glittery jewel-encrusted pocketbook in the shape of a frog. "Anybody can comfort you with apple pie or Valium."

I take it from her, pleased. "This is really for me?"

"Well, it's on loan," she says. "Nine thousand dollars retail. But keep it as long as you want. It's insured."

"Last time you lent me an evening purse I wore it to go to a formal dinner dance at the Plaza with Bill," I say, tears springing to my eyes.

She snatches back the gift. "Whoops, my mistake. Sorry, sweetie. I came over to cheer you up, not make you think about the creep." She rifles through a second bag. "Here. Try these. Chanel sunglasses. I love the shape and Coco's an inspiration to single women everywhere. Her lover dumped her—and she went on to create her zillion-dollar company."

I slip on the oversize tortoiseshell frames.

"Perfect," I say. "I don't know if they'll help me build an empire, but at least they'll hide my puffy eyes."

Bellini comes over and puts her arms around me. "No more crying," she says, taking a wisp of my hair and tucking it behind my ear. "You're perfect. This isn't your fault."

"Of course it's my fault," I say. "I've been replaying every second of our marriage again and again and again. Did I pay too much attention to Bill—or not enough? Did I plan too many evenings out, or too many at home? Did he hate my new perfume?"

"None of the above," says Bellini sympathetically. "You're a great wife."

"Then why did Bill turn out to be such a rat?"

"Not a rat, a vole. And, unfortunately, the wrong kind of vole," Bellini says firmly. "I read about it in *The New York Times*. Prairie voles are dependable mates. But if researchers tinker with just one gene, they become promiscuous—like meadow voles."

"So I got the guy whose genes gave him blue eyes and an eye for Ashlee?"

"Something like that. This is where we should be spending our research dollars. If scientists can genetically engineer voles and fruit flies, how hard could it be to change a man?"

"Very," I say dispiritedly.

Bellini sighs. "You're right. I guess all you can do now is go out and look for a prairie vole." Then she gives me a once-over, taking in my Nikes and shorts and thrown-together hiking gear. "From the looks of it, that's what you were planning before I even came in."

"A hike," I tell her. "Emily thought it would be a good idea. Get my blood pumping and get me out of the house."

"Smart girl that Emily. I came over to drag you out of the house, too." Then she pauses and grits her teeth. "You know I'd do anything for you. Anything. Do you want me to come with you on the hike?"

I'm genuinely touched. Coming from Bellini, an offer to go into the great outdoors for anything but a clambake in the Hamptons is friendship beyond the call.

"Your Manolos won't make it up the mountain. But I love you for asking. And for coming over." I give her a kiss on the cheek, and then it occurs to me. "By the way, how did you get inside the house?"

Bellini grins. "You'd already told me not to come over and I knew you'd disconnected the bell. But I had to make sure you were okay, so I found your key inside the second black umbrella hanging from the metal coatrack on the left side of the mudroom." She winks at me. "Easy enough. That's where everybody hides one."

Encouraged by Bellini's visit, I realize that I do know where I'm going after all. At least for this afternoon. I remember that Bill used to take the kids on day hikes, and the name of their favorite spot pops into my head. I type it into the GPS in my car. An hour later, I'm at the appealing little town of Cold Spring, which is packed with cute stores selling everything from silly knickknacks to serious antiques. I think about stopping to see if the jewelry's any better than on QVC. But, no, Emily won't count shopping as an aerobic activity. I drive on to the base of Taurus, just a couple of miles outside of town. I have a mountain to climb.

I get out of the car, do a few quick stretches, and put on my new Chanel sunglasses. I'm so chic that I might actually attract a vole out here in the wilderness. Prairie or meadow? I'd be afraid to take a new one home before I did a DNA test.

The sky is blue and through the cover of trees, the sun dapples the trail in front of me. It's incredibly peaceful. Nobody's around except me and two birds fluttering by, which are probably sparrows. Hawks? For all I know, they're penguins. Next time I sign up for something, it'll be the Audubon Society instead of the Duane Reade Rewards Program.

The hill is a little steep, but I'm not even panting. I'm in better shape than I think. I take a deep breath of the pine-scented air, which smells better than the sixty-dollar Diptyque candles I usually place around the living room. I think I'm getting the hang of this hiking thing. It's not so hard. In fact, those much-heralded exercise-induced endorphins must be coursing through my body, since I'm feeling almost heady. I take a swig from my water bottle, pick up my pace, and stride more determinedly. Hey, maybe I should be an Outward Bound leader. That could be the way I start my new husband-free life—as a strong, independent, mountain-climbing woman. Kilimanjaro, here I come. Everest is too clichéd.

My ascent is steady and, in just a few minutes, I seem to be at the top. I should have brought a flag to plant. Smugly I take in the panoramic view of craggy rock cliffs and verdant mountains. This wide field must be where I get to sit and eat my lunch. But I'm confused. A seven-minute climb is what Bill and the kids bragged about? I start to take off my backpack to lie in the sun when a few feet away from me, I notice a wooden sign that says "Trailhead to Taurus"—and has an arrow pointing to a serious path on a steeper hill. So this little climb was only the prehike hike. How Zen. Just when you think you've arrived, you realize you've only made it to the starting point.

I retie my sneakers, adjust the straps on my backpack and set out full of energy and determination. I quickly realize that I'm supposed to follow yellow markers on the trees. For the first few minutes of my trek, the path is well-worn, and even though the blazes on the trees are farther apart than I'd like, I'm not worried. But as I get deeper into the woods, the trail becomes more overgrown, and the dense canopy of autumn leaves obscures whatever yellow signposts might be ahead. I stop for a minute and look around, trying to get my bearings. Aha. There's a yellow swatch now. Heading off again, I plunge through some prickly thick vegetation and just barely manage to make my way through a mass of brambles. Am I the only person who's ever gotten this far? I struggle on for fifty yards and when I finally look up again, the yellow marker has disappeared and I'm standing under an oak tree whose leaves have just started to change. To yellow, goddamn it.

I'm not going to panic. I just have to get back on the trail. But the more I try, the farther away from it I seem to wander. Still, this isn't exactly the Lewis and Clark expedition. I dig into the pocket of my jeans and pull out my cell phone to call 911. I don't know how to pinpoint where I am, but surely the rescue squad will be able to find me. I flip open my high-tech, Internet-connecting, game-playing, video-streaming, picture-snapping phone, and confront a very low-tech message: NO SERVICE. Helpfully, however, the camera still seems to be working. At least I can photograph my last hour alive on earth.

No, I have to be realistic. I have water with me, plus two granola bars and a cheese sandwich. And given the number of Oreos I've eaten lately, I could live off my body fat for the next four months. Cheered that my chubby thighs could be lifesavers, I keep walking, and twenty minutes later I'm at another tree whose leaves are changing to yellow—though, for all I know, it's the same tree and I've just walked in a circle. If I ever get out of here, I'm moving to Manhattan. At least the whole place is on a grid. Nobody ever got lost walking from 62nd Street to 66th.

I'm getting tired and bend down to get myself a walking stick. I reach for a long branch lying on a pile of leaves and plant it firmly in front of me. Just the right height. This will help. But as I keep walking, my hand starts to feely itchy, and I look down to see that I have measles. I look closer. Shit! Even measles would be better than what's really on my arm—bright red creepy-crawly ants. They're feasting on my flesh and moving at warp speed up my elbow.

I jerk back, giving a loud yelp and throwing the stick over my shoulder. Suddenly, I'm under attack from a new, bigger, more aggressive enemy. The stick has apparently hit a hornet's nest and the hive's inhabitants are on the warpath. As they attack my face, I scream at the top of my lungs, but the angry hornets don't care. I stamp my feet and spin around, trying to swat them away, but they get madder and sting more vehemently.

"Help! Help!" I scream. I charge away, running blindly through the woods until my foot catches on a rock and I go sprawling, facedown, into a trickling stream. I lie there for a moment, trying to catch my breath. This is the part in the movie where Sam Shepard is supposed to swagger along and rescue me. I lift my head, but Sam must have missed his cue. At least the hornets are gone and the cool silty water feels soothing against my burning stings. Really good. I pat some of the muddy muck against the swollen bites on my face and then, just for good measure, I slather some on my neck and arms. If only I had a jar I'd take the stuff home and save the thirty-seven bucks I usually spend on that celebrated Mud Mask from the Dead Sea. It's probably the same basic formula, anyway. All I'd have to do is add some kosher salt.

I feel around for my foot, which apparently is still attached to my body. But my ankle is swelling. I don't think I broke it, but it's certainly sprained. Between my face and my foot, I'm practically a one-woman medical experiment. Maybe the Mayo Clinic is researching it right now: "Hornet Bites or Clumsy Fall—Which Causes More Extreme Swelling?" But I need to look on the bright side. With all my other body parts blown out of proportion, at least my waist will look thin.

I'm glad Emily can't see me right now. But I do hope she gets to see me again. I have to get myself out of here. I run my fingers through the stream, and then it occurs to me: I may not be Nature Girl, but a stream always runs downhill—and downhill should lead me toward the base of the mountain and my blessed car. Half-walking, half-crawling, I start to follow the stream. I'm achy, I'm miserable, but I don't have a lot of choice. Maybe singing camp songs will help. I warble "Frère Jacques" in both French and English, but have a little trouble making the rounds sound right all by myself. I kick into "Ninety-Nine Bottles of Beer on the Wall," and for the first time ever, I actually make it all the way down to two.

But I don't get to one because suddenly I see the road.

I'm so happy, I could jump up and down. Actually, I couldn't. Given my ankle, I'll have to settle for hobbling to my car.

Out of the woods at last—quite literally—I look up and down the highway for the small parking area where I left my Saab. I sigh. No Saab. But there is a sign for Cold Spring, and even with my bad sense of direction, I realize I didn't come out where I started and I'm at least a mile away from where I left the car. And that does it. After all this bravery, bravado, heroism, and stoicism, I give up. I'm tired of being an independent woman. It's time to plunk down and cry.

And I do. Right there on the side of the road. I just put my head in my hands and let go with long, loud, wailing sobs.

"Are you okay, miss?"

I look up, startled, and see that a green Jeep Cherokee has pulled up next to me and that a good-looking man is leaning out of the window. I try to wipe away my tears, but that just makes more of a muddy mess.

"I had a little trouble in the woods," I say, in case it's not obvious.

"Let me guess. You got on the wrong trail. Your car's in the lot by the park entrance. Happens to everybody," he says kindly. "Can I give you a lift?"

Cars are whizzing past, and I realize it's not safe to be sitting where I am. On the other hand, given my luck today, what are the chances that this good Samaritan is really a serial killer? Ninety percent? Ninety-five percent? At least that gives me a five percent chance of getting home safely, which is better odds than I had an hour ago.

"Thanks," I say, limping over to the passenger door. As I start to get in, he looks a little more closely and realizes how mucky and grubby I am.

"Hang on a sec," he says, reaching into the back and grabbing a towel. He lays it over my seat, as if he's protecting the worn leather from either a grimy six-year-old or a peeing puppy. But by now nothing can embarrass me.

"I live up the road," he says, trying to make me feel comfortable in case I'm worried about getting into a strange man's car. "I'm the local doc. Name's Tom Shepard."

I give him a grin. So Sam Shepard couldn't come, but he sent his brother. And this one's almost as handsome. Tall and dimpled, with that slightly craggy outdoorsman look. He's even wearing Timberlands. I try to tuck my Nike-clad feet under the seat so he doesn't notice.

"Hi. I'm Hallie Pierpont," I say. And then I change my mind. I've survived a day alone, and I'm going to survive a lot more. If I don't have a husband anymore, I'm not going to use his name. "Actually, I'm Hallie Lawrence," I amend, extending my hand.

"Nice to meet you." Now he returns my grin. "Hallie Lawrence. I went fly-fishing with a friend of mine last month, and he told me all about a college girlfriend of his with that name." He shifts the car into drive and heads down the highway.

"I hope he said nice things," I offer.

"The best. My friend's Eric Richmond. Any chance you're the same Hallie he was talking about?"

"Could be," I say, weakly.

Tom glances over, surprised, "Wow, how about that. So you do know Eric? I mean, not just from reading about him in *Forbes*?"

"I don't read *Forbes*," I try to say, but my throat seems to be closing. Either these hornet stings are causing anaphylactic shock, or I'm getting choked up at the memory of Eric, my great college romance, my first lover—who I dumped senior year, for reasons that I can't quite remember.

"I do know Eric," I say. "I mean, knew him. In another life." Come to think of it, if I'd stayed with Eric, I would have had a different life—that probably wouldn't have included climbing this stupid mountain.

Tom Shepard glances over at me, and I want to tell him that I clean up well. He's got to be wondering how the weepy, swollen, fumbling, mudwoman next to him can be the Hallie Lawrence he's heard about from the smart, hunky—and *Forbes*-worthy—Eric Richmond.

"Small world," says Tom, pulling into the parking lot where my Saab, my blessed Saab, is waiting.

"If you see Eric, say hello for me," I suggest, reaching for the door handle even though I'd like to sit here for a while and find out how my rural rescuer happens to know my college boyfriend. Two guys on a fishing trip talking about old girlfriends. Did Eric tell him about that night we got drunk on single malt scotch—he had fine taste even then—and slept together on the beach?

Unfortunately, Tom, like most men, isn't a mind reader. And instead of answering my unspoken question, he says, "Need anything else? Will you be okay getting home?"

"Of course," I say, trying to sound again like the confident, composed Hallie I was back in college. In fact, the confident, composed Hallie I was until a few short weeks ago.

I try not to grimace as I maneuver out of the high-set Jeep and land on my aching ankle. "Listen, you saved my life," I tell Tom. "I can't thank you enough."

"No problem. But if I were you I'd pick up some Benadryl on the way home. That face isn't looking too good."

At first I'm insulted, but then I laugh. "Thanks, doc," I say. Sure, I'm less than camera-ready at the moment, but this day wasn't so bad after all. I lost the battle with the hornets and the big hill, but I survived and I'm here. I made it. And best of all, now I get to go home.

Tom waves and drives away and I reach into my jacket pocket for my car keys. When they're not there, I fumble through my backpack, pulling out the contents piece by piece. Where could they be? I take a moment to think rationally, and then I spot them—locked safely on the front seat of the Saab.

I sigh. The adventures just keep coming.

Chapter TWO

I CALL THE LOCAL POLICE DEPARTMENT with my now cooperating cell phone to explain my problem.

"Maybe you could give me the phone number of a locksmith?" I suggest.

"Don't worry, ma'am. We'll send someone," says the desk sergeant efficiently.

Crime must not be much of a problem in Cold Spring, because almost before I hang up, three siren-blaring fire trucks, two speeding town patrol cars, and one mounted state trooper rush down the road to save me. The posse, however, doesn't include an ambulance, so I guess I'll have to buy the Benadryl on my own.

By nightfall, I'm finally home. I throw my dirty clothes in the laundry and my unsalvageable Nikes into the wastebasket. Standing in front of the refrigerator, I eat some leftover Nutella, straight from the jar. It occurs to me that when I thank Emily for nudging me out of the house, I'll spare her the less spectacular details of my day of independence, such as the fact that getting me home required one generous man in a Jeep and the entire Cold Spring rescue squad.

I turn on Vivaldi's cello concertos, wrap an ice pack around my ankle, and carefully slip the rest of my battered body into a warm jasmine-scented bath. With my foot dangling over the edge of the tub, I put a soothing gel pack on my face and run my fingers through the foamy bubbles. Closing my eyes, I finally relax.

When, of course, the phone rings. It has to be one of the kids. Any mother knows that when your kid calls from college, you pick up immediately. If you miss it and try to call back five minutes later, you're sure to be sent to voice mail limbo—also known as maternal hell. So I brace my arms against the side of the tub, keep my injured ankle outstretched in front of me, and try to lift myself up. I manage to hoist my body out of the bath along with about four gallons of water, and I careen across the Carrera marble floor toward the trilling bedroom phone.

"Hello," I say, eager to chat with one of my children.

I hear a click and then a deep male voice. "Hello, Hallie Lawrence Pierpont. I know you weren't expecting this call, but can I take just a minute of your time?"

"No, you can't have a minute of my time," I snap angrily. Damn, I got out of the tub for a telemarketer. "You can't even have a second of my time," I add venomously, preparing to slam down the receiver.

But I hear a chuckle. "So you haven't changed a bit, Hallie. Are you still as sexy as you used to be?"

Oh god. Can it be? Reflexively, I look down at my naked body and do the inventory. Tummy's fairly flat, breasts aren't sagging, but the thighs are a little generous. I start to run my hand over my hip. Wait a minute. Am I talking to who I think I'm talking to?

"Excuse me, do I know you?" I ask sheepishly.

"You told Tom Shepard you did," he says in a booming baritone.

Water is now dripping off my legs onto the antique Persian bedroom carpet. I start shivering uncontrollably, but maybe it's not from the cold.

"Eric?" I ask in a small voice.

"It's me. Hold on a sec," he says.

I hear muffled voices in the background and then Eric telling someone that he's busy now and the call from the ambassador will just have to wait. Good. It's been twenty years since I talked to him. I shouldn't have to wait another minute.

"So," he says, coming back, "what's been going on?"

I'm not sure of our time frame here. Does he mean since I got out of Tom's car or since the last time I saw him?

"Tell me everything," he urges.

Let's see, I definitely had some high points in my post-college life. I attended Columbia Law School, wrote three law journal articles, and argued a case before the Supreme Court. Okay, the State Supreme Court, but it was precedent-setting. I took Adam and Emily to Mommy and Me, Gymboree, soccer meets, and high school graduation—all within a week, it seemed. I learned how to bake banana bread. I finally read *Ulysses*. And I figured out which pipe to turn off when the washing machine overflows.

So where to begin?

"I have two wonderful kids," I tell him. "I had a terrific marriage until the jerk walked out." I take a deep breath. "And since Tom mentioned your name, I've spent the entire day thinking about you."

Oh no, did I really just say that? I didn't mean to flirt. Apparently, I've been married so long that I've lost my six-second censor delay—where you actually stop to filter what you're going to say before you blurt it out.

Clearly, Eric doesn't mind. "You've been thinking about me only today?" he asks suggestively.

I find myself smiling. "You might have crossed my mind a few other times."

"That sounds more promising," he says.

"So what have you been doing?" I ask.

"More interesting is what I'm doing next weekend," he says, ignoring the question and getting to the point. "I'm coming to New York. I just bought a new pied-à-terre on the sixty-seventh floor of the Time Warner Center with two-hundred-eighty-degree views of the city."

"Too bad you couldn't afford the three-hundred-sixty-degree view." I laugh.

There's silence on the other end of the phone. Apparently I've hit a sore spot. "They were all taken," he says tersely.

"I'm sure it's nice anyway," I say appeasingly. "I know it's the new number-one address in town."

"Why don't you come see it," Eric says. "I'll give you the grand tour of my apartment, and then we could get a nice little dinner. There are two fabulous restaurants in the building. Per Se's always good. Or Masa. Your choice."

Eric's not exactly living above the dim sum take-out place. Per Se's so exclusive that you need a copy of your financial statement just to get a reservation. As for Masa, two people can't eat there for less than five hundred bucks. And it's sushi. They don't even cook the fish.

"I'd love to. What time?" I ask, surprised to hear myself agreeing so readily. Clearly the filter's still turned off and I'm going out with a man.

"Around dinner. I'll call you when I get in, and you can just come over."

"Great, you've got yourself a date. I mean an appointment," I say, quickly amending my bold statement. Have we made a date? Probably not. Best guess is that Eric's married and is just meeting an old friend for dinner.

"Good," Eric says.

I play with my wet hair for a moment, twisting it around my finger.

"Before we get together, you have to tell me at least something about your life," I say. "Where do you live when you're not in New York? Are you married? Do you . . ."

I'm just starting to ask if he has any children, when I realize that I'll have to wait and find out in person. His mission accomplished, Eric clicked off the phone after the word "good."

By the next day, my ankle's feeling better and my face is almost back to normal, although, frankly, a case might be made in favor of the swelling. At least it plumped out the lines in my forehead. I could go back to work, but I've already told Arthur that I'm taking off the week. And I have a plan for today. My new motto: Don't get mad, get even. I've decided that I'll definitely feel better if instead of sulking, I do something completely vile to Bill.

I go to a box of old videos in the basement and pull out *The First Wives Club*. After twenty minutes, I turn it off. Way too tame. What I need is *The Godfather*. How satisfying to think of Bill and Ashlee waking up to a dead horse head in their bed.

I go online and Google "revenge" and I'm stunned to see ten thousand four hundred thirty-two websites come up. Clearly there's a multimillion-dollar industry being built on the idea that instead of turning the other cheek, you should slap someone else's. Eager online entrepreneurs have stepped in, offering to provide gifts that FTD never thought to deliver—dead flowers, doggie poop, or for those willing to splurge, cow patties from Hereford's Dairy (delivered to the door, fresh and warm). One idea does capture my fancy. According to the website, if I slip frozen shrimp inside a curtain rod in Ashlee's apartment, within two weeks the stench of decaying fish will render the place completely unlivable. She and Bill can hire all the fumigators, exterminators, or private investigators they want, but nobody will ever find the source. Yummy. A new use for shrimp that doesn't involve cocktail sauce.

Just reading about the revenge seems to have done the trick. I can stay above-it-all for the moment, knowing I have options just a click away. Besides, isn't living well the best revenge? And evidently living well is what I'm going to do next weekend. Per Se, Masa, Masa, Per Se. Maybe Eric and I will have dinner in one and dessert in the other and—well, a nightcap in his apartment. No, I'm not going there. I mean, I'm going to his apartment, but I'm not going to think about what might happen. Two decades since our college love and a lot has changed. Forget about his being married. What if he's bald?

Before my rendezvous with Eric, I have another engagement to think about—my maiden voyage at a party as a single woman (though am I still a maiden at forty-four, after twenty years of marriage and two episiotomies?). I pull out the boxed invitation that I received from my neighbor Rosalie Reilly a couple of weeks ago. Rosalie invited all the parents from Emily's high school graduating class to her get-together and the note, handwritten in gold leaf calligraphy, says, "Now that our little birdies have flown off, please come to our Empty Nest Party!" The note is sitting inside a handmade woven raffia bird's nest. Who but five-year-olds, mental patients, and lonely moms have enough time for arts and crafts?

I drive over to Rosalie's house because there's an unwritten law in the suburbs against walking, unless you have a dog at the end of a leash. Since she lives around the corner, I end up parking practically in my own driveway.

I ring the bell and smooth my perky polka-dot skirt; I might as well look cheerful. I'm armed with a bottle of Cabernet and a cover story.

"So good to see you," says Rosalie, kissing me on each cheek at the door. She steps inside and puts the wine on her foyer table, to join the anonymous lineup of a dozen other gift bottles. Next time I'm going to put a discreet "X" on the label and see how many parties it takes before the bottle ends up back at my house.

"Where's Bill?" Rosalie asks.

"He's in the city tonight," I say, not lying. Because why should I say any more? I'm not ready for all the sympathetic clucking and the "oh, my poor darling"s that my story is sure to elicit. Everyone will feel bad for me, and they'll even be sincere when they offer advice and names of divorce lawyers. But then tomorrow I'll be the lead item to gossip about over morning lattes.

I head toward a group of parents standing together—all of them the moms and dads of friends Emily made in her high school advanced placement classes. After the Ivy League-bound kids clicked, the grown-ups became a clique, too. I look around and realize that all the adults at the party are grouped according to their children's abilities. The parents of the kids who starred in all the school plays are standing by the bar, gesturing theatrically to each other. The jocks' parents are raucously drinking beer in the kitchen and jabbing each other good-naturedly. And those whose progeny were the school potheads are suspiciously gathered outside on the patio, doing God-knows-what. Lighting up and talking about rehab?

"Hi, Hallie," says the chorus of academically inclined parents as I join their circle. We kiss all around.

"Where's Bill?" asks Steff Rothchild (mother of Devon, now at Cornell.)

"Yes, where's Bill?" echoes Amanda Michaels-Locke (mother of twins Michael and Michaela, Princeton and Hofstra. Michaela had a tough senior year.)

"Bill, that's right. I haven't seen him on our usual 7:42 train this week," pipes up Jennifer Morton (Rory's mother. Duke).

Bill, Bill, Bill. This is the conversation I get from the intellectual parents? Maybe I'll go out to the porch.

"He's in the city," I say as brightly as I can muster, four words that I'm hoping will get me through the night.

"Oh, working late," clucks Steff. There's that judgmental cluck, and she doesn't even know the real news. "You can't let him do that. When the children are gone, hubbies and wives have to stay closer to each other." She tucks her arm smugly through her husband's, a woman who's clearly spent too many afternoons watching Dr. Phil. Her Richard takes a gulp of his vodka tonic.

"That's right," whispers Jennifer. "We don't want our men straying."

The vodka tonic must have gone down the wrong pipe because Richard starts coughing.

A tiny smile crosses Amanda's face, but she puts her arm around me. "So everything's good with you and Bill?" she asks solicitously. "You aren't missing Emily and Adam too much?"

"We're perfect," I lie.

Just then, redheaded Darlie rushes over, decked out in four-inch-high Jimmy Choo sandals and a Gucci miniskirt so tiny there's probably barely room for the designer label. Her half-dozen gold bracelets clang loudly at her wrist and, in its own way, her diamond necklace is no less quiet. But, then again, nothing about Darlie, the third wife of import-export king Carl Borden, is subtle.

Including her reason for joining us.

"Hallie, I heard about you and Bill," she hollers so shrilly that Rosalie's golden retriever, lying in the corner, yaps in pain.

Is it my imagination, or does the whole room stop to find out what daring Darlie has to say?

"Dumped, dumped, dumped," she exclaims, clamping her hand on me so firmly that her crimson-colored talons dig into the flesh of my upper arm. "I can't believe Bill left you like this."

Now the parents who had been grouped together by their children's activities have a more common interest. Me. They all drift closer to get the scoop.

"What in heaven's name are you talking about? Bill's just in the city tonight," says Steff. I can't decide if she's rushing to my defense or egging Darlie on.

"Am I the first to know?" asks Darlie proudly, scanning the room. She shakes her head. "Bill leaving and moving in with that Ashlee. Ashlee with two Es. I myself was horrified when I heard. She's twenty-eight. Barely older than your children."

"Emily's only eighteen. Ashlee's fifty percent older than she is," I say defensively, though why am I trying to defend Bill?

"Whatever," says Darlie, who's not here to discuss mathematical equations. Though she seems to enjoy geometry—she wants to keep talking about triangles. "Anyway, you have nothing to be embarrassed about—Bill chose well. Ashlee's gorgeous with those big brown eyes and that perfect body of hers. God, those abs. I'd die for those abs."

I wish Darlie really would die for those abs. In fact, right now would be a convenient moment for it. I should just keep my mouth shut and walk away, but I can't help myself. "Stick-straight blonde hair?" I ask, trying to confirm the image I've obsessed over for the last two weeks.

"No, nothing so ordinary. Short bouncy layers. Such shiny, glossy hair, Ashlee could be doing an Herbal Essence commercial."

Ah, yes, the shampoo commercial where the model washes her hair and has an orgasm. Couldn't Ashlee look like the woman in the estrogen-replacement commercial? The one who's not taking the drug?

"How do you know all this?" I ask meekly.

"Ashlee's my personal trainer at Equinox. She mentioned having a little something going on with one of her clients a while ago. She kept the details hush-hush, but she finally told me all about it last week. Really, Hallie, I felt so torn. You know I adore you, but Ashlee's just the nicest. I've been wanting her to find a man of her own for the longest time."

I wish she'd find a man of her own, too, instead of a man who has a family, two children, a ficus plant, three tropical fish—and happens to be married to me.

Then it clicks. My birthday present to Bill last year, to make him feel young again, was ten sessions with a personal trainer at Equinox. Apparently, a personal trainer with shiny, bouncy, orgasmic hair. Talk about planting the seeds of your own destruction. Why didn't I just buy him a tie at Lord & Taylor?

The crowd around us hasn't uttered a word since Darlie started her riveting story. But now Steff blurts out, "I can't believe this!"

"Yes, it's shocking," says Amanda. "Imagine that kind of behavior from Bill."

"Forget Bill," says Steff. "Richard just signed a year contract with Equinox. I'm canceling tomorrow. If he wants exercise, he can walk."

The other women in the group nod solemnly. I have a feeling the local sports store will sell out of treadmills tomorrow. Every wife in town is going to be installing a home gym.

The next morning, I find myself standing outside the Equinox gym at Forty-third Street, just a couple of blocks from Bill's office. I don't really know how I got here. If something awful happens to Ashlee when I go inside, I'll blame it on my dazed mental state. People get out of murder charges for eating Twinkies or popping Zoloft, so after the information I got last night from Darlie, I can certainly claim post-traumatic stress disorder. Not that I'll need a complicated defense. Get any three married women on the jury and I'm home free.

I can already visualize the bloody murder that I'll commit. The moment I'm face-to-face with Ashlee, I'll pull a sleek silver handgun out of my bag. No, wait, I forgot that I'm nonviolent. I've never held a gun in my life. I wouldn't know the difference between a Beretta and a barrette, and I'd never carry either of them. (Call me a hypocrite—I believe in gun control but not hair control). I poke around my purse. No scissors, no tweezers, no metal nail file. I could get on any airplane in the country. The best I can do is attack Ashlee with my emery board. Fine, I'll ruin her manicure.

Inside, I glance at the buff crew-cut guy behind the registration desk who's waiting for me to show my membership card.

"Hi, I'm here to kill Ashlee. Could you tell me where she is?"

Mercifully, I just think that. I don't actually say it.

"May I help you?" he asks, casually flexing his biceps when I continue to stand there silently.

Come to think of it, I don't really want to kill Ashlee myself, do I?

"Yes, yes, you could. Would you like to make a little extra money? I need to hire a hit man."

I'm pretty sure I don't really say that out loud, either.

"I'd like to check out . . . the gym," I say, stopping myself before I mention that I'm here to check out a certain bouncy-haired husband-stealing personal trainer.

"Great," he says brightly, flashing his laser-whitened perfect smile. "You're in luck. If you sign up today, I can offer an incredible package— twenty percent off the initiation fee, eighteen percent off the monthly fee the first year, and twelve percent off the second year. Plus two free smoothies."

"Not right now," I say. Even if I wanted to join, I'd need the chairman of Citibank to evaluate that deal—or at least Suze Orman.

"But it's a really good promotion," says buff boy, shaking his head. "It expires at noon. I don't want you to miss out. You just seem like such a nice woman." He puts his hand meaningfully over mine.

So Ashlee isn't the only one around here who seduces clients. I guess with all the competition for clients, gyms have to do more than offer a George Foreman grill to sign you up.

"Actually, I was hoping to start with a free trial day," I say, thinking this gym has already cost me dearly.

"No problem," he says, quickly filling out a pass and handing it to me.

I start to ask where I might find Ashlee, but somehow I don't. Either I can't bear to summon her up or I'm trying to cover my tracks. If she's going to end up dead today, I don't want the trail leading back to me.

I wander into the locker room to change into my workout clothes. I can practically hear the district attorney making hay out of that slipup. Since I'd thought to bring along gym wear, he'll up the murder charge to premeditated.

I pull on a white cotton T and shake out my hair. No, I'm not really going to attack her. I'm a lawyer; my weapon is reason. I'll stay rational and calm and explain why this is a bad deal for everybody. Lose-lose. Even if Ashlee's not worried about destroying my family, I can make the case that this is a terrible mistake from her point of view. Does she honestly want a man whose idea of a gourmet treat involves Orville Redenbacher's popcorn? Is she ready for a lifetime of anniversary presents from Home Depot? She's a young woman with her whole future in front of her. She doesn't need an old married guy who snores, pops Lipitor, and wrenches his back taking out the garbage. What a list. Come to think of it, maybe I don't need him either.

Suddenly full of courage, I walk over to a young Equinox staff member who's putting her gear in a locker.

"Do you happen to know where I could find a personal trainer named Ashlee?" I ask.

"Sure, she's right in there," she says, pointing to a curtained changing alcove.

I throw back my shoulders, lift my chin, and stride over with my best courtroom confidence. If ever I've needed to win a decision, it's this one.

"Ashlee?" I call out, my voice firm and friendly.

"It's me. Just a second."

"No rush," I say trying to control my breathing, which is suddenly too fast. Really no rush. Do I want to have this confrontation? What was I thinking?

Suddenly, the curtain pulls back and I see bouncy, glossy hair. It's Ashlee, in the flesh. Definitely in the flesh. She's upbeat, all smiles, and perfectly naked. And I mean perfect. Her skin is smooth, her breasts are perky, and—not that I'm looking—she has a teeny bikini wax.

"Looking for me?" she asks cheerfully. "I was just going to dash into the shower."

I try to answer but I'm speechless. So much for my being wise, mature, and telling her how to run her life. Right now I want to turn and run for mine. But the least I can do is make the situation real for Ashlee. I reach into my bag and, with a flourish, grab for the family picture I carry around in my wallet. Not the posed portrait, but the one of all of us frolicking on the beach in Nantucket, just last summer. Staring straight at Ashlee, I pull it out and hand it over.

"Here," I say. "This is what you should think about when you're with a married man."

Ashlee takes a long look at what I've given her. She looks puzzled, then she hands it back.

"Listen, I don't know who you are, but I really need to shower. Thanks for showing me that. See ya." She saunters away unfazed, her hair bouncing, her hips bouncing and, dammit, her cellulite-free thighs not bouncing.

I'm surprised at her composure. No reaction at all? She's a cool character. I look down at what I'm holding, and instead of seeing our family frolicking, I'm face-to-face with a bright logo: SAM'S CLUB. MEMBER #4555683310967. I gulp. That's what I handed her?

Mortified, I tuck it back into my purse, right next to the picture I'd meant to show. Tonight at dinner, Ashlee will regale Bill with her story about some crazy lady in the gym who was flashing her Sam's Club card.

I pull myself up straight, trying to regain some authority. I wag my finger in the air after her retreating back.

"Never forget, Ashlee," I call out. "I'm a discount shopper."

Chapter THREE

I RUSH OUT OF EQUINOX, feeling like a fool. I want to crawl into a hole and disappear. Or at least crawl into my bed and hide under my covers. But I've already spent too much time there, and all I have to show for it are a lot of cookie crumbs between the sheets.

But what else can I do? Clearly, I'm not ready to be part of the civilized world. Not that this world, particularly the corner that Bill inhabits, seems very civilized at the moment. I can't believe I told Eric I'd meet him. What makes me think I could make it through an evening with a man, any man? I acted like a blithering idiot with Ashlee, and I'll do the same with Eric. I have to cancel.

I walk for a while, then stand at the corner of Fifth Avenue and Fiftieth Street, hesitating. Go home or go on?

Bill found someone younger, prettier, and with a better bikini wax than me. (In fact, any bikini wax would be better since I've never gotten one at all.) The worst thing that could happen to a woman my age, right? But maybe there's another way to look at it. What's that expression about when a door closes, a window opens? Maybe I should start looking for open windows. And, goddamn it, if they're all slammed shut, I'll try to pry them open myself.

I didn't want to end this marriage. I was happy—or thought I was.

But it's gone and I can't go back. All I can do is move forward. And what better place to start than with someone I already know?

I march over to Saks to prepare for my date/my appointment/my evening—whatever it is I'm having—with my old boyfriend Eric. Maybe Ashlee looks good naked, but I'm determined to look good dressed.

I head up to the fourth-floor designer department and pick out several pairs of shoes to try, each over three hundred dollars. Discount shopping be damned. If I finally have something to look forward to again, I'm going to do it right. Besides, buying shoes in bulk is never successful.

"This pair definitely," says the gay spike-haired salesman, after I've tried all of them on and am back to pair number two. He swivels his hip and drapes an arm over my shoulder. "They're absolutely fantastic fuck-me shoes."

I pause in front of the mirror, contemplating the sexy open-toed Christian Louboutin sling backs that have wispy little feathers (sure to fall off) dusting the instep. Fuck-me shoes? I'm not sure what I'm expecting from the evening with Eric, but it's definitely not that. On the other hand, they are fabulous. Fuck me, fuck me not. What the heck; I'm buying them.

Am I trying to impress Eric? I never did that in the old days. Back then, I thought Eric was funny and smart and sexy and romantic—but I knew I was too. When he went off to business school at Stanford, I was still a senior in college and wouldn't dream of transferring across the country to follow a man. Plus, the three thousand miles between us gave me a good excuse. Yes, I adored him, but deep down in my heart I wanted to have new experiences. How can you pick the first guy you ever loved to be with for the rest of your life?

Eric did sneak back into my thoughts over the years. I heard he was a big success, and I sometimes imagined that if I'd married him, my life would be filled with nonstop parties and glamorous trips around the world. I envisioned staying at five-star hotels in Venice and ordering sumptuous champagne breakfasts from room service in Cannes, instead of (as per Bill) traipsing out to the coffee shop across the street to experience the local color. Local color, my eye. My husband is just cheap.

Friday morning, shoes at the ready, I start thinking about what time I should get dressed. Eric said we'd get together for dinner but I don't know when he eats. When my kids were little, supper was at five, but if Eric's spent a lot of time in Europe, he might think dinner is at eleven. I'd better hedge my bets: eat a late lunch but get ready early.

Around four o'clock, I hop into the shower and then start the rare (for me) process of putting on more than lipstick and blush. I almost never do my eyes, but tonight I might as well go for it. In my bathroom vanity, I unearth a crusted-over tube of $4.99 black Maybelline mascara, circa 2001. Doesn't look promising. In Emily's bathroom, I find an elegant container of Lancôme Définicils Long Lash Extra-Volume in navy blue that she's left behind. Definitely newer and higher quality. So do I use my old cakey, clumpy Maybelline, or commit the ultimate women's magazine no-no—sharing someone else's mascara? Well, Emily's my daughter, and everyone always says she has my eyes, so I might as well have her lashes.

In an hour, I've put on every bit of makeup I can find, and I move on to the Getting Dressed part of the evening. I decide on black pants, because they make me look thin and it won't seem like I'm trying too hard. What to wear on top? My pale yellow cashmere sweater is pretty, but what if it's warm in the restaurant? I reach for the sheer pink blouse, which is lovely—but too sheer? I put it back in the closet. Next to it is the black satin, which is very New York chic. And in black-and-black, I'll be prepared for any SoHo party or last-minute funeral.

I sigh. Eric hasn't called, so I don't have to decide this minute. I walk around the house in my black pants, three-hundred-dollar fuck me, fuck me not shoes, and my Lejaby nude lace bra. I glance at my watch: 6:15. I expected to hear from him by now. How silly of me not to have gotten his number so I could call him. Maybe the plane was late, although I don't even know where he's coming from. He could be kayaking across the Hudson for all I know.

I sit down at my desk, figuring I'll do some work. I glance over a law journal article, but the words blur in front of my eyes. Same with a memo from senior partner Arthur. I pay a couple of bills and answer some e-mails.

It's 7:30 P.M.

This is ridiculous. I pick up the phone to call information, but Eric's not listed and I don't know the name of his company. I hang up and pace around the room. Am I really sitting by the phone, waiting for a man to call? I didn't even do that when I was sixteen. I'm a successful, grown-up woman, and here I am, lolling around in a lacy bra, getting more anxious by the moment. What is it that reduces all women to teenagers when they're about to go on a date? And I don't even know if this is a date.

I'm starved, so I go downstairs to eat a low-fat yogurt. Somehow, my spoon wanders into the gallon of mocha-chocolate fudge ice cream. So I won't eat dessert at dinner. How good could the Japanese treats be at Masa anyway?

Masa. Per Se. Eric must have made a reservation at one of them. Finally, a constructive idea hits me. I'll phone them and find out what time we're expected.

But I strike out with both calls.

"I'm sorry, ma'am, our client lists are confidential," says the cool maître d' who answers at Masa. "I can't reveal that information." At Per Se, I'm transferred three times but get the same result. Who knew that restaurants were more secretive than the CIA? You'd think I were asking the Colonel for the classified ingredients in Kentucky Fried Chicken.

Stymied, I hang up and replay the conversation with Eric in my head. He definitely said he'd call me around dinnertime. And he was arriving this weekend. Oh, shit. Why did I assume "weekend" meant Friday?

By eleven o'clock, I'm pretty sure he didn't mean Friday.

And I'm right. When Eric calls, I'm sound asleep and it's two A.M., which officially makes it Saturday. Still in my clothes, I must have dozed off in the cozy club chair in my bedroom, reading *When Bad Things Happen to Perfectly Nice Married Women*.

"Hallie, it's Eric. I'm so sorry to be late," he says when I groggily pick up the receiver. "My pilot didn't show up and I had to wait two hours for another one."

"How incredibly frustrating for you," I say, trying to work up some sympathy for the travails of private-plane ownership.

"Anyway, I just flew in from London. You live at 21 Oak Street, right?" he asks.

"Twenty-seven," I say automatically. I stand up and walk across the room with the portable receiver, trying to stretch out from my bedless snooze.

"Oh, now I can see you," he says.

I look around the room, half expecting Eric to jump out of the closet, and I'm not far off. I go to the window and peer into the darkness. Under the street lamp, I see the outline of a long black limousine, pulling up in front of my house.

"Nice bra," Eric says cheerfully. "Is it new?"

I look down and realize that he must be in the car, staring into the bright lights of my bedroom. Instinctively, I throw back my shoulders—and then quickly reach for the tab on the shade. I pull it so quickly that it comes crashing down on my head.

"You okay?" Eric asks.

Damn Bill. I told him months ago that the shade was loose. Can I ask Eric to fix it? Or maybe his driver, pilot, housekeeper, butler, or maintenance man. Or wife. Remember, he may have a wife.

"I'm fine. But listen, I already ate dinner tonight. And it's after two. How about if I come by tomorrow? Lunch, dinner, I'm free for either."

"But I'm not. Change of plan. I thought I'd be here for the whole weekend, but I have to leave tomorrow to close a deal in Bermuda."

"Buying shorts?" I ask, joking.

"No, I'm trading long." And then he pauses. "Okay, I get it. Bermuda. Shorts. Very funny, Hallie." He chuckles. "Come on down. I want to see you. And hurry. Don't feel like you have to put on a shirt just for me."

I find myself smiling and grab for the sheer pink blouse. After all, he's already seen the bra.

When I step outside onto my dark cool porch, I see Eric leaning against the limo, arms folded, a big grin spreading across his face. I'm self-conscious as I walk carefully down the steps and across the long front walk, aware that Eric is taking in my every move. Thank goodness for the sexy shoes. As long as I don't trip, they do add a little wiggle to my walk.

Instead of worrying about the impression I'm making, I decide to concentrate on the handsome man in front of me. And he is still handsome. If it's been twenty years, I don't know where they went. His thick hair still falls boyishly across his brow and his strong body seems as lean and muscular as when he was captain of the crew team. Last time I saw him, he wasn't wearing a perfectly tailored pin-striped suit with French cuffs peeking out of the sleeves, but his gorgeously chiseled features are offset by the wry, amused smile that won me the first time.

"You must be Eric," I say, extending my hand with a little laugh.

"And you haven't changed one bit," he says, pulling me toward him and kissing me lightly on the cheek.

He opens the car door and we slide into the backseat of the limo. The driver offers a brief hello before closing the glass window that separates him from the passenger's compartment and pulling away from the curb. Eric reaches for my hand. Have I really not changed, or is it just that I'll always be the same in his eyes? How romantic. Or maybe he's just too vain to put on his glasses.

In the car, Eric tells me all about his various business deals, which seem to include commodities trades and international financing. In case he hasn't made the point about how successful he is with his limousine, private plane, and penthouse apartment, Eric announces that he was recently in *Forbes*.

"Did you happen to see it?" he asks.

"Your friend Tom Shepard mentioned something, but I never got to read the story."

"Check this out," he says, pulling out a laminated copy of the *Forbes* magazine article that he just happens to have in the backseat.

I'd like to know what it says. I'd definitely like to know what it says. But I'm as vain as Eric. No way am I putting on my reading glasses in front of him to find out. In fact, I've already Googled the menus at Per Se and Masa and made my choices, just to avoid this very situation.

"It's so dark, why don't you read it to me," I coo.

"The big headline is I'm 277."

I know it's not his age. It's certainly not his weight. And I'm hoping it's not his cholesterol. Does every man I know have to take Lipitor?

"You're 277 what?" I ask.

"On the list."

It doesn't immediately come to me what list he's talking about. "Don't worry. You're number one with me," I say.

He laughs. "Number one is Bill Gates. Or maybe some Saudi prince. I've done well, but I'm not competing with them yet."

Oh, a list of rich guys. I guess 277 is pretty impressive. Definitely better than I'd rank. I was proud when I opened the mail yesterday and found a preapproved Discover card.

"Then I guess it's a good thing you and I didn't stay together," I offer. "With me around, you never would have made the top three hundred."

I mean the joke to be self-deprecating, but Eric turns it around. "You're right. We'd have been having too much fun for me to concentrate on work. All that sex. Hey, for that chance, I'd be willing to drop off the list completely."

"We did have a lot of sex back then." I giggle.

"I still have the blue ceramic piggy bank. Do you remember?" he asks, as if I could forget. "A nickel in the slot every time we made love. I can barely lift the thing it's so heavy. I think our one-day record was fifty cents."

"A stellar twenty-four hours," I say, grinning.

"All that money sitting there. It's the only investment I've ever made that didn't keep growing. But I figure it'll pay off eventually."

"You can use my half to buy a lottery ticket," I tease, though I'm wondering if the investment he made is in me. And how he's hoping it will pay off.

"Ever have another fifty-cent day?" he asks, taking my hand and playfully stroking his finger across my palm.

"I've had fifty-cent years," I groan. "If you've ever been married, you'd know about those."

"I've been married three times, though I'm single at the moment," Eric adds hastily.

Three times? Obviously he's not averse to making a commitment, just to keeping it.

"What happened to your marriages? A few fifty-cent months and you quit?"

"No, it's just that I always have a mistress."

"Eric!" I gasp.

He laughs. "Work. My mistress was my job. Takes more time than any woman. And more time than any woman can put up with." Then he smiles and winks at me. "Besides, my darling, nobody could ever match your charms. Though I will say each of my wives reminded me a little of you."

"Is that a compliment?" I ask. "Were they five foot five with wavy brown hair? Greenish gray eyes? Or is it that they were all nineteen—like I was when we were together?"

"All of the above," Eric says, chuckling.

Having a chauffeur is definitely the way to travel. We're already in Manhattan and I didn't have to pay for a train ticket or sit next to a beer-swilling businessman on Metro-North. We pull up in front of the entrance to the Time Warner apartments and Eric jumps out before the driver can come around and open the door. I peer out of the car window, craning my neck up at the towering green glass building. Despite the hour, the street is bustling with late-night club-goers, chatting gaily as they hop in and out of taxis.

Eric swings open my door and extends his hand. When I got into the car half an hour ago, I didn't really focus on where we were headed, but obviously we're on our way upstairs. It's almost three in the morning. The restaurants can't still be open. I take Eric's hand and stroll with him through the lobby and into the elevator. As we walk by, the doorman, two lobby attendants, a concierge, and the elevator man all nod obsequiously and say, "Good evening, Mr. Richmond. Pleasure to have you back." Nobody bothers to glance at me. I'm obviously a transient.

Or a tramp. If Emily ever did something like this, I'd kill her. Wouldn't she realize what it means to a guy if you agree to go up and see his apartment at this hour? But I can easily convince myself that there's nothing wrong with what I'm doing. Eric's single and so, apparently, am I, at least in every way that matters. My wedding ring is off and so is my husband—off with another woman. If Bill can have Ashlee, I can have Eric. He doesn't even count. I already have that notch on my belt.

We step into his apartment and I gasp. Even before Eric turns on the pinpoint lights hidden in the ceiling, the room is already shimmering with the glow of the city. The glistening views reflected on all sides in the floor-to-ceiling windows provide all the decoration the room really needs. Some interior designer has been smart enough to realize the hard work has already been done and his job was just not to get in the way of the fantastic views. Muted low-slung sofas in soft grays sit on a quietly elegant beige carpet. An undulating glass coffee table almost disappears, except for the slim Giacometti sculpture sitting decorously on its surface. The one wall without a window manages to hold its own with a subtly spectacular Picasso.

Someone must have known we were coming, because the sleek steel table in the dining room is set for two. The tapered candles are already lit, and a generous dish of caviar is sitting inside a silver bowl filled with ice. Eric goes over to the waiting magnum of Dom Perignon, pops the cork, and fills two glasses, leaning over to hand me one.

I grab the glass and take a big gulp.

"Wait a minute. We need a toast," says Eric coming closer. He raises his glass and clicks it against mine. "To you. To us. To first love."

Now I bring the glass to my lips, but I can hardly swallow. The whole apartment could be out of a movie, and so could this scene. Is all this just a fantasy? Remember, Hallie, you haven't seen this man in twenty years.

"You know, you were my first love," Eric says as we sit down on a deep-cushioned sofa and he scoops some of the caviar onto a plate. He holds out a little spoon of beluga for me. "And you were my first lover. I've gotten even better in bed since then."

"I don't know if I have. I've been with the same guy all this time."
I'm not sure if that's a selling point or not.

He puffs up, clearly pleased with himself. "You've just been with
me and Bill?"

"Not just. But almost just," I say, skirting the issue. Men don't want
to know the exact number, anyway. If they did, what would be the ideal
answer? More than two (you have experience) but less than five (you're
not a . . . well, you know)? And who's going to admit the truth, especially if it's double digits?

I lean forward to take a taste from Eric's spoon. Mmm, that's good
caviar. I run my tongue over my now-salty lips and make a sucking
noise trying to get the wayward black roe out from between my teeth.
Very attractive. When will God or General Mills invent a food that you
can safely eat in front of a man? Everything either drips, crunches, or
sticks to your molars.

Champagne seems pretty safe. When Eric takes a tray of thinly
sliced chateaubriand from a side table, I decide to stick with the bub-
bly. He refills my glass for the second time. Or is it the third? What am
I trying to do—be like one of those college girls who downs a bottle of
tequila so she can claim "I didn't know what I was doing" when she
ends up sleeping with the guy?

More food keeps appearing, although I never see anybody bringing
it in. Eric must be so rich he doesn't just have a staff, he has elves.

Eric is as charming as I remembered him, and as the evening—or
morning—goes on, I begin to relax. And not just from the champagne.
I feel that magical mix of new excitement and easygoing comfort. The
conversation veers from Eric's brand-new business stories to old memories and we laugh as we catch up on almost-forgotten friends. Eric tells
me that the party-loving wrestler who lived downstairs in his freshman
dorm is now a missionary in Southeast Asia. I offer that the guy who
won the college beer-chugging contest (fifteen cans in fifty-seven minutes) is now a pilot for United Airlines.

"But he doesn't fly any major routes," I quip.

Eric laughs and pops a cherry tomato into his mouth. "People
change, don't they," he says. Then he looks at me seriously for a min-

ute. "I heard about your little sister, by the way. All those years ago. I'm so sorry."

"Thanks." He's touched a nerve, but I swallow hard and decide to let it pass. Determined to change the subject, I quickly ask, "How's your mom?"

"Doing fine. She just sold another one of her paintings. I've never figured out who hangs her stuff, but in Boca Raton, she's hot. By the way, she still asks about you. She never forgave me for not marrying you."

"A woman of fine taste," I say, feeling comfortable again. So this is the advantage of an old boyfriend. I feel that first-date sexual tingle but I'm cozy enough to kick off my shoes and curl my bare toes up on the sofa. I snuggle a little closer and rest my head on Eric's shoulder, taking in his subtle, rich scent.

"You've switched colognes. I miss the Old Spice," I say, teasing. "Remember? You used to come back from crew practice and instead of taking a shower, you'd douse yourself with the stuff."

Eric makes a face. "Not fair," he says defending his way-back-when frat-boy hygiene. "I always put on deodorant first."

"I know. A smell I'll never forget." I wrinkle my nose in mock horror. "Ban has been banished from my house ever since."

"Now I use L'Occitane, imported from France. I hope you approve," he says putting an arm around me and moving closer.

I don't know if it's the allure of the moment (and the hundred-dollar skin lotion) or the appeal of the past (and the remembered Old Spice), but I lift my chin toward Eric. And in case he doesn't know what I'm angling for, I slide closer and kiss him.

The kiss seems to have an immediate effect because I feel a pounding vibration between us. Eric reaches down, sliding his hand over my hip and toward his own. The vibrating intensifies.

"Cell phone," Eric explains, pulling back and grabbing the Motorola from his pocket. He glances at the number. "Got to take this."

I sit back, slightly embarrassed. I know my sex life with Bill had slowed down lately, but can I really not tell the difference between a pulsating phone and a throbbing man?

Eric has jumped up and is pacing around the room, barking orders to whoever's on the other end of the line. He's not happy about something in, as far as I can tell, a deal for orange juice futures. I personally think the future belongs to papaya, but Eric's not asking my advice.

He slams shut his phone and comes back to the couch. He starts to stroke my face, and runs a finger through my hair. But then he jumps up again. "I'm sorry, Hallie, but I'd better follow through on this problem or it's going to keep bothering me."

Well, I'm not going to let it bother me. I reach for some more caviar while he arranges a four-way conference call covering three continents. Given all of Eric's attention, the future of orange juice seems secure.

Eric finally comes back to the couch again, but he still seems tense. "Want a massage?" I ask, rubbing his shoulders.

"I have a better idea. I could use another kiss," he says, taking my face in his hands and pressing his lips against mine.

We embrace for a long time. His kisses are soft and warm, and his hands caressing me feel both familiar and new. I lean into his firm chest and pull him tight as both the space and the years between us dissolve. Time in all its essence disappears and when I finally open my eyes, I see the first whispers of light breaking into the dark sky outside.

Eric breathes softly into my ear, and when my whole body responds, he asks tenderly, "Will you come into my bedroom?"

I hesitate, and over my shoulder, I see him glance at his watch.

"Short on time?" I ask.

"Always," he admits. "But I don't want to lose this chance."

The phone doesn't ring, but the doorbell does. Eric groans and gets up. "It's just my assistant Hamilton. We always start early."

He lets in a nerdy-looking thirty-year-old who's holding a heavy briefcase. "Good morning, Mr. Richmond. I have those papers and we can . . ." Hamilton pauses, noticing me, and looks slightly abashed, though I'm probably not the first woman he's found lolling around Eric's apartment at the crack of dawn. But now he stammers, "Am I interrupting something?"

Eric glances at me with a little smile. "I don't know yet. We were just negotiating."

Hamilton disappears discreetly to a back room as yet unseen by me and Eric glances seductively at me and takes my hand. "Come on. Let's go put another nickel in the piggy bank."

I smile coyly. "Not on the first date. You know me."

Eric shakes his head. "I do, but you're not going to make me wait six months again, are you? This isn't really a first date."

All of a sudden, I feel hesitant. The night has been wonderful, but maybe it's gone as far as it should. Eric's a busy man now. I don't know that I want to take the next step.

"It's morning, and you have a lot to do today," I tell him. "Aren't you leaving for Bermuda?"

Eric strokes my hair with one hand and checks his BlackBerry with the other. "Come with me," he says, as he scrolls through his messages. I appreciate a man who can multitask, but does he have to do it when he's trying to seduce me? "Come to Bermuda this afternoon. Then I'm going on to London. I think I have a trip to Hong Kong after that. You could follow me wherever you want."

A knowing smile crosses my face. That's right. Eric's already told me that any woman comes second to his work. Two decades ago I wasn't willing to follow him across the country to graduate school, probably understanding even then that his priorities and mine would never be the same. Maybe my life would have been more exciting if I'd stayed with Eric, but it wouldn't have been my life. Even at twenty, I knew I didn't want to live in any man's shadow.

I stand up and wrap my arms around him. The very early morning sun streaking into the room is getting brighter and I give Eric a long kiss. "I love you," I tell him exuberantly. "I really love you."

"So we're having sex or are you coming to Bermuda?" he asks, slightly unsure of where we stand.

"Neither," I say. "Definitely neither. But you're still sexy and funny and gorgeous. Exactly what I remembered."

"Then why aren't you sleeping with me?" asks Eric, the man who never lets a deal slip through his fingers.

"Because I remembered a few other things, too."

Eric shakes his head and then smiles. "You're going to come back to me, you know. Maybe not tonight. But you'll come back to me."

"Awfully confident, aren't you," I parry.

"The key to my success," he says, kissing me one more time.

I slip into my high heels, give him one last hug, and head for the door. I'm a single woman now. I have to be careful how I spend my nickels.

Chapter FOUR

AS I'M LEAVING ERIC'S BUILDING, the doorman who ignored me when I arrived walks me toward the heavy glass door and pulls it open for me.

"I hope you had a marvelous evening," he says.

"Better than you can imagine," I tell him, tossing back my head and striding into the now quiet street.

He raises an eyebrow, clearly registering my remark. I don't mind burnishing Eric's reputation, and I haven't lied. It was a marvelous evening, though not the way the doorman thinks. I just had my first date in twenty-one years and everything went the way I wanted. I was charming and sexy, and I left a virgin. I can only hope Emily's dates end the same way. And just to prove that I'm not sexist, I hope Adam's do, too.

I stroll into early morning New York, feeling almost heady. The three A.M. revelers have finally gone to bed and the businessmen and store owners haven't started their day. Six forty to six forty-five may be the only time that New York sleeps.

I'm not ready to go home, so I decide to walk the few blocks over to my office. I'm officially starting back on Monday, but I might as well get a jump on organizing my sure to be overflowing inbox. A hansom cab comes clip-clopping by me, and the driver tips his cap. "Morning, ma'am. Need a ride through the park?"

"No, thank you," I say automatically. And then I think, why not? All these years in New York, and I've never splurged on a horse-drawn carriage. Sure, you're supposed to take this romantic ride on your first trip to Manhattan or with a man you love, but I'm playing by my own rules now.

"Wait," I call before he can get too far away. The driver stops again and I climb up into the buggy. I'm just settling into the faux-fur–lined seat when my cell phone rings.

"Hello," I say cheerfully, for once forgetting to screen the number before I pick up.

"Hi."

One syllable and my good mood disappears. And I'm not the only one affected. As if on cue, the dappled mare stops dead in her tracks and takes her daily dump. An apt editorial comment. Good horsey.

"Hello, Bill," I say. How is it that he happened to call me ten minutes after I left Eric? Did he pick up some electricity in the cosmos? A somebody-else-is-interested-in-her vibe?

"Hallie, I'm glad you're finally talking to me. Want to have breakfast?"

Does "hello" really count as talking to him? Maybe saying "Bill" was a little too intimate.

"Why are you calling me at seven o'clock?" I ask coolly, biding my time.

"I wanted to catch you before you went to the office," he says.

I pause. It's Saturday morning and my first day of even thinking about going to the office, and he knew that, too?

"Quick, what color pants am I wearing?" I ask, testing just how far his spousal ESP goes.

"Black," he says with assurance.

I sigh. That one was much too easy.

"We can get pancakes," Bill says, as if the lure of soggy, greasy, carb-ladened fritters can entice me. And I'm hungry, so it does. I should have eaten more caviar at Eric's. In fact, I should always eat more caviar.

"Okay," I say reluctantly. "Where should we meet?"

"Breakfast at the Regency," he says.

"Really?" I ask, shocked that my husband or former husband or soon-to-be-former husband picked the city's power breakfast spot.

"Just joking. There's a good diner on Ninth and Fifty-fifth. See you there in ten minutes."

He clicks off. A diner. What a surprise. I check my face in the compact mirror in my bag and note with satisfaction that my eye makeup is intact and my face is still flushed from Eric's kisses. I look down and wiggle my toes. Watch out, Bill, because I'm ready. Now I know why I bought these stilettos. Turns out they're my Fuck-You shoes.

I get to the diner and Bill is already comfortably settled into a red leather booth, filling in *The New York Times* crossword puzzle. The clues get harder every day, and here it is Saturday, and he's still doing the damn thing in ink. We used to work on the Sunday puzzle together, and I take some comfort in realizing that he's going to miss me every weekend. Not a chance Ashlee comes up with the five-letter word for the Swedish port opposite Copenhagen: Malmö.

"Hallie!" he says cheerfully. "Come sit down. I already ordered you a café au lait with skim milk and two Splendas."

"I only use one now," I say archly, sliding onto the banquette opposite him.

"You're looking great," he says, glancing at me appraisingly. "But isn't that blouse a little sheer for work?"

"I got dressed last night," I answer provocatively.

Bill doesn't seem to know what to make of my remark. "At least your clothes aren't wrinkled," he says, clearly not ready to imagine that I may have spent the night with someone else. He reaches over to smooth his fingers across my face. "In fact you're not wrinkled at all. Anywhere."

I'm pleased by the compliment—and the success of the QVC-ordered Victoria Principal anti-aging products that I now use daily—but I pull away from his touch. "Sorry, pal. You've lost your patting rights."

"Why? Doesn't twenty-one years count for anything?"

"Exactly my question," I say with an edge to my voice.

"Let's not go there," Bill says, shaking his head. "I just wanted to see you. I'm not looking for a fight this morning."

What would Bill and I have to fight about? Surely the fact that he's shtupping another woman shouldn't cause any bad blood between us. We don't even live together anymore. I can't complain that he set the thermostat too low or that he used up the last roll of Charmin Ultra and forgot to write it on the shopping list. In fact, I just bought a 48-pack all for myself. I'll never, ever have to worry about toilet paper again.

Oblivious, Bill starts chatting amiably, as if it were any other Saturday morning, telling me about the great movie he saw the other night and his newly improved tennis serve. I yawn audibly. I don't care if he aced Andre Agassi and Steffi Graf—and their toddler—all at the same time. If Ashlee's the one stroking Bill's body, she can be the one to stroke his goddamn ego, too.

The waiter brings over my Western omelet, which I'd ordered to send Bill the message that he doesn't know me as well as he thinks: I don't eat pancakes anymore. But the eggs look disgusting, and I just push them around on my plate.

"So, Bill, why did you want to meet?" I ask, taking a sip of watery café au lait.

"I don't want to lose touch with you." And trying to sound matter-of-fact, he adds, "Oh, and by the way, I remember you said that you got season tickets to the Knicks. The first game's not too far away, so I thought we'd make some plans."

I stare at him in amazement. "I got those tickets for you and me. For us."

"Well, 'us' is good," he says jovially. "We can go together. Ashlee won't mind. She doesn't even like basketball."

I take a bite of the disgusting omelet and almost gag. " 'Us,' is not good," I say.

"Why not?"

I shake my head. Bill's upended my entire universe and he's acting like he did nothing more scandalous than move the living room armchair a few inches to the left. Could he possibly not understand that his choice to be with Ashlee has repercussions? Losing courtside seats for the Knicks is the least of it.

"I got those tickets as part of my plan for life-after-the-kids-are-gone. You made a different plan."

Bill swipes a paper napkin across his lips to wipe away some errant maple syrup. "Hallie, be reasonable. We can still do things together. We're a family, and the kids being in college doesn't change that."

Unexpectedly, I sit back and start to laugh. I'm here at a greasy diner on Ninth Avenue, explaining to my Neanderthal mate why he's not going to see any three-point shots in person this season. I can only pray that Ashlee doesn't have premium cable and he won't get to see the games on TV, either.

"Unfortunately, darling, you did change our family. But one thing hasn't changed. You can still finish my breakfast." I stand up and slide my plate of eggs toward Bill.

"Thanks," he says, picking up his fork to dig in and flashing what he thinks is a charismatic grin. "Will you at least think about those Knicks tickets?"

"I will." I smile generously because that's what I typically do. I try to make everything work. I try to be nice. But not today.

"I'll think about the Knicks tickets and you think about this," I say sweetly. In one bold motion, I sweep my hand across the table, sending eggs, coffee, and half a glass of orange juice flying into his lap. A big blob of ketchup lands smack-dab in the middle of his white polo shirt. His fault—who uses ketchup on eggs anyway?

"HEY! What are you doing?" Bill screams, jumping up and smashing his knee against the table. I hope it's the bad one.

I toss back my head in satisfaction and stride toward the door. The websites are right that revenge is sweet. And in this case, it's also messy.

When I get to my office, I spend ten minutes sifting through papers and then stretch out exhausted on the sofa. But as tired as I am, I can't sleep, and I stare out the window at the water tower on the next roof. Not exactly the fourteen-million-dollar view from the Time Warner building (south tower), but in this office, my real estate passes for prime. If I stand in just the right spot and crane my head in just the right direction and it's a particularly clear day, I can even catch a glimpse of the Chrysler Building.

A lot's happened in the last twenty-four hours, but for some reason, one line plays over and over in my head. I keep hearing Eric say, *I heard about your little sister.* Though she was six years younger than me, I adored Amy and she idolized me. I read her bedtime stories, took her to school for show-and-tell, and helped her learn long division. (Why aren't fourth graders allowed to use calculators?) Studying in my room on sunny afternoons, I'd peek out my window and see my vivacious little sister turning somersaults in the backyard. After I went to college, Amy visited me often. We giggled together in my dorm room, and I let her meet all my friends.

Something I should never, ever have done.

My sweet sister Amy. Charming, funny, trusting Amy. I can still see her happy face that last day. Amy never dreamt that I couldn't protect her. I never imagined that I wouldn't get to laugh with my sister again.

I twist around on the sofa, trying to find a comfortable position to sleep in, but I keep thinking of Amy. I can't let Eric's comment make me relive that whole awful night. Restless, I head over to my desk to tackle the stacks of papers and messages that have piled up in my absence. After a few hours, my eyes are blurry from reviewing legal briefs and, exhausted, I finally lie down and take a long nap.

When I wake up, my office is dark and it takes me a moment to realize that it's Saturday night and I have nothing to do. Of course I could be flying to Bermuda with Eric in his private plane, so I guess this is my choice. My stomach is growling and I'm hungry. Dumping the eggs on Bill this morning was satisfying but not very filling. I check my watch, and it's after eight. I go out to my assistant's desk and flip through the loose-leaf notebook of take-out menus that she's so neatly put together: Mexican, Chinese, Italian, Indian, Thai, Cambodian, Lebanese, and Canadian. Canadian cuisine? I'm not in the mood for bacon or elk.

I close the notebook. I don't really want to sit here alone in an empty office building on Saturday night, anyway. I could go home and check to see if I've gotten my new DVDs from Netflix, or I could actually be brave and have dinner in a nice Manhattan restaurant alone. And why not?

I leave my office and stroll the few blocks over to the Brasserie, where I haven't been in years. A nice-looking crowd of people is milling around the entrance, and I figure I'll blend right in. The maître d' whisks the parties in front of me off to their tables, and when it's my turn, the young, dewy-skinned receptionist smiles distractedly at me.

"Please step to the side while you wait for the rest of your party to arrive," she says sweetly.

"I am the rest of my party," I say, trying to sound lighthearted.

But she doesn't get it and looks at me wide-eyed. Since she's miniskirted, beautiful, and about twenty-three, I'm sure it doesn't occur to her that anybody eats dinner alone.

An aggressive man behind me pushes me slightly and calls out to the young miss, "Excuse me, beautiful. We're all here. Party of four. Can you seat us?"

"Certainly, sir," she says, with more courtesy than he deserves, as she passes him on to the maître d'. Then she looks back to me, her problem client.

"Just *one*? You're by yourself?" she asks incredulously.

"Mmm-hmmm," I mumble, trying not to draw any attention to myself.

"All alone?" she asks. Her voice is loud so I'm sure everyone can hear, and her tone of voice suggests that given my pathetic situation, Sally Struthers might want to adopt me.

I think about explaining that I have a family, was married for a million years, and just canoodled with my ex-boyfriend. But instead I shake my head and sigh deeply.

"You come into this world alone and you die alone," I say solemnly.

She looks bewildered. Customers vying for tables have come up with a lot of persuasive arguments, but mine's an original. Who else has elevated getting a plate of steak frites into a metaphysical conundrum?

Amazingly, my ponderous pronouncement works, and a moment later, I'm being escorted to my table. We head to the dining area down a wide, theatrically lit staircase that's made for dramatic entrances. A wall of videoscreens plays back every arrival, and the restaurant patrons know to glance up every now and then to check out who's coming. My arrival will really give everyone something to talk about. Celebrities, politicians, and actors walk through all the time, but I'm that great rarity—A Woman Alone.

And for the rest of the meal, nobody will let me forget it.

"Waiting for someone?" asks the server, coming over to fill my water glass.

"Yes," I say. "Godot."

He hesitates. "And when will Mr. Godot be arriving?"

"Ah, that's Beckett's big theoretical question. Aren't we all waiting for Godot?"

The waiter shrugs. All he's waiting for is a good tip, and he's a little worried that he won't get one from me.

I'm ravenous and I scan the menu quickly.

"I'll have a mixed salad and the rack of lamb," I tell him.

"The lamb is prepared for two people," he says, pointing to the small print.

That explains the ridiculous price, but I want it anyway, so I just nod and close the menu. The waiter looks uncertainly at the second place setting, but decides to leave it. As he rushes away from the table, I realize that I have nothing to read and nothing to do but look at the animated couples all around me. I call the waiter back and order a glass of Shiraz.

"Nice choice," he says, and I smile, basking in his approval.

I eat a breadstick and curiously watch the scene unfolding in the restaurant. A mob of well-dressed singles trolls the bar, searching for the perfect mate. The thirtysomething couple on my left are clearly on a first date. He's flirting hard and trying to impress her, but she's looking bored and toying with the stem of her martini glass. Eventually he'll figure out that she's just not that into him. I shake my head, thinking how I'd hate to be going out with strangers again. I played that game once, and when I married Bill, I thought I'd won. Little did I know.

If somebody had told me that twenty years later I'd end up alone at the Brasserie on a Saturday night, would I still have picked Bill—the double-dealing, self-absorbed Knicks-ticket-demanding idiot who left me for Ashlee with two Es? And if not, who would I have married?

I take a sip of my Shiraz. Not to be too cocky about it, but I certainly had other choices—and not just Eric. I reel through the memories of my major romances and feel a little glow. I wonder where those guys are now. Could one of them be sitting somewhere alone tonight in a restaurant, too?

The waiter comes back, straining under the weight of his tray, and puts down the largest rack of lamb I've ever seen. He glances at the still empty seat across from me.

"You can serve us both," I say airily.

The waiter can't decide if I'm crazy or have a boyfriend outside puffing his third cigarette and cursing Mayor Bloomberg's no-smoking-indoors rules. But the waiter neatly fills both plates and scurries away.

I tuck into the tasty lamb and when I polish it off, I'm still hungry. I cheerfully switch my plate for the full one opposite me and keep eating. Sometimes waiting for Godot has its advantages.

Having a plan has its advantages, too—and under the influence of a good dinner and a bad bar scene, I think I've hatched one. I feel a shiver of excitement. If Eric found me, why can't I find all my other old boyfriends? It wouldn't be dating, exactly, just looking up people who once mattered to me—and could matter again. I fumble through my pocketbook and find a pen but no paper, so I pull the slightly soggy cocktail napkin out from under the wineglass. I write down Eric's name, add two others, and doodle hearts around them. Then, biting the edge of the pen, I reluctantly write down one more name.

Whatever did happen to those old boyfriends? All the men I didn't marry? It just may be time to find out.

Chapter FIVE

IF ANYTHING CONVINCES ME of the sanity of my plan, it's my Wednesday night at the opera.

The minute we get out of the cab in front of Lincoln Center, Bellini begins pulling at the front of her dress and hiking up the sides of her strapless bra.

"For goodness' sakes, you're acting like a thirteen-year-old girl at her first bar mitzvah," I tell her.

Bellini, who grew up in Cincinnati, has no idea what I'm talking about. She's probably never seen a chopped-liver sculpture, either.

"You're here to be supportive," she reminds me.

"So's the bra," I tell her. "I guess both of us are letting you down."

Bellini rolls her eyes. When she first asked me to tag along to this event a while ago, she explained that I'd be the married friend at her side who made it easier for her to meet men. Someone to talk to at intermissions so she wouldn't feel awkward at the Metropolitan Opera's "Meet at the Met" night—an event where listening to Mozart plays second fiddle to finding your future mate.

Little did either of us realize that by the time tonight arrived, I'd be single, too.

"Remember, you don't have to stand on the sidelines if you don't want to," says Bellini. "You look fabulous. You can join the hunt. In fact, you should."

"No way," I say, for the twelfth time.

"But you did great with Eric," she reminds me. "I'm so proud of you that you're bouncing back."

Bellini's right. I'm feeling better. But this isn't my scene. As we step into the lobby, I realize that the New York dating world is even tougher than I thought. For one thing, the place is teeming with beautifully dressed, perfectly lip-glossed women—and very few men. Could it be that the men in Manhattan would skip the opera to sit home, swill beer, and watch the third rerun of the World Series of Poker?

"Ready?" asks Bellini, squeezing my arm as if the starting gun is about to go off.

"I'd never be ready for this. But I can't wait to watch you."

Bellini looks around the crowd, spots an attractive man standing by the bar, and with her Ohio insouciance, casually strolls over and leans her elbows on the highly polished wood counter. "Come here often?" she asks, gamely.

Her target looks her over carefully and Bellini obviously passes the first hurdle, because he decides she's worth a response. "Not for the last twenty-six months. This is kind of my coming out party."

He puts his foot up on the bar rail and, as the cuff of his elegantly cut suit pants pull up, I notice a piece of jewelry at his ankle. Ever since Martha Stewart wore one, the anklet's become as recognizable as a Panther watch from Cartier. Except this little trinket probably comes from Sing Sing. Given the tracking band, it's clear to me that the man's under house arrest. I don't know if he's come to the opera to listen to music or to impress his parole officer.

"So, I see you got a few hours out tonight," I say, jumping into the conversation. "No opera for twenty-six months because you were too busy making license plates?"

Bellini elbows me. I figure she doesn't like my being rude to her potential New Year's Eve date. But on the other hand, I need to warn her, because even though she's an accessories maven, she might not have come across one of these little baubles in her buying for Bendel's.

"So, what'd they get you for? Insider trading or corporate stock fraud?" I ask.

"Nothing so mundane. I'm not one of those sleazoids from Enron. I'm an art thief," he says haughtily.

Apparently there is honor among thieves—or at least a pride in the pecking order. And this guy thinks art thief is close to the top. Look at how much I'm learning. Bill leaves me, and my world is expanding. Who knew divorce would be so broadening?

"So what do you steal?" I ask, as if this is now part of my normal conversation, just one of those getting-to-know-you topics.

"They only got me on conspiracy," he says coyly, "but it's been alleged that I steal Monets."

"Just like in *The Thomas Crown Affair*!" Bellini exults. "How fabulous. What an exciting life!"

I shoot Bellini a what-are-you-doing look. "I hated that movie," I say.

"But Pierce Brosnan was so sexy in the remake," Bellini says. And then, putting her finger against her inmate's—and I hope not future mate's—cheek, she says saucily, "You look a lot like him, by the way."

"So I've been told," he says.

Oh God, how did this happen? If three-hundred-dollar opera tickets net you an ex-con, imagine who you meet Ladies' Night at O'Malley's bar.

I tuck my arm through Bellini's and try to physically pull her away from Mr. This Is So Not the Right Guy for You.

"Let's go study the libretto," I say.

"I did that last night," she says, resisting my efforts.

But her admiration for a B-list movie and a possibly A-list art thief doesn't pay off. Her guy finishes his drink and slams it on the bar. "Listen, ladies, nice to meet you, but I'm off. Seem to be a lot of women here and it's time for me to meet a few other people." He pats Bellini on the back and swaggers away, and we watch him move toward a buxom blonde across the room. Clearly Bellini's strapless bra wasn't enough—she should have gone for a padded push-up.

Bellini blinks a few times and looks after him, crestfallen. "And he was so cute," she says.

"An ex-con," I remind her.

"Nobody's perfect," she says with a sigh. "He seemed very cultured."

"Right. He listens to music and steals art."

Fortunately, the lights in the lobby dim, signaling the start of the opera. "Come on, let's go hear some Mozart," I say soothingly.

"Mozart, I hate Mozart. I don't like any opera," Bellini complains. "Let's get out of here. It's Wednesday. Free drinks at O'Malley's."

But we never quite make it to the bar, because as we're strolling down Broadway, we're waylaid by a blinking neon sign in a storefront.

LAND OF THE MIDNITE SUN!
24 HR SUNLESS TANS

"Wow. The only thing open all night in Ohio is the emergency room," says Bellini, staring at the sign. Then she looks at me and laughs. "I guess in New York not being beautiful enough is the real emergency. You can probably get a manicurist to your house faster than an ambulance."

I grin and start to walk away, but Bellini quickly calls after me. "Wait a sec. Look at this: thirty-nine-buck special tonight. Let's do it. That's ten dollars less than I usually pay."

Than she usually pays? Bellini grabs my arm and drags me inside, and I notice that her hand on top of my pale skin glistens a rich nut brown. Since it's October and it's been raining for a week, it's suddenly obvious to me that my sweet Bellini isn't a sunless-tanning virgin.

I stand back while Bellini chats with the attendant at the desk.

"They can take us immediately," she says excitedly when she comes back—as if snagging a sunless tan at nine P.M. is as hard as getting a photo of Mary-Kate Olsen eating.

"Okay," I say with a sigh. "But what am I getting myself into?"

"The deluxe spray-tanning package. Nothing gives a girl a glow like a head-to-toe spritz. Takes about fifteen minutes and lasts a whole week. Well, maybe five days. Or three." She pauses. "Definitely two."

"Great. Because if there's one thing I want in my life, it's to look fabulous tonight when I go to sleep alone," I say as we head to the back. After singles night at the Metropolitan Opera, you'd think I'd be a little warier of Bellini's ideas, but what the heck. Maybe my skin will turn orange, but no man's ever going to see me naked again, anyway.

Bellini disappears behind a door and points me toward my own room. "Get ready. Your technician will be there in a minute."

I step uncertainly into a white tiled room with a bright light hanging in the middle. Draped over a hook on the door is a thin robe and what appears to be a paper G-string. I hold it up to the light and turn it slowly around in my hand, trying to make sense of the circular piece of elastic, no bigger than a rubber band, with the tiniest triangle of white paper attached to the front and an even narrower strip on the back. Or maybe it goes the other way around. I've never worn thong underwear, and now I know why. Whichever way I put this on, it's going to feel weird.

I slip out of my dress and spend as much time as I can neatly hanging it up. Then I confront the thong thing. Gingerly stepping into it, I pull up the elastic and realize that somehow I've managed to plant the modesty-protecting triangle over my left thigh. Very useful. I've always been slightly shy about my cellulite, but I have a feeling that's not what the patch is supposed to be covering.

Taking off the confounded thing, I'm trying to untangle the now-twisted strings when the technician knocks airily and bursts in without pausing for me to say "Come in." She must have trained under my gynecologist; he never waits either.

The technician offers me a big smile. She's tall, regal-looking, and magnificently dark-skinned. Either she's from Jamaica, or she's a walking advertisement for the company.

"I'm Denise. Ready to start?" she asks. She cheerfully takes the panties, puts them in the proper position, and holds them out for me. Once they're on, she eyes them critically, then reaches over to make a small adjustment. "You wouldn't want the tan line to be uneven," she says, as if the thong-shaped white patch will be previewed on the Howard Stern show.

She reaches outside the door and pulls in a heavy metal canister with a spray nozzle attached. I'm hoping it isn't filled with the same pesticides Lawn Doctor uses to kill off crabgrass. But clearly it's filled with some sort of potent chemical, because Denise pulls out a face mask and fastens it around her own nose and mouth. Well, at least one of us is protected. She doesn't even dare sniff the stuff she's going to be spraying all over my body and face. Good news is I won't get skin cancer from basking in the sun. Bad news is I might grow a third eye.

"So what color are you thinking?" Denise asks, fiddling around with the nozzle.

"Something like yours," I say, admiring her smooth, flawless complexion.

"I think chocolate brown may be a little dark for you," she says tactfully. "I'd recommend a deep beige."

Funny, that's exactly the shade the house painter suggested for my living room. Doesn't anybody look at me and think chartreuse?

Denise tosses out some instructions, and before I know it, I'm standing in front of her wearing nothing but a paper thong, which is now riding up my butt. With my legs splayed apart and my arms stretched out straight from my shoulders, I feel like a criminal waiting to be strip-searched. Hard to imagine that I'm submitting to this—and there's not even a policeman aiming a gun at my head. Sorry, officer, my only crime is that I'm too pale.

And, obviously, we're going to take care of that inexcusable offense right now. Denise comes at me with the hose and a fine mist hits my legs. It tickles, and I try not to giggle. Beauty is serious business. She sprays up and down my lower body, with the precision of an *artiste*, a modern-day Michelangelo creating the *David*. And that seems to be how Denise sees herself, too.

"Shall I do some body sculpting?" she asks. "I can slim down those thighs of yours and maybe narrow the hips a little."

I imagine her pulling a chisel out of her back pocket.

"Go ahead, chip away," I say.

Denise laughs. "No, it's just a matter of shading. I just make some areas darker than others and create an optical illusion."

"Can you do something about my nose?"

"Your nose is lovely," she says. "But I will work on the thighs."

She purses her lips and concentrates on the one area of my body that nobody ever wanted to focus on before. When she's done, she tells me it's time to tan my face—so I should close my eyes and hold my breath.

Trying to follow instructions, I clamp my fingers around my nose, as if I'm on a diving board.

"You might not want to do that," advises Denise, "unless you're going for the patterned look."

I drop my hand away and she turns her spritzer to me full-on. Quickly, my face, neck, ears, arms, torso, back, butt, and feet get colorized—probably with more finesse than Ted Turner exercised on those old black-and-white movies. Will Woody Allen object to my tan as much as he did to seeing *Gone with the Wind* in primary colors?

Denise puts her equipment away and gives me a friendly wave.

"Stay perfectly still for fifteen minutes," she says, as she disappears.

I stand in place for about two minutes, which for me is a record, then walk over to the full-length mirror. Yup, that's me all right—only darker and with an evened-out complexion. In fact, I look kind of sexy. For once in my life I have a healthy glow—though maybe the FDA wouldn't agree on the healthy part.

I shuffle around for about ten more minutes, then get dressed and go to the lobby where Bellini and I exchange delighted squeals. I'm feeling so good now I don't even mind going out with her for a drink, though I insist that we upgrade from O'Malley's to the lounge at the St. Regis.

In the classy hotel bar, we plant ourselves on high stools and I cross and uncross my shimmering honey-colored legs, admiring how they gleam. I hope I don't wear out the tan at the knee. In no time at all, I have two martinis and smile back at a man who smiles at me. I'm feeling so heady that I tell myself I'm going for this spray tan every week.

Well after midnight, I'm tired but Bellini isn't ready to leave. I excuse myself to go to the ladies' room and quickly lather my hands and

splash some cold water on my face. Bellini walks in then and gives a little shriek.

"You didn't wash, did you?" she asks in alarm. "You have to let the
color set for twenty-four hours."

I glance into the mirror again and see that my evenly tanned face is
now streaked with white stripes. I avert my eyes to the sink and, horrified, watch the glorious spray tan on my arms and hands swirl down
the drain.

"What do I do now?" I ask, holding out my arms to Bellini and re-
vealing the back of my hands, which seem to shine bright white.

"Max Factor Instant Bronze," she says firmly.

"If I could get bronzed from a tube at CVS, why did we do this?" I
sigh and stare at my mottled complexion. "What a disaster."

"Look on the bright side," says Bellini, the same woman who saw
husband potential in an ex-con. "At least you didn't get sunburned."

At my office the next morning, I sneak frequent peeks in my compact
mirror, trying to decide if I look more like a raccoon or early Michael
Jackson. Eventually, I turn my attention to something even more
distasteful—a file folder on my desk, filled with a stack of pictures. I
quickly flip through them. Naked woman. Naked man and woman.
Naked man and woman copulating.

"Eww," I blurt out. "This isn't what I needed to see before I've had
my first cup of coffee."

The beefy man across the desk from me goes to cross his arms in
front of his chest, but his too-tight suit pulls against his hefty arms and
he settles for putting his palms flat out in front of him. Joe Diddly may
be the most celebrated private investigator on the East Coast, but evidence suggests he's been spending too much time staking out Dunkin'
Donuts.

"Pretty good work," he says triumphantly. "I got him, didn't I?"

"Definitely," I agree. "But unfortunately the guy you got was our
client."

Joe reaches for one of the eight by twelve Kodachrome blowups, showing our client, Charles Tyler, being straddled by a young redheaded woman who works for him at the publicity department of Alladin Films—the very same colleague he claimed he'd never even met for a Frappuccino. Maybe so, but something frothy is definitely going on.

"You told me to follow the redhead, Melina Marks," Joe says, reaching into his briefcase for a white donut box. So I was wrong. He eats Krispy Kremes. He slides the box across the table and after taking a moment to choose, I reach for a chocolate one glazed with sprinkles.

"We wanted some information on her personal life, but not this," I say, delicately taking a bite. "Let me explain. Mr. Tyler's being sued for sex discrimination by a woman who works for him named Beth Lewis. Beth's colleague—the redhead Melina—got a promotion Beth thought she deserved. She claims that Melina only got the job because she was screwing their boss, Mr. Tyler."

Joe yawns. "That's not a case, it's a catfight. Sounds to me like Beth is just pissed that Tyler was sleeping with the other girl instead of her. Maybe she wanted her own shot at him. Think the guy's that good in bed?"

Dutifully, I take the photos, so I can answer Joe's question. One picture captures a particularly gymnastic contortion with the redhead's shapely legs wrapped around Mr. Tyler's neck. Looks to me like she's the one with the talents, but then I realize this is all beside the point.

"If what Beth claims is true, our client's in a lot of trouble," I say.

"Why?" asks Joe. "If there were a law against sleeping with people you work with, who'd ever go to work?"

"There is a law," I say in my best legalese. "The California Supreme Court just ruled that workers can sue if a colleague who's sleeping with the boss is shown preferential treatment."

"Preferential, shmeferential. Anyway, we live in New York," he says, licking chocolate off his finger.

I laugh, deciding that instead of educating him, I should try to get Joe and eleven of his brethren on our jury.

He pats the stack of photos. "Well, you wanted me to follow Melina and get you some background. I did. Sorry it's not what you expected."

"Definitely not what we expected. Mr. Tyler swore to my boss Arthur he was innocent."

Joe pauses and looks at me curiously, a new idea clearly crossing his mind. "So you and your boss, Arthur . . ." he says, wagging his finger back and forth. "You two ever do the hokey-pokey?"

I laugh. "Only at his three-year-old's birthday party."

Joe shrugs, then stands up to stretch his oversize frame. With his job done and me not supplying any good gossip, he tosses the now-empty box of doughnuts into the wastebasket. "By the way, tough break that your husband left you. Want me to follow him? No charge. Be my pleasure."

I make a face. "Thanks, but I already know what he's doing. I don't need to see it in black and white."

"Or color either?" he jokes.

I shoot him a look, wondering if he's making a veiled reference to my streaked tan. But then I decide I'm being oversensitive. "How'd you know about my husband?"

"I'm a detective. I know everything."

He gets up and paces around the room, then looks me up and down appreciatively.

"You'll be dating again in no time," Joe says. "When you meet a new guy, let me know and I'll do a background check."

"Thanks, but no new guys on the horizon," I say, and then I hesitate. "But how about an old guy? If I want to find somebody I haven't seen in twenty years. Think you could help with that?"

"You don't need me," Joe says, trying to button his suit jacket around his ample midsection. "A dozen online search engines can find anybody, anywhere, in a second."

"I tried, but the guy's name is Barry Stern. Type it in and a million people come up. I don't know if the Barry Stern I want is the neurosurgeon in Bel Air, the plastic surgeon in Boca, or the plumbing supplier in Brooklyn."

Joe comes back to sit down again. He takes out a dog-eared spiral notebook from his jacket pocket. Nice old-fashioned touch. And given his retro sexual politics, I wouldn't expect him to have a Palm Pilot.

I quickly fill Joe in on my idea of getting in touch with all my old boyfriends. I tell him about Eric, and then explain that I want to get in touch with Barry Stern, who I met one summer in a youth hostel, backpacking across Europe. We went off the next day and traveled together for four weeks, our student Eurail Passes making us feel like we owned the world. In Gaudi's park in Barcelona, we wandered in awe, admiring the serpentine mosaics, and in Florence, I had my first gelato at Vivoli's café, just off the Piazza Santa Croce. It tasted nothing like the Dairy Queen cones I was raised on. Barry loved art, and took me from museum to museum. At the Uffizi, we stood in front of Botticelli's *The Birth of Venus* and the long-haired, brilliant Barry regaled me with a story of how the artist had denounced his own glorious masterpiece late in life, regretting that he had painted anything so secular.

"I had a poster of her hanging in my bedroom as a teenager," said Barry, staring at the naked goddess with the swirling flaxen hair. I'd nodded approvingly. At least one boy in America hadn't gone to sleep every night under a picture of Farrah Fawcett.

"She's beautiful," I said admiringly.

"She is. But not as beautiful as you."

He'd kissed me then, a long, sweet passionate kiss, and I knew that Venus, the goddess of love, had done her job.

Now as I finish up my romantic reminiscence, Joe jots down a few notes. Professional that he is, he offers no reaction. Like any good psychotherapist—or a saleswoman at Versace who hears you're a size fourteen—he listens but doesn't raise an eyebrow.

"Did you ever see Barry after that?" he asks.

"No, he was still traveling. He went on to India and I had to get back to New York to start law school. We exchanged letters for a while, and suddenly they stopped. I kept writing, but I didn't hear back. I never knew why."

"Still have the letters?" Joe asks.

"I don't know. They're probably somewhere in the attic." I make a face, thinking about the boxes that I should have cleared out years ago.

"If you find anything that might be helpful, let me know," he says. He tucks the notebook back in his breast pocket, which means he won't be able to button the jacket again. Then Joe leans over my desk to close the folder of pictures from the Tyler case. He leaves his hand on top of it, tapping a warning finger. "Put these in a safe place. You don't want anybody seeing them who shouldn't."

"Of course," I say.

"And sorry for bringing you information about your client you didn't want to know. Sometimes when you go digging around in things, you find something different from what you bargained for."

I don't get up to my attic until the next night, and when I do, I bump my head immediately on a low-hanging rafter. I rub my forehead and look around at the dusty boxes of yellowed paperback books, broken lamps that I'll never rewire, and grubby garment bags that hold my once-favorite dresses in sizes six to fourteen, representing years of yo-yoing between pizza binges and Slim-Fast diets.

I duck and carefully take a few steps toward the Footwear Hall of Fame—two dozen pair of tiny red and blue Keds lined up on an old bookcase, all the shoes Adam and Emily wore until they were five. Next to them are the boxes containing every scrap of paper the children ever fingerpainted or put a crayon to, which I'm saving to donate to their future presidential libraries. But I'm never giving away the card Adam made one Mother's Day with a purple sun, a green flower, and the words I lov momy. Now he gets all A's at Dartmouth, but his spelling hasn't really improved.

I crouch down next to the huge wicker trunk that served as my first coffee table in my first apartment. I tentatively open it, knowing that over the years I made it the receptacle for everything I didn't know where else to store. I push aside the handheld mixer that I'm pretty sure doesn't work anymore and the box of earrings whose mates are long lost. I always figured I'd wear them as pins. And look at this—I saved Bill's mother's recipe for her famous lemon cake. Next time I see her, I can finally tell her the truth. It's dry and inedible, just like her Thanksgiving turkey.

I dig around and suddenly something sharp slices into me.

"Shit!" I say, pulling back my stinging hand. I wrap my cut thumb with the edge of my T-shirt and hold it tightly until the bleeding is stanched. I look into the trunk for the offending object and spot it immediately: the colorful blown-glass perfume bottle that was Bill's first gift to me. Years ago I accidentally broke the stopper, creating a sharp, jagged edge, but I couldn't throw it away. Damn Bill. Even when he's not around, he's hurting me.

I gingerly lift out the bottle and rummage more carefully through the trunk. And bingo. There, toward the bottom, is a small stack of thin blue paper, held together by a crumbling, stretched-out elastic band. Just seeing the long-forgotten aerograms that we once used for trans-Atlantic letters causes a nostalgic pang. I carefully unfold one. The paper is all but translucent and Barry's writing is teeny-tiny, so he can fit all the stories he wants to tell me onto one prepaid self-folding sheet. I run back down the stairs to the first floor to get my reading glasses and rush back up. In the dim light, I sit cross-legged on the splintery attic floor, though why I didn't bring the letters downstairs to a comfortable chair beats me. Nothing seems to be able to leave this attic.

In the first missive, Barry is at Heathrow Airport, waiting for his flight to India. He misses me passionately and I will always be his Venus. Next letter, he's been in Agra for almost a week and describes the Taj Mahal: "*. . . the perfect symmetry, the ethereal luminescence, the sheer scale. It was built as a monument to love, and I'd build no less for you.*" Wow, that's nice. I could be the eighth Wonder of the World.

But by letters three and four, my pull isn't quite so monumental. Now Barry's aerograms are filled with stories about prayer processions, rock-cut shrines, and a temple whittled out of the side of a mountain. He's made a pilgrimage to the Ganges to cleanse his soul in the holy waters, and he was just a little disappointed because some of the other pilgrims, joining him knee-deep in the river, were there to do their laundry. Barry also tells me about some great guru he's thinking of finding. He doesn't mention if he's the one who inspired the Beatles or some lesser-known guy who takes on acolytes who haven't gone platinum.

In the fifth letter, Barry has his journey planned. He'll go by rickshaw to the edge of town and then take a goat-drawn cart as far as possible into the hills. After that, he's planning on hiking for however long it takes to the guru's mountain shrine.

And that's where the letter trail ends.

I take off my glasses, misty-eyed at thinking of Barry, barely a year or two older than my Adam is now, so hopeful, so idealistic. Back then, Barry and I both thought we were wise and grown-up, incredibly knowledgeable about life. Little did we know how much we still had to learn.

Back all those years ago, I was heartbroken when Barry stopped writing. At first, all I could think about was how hurt I felt, but then I started to worry about him. Did something dreadful occur in the mysterious hills of India? Did Barry run out of water on his hike? Was he abducted by marauding tribesmen? Could he have fallen off the goat cart? I thought about it often, but I never knew.

Ten days later, Joe Diddly has the answer.

Chapter SIX

NOBODY HAS ANSWERED the phone at this place in the three weeks I've been calling, but Joe Diddly swore this was Barry Stern's current address. As long as Arthur needed me in San Francisco to take a deposition, I figured I might as well drive the extra seventy miles to the old Carmelite monastery. After my scenic trip through the hills, I pull up and see a sign for "Heavenly Spirit Retreat Center." I must be here. Either that, or I've died and Saint Peter's given the nod and passed me on through.

As I step out of the car into the bright sunshine, I smooth the skirt of the navy blue suit I'm still wearing from my morning in court. Now I wish I'd changed in the bathroom of the 7-Eleven where I stopped to pick up lunch—a box of Pringles, a bag of Doritos, and a greasy hot dog with everything on it. I'm sorry about those onions now, too.

I've already called Arthur to say that the deposition I took in the Tyler case wasn't encouraging. Beth Lewis's new boss on the West Coast, where she moved after leaving Alladin Films, claimed she was a perfect employee. Beth herself was calm and unshakable in her assertion that Mr. Tyler had no reason other than a personal one to pass her over.

Since there's nothing I can do about that problem now, I put it to the back of my mind and follow a row of slightly scraggly trees that line a grassy entranceway. I wouldn't quite call it a lawn—brown patches seem to outnumber green ones, and the clumps of crabgrass outnumber everything. But pretty wildflowers dot the landscape and I see a glistening pond off in the distance.

Turning in the other direction, I spot three people and I hurriedly walk over to them.

"Excuse me," I say. "Do you know where I could find the main house?"

The two women abruptly pull back and walk briskly away. Is my onion breath really that bad? The man doesn't answer me either, but he pauses briefly and jerks his head to the left.

"I'm looking for the main house," I repeat.

He jerks his head twice to the left. Either he has a mild case of Tourette's or he's trying to tell me something. Probably the latter, because he motions for me to follow him, which I do. We arrive at a large stone house and go inside to a bright, welcoming room. Two dozen people are scattered around, all barefoot and dressed in loose-fitting pants. Some are in little groups, holding hands, and everyone is sitting cross-legged on thin tatami mats. At least I think that's what they're called. Or maybe I'm confused and tatami is that sashimi I like.

For several moments, I stand bewildered, not sure what to do. Then someone catches my eye and glances toward an empty mat. When I don't move, he raises his hand slightly and makes a small gesture for me to sit down.

Okay, this is the Heavenly Spirit Retreat Center. Good guess says I've wandered into a meditation session. I slip off my pumps and plop onto a mat, glad that my skirt is pleated but wishing I hadn't worn panty hose. In fact, I often wish I wasn't wearing panty hose.

The woman next to me has her fingers tented together in a prayer-like position. Her eyes are closed and she has a peaceful expression on her face. The man on my left has his hands on his knees and is staring unblinkingly at his toes. I notice that both of my neighbors have perfectly squared shoulders and straight backs. I don't know what this meditating stuff does for your soul, but it certainly seems to improve your posture.

The room is silent and nobody moves. I decide to close my own eyes and concentrate on a happy memory. Let's see. There was my wedding day. Nope, take that off the happy memories list. Maybe the April afternoon strolling along the Seine in Paris? No, the man holding my hand was Bill. Something good that happened with the kids? A picture comes into my mind of Emily and Adam at the zoo when they were toddlers. Adam is jumping up and down to imitate the orangutans and Emily is mimicking their funny faces. I try not to laugh out loud. Then I remember Emily entertaining the monkeys with cartwheels, and a giggle escapes. It's just a little one, but it ricochets around the silent room like a gunshot. I look up, humiliated, but to my surprise, nobody has even batted an eyelash. Literally. What concentration. If you harnessed all the focused energy in this room, you could probably light up San Francisco for a week.

I have a feeling that I'm not supposed to be thinking about monkeys, gunshots, or California's energy crisis. Plus, my foot has fallen asleep and pins and needles are running up my leg. But they're nothing compared to the tingle I feel a moment later.

A gong sounds and suddenly the mood around me intensifies. There's a stir in the room as my fellow retreaters begin to hum. Quickly the hum builds to a drone and the drone to a chant: *om om om*. The buzz rings out like a chiming bell—or maybe a test of the Emergency Broadcast System.

The chant heralds the arrival of a man in flowing pants and a white caftan, who enters from a side door. The revered leader of the retreat— Rav Jon Yoma Maharishi.

Formerly known as Barry Stern.

Unwittingly, I grin and give him a little wave, but, fortunately, he doesn't notice. I'd laughed when Joe Diddly told me that the nice, arty, intellectual boy I once knew had become "a spiritual leader and teacher of enlightenment, merging the philosophies of the early Chan masters, the Zen Buddhists, and Swami Chinduh." (Why not throw in the philosophies of Dear Abby and the Reverend Al Sharpton just to be safe?) But Barry must be doing something right. The minute he walked in, my karma definitely improved.

Barry's audience—aka Rav Jon Yoma Maharishi's acolytes—are gazing at him in rapture. The chanting has continued and is only getting louder. I also stare at him intently. I don't mean to be harsh, but Barry hasn't held up over the years quite as well as Eric. I'm sure his soul is pure but his body is a little paunchy. Even under the caftan, I can see a bulging belly. I guess his retreats don't involve fasting.

Barry raises his hands and the chanting stops.

"Our satsang session now begins," he says in a soft voice barely above a whisper. "As you know, I will break the transforming spiritual silence of this weekend retreat only for this one ten-minute session."

A silent retreat would explain the guy with the jerking head—and the women who walked away from me. But only ten minutes to talk all weekend? My Sprint plan's a lot better.

"I will take questions on the pursuit of truth, the search for enlightenment, and the quest for selfhood," the Maharishi says. That seems like a lot to cram into ten minutes, and then he adds, "We can also explore the joys of oneness."

I wouldn't mind exploring the joys of twoness, since current experience tells me that oneness leaves something to be desired. But the woman next to me is nodding vigorously.

"Maharishi, I'm seeking cosmic consciousness. Can you enlighten us on how you found it?"

"Hmmmmm," says Barry, I'm not sure if he's thinking or chanting. "My journey began on a mountaintop and suddenly I felt I was floating in infinite space. All boundaries disappeared and as the doors of perception opened, there were no walls to hold me in."

As far as I know, there are never any walls on mountaintops, at least until the condo developers move in.

But the room is enthralled, and Barry continues. "I saw that life is One, that all the people in the universe, seen and unseen, known and unknown, experienced and not experienced, conscious and not conscious, glorious and not glorious . . ."

Yeah, yeah, all of us. Pretty and not pretty. Smart and not smart. Members of the Chaddick Tennis Club, not members of the Chaddick Tennis Club. Let's move it along.

". . . that everyone and everything that exists and has ever existed is really Love. And in its truest form, it provides an intensity that is joyous, transcendent, and almost overwhelmingly pleasurable for the human body."

Am I reading something into this? Sounds to me like he's saying that the goal of enlightenment is better orgasms. If the Sunday school pastor when I was growing up gave sermons like this, I might have spent more time in church.

A man in the middle of the room must think he's at a presidential news conference because he raises a finger and says, "Follow-up question, Rav?"

I nervously look at my watch. These people may be trying to get in touch with their inner peace, but I've been trying for weeks now to get in touch with Barry. The vow of silence must extend to the telephone. We've used up six minutes on just this one question. Only four more minutes and we're back to charades.

The follow-up query seems to take forever, and Rav Jon Yoma Maharishi's answer even longer. Now the tension in the room is palpable. With time running out, all the om-ing can't stop the anxiety from rising as people try to get in their questions.

"Is there a quick way to the bliss of Self-Discovery?" someone asks.

"Can you outline the top three tools for hopping on a spiritual path?" asks a man. He's clearly a corporate executive expecting to find the answer to life in a PowerPoint presentation.

Before Barry can answer, another exec-type shoots out, "Do you have a program for people who only have weekends to transcend their Ego?"

Fifteen seconds to go. Concerned about my own ego, I boldly stand and blurt out the only question that's on my mind.

"Do you remember me, Barry?"

Three dozen people turn around and stare. A few of them murmur the name "Barry" quizzically, over and over. I don't blame them. They've probably paid a lot of money to hear the Wisdom of the Rav Jon Yoma Maharishi. The Wisdom of Barry doesn't sound nearly as valuable.

Barry looks in my direction, but I don't see even a flicker of recognition in his eyes. I should be insulted, but instead I'm pissed. Come on, buddy. Eric said I haven't changed a bit.

The chanting begins again and the Maharishi faces the group, bows, and takes his cue to glide solemnly out of the room. I start to rush after him, but when I get outside, he seems to have disappeared into thin air. Did the change from Barry to Rav come with a magic Harry Potter cape?

I start to head back to my car to leave, but then I stop. I came all this way to talk to Barry, and while talking doesn't seem to be a popular sport around here, I'm not going to give up. And as long as I'm here, I might as well try to get some enlightenment.

I'd like to go rest in my room but realize I don't have one. I wander again toward the main area and see that everybody has come outside. I find my friend with the jerking head and make exaggerated motions to him suggesting that I need to register. When he doesn't get that, I lean my head to the side and close my eyes, hoping he'll understand that I could use a place to sleep. But he takes it the wrong way. He puts his arm around me, strokes my shoulder, and points toward his own room. This could be my one chance to experience the silent fuck, but I let it pass right by. I shake my head vigorously to tell him no.

For the rest of the afternoon, I roam the grounds like everybody else, figuring I'll try to give this spiritual quest thing a whirl. *Om, Om, Om,* I mumble to myself. Gosh, that's boring. *Rome, Home, Dome, Nome.* A little better. *Barry, Barry, Barry.* Maybe I can conjure him up.

And damn if a man doesn't suddenly appear in front of me. Not Barry, but then, I'm only a novice. What woman wouldn't be proud to summon up a man, any man, on command? This one—bald, tall, broad-shouldered, and dressed all in white—crosses his arms in front of his chest, looking surprisingly like Mr. Clean. He raises his hand and beckons me forward, wanting me to come with him. Setting off, Mr. Clean walks briskly ahead of me and I follow four paces behind. We go past the pond to a narrow path in the woods and I see a small cottage at the end.

And Barry is standing out front.

Mr. Clean goes inside and closes the door, but Barry stays where he is. Once I'm standing in front of him, I'm not sure exactly what to do. If he were really just Barry, I'd give him a hug. But do you touch Rav Jon Yoma Maharishi? Maybe I kiss his ring. No, that's the other guy. Barry takes the lead and puts both his hands on my head. Am I being blessed, or is he going to give me a kiss?

Barry steps back and slowly spreads his arms in a welcoming gesture. When I saw him this afternoon in the meditation room, I half-figured that his performance was just that, a show. But even up close, he exudes an aura of peaceful calm and serenity. And something in his deep gray eyes tells me that he recognizes me after all.

"Is it okay if we talk?" I ask, keeping my voice low. Maybe speaking doesn't count if we keep it under a certain decibel level.

Holding his hand against his chest, he shakes his head—but then pointing toward me, he nods almost imperceptibly. So I can talk and he won't. Sounds like a lot of marriages.

He sits down on a rock, and I squeeze in next to him on the hard, uncomfortable perch. But Barry seems perfectly at ease. I know his consciousness is on another plane. I didn't realize his butt was, too.

"So when did you become a Maharishi?" I ask brightly. Oh, great, I sound like an idiot. I haven't spoken for one afternoon, and I've already lost all my conversational skills.

Barry smiles beatifically. Obviously I need to work a little harder to get an answer.

"Five years ago?" I ask, persisting now in a question that I really have no interest in. "Ten? When you were in India right after I knew you?"

He doesn't give any indication of a response, but I'm not giving up. "Here's what we'll do. Just stomp your leg once when I get the right answer." I demonstrate, stamping my own leg a couple of times, like a horse.

Despite himself, Barry laughs. Now I take it as a personal challenge to get him to say something, anything. I try to remember what Adam did when he was nine to get the stone-faced Buckingham Palace guard to finally break down and grumble, "Go away, kid." If the Queen knew he'd talked, the guard would probably have been beheaded. What's the worst that could happen to Barry? He gets booted out of Nirvana?

But I don't have to try as hard as I thought. Fate does the work for me. Mr. Clean cracks the door open and holds out a portable phone.

"Psst, Maharishi. You have to take this."

I wonder what life-and-death emergency has gotten him to break his vow of silence.

"Your agent in L.A.," Mr. Clean says excitedly. I should have known. Hollywood trumps holiness. "Your prayers have been answered. She has interest in a talk show from that new cable channel—the Cosmic Consciousness Network."

I'm not sure CCN is as important as CNN, but thank goodness for digital cable or we'd all be stuck with only five thousand choices.

Barry slips off to take the call. I stand outside for about five minutes until he's done, and then he opens the door and invites me into the cottage. I can't wait to see how a maharishi lives. I expect it to be stark and austere—white walls and maybe a couple of hard-backed chairs. But instead Barry seems to have spent a lot of time at Crate & Barrel. Two green Ultrasuede couches crammed with cushy throw pillows face each other across a glass coffee table. The coordinated area rug is decidedly plush, and a comfy leather club chair is positioned near an elaborate Bose entertainment center.

"Can I offer you some soy milk?" Barry asks.

After twenty years, it's not exactly what I expected him to say to me, but it's a start.

"Sure," I say.

"Chocolate or vanilla?" he asks.

I didn't know it comes in flavors. "Strawberry?" I request, just to see how far I can push the envelope.

He slips into the kitchen and comes back with two glasses on a bamboo tray. He hands one to me, and sure enough it's pink. He's a Maharishi; he's supposed to have the answer to people's prayers. But as I take a sip of the yucky concoction, I remember the old adage—be careful what you wish for.

"So, Hallie, what brings you on this spiritual journey?" my maha-rishi asks as we sit down on the couch.

I don't know how long we have to talk, and I learned from the last session that I'd better be direct.

"I wanted to find you," I say. "Even after all these years, I have such happy memories of our time together."

"I do too," he says, clasping his hands over mine.

I gulp. "I couldn't figure out what happened when I didn't hear from you in India. I thought maybe you'd met someone else. Or you'd died."

"The person you knew did die," he says calmly. "And then I was re-born. I went to see the great teacher Advaita Ramana Maharaj and he taught me what it means to be free."

"But why did you have to be free of me?" I ask, the insecurities I felt at twenty flooding back.

Barry looks soulfully into my eyes and intertwines his soft, smooth fingers with mine.

"Because he found me," says Mr. Clean, coming over and territori-ally wrapping an arm around Barry's waist. "We found the light to-gether."

Ahh. Now I'm seeing the light, too.

Mr. Clean tenderly strokes Barry's arm. This is going to make it a lit-tle more awkward to talk about our great romance. Even the Pope gives private audiences.

But Barry is unfazed.

"Hallie, I did love you, but in a different kind of way. Perhaps you wondered why we never had sex."

"Not really," I admit. "I thought you were being a gentleman. Or you wanted our wedding night to be special."

In fact, I'd been kind of relieved when Barry didn't make any ad-vances while we were traveling together. We snuggled a lot, which was lovely, and coming off my intense relationship with Eric, that was all I wanted.

"Did you ever have a wedding night?" Barry asks carefully.

"A really good one," I say happily. "Breakfast at the Nevis Four Seasons is excellent." And as far as I can remember, our honeymoon was the only time Bill was ever willing to spring for room service.

"You picked a good husband?" asks Barry.

Did I? Who knows. I realize that's part of why I'm here and what I'm trying to figure out. Lately, I've been thinking I made a mistake in marrying Bill in the first place. But looking at Barry—and Mr. Clean, who's now nibbling his ear—I see that a matchup between us never would have worked out. I don't think I was destined for a life of soy milk and silence. Not to mention the other obvious problem.

"For a long time, I thought my husband was pretty decent," I say honestly. "Unfortunately, he's moved out."

"People move, people change," says Maharishi, practically chanting. "What happens in the present is temporal. Never let an incident of the moment make you regret the joys of the past."

Bill's being on Ninety-third Street seems more like a major crime than a minor incident, but I hear what Barry's saying. Just because something ends doesn't mean it wasn't worthwhile. My marriage is over, but for a long time it made me happy. I can't regret twenty good years, two terrific children, and a mortgage that's almost paid off.

But I can regret that Mr. Clean is pointing to the clock and spiritual silence is obviously about to descend again. An otherworldly glow returns to Barry's countenance. I may still be in the cottage, but I have a feeling he's back on the mountaintop.

"Will I see you at satsang?" Barry asks softly, ushering me toward the door.

"No, I have to get back home. Anyway, thank you. I think I got what I came for."

I put a hand on his shoulder and give him a light kiss on the cheek. And what the heck. I give one to Mr. Clean, too.

Chapter SEVEN

YOU'RE NOT SUPPOSED TO get personal with your clients, but something about Charles Tyler makes me want to hand him a Zoloft. For the last fifteen minutes, he's been squirming in his chair, chewing the side of his lip, and tapping the toe of his expensive Church's shoes against my highly polished desk. If he wears away the varnish, I'm going to tack a refinishing charge onto his bill. The more we talk, the more anxious Mr. Tyler seems to get. Since I'm not licensed to dispense drugs, I reach into my top drawer for the next best thing.

"Some Gummi bears?" I ask, holding out a half-eaten bag of the squishy candies. I used to carry them around to give the kids when they were little and I got hooked. I swear they're as addictive as nicotine. Maybe I should bring a class action suit against the candy maker.

"Thanks," says Mr. Tyler, reaching to take one. Then he changes his mind and sits back again. "Actually, no." A brief pause and he rocks forward and grabs a handful after all. "Well, yeah, thanks."

Instead of putting the candies in his mouth—which would mean he'd have to give up chewing his lip—he plops them on my desk. And a moment later he starts sorting them by color. There seem to be an unusual number of greens in this batch. I resist the urge to grab the sole red one.

"So, Mr. Tyler," I say, trying to regain some professional demeanor, "we haven't made a lot of progress. Let's go back to square one. You told Arthur that the plaintiff, Beth Lewis, is incorrect in claiming that you gave the promotion to Melina Marks"—I gesture toward the naked woman in the pictures—"because of your personal association. You told him you were innocent."

"I am innocent."

I sigh. As lawyers always say, if I had a quarter for every time a guilty client said he was blameless, I could buy myself a new Maserati. And take lessons to learn how to drive a stick shift.

"But the pictures would suggest that you are indeed personally involved with Melina Marks," I say, understating the case. Actually, the pictures would suggest that he and Melina have a future on the Playboy Channel—which might be a good thing, since if I can't figure out a defense, he's not going to have a future at Alladin Films.

"My involvement with Ms. Marks has no relevance."

I stare at him in disbelief.

"Your involvement with Ms. Marks is exactly what this case is about." I glance down at the glossy evidence. "And I'm going to jump to the conclusion that you do indeed have more than a professional relationship with her."

He looks sideways at the offending photos. "Perhaps I do."

"But you didn't disclose that important information to Arthur."

"He never asked. He asked if I'm innocent and I *am* innocent."

That's Arthur. Too polite to bring up the word "sex" in a sex discrimination suit. But I'm not.

"Let me be blunt. The plaintiff has charged that you're having sex with this woman. And you are having sex with this woman." I look up at him hopefully. "Unless there's another explanation for these photos."

For an answer he nervously uses his thumb to grind the lone red Gummi bear indelibly into my pristine mahogany desk. That refinishing charge is starting to look pretty reasonable.

"I'm unhappy to have you prying into my personal life," he says, finally.

In total frustration, I fling a paper clip across the room. "Mr. Tyler, help me out here. Everything Beth Lewis has charged in her lawsuit seems to be true."

"Not at all. Ms. Marks was promoted for perfectly legitimate reasons. I gave Arthur all the records that show she's done amazing publicity for some of our biggest clients. For example, Melina has handled Reese Witherspoon, while Beth never got above the Tilda Swinton level."

"Tilda who?" I ask.

"My point exactly. If Beth were a better publicist, you might know. Melina, however, is an exceptional employee."

"An exceptional employee who's having sex with her boss. How do you think that looks?"

I know exactly how it looks, down to the mole.

Mr. Tyler stands up. "Please, you've just got to get me off." He looks at me desperately, and I soften.

"Anything you can tell me that might support your case?" I ask. "Anything at all?"

He hesitates and reaches down to the carpet to pick up the paper clip I threw. He anxiously tugs at it, breaking it into pieces which he then plants like flagpoles in the gummy candy.

"I really can't say more about it."

I have a sneaking suspicion that if he wanted, he could make this whole problem go away. But right now only Mr. Tyler is going away. He shakily reaches for his briefcase and edges out of my office without so much as a backward glance.

After another two meetings, I start to scroll through fifty new e-mails. Could the deposed Nigerian prince who's offering to deposit ten million dollars into my checking account (if only I'll give him the number) be legit? Is it worth a free weekend at a new resort in Altoona if I have to sit through a two-hour presentation on buying a time-share? Good thing I'm such an important lawyer or I'd never be getting all this high-class spam. I'm just opening an e-mail that actually needs a response when Bellini calls.

"I'm around the corner from your office. Come meet me at Starbucks," she says.

"I thought you had a lunch date," I say. "Some new guy." Bellini recently signed up with a dating service to get fixed up for lunch at least twice a week. But so far the manicotti hasn't led to anything meaningful. She's been on three midday dates and only the restaurants have gotten rave reviews. There hasn't even been any sex *après* sandwich.

"I didn't like the guy I was matched with," Bellini says briskly. "I left before I even got a chance to eat."

Wow. I can only imagine what a disaster he was if Bellini, the patron saint of "he has potential," couldn't find a reason to stay long enough to wolf down a tuna salad.

Five minutes later, I find Bellini in Starbucks, sitting at a small round table with a greasy white bag in front of her from the pizza place across the street. She's busy pulling the mushrooms off the top of a slice and popping them into her mouth.

"I didn't know they sold pizza at Starbucks," I say.

"They don't. But nobody eats the lunch food they sell here. Seven dollars for the smallest salad you've ever seen."

I look around, and sure enough, everybody in the café seems to be digging around in her own personal deli bag. This Starbucks location is doing a landslide business—for the Korean grocer across the street. But I'm not going to worry about Starbucks' quarterly earnings reports because there's a long line of businessmen waiting for their four-dollar cups of take-out cappuccino. And from the number of people who are ensconced at tables typing away furiously at their laptops, maybe Starbucks is renting out office space.

"So what was wrong with this blind date? Hunchback? Cross-eyed? Two left feet?" I ask Bellini, running through the dating disabilities list. "Drinks Merlot instead of Pinot?"

"Stood straight, eyes were fine, and I didn't dance with him," she mutters. Then she looks up at me. "But if you must know, he didn't even order wine; he ordered seltzer. No lime."

I wait.

"And?" I ask.

"And nothing," she says. "That's the problem. He was boring."

Ah, now I understand. He probably wore a suit, has a job, and is nice to his mother. Not the right man for Bellini.

"I can't decide if your standards are too high or too low," I say.

Bellini laughs. "I'll go either way. I just can't stand guys in the middle." She wipes her fingers on a napkin. "But how about you? How was your weekend?"

"Quiet," I tell her.

I fill her in quickly on the Heavenly Spirit Retreat Center, and the details of my encounter with Rav Jon Yoma Maharishi. I've actually started to think of him that way because "Barry" is certainly long gone.

"So right after dating you, the guy turned gay," Bellini says, summarizing my story. "Nice work."

"I don't think that's exactly what happened," I say defensively.

"You should be proud," says Bellini. "It's easy to get dumped by a guy. It's harder to get him to dump the entire gender."

"I'm talented. Four weeks with me and a man's life is changed forever," I say.

I reach over and take a bite from Bellini's pizza. "Actually, it was good to see Barry. I always liked his openness and eagerness to explore the world, and I felt some of the same sense of discovery I did twenty years ago. He's the kind who introduces you to new experiences—Gaudi and Botticelli when we were young, silence and sat-sang now. But I think somewhere deep down I always knew he wasn't the man to marry."

"So the lesson for me is to rely on my instincts when it comes to guys," Bellini says.

"The lesson for you is to rely on *my* instincts," I tell her, remembering the night I had to drag her away from the art thief at the opera.

In fact, my instincts were on target with Barry. I didn't expect he'd become a maharishi, but given his wandering, ethereal spirit, I knew he'd never be the solid husband type, either. Not the man you'd turn to in the middle of the night to ask if he thought the bright red bumps on the baby were Magic Marker or measles. And, ultimately, I needed a husband who understood that having a family is the very best adventure.

Bellini reaches for a grape and peels the skin off before eating it. Talk about high maintenance. "So your old boyfriends now include one billionaire and one guru. I guess I'm not the only one who likes extremes. Who's next on your hit list?"

I think about the two other names I doodled on the napkin. One of them I can't call. I can never, ever possibly call, no matter what. But there's still the other one, and thinking about him makes me smile. Kevin, the first boy I ever kissed.

"Oh, there's someone," I say vaguely. "A guy I haven't seen since high school. But I had the biggest crush on him."

Just then a Starbucks barista comes by with a tray of samples. "Would you like to try our new Green Tea Wild Raspberry Mocha Frappuccino?" he asks, holding out a shot-glass-size plastic cup. "Or maybe a lemon poppy seed ginger low-fat scone?"

I like this place. You just sit here and they give you free food. I'm not thirsty, but I do accept his complimentary pastry.

Bellini reaches a manicured hand for the cup, and as she takes a sip from the tiny straw, she winks flirtatiously at the barista who—in Bellini's defense—at least has a name tag that says "Assistant Manager."

"Mmm, yummy," she says to him. "Did you make this yourself?"

He smiles. "Yes, with my very own hands."

"Nice hands," she says, batting her eyes.

He puts down the tray and pulls up a chair. "Mind if I sit down?" he asks.

I stand up abruptly. I'm getting out of here, but I've got to admire Bellini. The blind date might not have panned out, but the lunch-date concept was on target. Damned if she didn't meet someone over a muffin.

Since Adam had the good sense to have his birthday fall on a Saturday this year, I can spend the whole day with him. Well, until five o'clock, anyway. He has someplace he needs to go tonight. He hedged when I asked him the details, but I'm sure it's a date with that girl he's been telling me about.

I drove up early, and now as we walk across the Dartmouth campus, I try to figure out which of the perky, adorable friends who call out "Hi, Adam!" could be his current crush, Mandy. It's chilly in New Hampshire, and even though I keep tugging my oversize wool cardigan tighter around me, the hot-blooded college girls all seem to be prancing around in cutoffs and midriff tops. To get into this Ivy League school, you obviously need an A average and goose bump–proof skin.

So far the day's been perfect. We've hung out at Adam's dorm, had lunch, and opened his birthday presents. Adam liked the new digital camera I bought him, but he laughed when he saw the Swiss Army watch. I guess he'll put it in the drawer with the Timex and the fake Rolex, not to mention the Seiko, the Skagen and the Swatch I bought him in previous years. Eventually I'll have to accept that the new sundial is a cell phone. Time marches on, but without Bulova.

Adam eagerly takes me to the physics building and leads me to the lab where he's doing a research project with an esteemed professor. He tells me their work involves searching for neutrinos.

"You might find those in the breakfast aisle in the supermarket," I say.

"Is that a joke, Mom?" he asks, raising an eyebrow.

"Of course, honey." Though the truth is I could be chatting with a neutrino right now and not know the difference.

Adam gives me a little smile and launches into a detailed explanation of neutrinos, ghostly particles which can pass through metal as easily as we walk through air. Apparently, they're quite different from Cheerios after all.

"I'm so proud of you," I tell him, as we stroll outside again. And I am. It's nice when your children are young and the only things they know are what you've taught them. But it's even better when they grow up and can teach you.

Adam drapes his arm around my shoulder, and I'm pleased to realize that my grown-up son isn't embarrassed to be seen with his mother. We walk through a grassy courtyard where students are enjoying the sunshine. Blankets are spread everywhere, and some of the kids lying on them are reading and others are studying. Then I notice one young couple sitting close, gazing into each other's eyes. The boy's hands gently glide across his girlfriend's arms, he kisses her sweetly, and she melts into him. For a moment, I imagine how deliciously enraptured she feels. I sigh a little too loudly.

"What's wrong, mom?" Adam asks.

"Oh, nothing," I say, keeping my voice light. "Just all this young love on campus."

Adam kicks a stone that just barely misses the kissing couple. "Young love isn't all it's cracked up to be," he says.

"Having a problem with Mandy?" I ask, daring to go where mothers never should.

"Not a problem, really. I broke up with her two days ago."

"Oh, no. What happened?"

"Nothing."

"Nothing? You broke up with her over nothing?" I ask, trying to keep my voice in check.

"Yeah," Adam says. "Can we talk about something else?"

"No, we can't," I say petulantly. "This is important."

"What's so important? She was my girlfriend, now she's not my girlfriend. End of story."

"Adam! How can you be so flippant! I'm sure you hurt her terribly. I brought you up to behave better than that." I take a deep breath before continuing my rant. "Mandy deserved a little more from you." I've never even meet this girl, and already I'm taking her side over my son. Sisterhood is powerful, and all that. Or is it just that as a woman recently scorned, I'm feeling a tad sensitive?

"Mom, relax. Don't you think you're being a little O.T.T.?"

"I'm *not* being O.T.T.," I say huffily. Because how could I be when I don't even know what O.T.T. is?

"Geez, you're being just like Mandy. Over the top," he says, defining his terms. Look at that. If you just listen, you find out what you need to know.

We walk in silence for a minute. I'm thinking that I want to tell my son not to use Bill for a role model on how to handle a relationship. But I decide to be a little more even tempered.

"I just hate the thought of your trampling on anybody else's feelings," I say, with my familiar mantra. I've been repeating Mom's Three Rules of Dating forever. One: Emotions count. Two: Always consider the other person's feelings. And three: When it's time to get physical, make sure she wants to go ahead as much as you do. We had some confusion about that last one when Adam was five and wouldn't play softball with a girl named Lizzy because he worried that she didn't want to as much as he did. Maybe I started teaching about the birds and the bees too soon. On the other hand, my son may be the only genius nuclear physicist who actually goes out on dates.

"Why do you assume I'm the one who did the trampling?" he asks, irritated.

"Because men can be a little cavalier about these things," I say. And then I notice the chagrined look on my son's face.

"Okay, if you want to know, we were at a party and I caught Mandy kissing another guy in the bathroom." Adam shakes his head. "I can't stand cheating. I'd never do it myself, and I'm not going to let anybody do it to me."

I squeeze his hand. So Adam isn't Bill, after all. Or else he really is using his father as a role model. A reverse role model. And I've just made a bad mistake.

"I'm sorry, honey. I shouldn't have jumped to conclusions. Forgive me. I should know my son would never behave badly."

He gives me a faint smile. "Of course not. I was raised well. And you made me read *The Feminine Mystique* when I was fourteen."

"Which, as I recall, you hid inside your *Sports Illustrated*." I give him a little hug. "Break ups are hard, honey, however they happen. Trust me. I know. If you need to talk about it, I can stay as long as you want tonight."

"Thanks, Mom. That's okay." Adam pulls his cell phone out of his pocket to check the time. "You should go pretty soon," he adds, with a slightly anxious edge to his voice.

Why does he want me to leave? Now that I know he's not going out with Mandy, I wonder what he is doing tonight. I mean, it's his birthday. Adam's always made a big deal about being with family on his birthday.

Family. I should have thought of that. All of a sudden, I'm pretty sure I know why Adam's worried about my hanging around. Mom for birthday lunch, Dad for dinner. Everybody gets a little bit of him, and never the twain shall meet.

But my moment of clarity comes just a little too late. Because the twain are about to come into a head-on collision. About a hundred yards away, I get a glimpse of Bill. He's spotted us, too, and is now cheerfully striding across the field.

"Happy birthday to you! Happy birthday to you!" Bill sings out as he gets closer.

"Oh, shit," mutters Adam under his breath.

Poor kid, everything has suddenly gone wrong. Mandy cheated. His parents are about to confront each other. And his father never could sing on key. And then it just gets worse, because a bunch of kids who've been playing touch football nearby stop their game and decide to join the festivities.

"Hey, Adam, who knew?" calls out one, who looks like a linebacker. And then he, too, breaks into a chorus of "Happy Birthday," joined by his rowdy teammates.

"These your 'rents?" asks the linebacker coming over, tossing his ball from hand to hand.

"They were," mumbles Adam.

"What's the matter, you divorcing them?" asks the linebacker.

"No, they're doing that themselves," says Adam.

"Whoa, man," says the football player, raising his arms as if trying to block a pass—or, in this case, any more information. "Heavy, dude. Gotta go. Happy birthday. Wanna get drunk later?"

He's off before my dear Adam can tell him that he's only turning twenty and so wouldn't dream of letting a sip of Bud Lite pass his lips. As his mom, I'm sure he hardly even touches apple cider.

Meanwhile, Bill has taken the opportunity to put one arm around Adam and the other around me. "Hey, this is terrific. I didn't know we were all going to be together."

"I didn't either," says Adam.

"Great surprise to see you here, Hallie," Bill says jovially. He sounds a little too happy. Maybe I should let him know right now that he can stop trying so hard. I don't have the Knicks tickets with me.

"So," says Adam, "as long as we're all here, what do you guys want to do?"

I want to strangle Bill. I want to make Adam start wearing a watch. I want to head for the hills, or at least the highway.

"I think I'm going to get going," I say. "I don't want to hit a lot of traffic."

"Never any traffic in New Hampshire. It's not even deer season," says Bill, who doesn't seem to see anything awkward in our all being together.

I'm feeling incredibly awkward. But maybe leaving at this point would be even worse. Besides, this could be an opportunity to show Adam how mature his 'rents really are.

Both my men are looking at me expectantly. "Hallie, come on and hang out with us," Bill says. "It'll be like old times. When was the last time we celebrated Adam's birthday together?"

"A year ago," I say tersely.

Bill laughs a little too loudly, and punches Adam's arm. "What do you say, huh? Your mom has quite a sense of humor, doesn't she?"

"She's great," says Adam, kicking a stone again. "I wish you knew that."

"I do know that," says Bill. He turns to me, and now he punches my arm. "You're still great, Hallie."

I punch him back, harder than I'd intended. And then I punch him again.

"That's healthy, Mom," says Adam, who's taking a psychology class. "It's good to get out your pent-up aggression."

"I don't have any pent-up aggression," I say, punching Bill once more, just for emphasis. I seem to be developing quite a left hook.

"Why would I have any aggression against a lying, deceiving, unethical, vile, contemptible, depraved, despicable, abominable, loathsome"—I can't help it; the adjectives keep coming as if I swallowed a thesaurus—"horrid, horrible man?"

Adam clears his throat. "He's my dad."

I close my eyes for a second to pull myself back together. Bill has come up to celebrate Adam's birthday. I came up for the same reason. Having his parents fighting in front of him is exactly what Adam was trying to avoid. I'm not going to do that to him.

"He is your dad," I say quietly. "And he's a great dad. I'm sorry, Adam." Second apology to my son of the day.

Adam nods. "It's okay."

"How about if we all go out for ice cream before I leave?" I ask, figuring that I can make myself be nice for the duration of a medium-size Rocky Road cone.

"Great!" says Adam, cheering up a little.

"Great!" echoes Bill, looking relieved.

We head into the little town, where a crowd of students are lined up outside the ice cream shop. In Hanover, this forty-five-degree weather is practically a beach day. I manage to keep up a cheerful stream of conversation, and Bill and Adam both seem grateful. Before long, we're all telling stories—and I'm actually starting to relax and enjoy myself a little.

When we finally get to the counter, I decide to go for broke and order a large-size cup with whipped cream. I can keep up these good spirits long enough to work my way through a double scoop.

Or so I think.

We sit down on high stools and Adam is telling us that his research professor may include his name on a paper he's about to publish. Bill and I can't help catching each other's eyes. We're both proud of our son. Whatever's happened to our relationship now, we did a good job together raising our kids.

Bill's joking around, asking if there might be an investment market in neutrinos when I notice someone familiar waiting in the line for ice cream. Who could I possibly know in Hanover? I can't place her, but for some reason she's looking curiously at me, too. Bill has his back to the woman, but as she moves her gaze from me to Bill and Adam, a flash of understanding crosses her eyes. She tries to sidle toward the door, but a new crowd of ice cream-seeking students has come in, and she's trapped.

So am I. I've never seen the woman dressed before, but I know exactly who she is.

"Ashlee," I blurt out.

Bill looks at me, annoyed. "We're not discussing that now," he says.

"Then you shouldn't have brought her here," I grumble.

"I didn't," says Bill. He turns his palms upwards, gesturing toward Adam and me. "Just our little family threesome. Do you see anybody else here?"

"As a matter of fact, I do," I say, and I point an accusing finger at the young woman in the doorway, who is slumping her shoulders now and trying to make herself disappear. But a couple of guys who've come in behind her give her a little push forward.

"You're next in line," one of them says.

Ashlee's self-assurance seems to have drained out of her. She was a lot more poised when I saw her naked.

Bill turns around, his eyes following the path of my finger.

"Ashlee, what are you doing here?" he asks, his voice rising in indignation.

"Getting an ice cream," she says timidly. She looks thoroughly embarrassed. I don't know which is worse for her—having stumbled into our family party or being caught eating sugar.

Now Adam turns around, too, and then he stares at Bill. "Dad, you brought Ashlee to my birthday?"

"No, I didn't. I'd never do that," he says indignantly.

"Then what a coincidence," Adam says snidely.

"Obviously, they closed all the Häagen-Dazs stores between the Upper West Side of Manhattan and Hanover, New Hampshire," I say. And then I shake my head. "Imagine that happening on the one day that Ashlee had a craving for fudge ripple."

"A craving?" asks Adam. "Is she pregnant?"

"Oh my God, I hope not," says Bill, suddenly coughing so hard that he practically spits out his cone.

Now that my husband's close to hysterical, I feel a lot calmer. I run my spoon around the top of my cup and bring a small spoonful of whipped cream to my lips.

Ashlee, who's overheard most of the conversation, now comes tentatively over to the table.

"I just ducked in here to get a small sugar-free vanilla," says Ashlee, making it clear she hasn't done anything wrong—even to her diet.

Adam doesn't look at Ashlee but instead turns angrily to his dad. "So you were going to bring your new girlfriend to dinner?" he asks.

"Of course not," says Bill firmly. "Ashlee drove up with me, but she was supposed to go to the bookstore this afternoon. I told her she could even go to a movie."

What a generous guy. I wonder if he suggested she get the student discount.

"I'm sure your dad didn't intend for you to meet Ashlee," I say, as if I'm being exquisitely understanding.

Bill gives a grateful smile, glad that I've come to his defense. I smile back at him and then put my hand over Adam's and finish my explanation.

"He just brought his friend along so he could sleep with her. We wouldn't want him to have to spend a whole night in a hotel room all by himself, would we? You have to understand, Adam. Your father's a middle-aged man who thinks he can have everything he wants."

Right now all Bill wants is for Ashlee to disappear. And he has a quick solution. He reaches into his pocket, pulls out his wallet, and hands Ashlee a twenty-dollar bill. "Why don't you go down the street and buy me a Dartmouth sweatshirt. I like the gray with green lettering. Size large, not extra-large." He glances at me proudly, making sure I know about his newer, trimmer shape.

Ashlee looks startled by the request.

"Oh, buy a sweatshirt for yourself, too. Buy anything you want." He pulls out another twenty and tries to hand it to her, as if a girl could go on a wild shopping spree with forty dollars. Well, it's New Hampshire— maybe she could.

But Ashlee doesn't reach for the money and in fact seems offended.

"I have my own money, Bill," she says, annoyed. "You don't have to buy me off."

"I'll take the forty bucks," says Adam.

Bill hesitates and then forks the cash over to him. Adam needs it since college costs a fortune. Forget the tuition. The real expenses are late-night pepperoni pizzas, cases of Bull Run, and round-the-clock games of Texas Hold 'Em.

"I'm going to head out," says Ashlee, a little coldly, to Bill. And then to Adam and me, she adds awkwardly, "Nice to have met you."

I don't point out that she still hasn't been officially introduced to either of us.

She turns on her heel, but immediately comes face-to-face with Adam's touch football buddies, who have spotted him and swarmed over to the table.

"Hey, Adam, this your sister?" one of them asks.

"You told us you have a hot sister," another one chimes in.

"I do have a hot sister," says Adam, who's apparently told them about Emily. "But this happens to be . . ." He looks at his mom's rival for the first time. "This is someone who's just leaving."

"Hey, if you're leaving, come with us," says the first guy, clamping a strong hand on Ashlee's shoulder. She looks up at the handsome young athlete who's wearing a striped rugby top that accentuates his muscular upper body.

"Where are you going?" she asks.

"Back to campus to toss around a Frisbee."

"I'm pretty good at sports," says Ashlee, happy to have something to do other than shop for Bill's shirts.

The group consolidates and quickly heads to the door. A few minutes later, I'm also ready to say my good-byes. My ice cream is melted and I think I've run out of things to say. Besides, it's only fair that Bill and Adam get their long-planned father-son time alone together after all.

I give Adam a big hug. "Happy birthday, honey. I love you. You're the best twenty-year-old in the whole world. I couldn't ask for a more perfect son."

My son hugs me back and as I walk out, I offer Bill a little smile and bend down to whisper in his ear.

"Have a nice evening," I tell him. "And don't let it bother you for a moment that your girlfriend just went off with the entire football team."

Chapter EIGHT

I STILL KNOW his phone number. I haven't gotten in touch with Kevin Talbert since eleventh grade, and back then my girlfriends said I should wait for him to call me. I didn't listen to them then and I still prefer being the caller to the callee, so I confidently pick up the phone and punch in the number. How come I still have these ten digits lodged in my frontal cortex, but I can never remember my four-number ATM password?

After the first ring, I idly twirl the cord (note: You should always have one landline in case of an electrical storm) and think yet again how unlikely it is that Kevin hasn't moved since high school. Though maybe it's his mother who hasn't moved.

Kevin's mother. I hadn't thought about that.

I slam down the phone before anyone answers. I'm not always beloved, but I'm generally not someone who inspires hate—except in Jeanette Talbert. From the moment I met her when I was sixteen, she detested everything about me. She accused me of showing off when I became editor of the school newspaper and never forgave me for getting an A in Latin the same term that Kevin failed driver's ed. She complained about my clothes, and she actively hated my bangs—though heaven knows, she would have loathed my pimply forehead even more.

No, the slightest possibility of having to talk to the judgmental Jeanette is more frightening than facing the Soup Nazi. And why would I call Kevin anyway? I also have the number for 1-800-MATTRES (leave off the last S for savings) in my head, and you don't see me calling them.

But maybe they're calling me, because the phone rings.

"Hello," I say hopefully. Now that Bill's gone, I realize I'd like a new bed after all.

"Who are you and why are you bothering me?" asks a gruff voice.

The fact that this person has just phoned me—not vice versa—isn't worth mentioning, because I immediately recognize the snarl at the other end of the line: the dreaded Jeanette Talbert. From the tone of her voice, it suddenly occurs to me that Jeanette didn't hate just me. She hates everybody. I wish I'd known this when I was younger.

I don't answer fast enough, because her growl continues across the line.

"Stop pretending you're blameless. What do you think, I don't know how these things work? I caught you, I got you. I know you called me. I hit star 69."

I'm momentarily stopped by Jeanette actually uttering sixty-nine out loud, since this is the woman who called me a slut when she caught me innocently kissing Kevin. Out of all the possibilities for a call-back number, how did the phone company settle on this spicy combination? Is Chris Rock moonlighting as an AT&T executive? Thirteen-year-old boys must have a field day punching in *69 and cracking themselves up. But what number does Pat Robertson use when he wants to find out who called? Oh, right—he just asks God.

"Jeanette, is that you?" I ask, as sweetly as I can manage. "It's me. Hallie Lawrence."

"Hallie Lawrence, the slut?" she asks. The woman doesn't miss a beat. At least she's not senile.

"No, Hallie Lawrence, the school valedictorian. I used to be friends with your son Kevin."

"I know who you are," she barks. "Do you still have those awful bangs?"

"No, don't need them." If problems develop now on my forehead, I won't fool around with bangs. I'll go straight for the brow lift.

"So what do you want?" she asks.

Kevin's number. But that's a little too blunt. "I was just thinking of you and your family and wondering how you are. I always remember those wonderful dinners we had together." Particularly the chicken salad that was tainted with salmonella, though I'll never be able to prove she did it on purpose. Looking on the bright side, after twenty-six hours of projectile vomiting, I was two pounds thinner.

Obviously nobody's ever said anything nice to Jeanette about her cooking before, because she suddenly softens. "They were good times, weren't they," she says sentimentally.

"Yes, those were the days of our lives," I say, equally treacly.

"You could come over for dinner," Jeanette says unexpectedly. "I could defrost something. And I have some homemade potato salad I made just last week."

Oh, good. Salmonella and mold in one nutritious meal.

"I'd love to, but I'm on that new diet. I can't eat any food that starts with 'p,' " I say, thinking on my feet to save my stomach.

"No peanut butter?" asks Jeanette.

"Never."

"Pasta primavera?"

"Doubly bad."

"Reece's Pieces?" she asks.

I can tell that's a trick question. "Nope. You can't slip in a 'p' even in the second word."

"Strict diet," she says, impressed.

"I'm trying. But I bet Kevin still devours your potato salad," I suggest, making a clumsy detour to get the conversation where I wanted it headed in the first place.

"He would, but ever since he moved to Virgin Gorda he's not home very often. But he's happy there. So what more could a mother want?" she asks, somehow evoking pride and self-sacrifice in the same sentence.

"Virgin Gorda!" I say brightly. I seem to remember that's an island in the British Virgin Islands. Or maybe the American Virgin Islands. If they're all Virgin, they must have tough residency requirements.

"What's he doing there?" I ask, suddenly envisioning him married to an islander—who, I muse, is named Mary. I can see the wedding announcement now in the local paper: "Kevin Talbert Marries Virgin's Mary." Just imagine who their children would be.

"Kevin's an underwater photographer. Very successful. But he's so independent. I wish he'd settle down and get himself married."

I love this woman. I don't even have to pump her, and now I know everything.

"I'm separated from my husband myself," I say, the information highway now open. Besides, Jeanette invited me to dinner, so I think she's started to like me.

Or maybe not.

"Don't get any ideas," she says, suddenly gruff again. "You're not good enough for my Kevin."

"But you haven't seen me since high school," I say, pleading a case I'm not even sure I want to make.

"Kevin lives at the ocean," she says scornfully. "I don't care if you've given up the p's in your diet. Or even the q's, r's, and s's. I could never picture you in a bikini."

"I look just fine in a bikini," I say, unconvincingly.

"Maybe if you have clothes on over it," says Jeanette, and now protecting her beach-bum son from the possibly lumpy lawyer, she hangs up the phone.

I used to see my group of Chaddick moms all the time when the kids were in school, but now we have to plan special occasions to get together. For the lunch the next day at my friend Steff's house, I put on my usual slimming black pants (so I don't look like Jeanette's lumpy lawyer) and add a brand-new soft pullover. I'm particularly proud that it's a bargain, and I can't wait to share my big insider's tip—J. Crew sweaters are made from the same cashmere as the wildly expensive ones from Loro Piana. Though I'm not sure if the goats are fed the same hand-churned buttermilk.

"Hallie, I love your little sweater," says Darlie, the flashy tattletale who told all about Ashlee at our Empty Nest party.

"Thank you," I say, even though I can hear her condescending tone. Every group needs an outrageous member for the others to bond against, and Darlie is ours. She fingers the brand-new strand of expensive South Sea pearls at her neck, clearly given to her by her fourth husband, Carl, the import-export king. You pay a certain price for being married to a much older man—but he pays for everything else.

Glancing at the other women at the table, Darlie smugly repeats her catty compliment, "Love your sweater. Love your sweater. And love *your* sweater," she says in succession.

Now I notice we're all in nearly identical Crew cashmeres. I guess my insider's tip isn't exactly exclusive news. Whenever I think I'm in the know, it turns out everyone else knows, too. Forget Bob Woodward, my scoops wouldn't even be news to Geraldo Rivera.

"Yes, we all have good taste. Proper taste," says Jennifer, staring at Darlie's highly exposed cleavage.

"Boring," says Darlie, stifling a yawn. "But I guess at your age, proper is the only look to go for."

I want to point out that our age is her age. Despite her regular infusions of collagen, Hylaform, Restylane, Juvederm, and other anti-aging injectables, she can't change her birth certificate. Though if I know Darlie, she's tried to have that surgically altered, too.

"Here's to Steff," says Amanda Michaels-Locke, changing the subject by standing and holding her champagne glass in a toast. "Congratulations on your huge success."

"Thank you," says Steff modestly. And in this case, she should be modest. She's invited us to celebrate her new business, but the party may be a little premature. Right now all Steff has is the idea for her new business—a home ear-piercing kit for teenage girls.

"How did you come up with this brilliant concept?" asks Jennifer.

Steff smiles and leans forward to address the gathered group. "I saw a segment on *Good Morning America* that if you want to be an entrepreneur, you find a need and fill it. The best ideas are right under your nose. Or under your ears." She gives a little giggle.

"I think it's a great idea," says Amanda generously. "Especially now that Devon's off at Cornell, it's something new to do. How far along are you?"

Steff looks briefly worried. "I'm looking for somebody to build the machine, though I guess first I need someone to design it. And there are a few other details to think about. My husband, Richard, keeps babbling about budgets, unit price, and profits." She shakes her head. "Can't he see the potential? The world is full of teenage girls dying to pierce their own ears. You know how independent they are at that age. Can you imagine? This might be bigger than Barbie."

We all nod sagely, though it would probably be saner to have pre-pubescent girls piercing Barbie's ears than their own.

"One other thing. I'm really glad Richard and I are working on this together because it's important to have a project you can share. It helps keep the marriage close." She looks meaningfully at me, implying that if Bill and I had only joined efforts and invented a do-it-yourself butt tattoo kit, we might still be living under the same roof. But then she sighs. "I just wish Richard wouldn't keep throwing up so many roadblocks. In addition to everything else, he's got a real bugaboo about insurance. He seems to think people might want to sue us."

"What's there to sue over a pierced ear?" asks Darlie, touching the four-carat diamond stud hanging so heavily that it looks like it's about to rip the earlobe. Maybe that will explain at least one of the potential problems.

Everybody turns to me, the lawyer, for a professional opinion. "Nobody's going to sue our Steff," I say. And I'm pretty confident I'm right because there can't be a lawsuit without an actual business.

"I think Steff's a genius," says Rosalie, who threw our last party— the one with the handwoven bird's-nest invitations. Now she's busy with a crochet hook and already has a stack of small round weavings next to her. "In a few years, I won't have any more children at home, and I'm not even qualified to get a job. The last time I worked in an office, there was no such thing as e-mail and I still had to lick my own envelopes."

"Maybe you could make a business out of your crafts," says Steff, encouragingly.

"Or have another baby or two," says Amanda brightly. "Best thing I ever did was have that second set of twins."

"Yes, but you're a freak of nature," says Darlie dismissively. "The day Michael and Michaela started high school, you popped out Louis and Louisa."

"Without in-vitro," says Jennifer, admiringly. "Just plain old-fashioned sex. Who does that anymore?"

"And no surrogate," complains Darlie. "I'd never have a baby again without a surrogate. I have the name of the woman Joan Lunden used twice—just in case Carl gets any ideas." She strokes her three-strand diamond bracelet, making it clear that if Carl did get any ideas along those lines, they would be very costly.

"We're all at that age where we wonder about what matters and think about what's next," says Steff philosophically. True enough. Though I'd like to know what synapse in her brain took her from the meaning of life to at-home ear-piercing.

"There's always something next," says Amanda optimistically. "You just have to figure it out. Not get stuck. Have new adventures, try new things."

"I know exactly what you mean," says Darlie, nodding avidly. "I used to say I'd never wear any lingerie but La Perla. And now I've found this wonderful little shop on the Place Vendôme in Paris that makes everything for me."

"And maybe in ten years, when you're in your fifties, you'll find some fabulous Italian lingerie," suggests Amanda.

"I'll never be in my fifties," says Darlie, who's already working on how to avoid an entire decade.

"I didn't imagine I'd ever be in my forties or even my thirties," I groan.

"A century ago, the average life expectancy for a woman was forty-seven," says Jennifer helpfully, "which I guess made you middle-aged at twenty-three."

Darlie runs her fingers through her highlighted hair. "I read in a magazine that the perfect age is thirty-six. Hollywood may like young starlets, but the article said maturity brings a certain confidence to your beauty. And lucky me, I'm exactly that age."

We all try not to giggle.

"Thirty-six is when Marilyn Monroe died. Same with Princess Diana," says Jennifer.

"I didn't claim everything about it was perfect," says Darlie defensively. "I could be thirty-five if you prefer."

Amanda laughs. "Doesn't matter how old you are anymore. We're a generation of women without limits. You just have to stay receptive."

"I stay receptive to everything. Especially when the pro at the tennis club flirts with me," says Darlie, as usual offering her own spin.

There's a brief silence at the table.

Rosalie giggles. "Is he cute?"

"Very," says Darlie.

"Want to play doubles on Tuesday?" asks Rosalie, possibly crafting a future for herself that doesn't involve a crochet hook.

Steff, either worried about the food getting cold or Rosalie doubling up with Darlie on anything, raps her knife against her glass.

"I'm grateful to have such wonderful friends to celebrate with me," she says. "Lunch's on. Let's get over to the buffet."

We take our leaf-shaped plates from the elegant table Steff has set and head to her beautiful spread.

"I ordered in a very special lunch from that new store, Organic Edibles," Steff says proudly. "Everything's very healthy. Instead of industrial fertilizer, they raise their vegetables in one hundred percent pure manure."

Is that supposed to be appetizing? For healthy, I'd rather stick with Snickers bars and a One-A-Day vitamin pill.

"What's this?" asks Jennifer, picking up what looks like a flower.

"The best part. Everything in today's lunch is made with fresh nasturtium. Dig in," says Steff, as she heaps large mounds of the edible orange-and-yellow petals onto our plates. I look askance, trying to decide if I should eat this myself or save it to mulch the backyard.

I tentatively take an itty-bitty bite of a bitter-tasting bud and then surreptitiously spit it back into my napkin. Amanda's right. We really are lucky to be able to try everything. But maybe not everything is worth trying.

The cheapest time to buy airline tickets is supposed to be Tuesday night at midnight, which probably works fine if you don't have a job to get to early the next morning. I've been at the computer for two hours now, flipping back and forth from Expedia to Travelocity to Orbitz to Fly byNite.com. (Do their flights take off in the dark, or do they just take off with your money?) I could quit searching this minute, but I'll still get only five hours under the covers. If I fall asleep at my desk in the morning, Arthur will fire me, and I'll have to survive months of unemployment on the twenty-two dollars I've saved in this game of find-the-lowest fare. Definitely not a bargain.

Bleary-eyed, I stumble into the kitchen to pour myself a glass of water. I open the freezer to get an ice cube and find something better—some chocolate fudge cookies that I'd made for the kids and stashed in the freezer so I wouldn't be tempted. But I am tempted, so I reach for one and munch greedily. The cookies taste much better this way, and I'm pretty sure the freezing process kills off the calories. Plus everybody knows that any food you eat standing up doesn't count.

Revved from my sugar boost, I go back to the computer, determined that I'm going to buy the ticket on Expedia, stop worrying about a measly few dollars, and go to bed. But when I click "Purchase" I see that the fare has gone up ten bucks in the last ten minutes. I'm not wasting money! I'm not buying! I refuse! I quickly switch to Travelocity where the fare has soared twelve dollars. Time is money. On Fly-byNite.com the fare is down three dollars, but it doesn't seem worth the risk. Like a crazed day-trader, I'm desperate to close the best deal.

Somewhere in the back of my head I know that my real panic isn't over the money—it's that I'm planning a Thanksgiving getaway and buying only one ticket. But I've decided that's what I want to do and I'm going to do it. I click "Accept Terms and Conditions" on my nonrefundable ticket and make the purchase. There. Done.

I sit back and strum my fingers on the computer keyboard. I'm not going to be depressed. It was my idea to leave town and let Bill be with the kids for the holiday since I'll have them for Christmas and winter break. I'll probably feel awful not being at a happy family table this Thanksgiving, but at least I won't be home alone, eating a frozen Weight Watcher's dinner and watching the Macy's parade.

Exhausted now, I turn off the computer and go upstairs to my bed, where I lie awake, tossing and turning. What was I thinking? There are a lot of vacation spots in the world. I could have decided to spend the weekend skiing in Aspen, skeet-shooting in the Adirondacks, or ice fishing in Alaska.

But instead I picked Virgin Gorda. All the travel sites say there's no more beautiful spot. Still, I have to admit that what lured me weren't the sunny beaches and azure blue water, but something equally irresistible: the thought of seeing my high school honey, Kevin. Will I actually muster the courage to look him up when I'm there? And if I do, what will he think?

My list of things to worry about grows longer by the moment, but focusing on the big anxieties won't get me anywhere, so I do what every woman does—and obsess about my body. My encounters with Eric and Ravi both turned out well, but I didn't have to meet up with either of them in a bikini, or even a one-piece Anne Cole with built-in bra.

I flip onto my back and stare straight up. But the ceiling, slightly pocked and puckered from a recent rainstorm, just reminds me of my pocked and puckered thighs. I'll track down the painter tomorrow to ask him to do some scraping and spackling. But who can I find to do repair work on me?

The next morning at work, I call Bellini to tell her about my trip— and my ceiling. Immediately she's on the case.

"If you're going to a beach, you're going without cellulite," she says.

"Great. I knew you'd know how to get rid of it," I say to my friend with the silky smooth legs. The only dimples Bellini's ever had are on her face.

"Don't be silly. If I knew how to get rid of cellulite, I'd sell the secret and buy a house on Virgin Gorda. Or, come to think of it, I could buy Virgin Gorda."

"So fixing my legs is hopeless?"

"Nothing's hopeless. Drink plenty of water and call me in the morning."

"It is the morning. And why am I drinking water?" I ask, maybe a little too practical for this whole beauty business.

"Water's always good for you," says Bellini, "and I need time to pull out my files. I'll call you back."

Twenty minutes later, Bellini has turned into the Jonas Salk of chubby thighs. She believes there's a cure, and she's not going to rest until she finds it.

"I've found scads of possible solutions, so here we go," she says efficiently. "Number one: Do you have anything against needles?"

"A lot. I don't let needles anywhere near me. I don't even sew."

"Well, that lets out acupuncture, which probably works better on migraines, anyway. But some people swear by mesotherapy. It's a solution of enzymes and detergent, injected directly into the fat to melt it away."

"I can't even find a detergent that melts away ketchup stains," I say.

She sighs, and I can hear her crossing two things off the list that she must have scribbled.

"Okay, how do you feel about heat?"

"Yes, for showers, no, for salsa," I say.

"We could think about thermage. It's a new process that sends radio frequencies pulsating through your skin. Sometimes it burns a little."

"I could put up with burning," I say bravely. "But a radio frequency? I draw the line at listening to Garrison Keillor."

I hear another scratch mark.

"There is one other thing," she says a little hesitantly. "I'm not sure if it's real or an urban myth. I heard about a woman at a spa in the city. If you want to meet me tomorrow, it's worth a try. She's called the Cellulite Exorcist."

I travel down to SoHo from my office in midtown, which for me is like making an exotic sojourn to Paris. Unlike the sterile lineup of skyscrapers where I work, this neighborhood boasts charming boutiques, outdoor cafés, and expensively dressed women brandishing logoed shopping bags. Art galleries used to be the attraction here, but rent got too high and most of them were replaced by designer-name stores. Now the chic shoppers who come here are saved the trouble of pretending that they're as interested in Chagall as they are in Chanel. Unless they totter twenty blocks on their stilettos to the newest art mecca, they're mercifully spared the embarrassment of trying to make intelligent comments about Jenny Holzer's neon word sculptures.

I glance again at the address Bellini gave me and make my way toward the cellulite spa, which seems to be right next door to the overpriced food emporium Dean & DeLuca. Very convenient. You can wolf down a last snack of thirty-dollar imported triple-creamy Camembert and race over to have the fat extracted the moment it lands on your hips.

I tentatively step inside and find pretty modern digs for an exorcist. I can't imagine Linda Blair spewing green vomit in this soft-toned pink waiting room. But if I'm not mistaken, the slim woman sitting on a sofa in a corner is a different Linda—Evangelista. She's flipping through a *Vogue*, probably checking to find a picture of herself and see if she's made a comeback.

Since Bellini hasn't arrived yet, I take a seat across from Linda, who's wearing tight jeans and a turtleneck with high-heeled fur boots. Very chic and paparazzi-ready. I've been looking at pictures of Linda in magazines and on billboards for so many years that I have the momentary sense we're friends.

"So who paid you ten thousand dollars to get out of bed this morning?" I quip, paraphrasing her famous line about how much money it would take to entice her into a photographer's studio.

She peers up from her *Vogue* and shoots me an icy glare. Supermodel eye contact. I can practically see us becoming pals and renting a house together next summer in Nantucket.

"Sorry," I say, trying to get back on better footing. "I didn't mean to bring up a sore subject. You made one stupid comment in your life and it's all anybody remembers, huh?"

Bellini walks in just then, waves cheerfully, and sits down next to me.

Skipping hello, she leans over and in a stage whisper that would wake Hamlet's ghost, "Psst. I think that's Christy Turlington."

"Linda Evangelista," I tell her smugly.

"You're right. Geez, I wonder who paid her ten thousand dollars to get out of bed this morning," Bellini says.

Linda throws down her *Vogue* and storms toward the door. Apparently no amount of money would be enough to keep her in the same room with us. I think we've upset her more than we realized, because, through the window, I see her heading straight into Dean & DeLuca.

"Linda, don't do it!" I call after her, opening the glass a crack. "You're still beautiful! Do cigarettes! Do booze! Just don't do cheese, please! Promise me you won't do the triple-fat cheese!"

Bellini rushes up next to me. I think she's going to pull me away from the window, but instead she leans out, too.

"Linda, come back. Do you really have cellulite? How can somebody as skinny as you have cellulite?"

We both move away from the door and collapse in giggles.

"With that body, she can't have cellulite," I say. "She must have just been here reading the magazine."

"Not necessarily," says Bellini. "We're all sisters under the skin."

"Are we all lumpy sisters?" I ask.

"Not for long," Bellini promises.

My appointment is next. The attendant appears and leads me into the treatment room, and I insist that Bellini come with me and stay at my side. Like a thirteen-year-old on a double date, I'm not going through this alone. The attendant hands me a white stretch one-piece unitard and tells me to change. The Cellulite Exorcist herself will be in momentarily.

When she's gone, I hold the stretchy material in my hand. This could be as challenging as the thong in the tanning salon. I haven't worn a leotard since I was a dancing oak tree in the second-grade Arbor Day celebration. That was the day I tripped over one of my own branches and gave up a promising ballet career forever. Since then, the shape of leotards—and of me—has changed considerably.

"How am I supposed to get into this?" I ask, pulling the unitard up to my knees but not able to tug it an inch higher. "And what is it, anyway?"

"A body-sleeve pressure system," says Bellini, reading from the sheet the attendant has left behind. "It helps squeeze the impurities from your cells and stimulates the lymph drainage system."

"By cutting off my circulation?"

"By whatever means necessary. Besides, they developed this at NASA."

"When do I get the Tang?" I ask.

"In this place, we're all drinking the Kool-Aid," Bellini says with a sly grin.

I grimace and tug harder. Of course I'll be thinner when all this is on, because there won't be any air left in my body. Fighting the tight material over my thighs and hips, I twist around getting my arms into the slinky sleeves. At last it's on. Encased like the finest Jimmy Dean sausage, I roll onto the leather-covered treatment table and stare at the ominous piece of equipment looming over me. I'd hightail it out of here, but I can't move. That's probably the real purpose of the suit.

"What is that thing?" I ask, pointing to the menacing machinery with the scary suction hoses attached. "It looks like an old Hoover vacuum."

"Not a Hoover or even an Oreck," barks a brittle voice.

"A Dustbuster?" I ask meekly, turning to the black-clad figure who has just swooped in. She's barely five feet tall, but fills the room with her mass of frizzy red hair and swirling black cape. Clearly the Cellulite Exorcist has arrived.

She flicks some switches, and a moment later, when the machine sputters on, she comes menacingly toward me with a thick pulsating hose.

"Um, could you please tell me what you're doing before you start?" I ask, ever the educated consumer. Though if I were really an educated consumer, I probably wouldn't be here to begin with.

"Shush. You must stop thinking and just believe," she says.

"We do believe," Bellini says, as if trying to keep Tinkerbell—and my hopes—alive. "How can we not believe? You're the Cellulite Exorcist, right?"

She spins around, clearly irritated. "The Exorcist? Nobody calls me that to my face. I have serious credentials. Medical credentials."

"What are you?" asks Bellini, a little worried about what she's gotten me into.

"A veterinarian."

Okay, I have self-esteem. That doesn't mean she thinks I'm a pig.

"My being a vet isn't as strange as you think," she says, as she attaches the nozzle to my upper thigh. "This procedure is called Endermologie, and it started as deep-tissue massage for injured horses. Then an esteemed colleague realized the amazing side effect. None of the horses had any cellulite."

I rack my brain, trying to think if I'd ever seen cellulite on Secretariat. Definitely none on Seabiscuit.

All of a sudden, I feel a pulling on my skin, and I grab onto the edge of the table so the machine doesn't suck me in—though clearly I've already been sucked in.

The Exorcist vacuums the machine over me like I'm a saggy couch, explaining that the motorized rollers are lifting, stretching, and spinning, to increase collagen production and make the skin smoother. And best of all, we're getting rid of the hardened connective tissue, though I was kind of used to that old hardened connective tissue. Isn't it the only thing holding me up?

"I feel the problem leaving your skin," the Exorcist intones. I suddenly picture her dangling a cross over my dimply thighs. And why not? Cellulite is clearly the work of the devil.

"Do you feel the subcutaneous fat and the toxins breaking down?" she asks grandly.

Actually, I feel the social contract of the twenty-first century breaking down. I'm an attractive intelligent woman with an Ivy League law degree and a good sense of humor, and I'm lying here with an Exorcist, a vacuum cleaner, and a slim hope of thinner thighs. Yes, civilization as we know it is about to come to an end—or else it's advanced beyond our wildest dreams.

When the Exorcist finally turns off her whirring machine, she pats the back of my thighs.

"Good start," she says definitively. "We'll do this twice a week. Fourteen more sessions. I'm sure you'll see some improvement."

Twice a week for seven more weeks? That's a longer commitment than George Bush made to being a compassionate conservative.

"I don't have that kind of time. I'm leaving for the Caribbean," I tell her.

Her eyes light up. "It's not unheard of for clients to take me with them on vacation," she says eagerly.

I think about that one for a minute. My own personal exorcist on call day or night to break down my subcutaneous fat—not to mention breaking down my bank account.

"Thanks," I say, managing to get off the table and stand on my own two feet. "I'm flying solo."

Chapter NINE

FOR ABOUT THE SEVENTEENTH TIME, Emily calls from her dorm to ask me if I'm really going to be all right by myself at Thanksgiving. I'm determined to put up a brave front, so I shrug off her concerns.

"It's only a holiday about eating a dead bird," I say lightly. "Plus, I've never liked cranberries. Gravy is always lumpy, pecan pie is bad for you, and who wants to eat sweet potatoes slathered with marshmallows?"

"You love marshmallows," says Emily, who knows me too well.

"Only in s'mores and Rice Krispies treats," I say. "Besides, you'll enjoy being with Dad."

"You're sure Daddy's not going to have that woman with him?" Emily asks.

"No, you're going to Grandma Rickie's, like always. Daddy would never go to his own mother's house with Ashlee."

"Please don't say her name out loud," says Emily. "It makes me sick."

The other phone line rings. "Hang on a sec," I say seeing caller ID flashing Adam's number. "You're brother's on line two."

Instead of putting Emily on hold, I hang on to the phone with my left hand and pick up another portable with my right. With one phone cradled to each side of my head, I'm surrounded by my children.

"Hi, Adam," I say.

"Hi, Mom. Listen, I just wanted to check in. Are you sure you're going to be okay for Thanksgiving?"

"Yes, I'm going to be fine," I say.

"How's Adam?" Emily asks, from the phone on the left.

"Your sister wants to know how you are," I say turning to my right as I play, well, telephone.

"Tell her I'm fine."

"He's fine."

"But I'm worried about you," Adam shouts, trying to get some attention.

"He's worried," I report dutifully to Emily.

"Me too," says Emily, loudly enough that I'm pretty sure Adam has heard without my being middleman. Or middle mother.

"Why are you worried?" I ask, holding both phones close to my mouth so I can talk to my two children at once.

"Because you're our mother."

"Because more people commit suicide during the holidays than any other time of year," Adam adds helpfully.

"I'm not committing suicide," I say.

"What did you say about suicide?" screams Emily. "Suicide? I knew it. You're depressed."

"Of course she's depressed," says Adam. "How could she not be? We won't be with her."

"It's unhealthy to be alone at Thanksgiving," says Emily.

"The only thing in life that's probably *not* unhealthy is missing a carbo-calorie-laden Thanksgiving dinner," I insist. "And I've planned a lovely getaway. Of course I'll miss you, but I'll be all right. What bad can possibly happen on a beach?"

"You could forget your sunscreen, get skin cancer, and die," says Emily, who's apparently more upset about all this than I'd imagined. "Or even worse, you just suffer and I have to leave school and take care of you."

"No, I'd take care of her," says Adam heroically.

"I'm the daughter. I get to do it."

"You couldn't even sit through *Terms of Endearment*," scoffs Adam. "As soon as Shirley MacLaine started hollering for morphine, you ran for cover."

"Did not. I had to go to the bathroom," retorts Emily.

The moment every mother dreams of. My children are bickering over who gets to sit by my bedside and give me the cyanide pills.

Still, the stereophonic screaming is starting to give me a headache. I gingerly place the two phones on the desk, facing each other, and walk away. Let the kids battle this out. I have to pack.

But I don't pack lightly enough.

"You'll have to check that bag. It's too big to go in the overhead," says the flight attendant at the gate, as I try to board the plane at Kennedy airport. It's Wednesday of Thanksgiving weekend and, as expected, the terminal is in turmoil.

"But it's a carry-on," I tell her, tugging at the leather tag on the Tumi bag. "Look. It says so right here: *carry-on*."

"Only when it's empty. Now it's way overstuffed." She pokes her finger at the bulging bag and shakes her head. "Let me guess. You needed six pairs of shoes for three days away."

"Five," I say defensively. "Though to be honest, I probably didn't need the pink mules since I had beige ones. But honestly what would you wear with the Marc Jacobs white eyelet dress?"

"Not beige," she says wrinkling her nose.

"Exactly. But I needed beige to wear with a khaki skirt."

"I see your point."

Behind us, people in line to board the plane are getting a little restless. But that doesn't put a crimp in our leisurely conversation.

"Do you mind unzipping your case?" she asks me.

"More security checks?"

"No, I'm just dying to see the new Marc Jacobs dress. I think Lindsay Lohan wore it to a movie premiere last week."

I heft the bag up on the table and start to open it.

"Excuse me, miss," says the next man in line, obviously eager to get on the plane. "If it would help speed things along, I have some Calvin Klein underwear I could show you."

The flight attendant eyes him dubiously, probably because he's not even carrying a suitcase.

"Why don't you just board," she says to me. "Take your carry-on. I'll stow it for you later in the first-class closet."

"Thank you," I say, relieved to be on my way. "And take a look at the dress whenever you want. In fact, take the whole dress if you want."

Three hours later, rushing between terminals in the San Juan airport to catch my connecting flight, I start to wish I'd checked the over-stuffed suitcase after all. Or at the very least, that the attendant had confiscated the dress and a few pair of shoes and made the bag a little lighter. I arrive at the gate sweaty and out of breath with three minutes to spare. Predictably, there's an announcement at that very moment that the plane will be two hours late.

I drag myself and my bag over to the airport's food court where, no contest, Cinnabon beats out Salad King for my business. With my sweet treat in hand, I sit down at a small plastic table, alone. Around me kids run up and down screaming, babies howl, husbands and wives argue over who has the boarding passes. The din is unbearable. Yet suddenly even the tumultuous family scenes all seem very appealing to me. Adam and Emily were right that it hurts to be by yourself over Thanksgiving.

I check my watch. Only an hour and fifty minutes left before my flight boards. What to do to pass the time? I could buy a few more Cinnabons, but that probably guarantees I'll get a personal phone call from Anne Cole asking me never again to appear in public in one of her bathing suits. No, I'll just read the *People* magazine I bought—and see which celebrities split up this week. I glance at the back cover, which has an ad from Citibank warning about identity theft. How fitting—because I'm pretty sure someone has stolen my identity. What else could have happened to the happy lawyer-mother-woman-wife who always had a family around her at the holidays? Where did she go?

Oh, buck up, girl. She's right here. Stop wallowing in self-pity and pull yourself together. I fumble in my leather tote for a ballpoint pen. I don't need a turkey to remind me to be thankful. In the white space around the ad, I carefully write "Ten Reasons Why I'm Grateful." Then, just to be safe, I cross out the "ten" and write "five." Now's not a time to put myself under extra pressure.

1. Adam.

2. Emily.

I pause and chew the end of my pen. Is that cheating? Yes, definitely. I turn the magazine around and start again.

Five Reasons I'm Grateful.

1. Adam and Emily.

2. A job I like that gives me satisfaction.

3. Good friends.

4. Curly hair that doesn't frizz too much in humidity.

Okay, now for number five. I know there's a five. There's probably fifty if I really think about it, but I just have to come up with one more. That's not really hard.

5. I like who I am.

I study my list carefully and give a little smile. After everything that's happened recently, I'm doing pretty well. I always knew I was resilient, but I think I've surprised myself. It's not the circumstances of your life that make you happy or not, it's how you face them.

I toss away the mostly uneaten Cinnabon and wipe the sticky frosting off my hands. As I turn around, I'm hit squarely in the face by a flying French fry, propelled by a seven-year-old boy.

"Very inventive," I say to him, wiping a bit of ketchup off my cheek. "It's not every little boy who can make a slingshot out of straws."

His parents look horrified, but I flash them a big smile, determined to accentuate the positive in everything. At least until I have to put on that bathing suit.

The pictures on the Web didn't lie. Virgin Gorda's white-sand beaches are the most gorgeous I've ever seen, complete with hidden coves and oversize rock formations. The water is sparkling and my spacious pink stucco cottage is charmingly propped up on stilts, giving me a breath-taking view of the sailboats that dot the harbor. Perfection. I feel a little pang as I realize that the cottage has a second bedroom. If only Bill hadn't been so stupid, we could be here with the kids, all of us to-gether. If only if only if only. If only pigs had wings. I can't think about what isn't; I'm here for what might be. And today what might be in-volves a long walk on the sunny beach and a swim in the salt water. To-morrow, with my new island tan (definitely better than the spray-on variety), I'll think about looking for Kevin. I already know he lives on the other side of the island. It will take a long drive over undulating is-land hills to find him.

I put on a pair of shorts and a T-shirt and slip my feet into my rub-ber flip-flops. Those four other pairs of shoes, not to mention the skirts and sundresses, will probably never leave my suitcase. And, oh yes, I brought along two bulky sweaters. The Weather Channel reported the Caribbean at a balmy eighty degrees, but standing in thirty-degree New York, I couldn't quite imagine balmy. The unwritten law of vacation packing is you take it all and never wear any of it. And somehow, I never learn. Next time, I'll do the exact same thing.

Stepping outside to go exploring, I breathe deeply. The sweet smell of freesia fills the air. The island isn't exactly overinhabited. I see beach on one side and scrubby island vegetation on the other. As I walk down a quiet dirt road, two goats start to follow me. And to think that Adam and Emily were worried that I'd be alone.

In the warm bright sunshine, the idea of looking up Kevin is start-ing to seem a little dim. No reason to think we'd have any more in com-mon now than we did back in high school, when I was on the fast track to Columbia and he was just fast. We were quite a pair, Kevin in his black motorcycle jacket and me in my little cotton cardigan. Talk about opposites attracting; I once told him we made about as much sense to-gether as a penguin and a zebra.

"But those do make sense. They're both black and white. They have a lot in common," he had said earnestly.

I'd marveled at his wisdom. At the time, his meaningless reply seemed so brilliant that I was sure only I understood Kevin's genius. He'd held my hand as we walked away from school together, in the flush of first love. We'd skipped out of class—a new experience for me, but that was Kevin's bad boy appeal. He made his own rules, and I was dazzled.

But how desperate am I, looking up the boy I kissed in high school? Our relationship would all seem very innocent now. His hand never got above my knee, but I broke his thumb anyway. I swear it was an accident. One night, he leaned in for a last good-night kiss just as I was closing the car door. Slam, bang, snap. Kevin showed up the next day with his arm in a cast. He never spoke to me again. The darnedest things can end a relationship.

My little walk has taken me into town, where I wander by a sail shop, a store selling fishing bait, and a pretty outdoor café. I sit down at one of the metal tables, shaded by a red and white Campari umbrella. Every café in the world seems to have the same sunshade. It could be the company's become more famous for their umbrellas than their liquor.

"Welcome," says a tall island waiter who's made his way slowly to my table. "Drink?"

"Sure. How about a Campari and soda," I say, feeling a new loyalty for the brand that's been kind enough to shield me from sunstroke.

"Campari? Never heard of it. But I can offer some excellent local rums," he says in a lilting accent.

Did the rum people pay for the chairs? I'd hate to support a nonadvertising beverage. "Rum is fine. What do you suggest?" I ask.

"I'll mix you something special. I'll make it a double," he says, giving me a little wink.

While waiting for my double I-don't-know-what, I idly watch the street scene in front of me. A low wooden fence separates the café from the street, and some native children in bright red shorts and bare feet run by, followed by a couple of barking dogs. A man pulling a cart of fruit smiles at me and hands me a fruit across the fence.

"Guava?" he asks. "Just picked. Fifty cents."

"No thanks," I say politely.

"Mango?" He holds out the fresh, sweet-smelling fruit, but I shake my head no.

"Here." He puts it on my table. "For you. My gift. Happy Thanksgiving."

That's nice of him to celebrate Thanksgiving, considering that Virgin Gorda is a British territory. The only reason we got to have the turkey-and-pumpkin-pie feast in the first place was because the Pilgrims fled the English colonies. Thank goodness all is forgiven and we can enjoy the blessings of Elton John.

A few yards away, I notice a woman sitting on a mat, weaving a beautiful reed basket. Some tourists stop to admire her work and choose one to buy from the stack next to her. Maybe I should tell Rosalie there's a business opportunity down here for her. If her raffia nests and crocheted squares aren't a hit, she could always set up a Campari stand.

A good-looking man walking by stops and props himself against the fence next to the basket weaver. He opens the Coke bottle he's holding and takes a long sip. His hair is streaked blond from the sun and he's deeply tanned. His face is lined in that sexy crinkled-eyed way that makes men look athletic and rugged—and just makes women look ragged. He's wearing khaki shorts and a white T-shirt with ripped-off sleeves that accentuate his broad shoulders and muscular arms.

Slung over his shoulder is a well-padded blue nylon bag. He reaches inside and pulls out a long-lensed camera. It must be a brand-new toy, because he flips through an instruction booklet, then holding the Nikon SLR in front of him, he snaps a few shots. Checking the digital images he's taken, he makes some setting adjustments and starts snapping again. In rapid succession, he captures the romping children, the fruit man, and the basket weaver, then turns around to snap the waiter, the couple at the next table, and then, apparently, me.

The camera seems to stay focused on me for a little too long. Then the photographer slowly lowers the lens and stares at me full-on.

"Goddamn," he says exuberantly. "Hallie Lawrence. I know that's you."

He takes half a second to put the lens cap on his expensive camera, then rushes over, captures me in a bear hug, and scoops me up from my seat. He starts to swing me around, but embarrassed, I flail my legs and accidentally smack his knee with my foot.

He puts me down and gives a grin. "That's the Hallie I remember," he says, shaking out the leg. As a reminder of what he means, he wiggles his thumb at me. "Years of physical therapy, but it's almost perfect."

"I've been worrying about that thumb for years," I say. I laugh and shake my head. "Kevin, I can't believe it's you. What a coincidence."

"Yeah, yeah, of all the gin joints in all the world." He flashes a wide smile and I blush, remembering the night he took me to the drive-in when they were showing *Casablanca*. We didn't see much of the movie, but we always said it was our favorite.

He traces an affectionate finger across my cheek. "My mom told me you'd called—and I was hoping you'd track me down."

"I'm just here on a vacation. A long weekend," I say lamely.

Kevin nods. "You're looking great. Mom also said you're separated. Sorry to hear it. Well, not really. How about having dinner with me tonight? I know a great romantic spot."

I swallow. Isn't this a little fast? Don't we catch up on old times and have coffee first before "romantic" enters the equation? On the other hand, Kevin never held back. I'm not here for long and playing hard to get won't work.

Still, I stall for time. "Yes, I'm separated. How about you?"

"Didn't my mother tell you that, too? I haven't settled down, as she puts it."

"Girlfriends?"

"Dozens of them. But no one at the moment. At least nobody who matters."

I don't ask what would make somebody matter. All he's asking for right now is dinner.

"I'd love to see you tonight," I say, wondering if I'll be pulling out the pink mules after all.

"Don't plan on getting home early," he says with a smile. And then, in case I don't understand what he has in mind, he unexpectedly grabs me and suddenly we're locked in a close embrace that's nothing like I remembered. Kevin's arms feel strong around me and his once abrupt boyish kisses are seasoned with a manly tenderness. I think I should pull back from the kiss, but for some reason I don't.

Kevin steps back first. "Do you mind meeting me at the restaurant? I have a photo shoot tonight." He checks his watch, which is either an underwater Breitling or a good imitation. "In fact I should get over there now. But I'll be done by nine. Take a cab from your hotel and tell the driver the Top of the Hill. Everybody knows it."

He puts his arms around my waist and kisses me once more. My heart flutters just like it did in high school as we promise to meet later. I'm floating as I walk back to my cottage, and not from the double rum. I repeat to myself twelve times the name of the restaurant where I'm supposed to meet Kevin. That Marc Jacobs dress is going to see daylight after all. Or moonlight. I imagine us sitting at a table for two, stars twinkling above as a gentle breeze flutters through my hair. We'll say sweet things to each other. I'm going on a date, a real date—and why not? Kevin did give me an awfully nice kiss.

I walk up the steps to my cottage and feel myself bubbling over with girlish anticipation. On my sunny balcony, I perch on the edge of a chaise lounge, but I'm much too keyed up to sit. I stand and spin myself around, like an ingenue on a Broadway stage.

Tonight, tonight, won't be just any night!

Good thing that my balcony is hidden away behind some trees so nobody has to witness my performance. That's the advantage of being alone. I can be as giddy as I want.

Tonight, tonight, I'll see my love tonight.

Okay, that's an exaggeration. He's not really my love. But hey, you never know.

I segue into "I Feel Pretty," and twirl my arms overhead like some deranged dancer. Geez, no wonder I didn't get into the high school musical. But today I'm getting the chance to do high school all over again.

Oh, so pretty! I sing loudly enough—and off-key enough—that I flush a couple of birds out of the bushes.

I feel pretty and witty and bright!

Now I'm singing so loudly that the birds have made a snap decision to fly north—even though it's the dead of winter up there.

"You *are* pretty," says someone from inside my cottage. And then there's a barrage of giggles.

"Witty and reasonably bright," says another voice, this one deep and male.

"Adam?" I ask incredulously.

"SURPRISE!" say my two darling children, bursting through the door onto the balcony. I stare at them in disbelief. To paraphrase Kevin—not to mention Humphrey Bogart—of all the islands in all the world, how'd they end up on this one?

"What are you doing here?" I ask in a tone that comes out more like an accusation than a welcome. I can't believe they caught me *in flagrante*—singing songs from *West Side Story* on my east-facing balcony.

"We wanted to surprise you!" says Emily, throwing her arms around me.

"We couldn't stand the idea of your being all alone on Thanksgiving," adds Adam. "Dad said he understood and he bought us the plane tickets."

"How thoughtful of him," I say, still trying to recover from the arrival of my unannounced guests.

"Real thoughtful," grumbles Emily. "He and Ashlee took us to the airport and then got on a flight to Vail themselves."

"And you guys . . ." I pause.

"We're here for the whole long weekend!" says Emily exuberantly.

"We're here for you, Mom," says Adam, plopping an arm around my shoulders. "We're not going to leave your side for a moment."

Ah, yes, what mother wouldn't want to be me right now? Two loving, thoughtful, wonderful children who truly care about their mom. And now I have just what I'd wanted a few hours ago—Adam and Emily here with me. Filling my heart and the other bedroom.

And obviously filling my dinner hour.

"What do you feel like doing, Mom?" Adam asks. "A walk on the beach? A swim? Collecting shells?"

Actually what I feel like is giving myself a pedicure, making sure my legs are shaved, and putting on my sexy dress to meet Kevin. But "Mommy has a date" is not the conversation I'm going to have with Adam and Emily. They're here to be with me, and I'm not going to be with anybody else. It's dreadful enough that Bill's flaunting his love life. Mom at least has to remain maternal (which means sexless) in their eyes. Bad as it is for me to imagine Emily with a guy, it would be a lot worse for her to imagine the same about me.

"Let's go to the beach," I tell the kids. "I just have to do one quick thing. I'll meet you."

I hear their sandals scrape against the wooden steps as they clatter down to the beach, whooping their delight to be outside, racing to the waves, just like when they were little.

Once they're out of view, I open the top drawer next to my bed and find a local phone book. Much more helpful than the usual Gideon Bible. Kevin's home number is listed, and when I dial it, I get his voice mail. *"Kevin here. Actually not here. Leave only good news."* Beep. Since my message doesn't qualify as good news, I hang up. Then I quickly dial again, but I seem to have missed my window, because this time the message is followed by an electronic voice informing me: "Mailbox full." How did it know what I was going to say? Kevin is clearly serious about filtering out things he doesn't want to hear.

Now what? I can't just not show up, and I'm definitely not showing up with kids in tow. I call the restaurant and tell the owner to let Kevin know that I won't be able to join him.

"You're blowing off Kevin Talbert?" he asks indignantly. "Kevin's a good guy. What's your problem?"

It's a small island, and the locals clearly stick up for each other. Maybe just as well I had to cancel. If the restaurant owner didn't like my looks, it probably would have been a short evening, anyway. Worse than having to pass muster with the evil Jeanette.

"Please explain something came up. I'm so sorry," I say unctuously.

"Fine," he says curtly.

"Make sure he knows I'm really sorry."

"Do you want to make another date with him?" he asks, suddenly turning into Kevin's social secretary.

Would I ever. But by the time the kids leave, I'm leaving, too.

"Tell him I'll call him," I say.

"I'll tell him you're blowing him off," he says, hanging up.

I stare at the phone, annoyed. Now I remember what's so wonderful about dating. Nothing. Everything you do is wrong. I'll try to fix this later, but for the moment, I'm better off sticking to what I do well, which is being a mom.

I go out to the beach, which is deserted except for a woman lounging on a blanket with a small baby. Her ample cleavage spills out of an inadequate bikini top. Given those breasts, I try to decide if she's the baby's mother, the nanny, or the wet nurse.

I wander to the other side of some rocks where my children have set up camp. Adam is running along the sand trying to get a colorful kite to fly in the gentle wind and Emily is in the ocean, paddling on a boogie board. Next to their oversize striped Ralph Lauren beach towels are a cooler, two blue sling chairs and a small Weber grill. Damn, my kids are amazing. I wonder how they got all that into their carry-ons.

Chapter TEN

WE SPEND THE NEXT THREE DAYS touring the island by moped, snorkeling around the shallow coral reefs, and horseback riding along the beach. We even take a midnight boat ride to observe the phosphorescent fish that flash bright neon colors when they mate. Under the half-moon, we lean over the side of the boat, and all around us the water is glowing with tumescence. At least the fish are having sex.

On our last day, Adam wants to go scuba diving—something we haven't done in years.

"I'm not sure I remember how," I tell him.

"You never forget. It's like falling off a bike," he says.

"Falling off a bike I can do," I say, wondering why everyone always invokes that image. "It's the riding part I'm not so good at."

But Adam makes all the arrangements and at seven A.M. we're standing outside, ready for the van that will take us to the dock. Furtively, I slip back inside the cottage, figuring this might be a good time to reach Kevin. The last dozen times I've tried, I got the same "mailbox full" message. You'd think he could have emptied it by now. But again I get no answer and the same message. Damn.

At the dock, we're fitted out with tanks, wet suits, flippers, masks, regulators, buoyancy-control vests, and a weighted belt to hold us under the water. Eyeing us, the scuba master recommends a seven-pound belt for Adam and twelve pounds for me.

"You mean the other way around," I say confidently. "Adam's much bigger. He'll need more weight than me to stay underwater."

"But he's all muscle, which sinks. And you're . . ." He doesn't bother to finish because we all know what he's thinking as he looks at me. Fat floats.

All of the equipment gets loaded onto the well-scrubbed white fiberglass boat and as we go aboard I try to remember what I learned in those scuba certification classes years ago. Let's see, I'm supposed to stop every ten feet or so to hold my nose and blow—which either clears my ears or makes my head explode. I should keep one eye on the depth dial and another on the meter that shows how much air's left in the tank, which by my calculation leaves no eyes for the whole point of this expedition—seeing the coral. What I really need is a gadget to tell me whether that fishy over there is a bass or a barracuda. I could use one to identify men, too. I know my star Adam would be a starfish, Eric a shark, and Bill a big old blowfish. But Kevin? If only I knew. And now I probably never will.

The cute blond scuba master, who looks all of about twenty, introduces himself as Nick and comes around to check our tanks and regulators.

"Nervous?" he asks me. My shaking hands must be giving me away, and he knows his job is to calm me down.

"Do you remember the most important rule of scuba diving?" he asks cheerfully.

"Yes," I say, as it all comes back to me. "Always breathe steadily. Never hold your breath underwater."

"No! That's rule number two! The most *important* rule. Wear black. It looks sexy!"

He guffaws, then gives me a congenial slap on the back. Great. I'm risking my life to go a hundred feet underwater, and our leader thinks he's Conan O'Brien.

Adam and Emily double-check my equipment, and then the scuba master double-checks their double-checking. I'm briefly moved by their concern—but then I realize it's not just altruism. Nobody wants a good dive cut short because Mom drowned.

We're ready to head out, and the captain revs the motor. Then, just as we're pulling away from the dock, there's a commotion and two men from the scuba shop rush out, waving their arms. After a quick conference on board, the captain swaggers over to us.

"There's a problem with another boat. We're going to pick up a couple of divers at Pine Cay."

"Good, more people," says Emily, who's maybe getting a little tired of this vacation that's all mom all the time. I know just how she feels.

We move slowly through the water, but as soon as we're past the sign that says "NO WAKE AREA . . . 5 KNOTS" the boat lurches quickly forward over the waves. Adam and Emily stand in the bow, enjoying the salt spraying over their suntanned faces and chatting with Nick, the hunky scuba master. Thank goodness, someone for Emily to talk to. But then I notice said boy draping his arm casually around my daughter's shoulders. In other words, making a move on her. He's wearing a skimpy Speedo (black, of course), and my little Emily's clad in only a tiny Guess bikini. Good thing it's pink, not black. Maybe Nick won't think she's sexy.

Fat chance of that. Actually, slim, curvy, voluptuous chance. Mom needs to intervene.

"Isn't it time to put on our wet suits?" I ask, standing up.

"Not until we're at the dive site. We'll get too hot," Nick says.

Too hot is exactly what I'm worried about. ·

I throw Emily a towel. "You must be chilly. Wrap up," I suggest.

She laughs, and tosses back the towel. "Don't worry, Mom. Nick's keeping me quite warm."

I sit back down and distract myself by looking at the scenery. The clear blue water is dotted with islands so small they look like nothing more than big rocks, which is probably why the guidebook gets to claim sixty islands in the British Virgin Islands. I guess if three hundred square feet and a Murphy bed counts as an apartment in Manhattan, a clump of trees on a boulder should qualify as a tropical paradise.

The waves are choppy, the boat is going faster, and embarrassingly

I'm starting to get queasy. I rub my temples. Come on, now, that queasiness is probably only from looking at the sexy bodies standing in the bow, one of whom happens to be my daughter. It's all in my head, all in my head. I swallow hard. No, it's also in my stomach. And it feels like whatever's in my stomach won't stay there for long.

"Nick," I call out weakly. "Can you come here? I'm not feeling very well."

He unwraps his arm from Emily, who rolls her eyes.

"Oh god, Mom. You'll stop at nothing," she says, mildly irritated.

"I mean it. I'm afraid I'm going to throw up," I say as they both come over.

"You don't have to throw up. Nick and I aren't doing anything," Emily says, still sure that I'm faking.

But Nick must have noticed that I'm green around the gills because he immediately gets me a cold pack and holds it behind my neck.

"Find a spot on the horizon and look at it," he advises. "That sometimes helps."

I focus on a yellow buoy in the distance. Bad choice. It's bobbing in the waves, and as my head goes up and down following it, I only feel worse.

"Any other bright ideas?" I ask him.

Adam joins us as the boat starts to slow down. "We're getting close to the island where we're picking up those other people," he says. "You should go for a quick swim. You can't stay seasick in the water."

"He's right," says Nick, who, let's face it, would be just as happy to get me off the boat anyway.

Emily hands me a pair of goggles. "Jump, Mom, jump."

My, how things have changed. Not too long ago, Emily was trying to prevent my suicide.

The captain ties up the boat at the dock to pick up our additional passengers and I slip over the side into the cool water. Almost immediately, I do feel better. I swim away, hoping everyone's impressed with my strong Australian crawl stroke. I stop to look back, but our new arrivals seem to be struggling to drag a lot of equipment onto the boat, and I figure they'll be taking some time. After swimming fast for awhile, I start to feel cold and tired, so I head back. All's well until I get to the ladder at the side of the boat. Trying to climb up, I catch my flipper on a rung and fly backwards. At the flopping sound, everybody gathers at the stern.

"Take off the flippers and give them to me," Adam says, reaching out a hand.

Now thrashing in the waves, I try to reach my feet but they seem kind of far away. My knee smashes into my chin, but I finally manage to pry one flipper off—and it immediately floats away.

Nick dives in. I think he's going to help me up the ladder, but instead he goes after the wayward gear.

"Anything lost comes out of my salary," he explains, swimming away.

I wonder how much he'd be charged if he lost me. Probably less than the price of a life vest.

I swim back to the ladder and taking off the second flipper, give it to Adam, who is standing in the stern. He reaches out to me, strong, stable, and sturdy. But I lose my balance on a slippery rung anyway, and this time hit the water with such a resounding splash that people on a neighboring sloop applaud.

I'm totally mortified, not to mention cold, and I can barely see because my hair has fallen in clumps over my face. The search for the Loch Ness monster could end right here.

Adam practically drags me onto the boat and I collapse in a shivering puddle. I look up at the circle of concerned faces above me—the captain, Nick, Adam, and Emily. And the two newcomers. I must have swallowed too much salt water and turned woozy because one of them looks just like Angelina Jolie. And the other one? Oh my God, it's Kevin.

"Are you all right?" asks the pretty woman, who I'm now convinced really is Angelina. Anybody could have that dragon tattoo on her arm, but who else would be wearing a UNICEF T-shirt?

"Thanks. I think I'm okay," I say.

She reaches into her own bag and pulls out a fluffy towel that she wraps around me. "Can I get you some water? Some juice? What will make you feel better?"

I've always wanted to meet Brad Pitt, but it might be too soon in our friendship to ask.

"Juice would be good," I say.

Sure enough, the goodwill amabassador and mother of an ever-burgeoning brood reaches into her case again and pulls out a box of Mott's fruit punch. She takes the little straw off the side of the box and pokes it through the foil hole on top.

"Here you go," she says, smiling solicitously at me, a mom in the know. Just a few short years ago Angelina was the brother-kissing wild woman who wore a vial of blood around her neck. What would she have offered me then?

Kevin rubs a hand over Angelina's back.

"Listen, just a few more minutes and then I want more of what we were doing before. Got me?"

"Got you." She puckers those Angelina Jolie lips and kisses him on the cheek. "I love everything you were doing."

Kevin doesn't bother saying anything, but he gives me an arrogant glance and saunters away. Great. What kind of world are we living in if you stand a guy up for dinner and he throws it in your face by turning up with Angelina Jolie?

The boat putts over to our first dive site, and Angelina slithers into a black wet suit. Kevin puts an arm around her and pulls up the zipper in the back.

"Hard to reach on yourself," he says.

"No, it's not. There's a long string attached to the zipper on every wet suit, for just that reason," I say, holding it out to demonstrate.

Kevin ignores me completely, which is worse than any nasty comment he might make.

"Angie, are you set? I need you sexy, sexy, sexy underwater," he says.

"That shouldn't be hard for her," says Adam, who's been staring gape-mouthed at Angelina since she came on board.

I'm stewing as Angelina and Kevin don the rest of their scuba gear. Angelina and Kevin, isn't that cute? Maybe I can stencil their names in a little heart on the girls' room wall, just like I did all those years ago: Hallie ♥ Kevin. Kevin, bless him, carved the same on a tree, then got suspended from school for vandalism. And he's probably been black-balled from the Sierra Club ever since.

Even on my best day, I couldn't compete with Angelina Jolie, and today we don't belong in the same ocean, never mind the same boat. While Angelina struts around the boat, the Queen of the Sea, I'm sitting huddled in a corner with goose bumps, matted hair, bruised legs from my falls, and a bruised ego from Kevin's indifference. Angelina's tank is already strapped to her back, but she still moves gracefully to her apparently bottomless bag. I'm waiting for her to pull out one of her babies, or at least the remains of Billy Bob Thornton. But instead she finds a small tube that she glides across her famously full and seductive lips.

"What's that?" asks Emily, who's been watching almost as intently as Adam. "Lip Plumper? Du Wop Lip Venom? Tabasco sauce? I hear it puffs up your lips just as well as the stuff you buy at Sephora."

"Just Chapstick." Angelina proudly traces a finger around her sumptuous lips. "These babies are all natural."

"Please tell me. I'm dying for lips like yours. You must have one secret to share," begs Emily. I'm guessing Angelina's sexy lip secret involves sucking exercises, but I don't say anything.

Scuba master Nick is now keenly interested, too, though it seems to be my daughter's lips that he's staring at. On the one hand, I'm proud that in his eyes, Emily outshines the star. But on the other, I hope he realizes that all Emily sucks is Popsicles.

"I don't know what's so good about having a fat lip. I remember when we all wanted to be thin-lipped blondes like Christie Brinkley," I say.

"Who's she?" asks Emily.

Who's Christie Brinkley? How quickly those fifteen minutes fade. "We used to think she was the most dazzling woman in the whole world," I tell them. But times have changed, and today she'd never make the cover of the *Sports Illustrated* swimsuit issue. Forget her stunningly slim, straight All-American style. Now you need Angelina lips, Gisele Bündchen curls and curves, and a J.Lo butt.

"A lesson for you," I say, the voice of mature reason. "Remodel yourself to look like today's idols, and in a few years you'll be as out of style as Frye boots."

"I love Frye boots," says Emily.

"Me, too," reports Angelina. "I have five pair."

I sigh. If the cowboy craze has come back in style, maybe there's hope for my thin lips. Everything goes in cycles.

But if I thought Kevin's affection for me would be cycling back, I don't see it happening any time soon.

"Into the ocean, gorgeous," Kevin says, strolling over, and I know he's not talking to me. He coos to Angelina as he adjusts the mask over her eyes and nose and helps her ease into the water. He has an expensive underwater video camera slung around his neck, which isn't surprising. If you're spending time scuba diving with Angelina Jolie, you want to be able to prove it.

The kids are on the other side of the boat now, getting ready for the dive, and Kevin has paused for a moment before joining Angelina to spray defogger on his mask. I grab the moment. In fact, I grab his hand.

"Listen, I'm sorry I couldn't make it the other night. My kids showed up unexpectedly. I tried to call you a dozen times, but you must be the most popular guy on the island. Your message machine is always full."

Kevin doesn't even look up. "No big deal. No problem," he says, in a tone that lets me know it really is. I remember that voice—it's the same one he used when I tried to apologize in high school for his finger. Back then I broke his thumb and he wouldn't forgive me. Now I've broken a date, and it's the same story.

But we're all grown-up now.

"I came to Virgin Gorda because I wanted to see you," I say, laying my cards on the table. "And after we ran into each other, I wanted to get together with you even more."

"Too bad it didn't happen. Timing is everything," he says as he starts to descend the ladder. Then he adds, "Really, forget about it. I have."

"Hard to forget that kiss," I say bluntly.

Kevin pauses briefly on the ladder to stare at me. But a moment later, he's disappeared underwater—to swim with the fish, and with the sexy, black-clad movie star with the trout pout.

Great. I gave up any chance of being with Kevin to keep my private life discreet, but Emily feels no such compunctions. I'm very lucky that my eighteen-year-old daughter confides in me but less than lucky that her honesty keeps me awake at three in the morning, as I imagine what she and scuba boy Nick could possibly be doing.

"He's gorgeous, isn't he?" Emily had said jubilantly after our family farewell dinner earlier tonight. We'd come back to the cottage—me, to go to sleep, and Emily, to put on a shorter skirt and head back out again.

"Yes, very cute. But if you're meeting Nick at a club, maybe Adam would like to join you."

"No, I'm kind of tired. Think I'll just turn in," her big brother Adam had said, not picking up on my cue. Or picking up on it and deciding to take Emily's side. Adam made a show of opening the sofa bed in the living room and plopping down with a yawn.

Now I consult the bedside clock again, which has advanced a full two minutes since I last checked. How late can the clubs in Virgin Gorda be open, anyway? What if Nick took her back to his house to show her some Virgin Gorda version of his etchings? Maybe his sea urchin collection. Emily might go for a line like that. She always loved sea urchins.

I finally fall asleep—and I don't see Emily until I wake her the next afternoon.

"Have fun last night?" I ask, trying to sound nonchalant. I putter around her room and find a pair of shorts and a hair clip, which I toss into her suitcase.

"Sooooo much fun. Nick's been down here teaching scuba for six months. He dropped out of the University of Minnesota and said he's never been happier."

"And never been tanner," I suggest.

"Or hotter," Emily adds with a grin. "He's really hot."

I stare at her.

"Hot, Mom. Like it's cold in Minnesota. Cold in New Haven, too. Maybe I should spend some time here with him. I can see why it would be nice to be hot with Nick."

I look at her plaintively. "You're a freshman at Yale. Do you know any adjectives other than 'hot'? Are you trying to say that you're attracted by the concept of warm sunshine pouring down on you in the midst of the frigid northern winters?"

"No, Mom. I'm trying to say that I'd like to be hot with Nick." Emily jumps up from the bed and gives me a hug. "You're a smart lawyer. How hard is it to understand? College boys are just boys, but Nick is a real man. Think how much more I'd learn if I left Yale and just hung out with him for a semester."

"I can imagine what you'd learn," I say a little too snidely.

"Real life matters, too, Mom," says Emily, catching my tone and immediately turning defensive. Actually, offensive. "I'm serious about coming back to be with him. You never took chances, but maybe I should. You're a lawyer, you were loyal—and look what it got you."

I stare at my daughter for a moment, stunned. In her eyes, has my life really been that bad? Added up to so little?

"Look, we're talking about you, not me," I say, trying to hide my hurt feelings and be reasonable. "I'm sure Nick was cool. Or hot. Or whatever. But what attracted you to Nick for one night in a club probably wouldn't be enough to get you through a whole semester."

"You can't tell," says Emily with a sly smile. "I've heard wild physical attraction can get you through a lot."

"You'll forget about him the minute you get back to Yale," I promise her.

"Some people you never forget," says Emily, looking at me meaningfully.

I clear my throat, because I can't disagree. I'm sure Emily doesn't know about my secret list and the old boyfriends I've been looking up, but she's already figured out for herself that certain people have a lasting impact.

Adam appears at the open door. "Mom, what time do we have to leave for the airport?"

"This very second," I say, thinking I can't wait to get Emily off this island.

I bustle around, getting everything into the rental car. My own flight's not scheduled until tomorrow, but now I wish I could leave the island with the kids. There's nothing left to do here and certainly nobody left for me to talk to. I've had enough of hot guys in the sun. I tuck my own suitcase into the car, hoping that I can switch my flight.

The airport is nothing more than a windswept field bordering a pebbly path, which I guess is supposed to be the runway. The windsock blowing in the breeze is literally a sock. I'm praying that the pilots have more sophisticated weather technology somewhere, but if they do, I don't see it.

I beg the man at the ticket counter to get me on the kids' plane, but he just laughs at me. Finding an open space on a four-seat puddle jumper is harder than getting warm macadamia nuts in coach on a 747.

"Sorry you have to stay here alone," says Adam, hugging me before going out to the plane, which is only slightly larger than the one he built out of Legos when he was ten.

"Don't be silly. Just one more night and then I'm following. You two were the best to come down. It meant the world," I say, hugging them both tightly.

"If you're lonely, you can call Nick," advises Emily. "He's very . . ."

"I know. Hot," I say, interrupting, and giving my daughter another hug.

The kids leave, calling good-bye to me as they climb up the steps to the plane. I keep waving frenetically long after they've stopped looking—just like I used to when their camp bus pulled away each morning. I wait until the plane is in the sky, and still I keep watching. There's nothing to do now but head back to my empty cottage.

Alone and suddenly feeling lonely, I walk listlessly toward my rental car. What a sight I must be. I'm dragging my feet glumly in the dirt, my head is down, and I'm not paying attention to much around me. I'm a few steps from my parking spot when I hear a noise. Somebody comes up behind me and grabs my arm. I gasp in panic, and then spin around to face my assailant, and gasp again.

It's Kevin, wearing his usual shorts and a T-shirt—and a Humphrey Bogart fedora.

"If you get on that plane, you'll regret it. Maybe not today, maybe not tomorrow, but soon, and for the rest of your life," he says.

"I will?" I ask, hesitantly. What's he doing here? Is this the same man who ignored me on the scuba dive yesterday?

"Worked on Ingrid Bergman," says *Casablanca*-quoting Kevin.

"Just one little problem. I believe Humphrey said 'If you *don't* get on that plane you'll regret it.' He was trying to convince Ingrid Bergman to *leave*."

"That's one way to interpret the script," says Kevin.

"And what's your way?"

"That he secretly wanted her to stay. But he was too much of a jerk on the boat to say so."

"I don't remember any boat scene in *Casablanca*."

"Good. Then maybe you forgot yesterday's boat scene, too."

"Hardly," I say. "But I'll get over that you acted like I didn't exist. After all, you were very occupied fawning over Angelina Jolie."

"That wasn't fawning. In Hollywood it's called auditioning," says Kevin, contritely. "The director had called me for the gig as underwater photographer on her next film, but Angelina gets approval on everyone. We went diving together yesterday to take some shots and see if she found me compatible."

"Did she?" I ask.

"Compatible enough to get the job but nothing more, if that's what you're asking."

"I wasn't asking. Not my business."

"I'd like it to be your business." He looks soulful for a moment. "I spent the weekend sure you'd blown me off and didn't want to see me. It meant a lot what you said on the boat. And this morning, I realized how much I wanted to see you before you left."

I'm not sure what to say. "I'm glad you're here," I say softening. And then I add, "I didn't really understand what was going on with you and Angelina. But I'm glad you got the job."

"My magnetism apparently paid off with her. Now I want to see if I can make it pay off with you," he says with a smile.

"You didn't really say that," I say with a giggle. The line is a little corny, but I have to admit I'm feeling the draw of his force field. So I add, "But go ahead, be magnetic."

"What magnets do best is pull things toward them," Kevin says. And wrapping his arms around me, he does exactly that. Then he dips me over his strong arm, holds me tightly, and kisses me. When I stand up again and catch my breath, I'm flushed. But that's just the start. We stand on the field kissing until someone drives by in a pickup truck, kicking up a storm of dust.

"Hey, Kevin, take it home," calls the guy behind the wheel, leaning out the window and laughing.

"Get out of here, Dave. You're just jealous," Kevin retorts, waving him on.

Dave beeps his horn a couple of times and floors the truck.

Kevin turns back to me. "My buddy Dave didn't have a bad idea. I should take you home. I mean, to my home. We can watch *Casablanca*."

I playfully tug on the rim of the fedora, pulling it down over his eyes. "What an offer. But you didn't need this whole getup to keep me here. My flight's not until tomorrow anyway."

"Good, then I'm kidnapping you for twenty-four hours."

I don't need any convincing. I climb into Kevin's old MG convertible, and in the late afternoon heat, we drive across the island, catching up on our stories. Kevin came to this island years ago expecting to do nothing more than spend his life as a carefree scuba diver. Eventually he realized he had to make his passion pay. When a local rum company wanted to shoot an underwater commercial, he signed up for the job,

figuring he could breathe and click a camera at the same time. A star—
or at least a part-time career—was born.

"Since then, I've done some Hollywood gigs, but it's not all glam-
our," he says. "After *Waterworld*, you couldn't get most directors to shoot
inside a toilet bowl. So I went into the service business."

"Just who do you service?" I ask.

"Tourists. People love vacation videos of themselves diving underwater. And even better, destination weddings are all the rage these days.
It's really boosted my business. You'd be surprised how many people
want to come to the islands to get married underwater."

"I would be surprised," I say, wondering if Vera Wang's white lace
wet suits have a detachable train. And whether the bridesmaids' bathing
suits all have empire waists and are an awful shade of puce. Then making a slightly awkward transition, I ask, "But you never got married
yourself? Not once? Not even on land?"

Kevin swerves to avoid a rabbit that runs into the road. Or maybe
to avoid my question.

"I was waiting for you to come back to me," he says getting the
car—and himself—back in control.

"Baloney."

"Correct." Kevin laughs. "The truth is I never met the right woman."

He glances away from the road to look at me and see if I'm buying
it. I shake my head dubiously and Kevin grins.

"How about I like being footloose and fancy-free?"

"Warmer," I say. "Now you're supposed to explain how hard it is
for you to commit. And that you suffer from Peter Pan syndrome."

"Good ones," he says impressed. "Are those working for you?"

"Pretty well. I'm not exactly in the mood to defend marriage these
days." I reach to pull back my hair, which feels good blowing in the
breeze. At home in the summertime, I wouldn't even dream of rolling down my car windows. Like everyone else, I travel temperature-
controlled and hermetically sealed. But here I'm loving the freedom of
Kevin's open-topped coupe. I'm on vacation, I'm on the road, and anything goes.

"Marriage doesn't sound so bad to me anymore. I guess you always want what you don't have."

"You've probably had plenty," I say. "My bet is that you've been here long enough that there are no virgins left on Virgin Gorda."

"Ah, but there's a constant influx of tourists."

"I hear the Chamber of Commerce lists you as a national resource."

Kevin's face crinkles appealingly as he breaks into a long laugh. "You have the wrong image of me. I've had my moments, but despite what my mother thinks, I'm not the playboy of the Caribbean. These days I'm happy coming home to peace and quiet."

A few minutes later, we arrive at Kevin's rambling wooden house, tucked into the rocks, high above the water. It's definitely peaceful, but the roar of the waves and the cackling of the seagulls don't sound quiet to me at all. As Kevin shows me around, I'm impressed that every room looks out on the sparkling blue ocean. I make a mental note to lord it over Eric. Kevin may not live in the Time Warner building, but his cliff-side perch has a breathtaking 360-degree view.

We go outside and walk down to the water's edge. The deep blue Caribbean sea seems to stretch forever, a shimmering mosaic of turquoise and azure waves.

"How about a swim?" he asks.

"I don't have a suit."

Kevin gestures to the deserted landscape. "You may notice that there aren't a lot of people around." He takes off his shirt and puts his arms around me. We kiss and I feel the waves lap at my ankles. A moment later, he tugs gently at my shirt.

"I was crazy about you in high school, but you were such a good girl, I never got to see your breasts."

"Have you been thinking about them for the last twenty years?" I ask, teasing.

"No," he says honestly. "But definitely for the last twenty-four hours."

Laughing, I scamper away into the water, and dive bravely into the breaking surf. Kevin follows and playfully swims alongside me.

"Should I beg?" he asks.

"That would help," I say, only half-joking. The truth is, nobody except Bill has seen these breasts in maybe forever. Unless you count the spray-tanning tech and Biddy, the bra saleslady at the Town Shop. She's an expert, and she assures me that mine are quite nice. But still, I pirouette away, splashing a storm of water into Kevin's face.

"Feisty," he says, swimming after me.

"I'll let you catch me," I say, slowing down.

"I would anyway," he retorts, kissing me as we both tread water. "You can swim but you can't hide."

What the heck. This wet T-shirt's obviously not concealing much anyway. And if I loved the freedom of Kevin's convertible, I'm even more emboldened by the freedom I feel in the vast, limitless ocean. This is a deserted beach, for heaven's sake. I wiggle away and duck under water, emerging a moment later holding my T-shirt and bra. I make a show of tossing them into a wave while smiling at Kevin.

"Very nice. Worth the wait," he says admiringly, paddling over to cup his hands tenderly around my breasts.

But I jerk away. What am I doing? I'm not the topless type.

"My T-shirt! I love that T-shirt!" I say, pulling away, panicked that my favorite Juicy Couture is being carried out to sea. And even more panicked that after all these years, Kevin's made it to second base. Though I don't think there are bases anymore. In the lingo of the MTV generation, does this mean Kevin and I have "hooked up"?

I swim as fast as I can toward the errant red T-shirt, which is bobbing up and down in the ocean like a warning sign. "*Stop!*" it's screaming to me. "*Stop Whatever You Were Thinking of Doing!*"

"I *did* stop," I tell my Juicy, at least in my head. "I'm sorry I threw you away. Now I need you back."

"You have me back," says Kevin, who's effortlessly floating on his back next to me. Is my fast swimming really that slow? And even worse, did I talk to my T-shirt out loud?

"I didn't mean you," I say keeping my back to Kevin as I stop to tread water and catch my breath.

He looks around the empty sea but graciously doesn't ask which imaginary friend, or fish, I might be having a conversation with.

"Let me get that shirt for you," Kevin says, and I watch as he propels his strong arms through the water to retrieve it. He returns quickly and slips the shirt over my head.

"There you go. Feel better?" he asks gently.

Embarrassed by the whole episode, I smile and nod my head. How can I tell Kevin that taking off my T-shirt felt too reckless? After all the years of being with nobody but Bill, I want to move on, but I'm not sure I know how. And even scarier, I feel a real attraction for Kevin—not just the old one, but a brand-new appeal.

"Sorry for being an idiot. I don't really know how to do this anymore."

"Do what?"

"Be with a guy."

"I'll tell you how to be with this guy. Just relax and don't worry, okay? There's no rush. Remember, we're on island time."

I kiss him gratefully on the cheek. And then I look anxiously toward the shore, which now seems miles away.

"We've drifted," I say worriedly.

"I've already told you. No worries when you're around me. I'll get you home safely. Climb on."

Following his directions, I lie on Kevin's back, fasten my arms around his shoulders and wrap my legs at his waist. Hmmm? Is this really the most efficient way to get someone to shore? I don't remember this position from any Red Cross lessons. But Kevin must know what he's doing. I relax and let my now-chilled body sink into his muscular form. Beneath my wet T-shirt, my nipples rub appreciatively against his smooth, wet skin.

Yup, Kevin definitely knows what he's doing.

Chapter ELEVEN

BACK AT THE HOUSE, Kevin disappears into the kitchen to whip up what he promises will be the best dinner of my life. I duck into the bedroom to change out of my wet T-shirt and soggy shorts and put on one of Kevin's shirts. It's long enough on me to be an improvised minidress. I glance in the mirror. Not a look I'd wear in New York, but not half-bad, either. For once, I'm not worried about my thighs. The Cellulite Exorcist might have recommended fourteen more weeks of treatment, but having a man find you attractive works even better.

"Whatever's on the grill smells fabulous," I say, joining him in the kitchen.

"Nothing on it yet. You're smelling the charcoal," he says with a grin.

"Mmm, well, then, maybe we should have that."

"Good idea. I'll save the steaks for someone else," he says. "Should be another date coming over later."

"Blond or brunette?" I ask.

"Don't remember. Which one would make you more jealous?"

"You don't need to make me jealous," I say, laughing. "We're not in high school anymore."

Kevin stops mixing his marinade and puts his arms around me. "I'm glad we're not in high school. I think I was too young to really appreciate you back then. I like you even better now." He kisses me gently. It's a sweet, romantic moment, which, of course, I can't leave alone.

"You only like me more now because you finally got to see my breasts," I tease.

"Well, that helps," Kevin agrees with a smile. He pauses and flexes his fingers. "And you haven't broken a single digit yet."

I laugh and look around, ready to offer to help. But just as I'm about to explain how talented I am at tossing a salad, the doorbell rings.

Kevin looks up, surprised.

"Your other date," I say calmly. "Should I sneak out the back?"

"I have no idea who that could be," Kevin says. He wipes his hands on a dish towel and heads to the front door. A moment later, I hear loud, cheerful voices offering a chorus of congratulations.

"Hey, good work getting that movie gig with Angelina Jolie, Kev!" booms one guy.

"You work, we all work!" says another. "Thought we'd come over and surprise you with a little party to celebrate."

"PAR-TEE!!" holler a couple of other revelers.

"Hey, guys, thanks," says Kevin. "But this might not be the best time. I have someone here."

"You bagged Angelina already?" asks a male voice admiringly.

The crowd who came to party now push past Kevin, in search of the star. But as they head into the kitchen, all they find is me.

"Hi," I say tentatively to Kevin's buddies, who troop in bearing six-packs of beer and big bags of chips. Two of the women are carrying plastic bowls filled with food.

"My famous pasta with mango and black beans," says a well-tanned woman in shorts and a colorful tank top. She puts her container on the counter and holds out her hand to shake mine. "Hi, I'm Susie. I sometimes work with Kevin on shoots."

"Hi, I'm Hallie." *I sometimes ride on Kevin's back* is the first way I think of identifying myself, but I amend it. "I'm an old friend."

The rest of the group—a good-looking collection of scuba instructors, sailors, and other assorted ex-pats—also make their introductions. Most mention what a great guy and good buddy ol' Kevin is.

"Don't let them fool you," says Kevin, coming over to put an arm around me. "Half this crowd of beach bums have come by figuring I'll hire them to work on the movie with me."

"Well, won't you?" asks Kevin's friend Dave, wearing a T-shirt that says "Divers Go Deeper."

"What choice do I have? My good buddies. The best of a bad lot," says Kevin with a fake sigh.

They pop open cans of beer and rowdily toast Kevin. One guy breaks open a bag of chips and Susie busily takes the Saran Wrap off the food and passes around paper plates. So much for my quiet romantic dinner with Kevin. Someone turns on the CD player and the thumping beat of Latin music fills the room.

"Salsa!" calls out a woman named Carla whose long red hair swings practically to her waist. She wiggles her hips and snaps her fingers over her head, then grabs Kevin. "Come dance with me," she says.

They sidle into the middle of the living room. Two guys push the furniture against the walls, creating a makeshift dance floor, and quickly the rest of the party pairs off, moving to the beat. Mr. Divers Go Deeper grabs my hand. We don't really need to talk; his clothing tells me all.

"Salsa me, baby," he says sashaying in front of me.

I shake my head. I can't dance. And even if I could, I'd worry that the bottle he's now jubilantly waving in the air would send beer raining all over me.

"No, thanks. I have no rhythm," I say truthfully.

"I'll lead," he offers.

"But I can't follow."

"You can follow me," says Kevin, coming to my rescue. He hands off Carla to my would-be partner, and the new twosome glides into the center of the room.

"Waltz?" I ask Kevin hopefully as he pulls me into the classic ball-room dance position. "I can probably handle three-quarter time."

"This is four-four time. Just remember the first step occurs on beat two, not beat one."

"That clarifies it," I say, refusing to move my feet.

Kevin starts to dance, practically dragging me.

"What are you waiting for?" he asks.

"Beat two," I explain.

"I'll count out loud," he says patiently. "One, TWO."

He steps forward and so do I. Almost immediately, we bang smack into each other.

We both step back to rub our foreheads. Then Kevin bravely resumes a dance position and soldiers on.

"Just mirror what I do. Listen to the music and move to the tempo," he says good-naturedly.

I've always prided myself on moving to the beat of my own drummer. But on the dance floor, that doesn't seem to be working to my advantage. I look around and watch in amazement as the various partners launch into complicated patterns of dips and dance steps.

"How come everyone knows how to do this?" I ask.

"It's just a matter of swaying your hips in rhythm with mine," Kevin says.

I try to mimic his movements one more time, but then I sigh.

"It's hopeless."

"Never," says Kevin. "It's instinctive. To quote George Bernard Shaw—and I'd like to point out that very few men do—dancing is just the vertical expression of a horizontal desire."

I think about it a minute. "Horizontal desire, check. It's just the vertical expression that's giving me trouble."

"Better than the other way around," Kevin says. Then spinning me toward him, he whispers, "Let's try again—and focus on that horizontal desire."

This time when Kevin puts his hand on my back and draws me closer, I just relax and stay attuned to his gentle lead. We start with small steps, and I let his hand holding mine guide me around the dance floor. Look at that. Nobody's laughing at me. In fact, nobody's even noticing. Except Kevin.

"You're doing great," he says encouragingly. "Ready to try some swivels?"

"I'm ready for anything," I say throwing back my head.

"What I like to hear." Kevin starts to explain something about twisting my hips one way and transferring my weight to the other foot. Then there's something about bending a knee.

"Why don't you just lead," I suggest.

"You told Diver Dave you don't follow."

"I wouldn't follow Diver Dave. But I'd follow you."

Someone turns the music a little louder, and the new tune bouncing off the walls is even faster paced. Kevin and I are whirling around the room—and colorful visions are whirling in my head. I feel giddy in his arms, and instead of analyzing why, I'm just enjoying it.

We dance the whole night away. At one point Diver Dave cuts in, and I don't even mind. I take a break to grab some food in the kitchen and talk with Susie and Carla. It doesn't take long to get their stories. Before escaping to the islands to become a scuba teacher—and Kevin's occasional underwater assistant—Susie was a loan officer at the Montreal branch of the largest bank in Canada. Carla was the vice president at a sales company in Philadelphia.

"How'd you get down here?" I ask.

"Plane," Susie says and laughs.

"I mean, why? What made you come? Or more to the point, why'd you stay?"

Susie looks around the room, at the friendly, easygoing crowd milling under the whirling ceiling fans. The double glass doors off the living room are open to the vast expanse of ocean, which is sparkling under a full moon.

"Better question. Why would you leave?" asks Susie.

"Happens to a lot of us," says Carla. "I jumped off the merry-go-round for what I thought would be a two-week vacation. But then I thought, what about the other fifty weeks of the year? Shouldn't you try to be happy every day of your life?"

I take a sip of beer. Happy every day of your life? Being a mom means you feel happy if your kids are happy. You stop thinking about finding happiness yourself.

"What about your jobs?" I ask.

"Amazingly, the bank has survived without me," Susie says, and laughs again.

"And, amazingly, I survived without the corporate world," says Carla.

"Very nice to trade in three-piece suits for two-piece suits. You get a much better tan in a bikini," says Susie.

"So what's the story?" asks Carla, smiling at me. "Are you staying down here with Kevin?"

I start coughing on a gulp of beer. "Not at all. Nothing like that. I'm going back to New York tomorrow." As I say those words, it dawns on me that I wish I had a little longer to enjoy swimming in the ocean, swigging Corona from a bottle, and reveling in my newfound talent as a salsa dancer. And I wish I had a little more time with Kevin.

But everyone in the room seems to want a little more time with Kevin because, well after midnight, the party is still going strong. Not until almost 2 A.M. does Diver Dave mention that he has a boat going out in the morning and really needs to get his full four hours of rest.

"You definitely need your beauty sleep," jokes Carla. "You'll get better tips from the tourists if your eyes aren't puffy."

"I rely on the tightness of my Speedo to get good tips," says Dave.

"You learned that trick from me," quips Carla, and she throws him a kiss as he heads toward the door.

The rest of the group helps clean up the kitchen and push the furniture back to its original places in the living room. Nobody seems to notice the carpet of chips on the floor or the beer-can sculpture on the mantelpiece. But at least they've tried. They take a long time saying their good-byes, but finally only Kevin and I are left.

Suddenly exhausted, I sit down on the couch and Kevin comes over to me.

"It's really late," he says, draping an arm over my shoulders. "Why don't you stay here instead of going back to your hotel? I'll drive you to pick up your car at the airport in the morning."

I give him a hesitant look.

"You can stay in the guest room," he says.

"It's a deal."

He leads me to a pretty, pale blue room with a double bed and the same patterned pastel spread you find in every hotel room on every island in the world. I look for the usual shell-framed painting of a beach, but instead three vibrant poster-sized underwater photographs grace the wall.

"Yours?" I ask Kevin, admiring the brilliant clarity and the way he caught a moment with angelfish lined up and looking like they were throwing him kisses.

Kevin nods. "Took these years ago."

"You're good," I say.

"Very good. And I keep getting better."

"You do." Still in my improvised minidress, I pull back the bed-spread and lie down on the crisp, cool sheets, then stretch out my arms and yawn.

"Mind if I join you for a moment?" asks Kevin.

I pat the space next to me, and Kevin slides in and cuddles me close. "This has been fun," he says.

"A great day. A happy day," I say, and with my head snuggled tightly against his strong chest, I immediately fall asleep.

I wake up in the morning later than I'd planned and look over at Kevin, still asleep in his shorts and T-shirt. Breakthrough: I've spent the night with a man. In fact, if you take a literalist interpretation, we've actually slept together.

Somehow during the night, Kevin's arm has ended up curled around my waist and my leg is intertwined with his. I gently pull away to get up, and Kevin flutters open his eyes.

"Mmm, that was a good night," he says.

"Did anything happen in bed that I should know about?" I ask, teasing.

Kevin rolls over groggily. "I'd never waste my talents. You should be fully awake to appreciate me."

"Cocky, aren't you?" I giggle and punch him lightly on the arm. For-tunately, he doesn't comment on my bad double entendre.

He starts kissing me lightly on the neck, but then I glance at the clock and jump out of bed in a panic, the happy, calm spell I've been feeling broken.

"What's wrong?" asks Kevin.

"I can't believe I slept this late. I have to get back to the hotel to check out, and then to the airport to turn in my rental car and get on the flight." I shake my head and then repeat, "How did I sleep this late?"

"You were relaxed. Maybe you felt good lying next to me," says Kevin.

"Well, now I feel a little crazy," I say. I rush into the bathroom to splash cold water on my face, then grab my pocketbook, smear on some lip balm, and check that my passport is still in the little zippered case.

Meanwhile, Kevin hasn't moved. Doesn't he realize that I don't have my car here? I need him to drive me back. I have a million things to do today. But Kevin just lazily rubs his hand across the pillow.

"Look at that beautiful day out there, will you?" he asks, pointing to the sunshine streaming in the window.

"Beautiful, wonderful, very yellow sun. Now come on, please." I go over to the bed and tug at Kevin's arm. "Help me out here. My flight's in a few hours."

"And there's another flight tomorrow. And the day after that." Kevin rubs my hand.

"But my flight's today."

"Doesn't have to be." He plays with my fingers. Slowed down by his lack of reaction to my frenzy, I sit down on the bed next to him.

"Stay with me," Kevin says. "Don't you remember what I told you yesterday? If you get on that plane, you'll regret it."

"I will?"

"You'll always wonder what might have happened. We'll both always wonder."

Kevin's fingers dance across my bare thigh and I close my eyes for a moment.

"What will happen if I stay?" I ask in a soft voice.

For an answer, Kevin gently pulls me close. He holds me tightly, then rolls over so I feel the full weight of his taut body against mine.

Instead of telling him how much I want to stay, I just melt into him as we kiss. This is what I've been running both toward and away from since the day I got to the island. Am I going to finally give in and let myself feel again? Take the chances that Emily says I've never taken?

"I want to make love to you," says Kevin, his breath warm against my ear. "Passionate love, but slowly, very slowly." My heart pounds against his chest and I slide my hands under his shirt and feel the strong muscles along his smooth back.

Take a chance. Go for what I want.

"I'm not sure I remember how to do this anymore," I say, whispering and pulling him closer.

"Then let me remind you." He reaches down and pulls off my T-shirt and takes off his own. I feel the thrill of naked skin against skin, and this time, I'm not embarrassed for Kevin to see my body. Or stroke it. Or make love to it. Just like when we were dancing, I blissfully follow his lead.

And follow and follow. And lead. And then follow again.

Since Bill left me, I wondered if I'd ever make love again. I didn't think I would; I didn't think I wanted to. After all these years, how could I be with someone new? But as my body merged with Kevin's— over and over—I felt as if parts of me were being roused from a long sleep.

"How many times can we possibly make love?" I ask Kevin, late that afternoon when we're nestled in a hidden cove on the beach.

"Mmm, maybe just once more," Kevin says, coming closer.

"Uck, you're sandy." I giggle and push him away.

"One day and you're already tired of me?" he asks.

"Never," I say, kissing him.

Kevin stretches out, his chin propped in his cupped hand, and I run my hands appreciatively—yet again—over his gorgeous body.

"So what do you think?" he asks.

I turn onto my back and look up at the sky. "I think you're an amazing lover."

"How big is your database?"

"Small. But I read a lot." I don't mention that the books tend to be law texts, not Harlequin romances.

"And what else do you think?"

"I think Arthur's going to wonder if I was abducted by pirates."

Kevin looks at me quizzically. "Arthur? So you do have a boyfriend back home."

I laugh. "No. Arthur's my boss. He's expecting me in the office tomorrow."

"That's easy, then. Call him and tell him you'll be a day late." Kevin reaches over and strokes my breast. "Better idea. Tell him you'll be a week late. You can stay with me for as long as you want, you know."

"I don't have any clothes here. My suitcase is still in the rental car I left at the airport," I say, as if the only thing keeping me from moving in with Kevin is an extra pair of Levi's.

"Forget clothes. I don't want you ever to wear clothes again," says Kevin. He reaches over and caresses the curve of my waist.

We slowly head back to his house, arms wrapped around each other. I realize Kevin's right. There's no way I want to go back to New York right now. "I'm going to call Arthur," I tell Kevin once we're inside. It's not like me to run out on work, but it's just for a few days. Plus, I pass the Susie-Carla litmus test of why you shouldn't rush back to your real life. I feel happy.

And I feel even happier two days later when Kevin and I agree that I should at least stay on the island until the supply boat arrives with his order from Amazon.com for a new espresso machine and a copy of *The Complete Illustrated Kama Sutra*.

"I don't want you getting bored," he says, explaining his purchases.

"One more cup of bad coffee and I'm out of here," I laugh. But he could have saved his money on the book. Kevin's repertoire doesn't need any help.

"How many positions are there in the Kama Sutra?" I ask, curious.

"Sixty-four."

"It will take serious work to get through it all."

"We'll take as long as we have to."

One thing I know is it's going to take long enough that I have to call Arthur again. When he answers, I explain that I'm delayed and am taking some more of my vacation time.

"What's going on, Hallie?" Arthur snaps. "It's not like you to be this irresponsible."

"I know," I blurt out cheerfully. But I quickly recover, realizing that Arthur wasn't tossing me a compliment. I'd expected my usually accommodating boss to be a little more supportive, but since he's not, I quickly change my tone.

"I can do some work from here," I say in what I hope is my best professional voice. "With phones, Internet, e-mail you'll never miss me."

"I don't really like the idea," says Arthur, "The Tyler case is coming to trial soon. I need your full attention."

And what makes him think that he doesn't have it? Can he tell from my tone that I'm holding the phone with one hand and slathering on sunscreen with the other?

"I'll get you anything I can for the Tyler case," I say, the tube of sunscreen slipping from my fingers. I watch it bounce across the floor. Exactly what rabbit am I going to pull out of the hat to save the Tyler case? My luck it'll be Jessica Rabbit, the sexed up 'toon. And it'll turn out she works for Alladin Films and is screwing Mr. Tyler, too.

"The best thing you can get me is Mr. Tyler," says Arthur gruffly. "I've been trying to find him for three days, and he hasn't answered any of my messages."

"I could always look around here," I joke.

"Why don't you do that if you're not too busy," says Arthur snidely, as he hangs up.

To keep Arthur happy, I decide to do a little work after all. I check behind the pillows, under the bed, and in the bathroom for Mr. Tyler. Nope, he's not here. Well, this should count for at least one billable hour. Next, I'll go to the beach to look for him. But first I make a quick call to check in with Bellini again. Someone in New York should know where I am.

"What do you mean you're still on Virgin Gorda?" she asks when I reach her at her office at Bendel's.

"You should see how exquisite the beaches are," I say languorously.

"Right," she sighs. "Listen, I don't have time for another travelogue right now. Could you just give me the news? I have a rep waiting to sell me sequined handbags and another who insists next season will be all about appliqué. Sorry, but I'm under so much pressure."

I step onto the deck and watch a pretty forty-foot catamaran sail by. The three people lounging on board wave and I leisurely wave back. Yes, so much pressure. Bellini's panicked because Bendel's bottom line depends on her choice of sequins or appliqués. Arthur's frantic that he might lose a case—and has misplaced a client. For me, just a little relaxing in the warm sunshine and it all seems so far away.

But if Bellini needs me to cut to the chase, I will. "The news is that Kevin turns out to be a scuba-diving photographer *extraordinaire*. And when it comes to sex, he's even more *extraordinaire*."

"Sounds good," she says.

I smugly lean against the railing and wave at another boat. "I may never come home."

"Of course you will. You're just having a fling."

I think about it for a second. "No, not a fling. What if this is serious? Is there any reason I couldn't stay here?"

"You just met the guy. You have two kids. And you hate piña coladas. How are those for reasons?"

Since I've been going through the same arguments in my head for the last few days, I'm ready to rebut.

"My kids are at college. Piña coladas are passé. And I've known Kevin for twenty-five years. For heaven's sake, I even know his mother." That stops me. Jeannette Talbert definitely does not belong in the plus column.

"Oh, stop being silly," says Bellini. "He's a scuba diver and he lives on an island. He's not appropriate for you."

"Not appropriate?" I start to laugh. Bellini judging me for dating someone inappropriate is like Rush Limbaugh attacking drug addicts. Or Bill O'Reilly railing against sexual deviance. Or the Catholic church sermonizing about . . . well, about anything these days.

"Hallie, I'm the one with the low standards," Bellini bursts out, exasperated. "We all rely on you to be the paragon of virtue. The pillar of the community. The epitome of appropriateness."

"Well, maybe I'm tired of being a paragon and a pillar. Not to mention an epitome."

"It's who you are. It's how you're built."

"You make me sound like an ancient Greek amphitheatre. I've had enough of that. I want to be"—I pause. What do I want to be?—"the Guggenheim Bilbao. You know, that crazy museum in Spain with the curvy roofs. New and modern and something everyone talks about."

"Keep this up and everyone will be talking about you, that's for sure."

"I can't believe you're so disapproving. You're the one person I thought would tell me to go for it."

"I'm just being rational," says Bellini.

"It doesn't become you."

Bellini sighs. "Okay, look. Enjoy the sex. You're using condoms, right? And backup birth control? You know to reapply the spermicide every time you make love. And just to be safe, use a gob more than they say on the directions."

I wrinkle my nose. "Bellini, if you want me to enjoy the sex, shut up. I know what to do so cut the public service announcement. What happened to spontaneity?"

"Don't you dare think about spontaneity! I'm serious about reapplying every time, even if you're doing it twice in an hour." She pauses. Then lowering her voice she asks, "By the way, does he do it twice in an hour?"

"Three times," I say.

"Now I know you're lying." She laughs. "But while we're on the subject, what have you told your kids?"

"Nothing."

"You're lying to them?"

"I would never lie to my children," I say righteously. "I talk to them all the time. They call my cell phone. They just never think to ask where I am."

"Well, it sounds like you have things under control," says Bellini dubiously. "I'll call you soon. But meanwhile, I've got to get the Bendel's pocketbook crisis under control."

"So what'd you decide about next season? Sequins or appliqué?"

"Neither," says Bellini. "You're not the only one who can head in a whole new direction. Hold on." I hear her call out to her assistant to get rid of both of the sales reps who are waiting in the outer office.

"Time to shake things up around here," she announces. Then in one short sentence, Bellini makes her mark on fashion accessory history.

"Get me those evening bags in plastic."

Plastic bags? Good idea. But maybe I'll just get mine at A&P.

Chapter TWELVE

IT AMAZES ME how easily I've slipped into island life—and can now slip into a sarong. Being outside every day running on the beach, swimming in the ocean, and having sex everywhere, I'm in my best shape ever. I've heard that the average woman gains two pounds every year she's married. Maybe when you're separated, you lose two pounds a year. If I stay single another twenty years, I could end up anorexic.

But at the moment, I have the best of everything. I'm feeling trim and healthy—and I have Kevin. Talk about slipping into things. With stunning ease, I've abandoned my world and moved into his. My morning wake-up call is suddenly the lapping waves, not a blaring alarm clock. Instead of stuffing an oatmeal breakfast bar into my mouth as I run for the commuter train, I sit at leisure with Kevin on his deck, watching the seagulls, sipping freshly brewed coffee (that new espresso machine was a good idea), and nibbling ripe fruit. The Kama Sutra manual was a good idea, too—but we don't usually get to that until lunch.

I like being at Kevin's side, even though that means I'm spending a lot of time underwater. My diving skills have improved and I'm happy

to help out occasionally on his jobs. I rarely even visited Bill's sleek office when we were married, but I like going to work with Kevin. Maybe
it's because his workplace is the ocean, and being with him seems com-
pellingly exotic.

Kevin's movie job with Angelina isn't starting for another month,
and in the meantime he's back to taking photos of scuba diving
tourists. But today's assignment, shooting a marriage ceremony, is unusual, at least for me. Having been to a lot of weddings, I've seen barefoot brides romping through fields in Vermont and grooms walking
stiffly down the aisle at St. Patrick's Cathedral in morning coats and top
hats. But I've never seen a couple exchange vows a hundred feet under
the sea with air tanks strapped to their backs. Everybody gets a little
short of breath before they say, "I do," but this will be the first bride and
groom I know who actually require oxygen.

"What if they drop the ring underwater?" I ask Kevin, as we're
bounding by speedboat out to neighboring Guana Island, where the
happy couple is getting married.

"If the ring drops, we call the Coast Guard," Kevin says.

It takes me a moment to realize he's teasing. "*Coast Guard: Ring
Rescue Team*," I parry. "I think it's on CBS on Sunday nights."

Kevin laughs, and as we pull up closer to Guana, a flock of fluffy
white birds lazily hunting food scatter, their noisy calls quickly replac-
ing the whir of our motor. From the edge of the dock, a tall broad-
chested man waves, then comes over and extends a helping hand as we
get off.

"Hey, Henry, good to see you," says Kevin, shaking the man's hand.

"You, too. Welcome," says Henry. He looks at me appreciatively,
then asks Kevin, "Is this a new friend of yours?"

"Actually an old friend. Meet Hallie." Kevin puts his hands posses-
sively on my shoulders. "Will you take care of my girl while I go get set
up for the wedding shoot?"

"I'm always happy to take care of your girls," Henry jokes.

Kevin laughs then grabs his photography equipment, and heads
off.

"Pretty place," I say to Henry as he helps me tie up the boat and we wander along the shore. "Worked here long?"

"I suppose you could say that," he admits with a sweet grin.

A flock of flamingos parade past us, graceful long-legged, long-necked beauties that look like they should have a ballet written about them. The divas of *Swan Lake* have ruled for too long.

"How beautiful," I say, watching them.

Henry looks after them proudly. "Guana's a wildlife sanctuary. A few years ago, Caribbean flamingos were endangered, so we repopulated. We have a lot of animals you won't find elsewhere."

As if to prove it, a large insect starts to crawl up my leg, and I give a little squeal and flick it off.

Henry bends over and cups the beleaguered bug in his hand. "Hundreds of species of bugs live here, including three types of beetle." He stares briefly at the insect, then puts it down gently on a leaf. "Did you know there are more beetles in the world than any other species? There's an old story about a biologist who was asked what nature has taught him about God, and he replied, 'He has an inordinate fondness for beetles.'"

I laugh and flex my leg. "You seem to know a lot about this place," I say.

"I should," Henry says, adjusting his broad-brimmed hat. "I own it."

"You *own* it?" I ask surprised. "Does that make you the king? The dictator? What do I call you?"

"Henry," he says simply.

"I might go for King Henry," I say, curtseying.

Henry chuckles. "Actually, I own two islands. I bought Guana back in the seventies."

"Smart investment. What are you thinking of buying next?" I ask him.

"A new fishing rod."

"Nice to have goals," I say.

Henry smiles and sits down again on the dock. "So how about you, Hallie? What's your story?"

"Everything about my story seems to be changing," I tell him. "Right now being with Kevin seems to be the main theme."

Henry picks up a stone and tosses it neatly across the water. Three skips. Not bad. "Kevin's a fun guy. A very free spirit," he says. "I admire that in a man. Although after a while, some women get tired of it."

I pause and run some sand through my fingers. "Is that a warning, King Henry?"

"Just an observation," he says.

We look at each other, and then Henry stands up. "You should probably be getting over to the wedding." He points down a path and offers directions to Muskmelon Bay. Then he gives me a small hug and kisses me on each cheek. "Have fun. Enjoy yourself with Kevin. That's a lot more important than owning islands."

I hug him back. "You're the nicest king I've ever met," I say.

I give Henry a little wave then walk toward the site of the nuptials. An unusual lizard skitters across my path, and instead of jumping out of its way, I stop to admire it. After all, it's one of God's—or at least Henry's—creatures.

When I get to the edge of the bay, I peer into the clear blue water, looking for bubbles and signs of Kevin. My boyfriend is out there somewhere. My boyfriend. That's a nice thing to have again, despite Henry's word of caution. Guana seems to be a good place for cultivating things. Maybe a boyfriend becomes . . .

"Aquaman!" I call out as his head bobs out of the ocean.

Kevin waves to me and swims to shore. He hauls himself out of the water. "Hey, Aquababy," he says, pulling off his mask and dripping water all over me.

"Stop it. You're getting me wet."

He laughs and spreads his arms to the vast ocean. "That's what we do at underwater weddings," he says.

I speedily suit up and check my equipment, thinking how just a few weeks ago I needed help from my children, Nick, and the speedboat captain just to get into the water—and once there I flipped my flippers like burgers at a barbecue. But now being in the ocean is no big deal. Second nature. And I'm getting a second chance at more than just scuba diving.

Holding hands, Kevin and I dive down to the ceremony site. Since it's a wedding, I think I should fuss, but there's not a lot to do with the natural habitat. The living coral reef, glittering like a thousand crystals, is more beautiful than any marble altar, and the purple sea fans wafting in the current are more stunning than fifty thousand roses.

A few minutes later, I see the bride and groom slowly dropping down from the surface to join us at eighty feet. They glide toward us in matching sleek black wet suits, and given the spandex, the masks, the hoses, and the tanks, it's a little tricky to make out who's the he and who's the she. Could be the perfect solution for gay marriage. Don't ask, and there's no way to tell.

Accompanying the couple is Susie, Kevin's sometime assistant, who will also be presiding over the nuptials. She might have abandoned her banking career when she came to the islands but she definitely kept her business sense. To supplement her services as a master scuba diver, Susie became certified as a justice of the peace and a bartender. Clever career move. Who doesn't need a drink after a wedding?

When the couple approaches, the bride (or at least the smaller of the two) grabs some seaweed to hold in front of her as a bouquet. Kevin removes his mouthpiece and blows out musical bubbles.

"*Dum dum da-dum*," he exhales, to the beat of "Here Comes the Bride." He quickly puts the tube back in his mouth to breathe again. Good thing the bride's not swimming down the aisle to Wagner or Kevin would pass out before the last note. Musical accompaniment finished, Susie gathers us close, and at last, the wedding is in full swing. A colorful school of parrot fish gathers to witness the holy union and a large loggerhead turtle appears to stand up for the groom.

With nobody to give the bride away and none of the fish objecting, the proceedings go rather quickly. Kevin starts snapping pictures as Susie performs the ceremony by pointing to the groom, pointing to the bride, and making a question mark with her finger. The groom forms the okay sign by making a circle of his thumb and forefinger, the underwater version of "I do." Susie reverses the process, and his beloved nods, pledging her troth. I'm sure Susie would never slip anything by her, but how's an underwater bride to know if she's agreed just to love and cherish—or also to obey?

The happy couple mash their masks together, trying to kiss, and as an ultimate sign of oneness, they both take a swig of air from the same tank. In the excitement of the moment, I give the thumbs-up sign, forgetting that for scuba divers, that means it's time to go back to the surface. Everybody dutifully starts to ascend. Oh, well, the only thing the bride didn't get to do was throw her bouquet and I didn't want a face full of seaweed, anyway.

Kevin and I are the first out of the water, and we pull off our equipment quickly. The newlyweds surface and I hold out a hand to help them ashore.

Through his mask, the groom looks at me and is so startled, he almost falls back into the water. As I hoist him to land, he quickly scuttles behind his bride.

"What's the matter, honey?" she asks, taking off her goggles. She pulls out the elastic band holding her hair in a ponytail and swings her thick red curls. The groom, meanwhile, is whispering in her ear and urgently tugging at her wet suit.

And suddenly I realize that I know both of them. I've met the groom, nervous in my office, and seen the bride naked in a photograph.

"Mr. Tyler?" I ask incredulously. "Is that you?"

Instead of answering, he hurriedly grabs the bride—who I can now identify as Melina Marks—and spirits her into a speedboat moored at the beach. He heaves the boat into the water and yanks the cord to start the motor.

I start to run after them, but they shove off, sending a fine wave of salt water splashing back in my face. Susie joins me at the edge of the water.

"I hope I didn't do anything wrong at the ceremony," she says, watching the couple zoom away.

"You were perfect," I promise her. We continue to stare out to sea until the boat is barely a speck in the distance.

Susie sighs. "I have to fill out the license, and I don't even know their names. Who was that masked man?"

All those years watching reruns of *The Lone Ranger*, and I never thought I'd actually get to answer that question.

"His name's Charles Tyler. He's a client of mine," I say. "When my boss told me to find him, I figured I should look under every rock, but it never occurred to me to look under an air tank."

"Why was he so panicked to see you?"

I shake my head. "Probably because it's not too prudent in the middle of a sex discrimination trial to marry the woman you're accused of sleeping with."

I wander around Guana for a while, waiting for the speedboat to reappear, but it never does.

"You think we should go looking for them?" I ask Kevin.

"We can try. But they could be anywhere by now—or at least anywhere you can get to on a tank of propane."

With no real alternative, I leave a voice message on Mr. Tyler's cell phone, congratulating him on his wedding—because what else can I say? You stupid idiot, you're going to lose your career and your new wife is going to lose her job. I beg Mr. Tyler to call me, even though he's now officially on his honeymoon.

We leave Guana, and I'm agitated all the way home. As our small boat crashes through the rising waves, the pounding of my butt against the seat is nothing compared to the pounding in my head, courtesy of Mr. Tyler. When we go out to have drinks with Susie and Dave at an outdoor bar that night, it's all I can talk about.

"I still don't understand why you're so worked up," says Kevin for about the tenth time.

"Worked up? I'm not worked up," I say, getting more worked up at the thought of having to defend my worked up-edness.

"No, Kev's right. You're worked up," says Dave, who tosses a peanut in the air and catches it in his mouth. "What's the big deal?"

"My client's acting very strangely. I know something's up with him, but I can't quite put my finger on it." I take a gulp of my drink. "It's driving me nuts not to have a handle on this."

"Who cares? End of the day, you have a beer and leave your work behind," says Dave.

"My work *interests* me," I say, remembering that it once did. "I don't like to leave it behind. Sometimes it stays with me all night."

"My work sometimes stays with me all night, too," says Dave with a leer. "Always some sexy tourist who wants the scuba master to show her more than the reef. So she comes home with me and I introduce her to the big eel."

"Oh, Dave, you're gross," says Susie.

"The big eel?" asks Kevin bemusedly. "Is that what you call it? I thought the last woman who slept with you referred to it as the little squid."

I sit back in my chair and shake my head. A few short months—and a lifetime—ago, I was with Bill at dinner parties in Chaddick, sipping Château Margaux and discussing the effects of Amazonian deforestation on environmental change. Now my environment really has changed. I'm swilling whatever's on tap and discussing whether a man I don't even like has a little squid or a big eel.

"So about your case," says Dave, done discussing his endowments. "This whole sex discrimation thing sounds like bullshit to me. Welcome to the world. Of course you get things because you look good and someone wants to sleep with you. It's natural selection. Downright Darwinian."

I pause, impressed that Diver Dave is referencing Darwin. But not so impressed by his take on the topic.

Or by Kevin's.

"Come on, Hallie. I hire the people I like. Why shouldn't everybody?"

"But do you sleep with all the people you hire?"

There's an uncomfortable silence at the table. Susie and Kevin exchange a glance.

"He never slept with me," says Dave, tossing up another peanut, which bounces off his cheek.

Susie gets very busy spreading a pat of butter on her bread. "Back to Mr. Tyler. Since I've just made them husband and wife, doesn't that help your case, Hallie? I mean, it's all legal now."

"It makes it less sordid, but it doesn't help the case. Now that he's married Melina, it's hard to say he wasn't favoring her."

"Ooh, teacher's pet, teacher's pet. What is this, fourth grade?" asks Dave, now holding the edge of his paper napkin into the candle flame and watching it burn. "I've had enough with political correctness. It just keeps you from having a good time."

"We wouldn't want anything to get in the way of any of you having a good time," I say a little too archly.

Kevin puts his hand on mine and pats it soothingly. "Come on, Hallie. Loosen up. You're not in New York anymore."

"Maybe I should be," I say softly.

He shakes his head. "Let's not argue about this. It's your job, and I bet you're good at it." He kisses me, and as usual at Kevin's touch, I start to relax. But then he can't leave well enough alone. "And look at you. I can't imagine it hurt your career that you're a great-looking babe."

I'm flattered and insulted at the same time. I'm sitting here with a couple of guys who think life is a frat party, but at least one of them calls me cute.

The next morning while I'm wandering through town, Emily calls my cell phone, sounding a bit too cheerful. Since it's final exam period at Yale, I expected she'd be a little tenser than this.

"I just have one ten-page paper left to finish on the rise and fall of Old World civilization," she explains.

"It's only four thousand years of history. You should be able to knock if off in an hour," I say sardonically.

A seagull squawks in the background, and I cover the speaker with my hand, hoping Emily won't hear. If she does, I can always tell her I'm in the subway. Lots of strange birds there. I don't like to lie, and since I'm not quite ready to admit that I'm hanging out with Kevin, I'm grateful that Emily never thinks to ask me where I am.

"Any interesting guys at school?" I ask her.

There's a long pause. "I'm too busy working to pay attention to guys," she says.

"Working is good, but you should still have a little fun at school," I tell her. "Best years of your life and all that."

I hear a strange squawk, but this time it sounds like it's coming from the receiver. Emily seems to muffle the phone herself, because I can barely hear what she says next.

"What?" I ask.

"Don't worry, I'm having fun," Emily says, a little clearer now.

"Good, so what else is going on?" I ask.

"Real busy. Just wanted to check in and let you know I'm fine." She pauses, and then adds in that fake-chipper voice again, "If you have trouble reaching me in the next couple of days, just figure I'm holed up in the library."

"My poor sweetie. I'll be thinking about you," I say as we hang up.

I feel briefly guilty about my daughter's working so hard in a chilly library while I'm strolling blissfully in the island sunshine. It was fun to have her down here. Maybe I should have bought her that trinket she liked so much, even though it was too expensive. Leave it to my daughter. On an island where vendors hawk two-dollar puka beads on the beach, she managed to find a freshwater pearl necklace with a Tiffany price tag.

I turn around and head over to the little shop that had the necklace, looking forward to surprising Emily. But when I get there, the necklace is gone. The shopkeeper Imelda remembers me from my last visit and shrugs when I ask her about it.

"Sold the pearls this morning," she says.

I look chagrined. "Darn, I wanted them for my daughter. She liked the necklace so much when we were here a couple of weeks ago. I should have bought it for her."

"Someone else bought it for her," says the shopkeeper. "She came in with that nice scuba teacher, Nick. What an adorable couple."

I stare at her briefly, then shake my head. "If you saw her this morning, it wasn't my daughter. She's at college. I just talked to her."

"You might have just talked to her, but I just saw her," says Imelda firmly. "Her name's Emily, right? We even discussed that she'd been in before with her mom."

I stand there, bewildered. Emily already got the necklace? And Nick bought it for her? And they're an adorable couple?

"Maybe they were in a few weeks ago," I say to Imelda, hopefully.

"It was this morning. What part of 'this morning' don't you understand?" asks Imelda, irritated that I'm doubting her.

Which part don't I understand? The part where my daughter called me and said she was writing a paper. The part where I told her to have fun. The part where I worried that she was holed up in a library when apparently she's holed up with Nick.

Baffled, I walk out of the store. How could Emily be on the island without my knowing about it? Wouldn't she have told me? On the other hand, I'm on the island and Emily doesn't know. But that's different. I'm the mother; I'm supposed to know everything.

I head over to the dock to look for Kevin. He's standing by a diving boat packed with bikini-clad tourists that's about to go out. I grab him.

"Do you know where Nick is?" I ask.

"Nick, the young scuba stud?" he asks. "What do you need him for? Already looking to replace me?"

"No, I love you," I say distractedly. "I just need Nick."

"You love me?" Kevin asks, surprised.

I'm suddenly embarrassed, realizing we haven't used that word with each other yet. "Not really love you," I say.

"Then how would you describe it?" Kevin crosses his arms and a small smirk crosses his face as he waits for my answer. A couple of the scuba-ready tourists lean out of the boat to hear more.

"I like you. I really, really like you. I hope you really, really like me," I say, flustered. Oh God, this is practically the speech that brought Sally Field down. And it's probably not going over any better with Kevin and the tourists than it did at the Academy Awards.

"Oooh, she really, really likes you," calls out one of the teenage girls who's hanging over the railing.

"I really, really like you, too, Kevin," snorts the captain from the bow. "Now can you get your ass on the boat so we can get moving?"

Ignoring the hecklers, Kevin wraps his arm around me and gives me a kiss. "I'm glad you love me, because I love you, too. I'll show you how much tonight," he says.

"I can't wait," I say, kissing him back and momentarily forgetting why I'd come.

But Kevin has a job waiting and I have a daughter waiting—somewhere. Though she's certainly not waiting for me to show up.

Kevin hops on the boat and then helpfully calls out over the sound of the motor, "Nick's up at the dive shop. But keep your hands off him!"

I rush up to the shop and fling open the flimsy screen door.

"Hallie, baby, how ya' doin'?" calls out the guy inside.

Alas, it's not Nick. Double alas, it's Diver Dave.

"Is Nick around here?" I ask him.

"Nope, just me. Isn't that good enough?"

"No," I say bluntly. "I need Nick."

"Whoa! Old Nickerino sure is getting more than his share of the action today." Dave steps out from behind the counter. "He just went off on his moped with some cute little girl."

"That cute little girl's my daughter!"

Dave raises an eyebrow. "Couldn't be. You're not old enough to have a grown daughter."

"Thanks. I started early," I say. I shake my head. "Anyway, I'm definitely not old enough to have a daughter who's screwing around with Nick."

"No mother's old enough to face that," agrees Dave. "Come on, we'll go find them."

He flips the hand-printed sign on the shop door from OPEN to CLOSED. I guess nobody's going diving again until we let old Nickerino know that you don't screw around with somebody's daughter. Does it ever occur to these guys that everybody is somebody's daughter?

I follow Dave out the door to his shiny black-and-silver motorcycle.

I've never been a biker babe before, but Dave tosses me a beat-up helmet and before he straps on his own, he pulls a black Jerry Garcia T-shirt on over his white tank top.

"Better image for the Harley," he explains, straddling the seat and motioning me to sit behind him.

"I don't understand why you bikers revere the Grateful Dead," I say, tentatively approaching the saddle. "I want to make it clear that if we end up dead, I'm not going to be grateful."

"Trust me. Every woman's grateful after she's been with me," says Dave, although this time when he winks, it's more self-knowing than salacious.

He starts the Harley, and it makes the intimidating VROOM that usually heralds the Hell's Angels. We jerk forward and I grab onto Dave's waist. A little scary to be on this thing, not to mention scary to be this close to Little Squid-Big Eel Dave. Though with a name like that, he could be the chief of the Cherokee Nation. The right person to . . .

"Find my daughter!"

"Will do! I can catch up to any crummy little moped!" He takes a turn a little too fast, which makes me grab him even tighter.

Up ahead of us, I see a speck on the road that, sure enough, gets closer and closer. Dave picks up speed, overtakes the moped, then makes a stunning U-turn, completely cutting them off. The moped skids in the dirt and almost falls over.

"I wanted to find Emily, not kill her," I squeal.

"Yeah, but I bet you'd like to kill Nick," Dave says. Our monster-size Harley and Nick's miniature moped are both stopped, facing each other across the road, a High Noon standoff.

From his moped, Nick screams, "Dave, what the fuck are you doing? What do you want?"

"Give up the girl!" Dave hollers out to him from his seat.

Emily just puts her arms tighter around Nick's waist. "Mom, is that you?" she asks incredulously. "What are you doing here?"

"Looking for you," I say. "I can't believe you came back to see Nick."

Emily shakes her head. "I don't get this."

"I don't either. You told me on the phone this morning you were writing a paper."

"I am writing a paper. My laptop's at Nick's house."

"But you wanted me to think you were at Yale," I say accusingly.

"And you wanted me to think you were in New York," she shoots back.

We glare at each other.

"Who's that guy you're with?" Emily asks, pointing at Dave.

"I'm her boyfriend's best friend," says Dave.

Emily looks stunned. "Mom, a boyfriend? You have a boyfriend? That's so tacky."

"No, it's kind of sweet," says Dave, thinking he's being helpful. "They're living together and . . ."

"*Shut up*, Dave," I say loudly.

Dave shuts up, but it's about half a sentence too late.

"You're living with someone?" Emily asks, her voice rising along with her level of indignation.

"Not really," I say, thinking that my passport's still stamped "Visitor" and I'd need at least two more suitcases full of clothes to be considered a permanent resident.

"She's just shacking up," says Dave, who can't seem to leave bad enough alone. "Kevin's a great guy. He's about to shoot a new movie with Angelina Jolie."

"Is that the guy I met on the scuba boat at Thanksgiving?" Emily asks, still trying to make sense of the situation.

"No," I say, having promised myself that I wouldn't do a Bill and introduce my children to anyone I was dating. But since I've also promised myself that I'd never lie to my children, I then amend, "Yes."

"Multiple choice?" asks Emily.

"Correct answer is yes," says Nick. "They're always together."

"Nick, how come you never told me?" Emily asks, still sitting behind him and now giving him a little punch.

"I figured you knew. And your mom's the last thing I want to talk about when we're in bed."

"Hey, Nick, you bought a real bed? You finally traded in your futon?" Dave asks.

"Of course," says Nick, leaning back on the seat to give Emily a little kiss. "You don't sleep with a girl like Emily on the floor."

"You don't sleep with a girl like Emily *anywhere*," I say.

Nick revs his moped, hoping to drown me out. Dave does the same with the Harley, blotting out Nick's words. So this is how men take each other's measure. They test to see who has the bigger engine.

"*You don't leave Yale to sleep with a scuba diver!*" I scream to Emily, over the loud vrooms.

"You left a fancy law firm to sleep with one!" she hollers back.

"My scuba diver takes photographs!" I roar, as if that's the point.

Nick decides he's had enough and turns the moped. Just as he's taking off, a black BMW comes hurtling toward us.

"Watch out, Nick!" I yell.

Dave swerves our Harley out of the way, but Nick doesn't hear.

"Nick!!" I scream, almost hysterical.

The BMW careens to a screeching halt just as Nick, finally aware of the danger, spins toward the side of the road. Nick and Emily tumble off the bike into a grassy patch and as Dave and I rush over, I hear a car door slamming.

"Oh my god, is everyone all right?" asks the ashen BMW driver, now at our side.

"I'm fine," says Emily, standing up. She has a little scratch on her knee. She looks at Nick, who's rubbing a bloodied elbow, but seems otherwise okay. Stunned from the fall, Emily bursts into tears and rushes into my waiting arms.

Shaken, the driver sits down on the edge of the road and puts his head in his hands. A woman gets out of the car and joins him. Seeing who they are, I'd laugh if I weren't so upset.

"I'm sorry, Hallie," says the upset driver, also known as my runaway client Charles Tyler. "I don't mean to cause so many problems for you."

"I didn't mean to cause problems either," says Emily, still sobbing. "I should have told you what was going on."

"I should have told you, too," I tell my daughter, kissing her on the top of the head.

I look from Emily to the newlyweds, expecting them to chime in that they, too, have a few things to tell me. But instead Melina puts a steadying hand on Charles Tyler's trembling shoulder and gives me a feeble smile.

"So, counselor," she asks, "are your rates any lower for roadside consultations?"

Chapter THIRTEEN

WITH EMILY, Nick, Charles Tyler, and Melina Marks all crowded into my island escape, real life has come crashing down. Instead of being able to focus on the wonderful, sexy man next to me in bed, my mind races off in a million directions.

"Is the butterfly position not working for you?" Kevin asks solicitously, as he hovers over me that night in bed.

"Not really," I admit. Candles are twinkling on the nightstand and soft music wafts in from the living room, but for the first time ever, Kevin's touch isn't yielding its usual magic.

"No problem." He leans over to look at the book propped by the bed and flips a page. "This picture looks promising. Let's see. Starts with you putting your left leg on my right shoulder."

He kneels on the bed and I dutifully place my leg in the correct location. But I might as well tell Kevin right now that none of the pages of the Kama Sutra are going to bring me any pleasure tonight. In fact, I wouldn't be able to get any satisfaction even if all four members of the Rolling Stones were joining us in this tantric pose.

But for Kevin's sake, I might as well try. I close my eyes, lock my jaw, and grit my teeth.

Above me, Kevin laughs. "That's not exactly the face of a contented woman," he says.

"No, it's the face of a confused woman," I say, pulling back my leg and sitting up.

"Should we try an easier position?" he asks.

I give a little smile. "The sex isn't what's confusing me," I say, though maybe all this delicious sex has been distorting my perspective. Seeing Emily made me realize that I've been floating along happily, dreamily, with Kevin, without making any real decisions about what comes next. Part of me knows I can't stay here forever with this man from my past. But another part of me wonders why I would ever leave when everything in the present is so terrific.

Kevin tenderly pulls a sheet up around me. "You had a tough day," he says sympathetically.

He's right. The near-accident and the shock of finding Emily with Nick hit me like a cold bite of sorbet. My brain froze, and my head's been throbbing ever since.

"I got Mr. Tyler to promise to go back to New York and check in with Arthur. He said he'd meet with me in my office within the week."

"Will you be there to see him?" asks Kevin, slightly surprised.

I play with the corner of the sheet, tugging at a frayed edge. "I guess I will," I say quietly.

"Is that what you want, to go back to New York?"

What I want to do is suddenly all mixed up with what I should do and what I have to do. I can't tell Emily not to run off to an island—and then run off to an island myself. When we went off for a mother-daughter talk late this afternoon, Emily assured me that she'd only come to Virgin Gorda for a three-day getaway with Nick. How could I admit to her that I secretly think about abandoning real life and staying here forever?

"What I'd really like is to be here in bed with you always," I tell Kevin, my hand resting on his shoulder.

"Good," says Kevin, flicking through his sex manual. "We're only on page twelve. And there are plenty more books where this one came from."

I lie back on his soft pillows. Right after Bill left, the major sign of my depression was that I didn't want to leave my bed. Now the major sign of my happiness is that I don't want to leave Kevin's bed. But I have to. I stretch out next to Kevin and kiss his shoulder.

"I'm thinking I need to go back to New York to take care of some business and spend the Christmas break with the kids," I say carefully. "But after that, do you want me to come back?" I feel my breath quicken, having put the question on the table. Or at least on the sheets.

"Of course I want you back," he says.

I roll over to face him, working up the courage to ask the even bigger question. "Do you think you'd ever come to New York? I mean, move there again, to be with me?"

I bite my lip, waiting for his answer. But Kevin doesn't need much time to think about it.

"I left New York long ago. It was never my scene. For someone smart and ambitious like you maybe it works, but not for me. I got to Virgin Gorda and knew I'd found home. This is a much better place for me to live."

We're both quiet for a moment, reflecting on what makes a place feel like home. Then Kevin strokes my hair and tries to ease the tension of the moment. "Besides, how could I go back to New York? I don't think Angelina is going to want to shoot her movie in the Hudson River."

"There's always the East River," I say, rubbing my finger across the sunburn on his nose. We both laugh, but I have his answer, and I have to admit it's not a surprise. If Kevin and I are going to be together, it'll be on his turf. A lot of people come to the Caribbean and dream of staying, but Kevin actually did it. Could I?

"Virgin Gorda really is an amazing place," I say, giving Kevin a kiss. "It's very seductive. You're lucky to have found it."

"And I'm lucky to have found you again."

Kevin slides on top of me so every part of our bodies is touching and our faces are just inches apart. My favorite position. Who needs fancy gymnastics when those missionaries had it right all along?

"Three weeks," I whisper as he moves rhythmically against me and horizontal desire takes over. "I'll be back in three weeks. Four at the most."

Two days later, my nails are digging into Emily's arm as our four-seater plane bumps terrifyingly across the sky.

"Calm down, Mom. I can't concentrate on my book," says Emily, who's trying to read *Don Quixote*.

"We can rent *Man of La Mancha* when we get home," I say, removing my trembling hands from my daughter's flesh.

Emily laughs. "Right. And instead of taking my English final, I'll just sing 'The Impossible Dream' to my professor. But relax, Mom. This flight's perfectly safe."

"Perfect conditions, beautiful day," agrees the pilot, turning around with what he thinks is a comforting smile. But he's only about a year older than Emily, and instead of an official uniform, he's wearing a tank top and Boston Red Sox cap.

"Get your eyes back on the road," I tell him.

"Yes, ma'am," he says, giving a little wink to Emily that says "We understand these old folks, don't we?"

Emily takes my hand. "I'll always remember these days on Virgin Gorda," she tells me dramatically, sounding like an ingenue on *The Young and the Restless*.

"You had a good time?" I ask, knowing that the secret to talking to your children is the open-ended question.

She nods. "A really, really, really great time. And thanks for being so cool about my being here, Mom."

"Kevin says Nick's a nice guy," I tell her, now that I've snatched her safely away from him.

"He is," she says happily. Then lowering her voice she adds, "You know, Mom, I went to college a virgin."

"Thank goodness."

"I'm glad I waited," she says. "There are a lot of things you do for the first time freshman year. Live with roommates, get a credit card, do your own laundry, have sex."

Apparently I saved money in a 529 plan all those years so my daughter could go to Yale—and learn to do laundry and have sex.

"Did I remember to tell you to use Tide? The 'mountain fresh,' not 'original' scent?"

Emily laughs. "It's okay, Mom. We can talk about this. We're both adult women now." There's a tinge of pride in her voice at her new status.

"So you and Nick . . ."

"Did it," says Emily. Then she adds theatrically, "You know, you always remember your first time."

"Yes, you do," I say smiling. I'm glad she remembers, since it was less than forty-eight hours ago. But twenty years from now, she'll still remember. And maybe she'll be like me, wondering what might have been.

"Are you and Nick going to try to keep this relationship going?" I ask gingerly.

"I think it's kind of unrealistic." Emily looks out the window, then back at me. "Nick and I do kind of live in different worlds. I mean, we love each other madly and all, but I have a busy semester coming up— five classes."

"Five classes is a lot," I agree.

"It kills me, because Nick's so great." Emily fishes a slightly used tissue out of her pocket and blows her nose loudly. She hugs herself and crumples forward in her seat, and I rub her back sympathetically. Then she pulls herself together and straightens up. "I have to be sensible," she says, giving one more blow before putting the tissue away. "These long-distance things never work."

They don't? My now-worldly daughter seems pretty confident about the topic that I've been mulling—without an answer—for days.

"Anyway," says Emily, "I spent all the money I saved this summer on the airplane ticket. I wouldn't be able to come down again for months."

"I could always buy you a ticket," I blurt out in the spirit of romance, rather than rational mothering. Then I quickly amend, "That is, if I happened to be on Virgin Gorda anyway, and you wanted to visit me. And see Nick."

"I'd *looove* to see Nick again," says Emily, practically swooning. But then she suddenly looks at me aghast. "But wait, why would you be here? Not to visit Kevin again, I hope."

"Maybe," I say timidly, as if I'm the daughter now, answering to an all-knowing mother.

"He's not your type," says Emily resolutely. "In my heart, I know Nick's not my type either. They're both cute, but they're not our type."

"And why not?"

"It's just opposites attracting. Someone told me every man wants a good girl who'll be bad just for him. And every woman wants a bad boy who'll be good just for her." She sighs. "Like it or not, you and I are good girls, Mom. Kevin and Nick are island boys. It'll never work."

Never work? Now it's my turn to look out the window. Emily's doing exactly what she should, making a man a part—but not all—of her life. As long as she's going back to school, I can't even complain that she flew down to be with Nick. Still, it makes me a little wistful that she feels her romance has to be over before it's really begun.

As for Kevin and me? Emily's probably right about good girls and bad boys. But maybe Kevin will be good just for me. He certainly has been so far.

When the airport cab pulls up to my house in Chaddick, a small crowd is gathered on the lawn. I've been away for a while—how long has this party been going on? I step out of the car, take my luggage from the trunk, and wave to a couple of friends. Amanda, with her four-year-old twins in tow, is passing around hot cider and homemade cookies. I'm touched by this neighborly homecoming, though come to think of it, nobody knew I was coming home.

I notice Rosalie walking around with a basket and picking up pine cones.

"These make beautiful holiday centerpieces," she says, giving me a little welcome-back kiss on the cheek. "Particularly festive with a touch of gold spray paint."

"Nice," I say. The sky is steel gray and the chilly air cuts right through my coat. Not only is it colder than Virgin Gorda, it's a lot colder than when I left.

I look around at the dozen people milling around on my lawn and try to figure out what's brought them here. It's too late for Octoberfest and too early for Boxing Day.

"What are we celebrating?" I ask her.

"Bill," she says, suddenly swooping down to beat out a passing squirrel for a Grade A acorn. She plops it victoriously into her basket.

We're celebrating Bill? The horrible thought suddenly crosses my mind that he and Ashlee must be getting married and everyone is here cheering him on. Have I been away so long that the whole town is now on his side? Before I left, I had the sympathy vote all tied up. Now I take an island escape, and Bill becomes the local hero.

But instead of champagne corks popping, I hear the whir of a chain saw. I spin around and see Bill, power tool in hand, playing Paul Bunyon with a downed branch from a maple tree.

So that's it—we're celebrating the triumph of suburban manhood. Nothing attracts a Chaddick crowd more quickly than the primordial struggle of man against nature, especially when man comes equipped with a twenty-four-inch lumberjack special.

I catch sight of Bill now halfway up a ladder that's leaning precariously against the maple. I stride determinedly over to him.

"What are you doing?" I ask.

"A branch fell down in the storm last week. Needed to clear it up. And I want to take down this other limb before another big wind does it for us."

I guess it's infinitely better that we're celebrating Bill's pruning a tree rather than tying the knot. On the other hand, I've started to think of this as *my* maple, not his.

"Bill, get down from there," I call out to him.

"Don't worry, honey. I'm okay," he says.

"Don't call me honey," I yell back, irritated. "And I'm worried about the tree, not you."

Our neighbors are watching intently now as Bill yanks the cord and the chain saw whirs menacingly to life. I hear the collective intake of breath from the throng. It's not that anybody really *wants* Bill to cut off his thumb, but the scene provides the same macabre fascination as an out-of-control truck on I-95. Who knows what will happen?

Bill goes to work, anchoring his boot against a rung of the ladder to brace himself. With two hands, he steadies the vibrating tool in front of him and begins his version of the Chaddick chain saw massacre. Smoke billows from the machine and chips start flying everywhere. A moment later, the bough starts to break.

"Timmm-ber!" call out Amanda's twins gleefully.

People scurry away as the branch crashes to the ground with a resounding thud. Then there's a flutter of applause for Bill, the champ.

Disgusted, I turn to go into the house. My feet are freezing. I left Virgin Gorda wearing sandals, and even though I've already added a pair of wool socks, my body's thermostat is not set to be back.

And I'm not set to be back, either. I go into the house, thinking about the warm good-bye I had with Emily at Kennedy Airport when I put her into the van heading back to Yale. I can't even think about my good-bye with Kevin. He kissed me before I boarded the plane, murmured for me to come back soon, very soon, and tucked a wildflower behind my ear. Unwittingly, I touch it now as I glance at myself in the hallway mirror. I'm tanned, my hair has light streaks from the sun—and my flower has wilted. I bring it into the kitchen and put it into a little china teacup that I fill with water.

I place the cup tenderly on the windowsill. It's always hard getting re-acclimated after I've been away, but today seems worse than usual— and not just because I'm already missing Kevin. I slowly look around the room. I know I left the kitchen spotless, but now I see dirty glasses on the counter and crumbs dotting the floor. A plate with a half-eaten bagel has been abandoned in the sink, and instead of being scattered by the slot at the front door, the mail is piled high on the table. I go upstairs, dragging my suitcase behind me. The duvet is spread over the bed in my room, but it looks clumpy and the pillows are in the wrong order. That can mean only one thing: Bill has made the bed. Why is it that no man knows the difference between a European square, a sham, and a basic king-size down pillow? Do you really need to watch designer Nate Berkus on *Oprah* to figure out that the small one with the decorative design goes in front?

I straighten the linens, almost more annoyed that Bill mis-made the bed than that he's been sleeping in it. Almost. Because what the heck has he been doing here anyway?

I take off my sandals and dig through my closet for a pair of shearling-lined boots. I pull them on, but they squish my toes and hurt my ankles. Ouch. After all that island freedom, my feet aren't ready to be bound again. I somehow manage to zip the boots and march back outside, where woodsman Bill is still accepting kudos and letting neighbors cart away the newly cut logs for their fireplaces. I hope they're not expecting to cut down on fuel costs this winter, because that firewood needs to dry out for about five years before it will burn.

Bill clumps over to me in his muddy boots. "So, how you doing, stranger? Haven't seen you in ages," he says.

"She hasn't been around in ages," pipes up Amanda.

"I've been taking in your newspapers," says Rosalie. "It's a pretty big stack. If you don't want them, I could use them for a crafts project."

"And we just got a puppy," says Amanda, vying for my now-valuable cache of old issues of *The New York Times*. I think I'll give them to Rosalie. I like the idea of preserving Maureen Dowd's columns as papier mâché picture frames.

Bill scoops up some kindling in a canvas carrier. "Have you been away ever since Thanksgiving? I know you weren't home last night, anyway."

"Not really your business," I say snippily. "And what are you doing at the house? Not enough trees to chop on Ninety-third Street?"

"I live here, too," he says.

"Not anymore."

One of Amanda's twins starts to cry. "Mommy, they're fighting. Make them stop fighting."

I snicker. This is what happens when you send your toddlers to a Montessori school. They expect everyone in the world to get along.

"Maybe we should continue this conversation inside," Bill says. "Light a fire and have a couple of drinks."

"I don't want to be inside with you," I say.

"Of course you do," prods Rosalie. "You two should make a romantic fire and patch things up. It would be so wonderful to have Bill back for Christmas. I was hoping we could all go caroling and we don't have enough tenors."

"I'm a baritone," says Bill, defending his testosterone levels. As if the tree-pruning weren't enough.

Amanda knows when it's time to leave. Turning to the twins, she says, "Come on kids, let's get some hot chocolate back at our house." And to entice Rosalie off the premises, she adds, "You come, too. I have some bottle caps at home I've been saving. You can make them into a belt."

When they all head off, I don't make any move to the front door, even though at this point I'm freezing.

"So why were you here last night? Was that Ashlee girl with you?" I ask, practically spitting the name.

"Of course not," he says piously. "I'd never do something like that. The marriage bed is sacred."

Glad to know where he draws the line. Desecrate the marriage, but not the bed.

"So where is she and why were you sleeping here?"

"Ashlee went off to a Mega-Vitamin and Mineral Conference in San Jose. She wanted me to join her, but if I'm going to do drugs, it's not going to be potassium."

He pauses, waiting for me to laugh—which I don't. So he moves on to the heart of the matter. "And frankly, Ashlee and I needed a little time apart. We're on a break."

I wonder which one of them has put on the brakes. Their little joyride plowed through our marriage, and if it's coming to a screeching halt, hallelujah. Maybe Ashlee got tired of a midlife crisis playboy or Bill was bored by his New Age plaything. New Age or old age, they were definitely the wrong match.

"And you want to stay here on your break?" I ask.

"Right," he says with a big smile.

"Wrong."

As usual, Bill only hears what he wants. He puts his arm around me. "Come on, Hallie. You must be cold. Let's go in. You could make me some of your famous lasagna."

I laugh ruefully to myself, remembering that the night Bill told me he was leaving, I offered that very same lasagna—as if some tomato sauce and mozzarella would save our marriage. Couldn't then and won't now.

I put my arm around him, and oozing false sympathy, I say, "Oh, darling, you can't stay here because you need to take some time and enjoy living on your own. Stock up on Oreos. Watch the Home Shopping Network. It worked for me when you left, and I emerged a better, smarter, tanner person."

I open the front door and step into the house, leaving him outside. "Go, be on your own, sweetheart. Get severely depressed. Think that your life is over. I'd hate for you to miss the experience."

If Bill has a response to my wise and caring advice, I don't hear it because I close the door firmly in his face. I'm going upstairs to rearrange the pillows.

Chapter FOURTEEN

NOW THAT I'M BACK IN NEW YORK, I take twenty-four hours getting re-acclimated before heading to my office. As I dodge across Madison Avenue to my first morning at work, a taxi almost runs me over.

"Watch it, lady," the cabbie screams. "Don't ya know how to cross a street in New Yawk?"

Apparently I've forgotten. I'll have to accept the blinking "Don't Walk" warnings until I get back my Manhattan edge. A couple of weeks on Virgin Gorda, and I don't even remember how to jaywalk.

Somehow, I make it alive to my law firm, and the moment I walk in, I'm glad to be back. In a funny way, my office feels more like home right now than the house does. Even as I moved up the ranks, I kept the same desk, and as I settle down into my familiar Aeron chair, it occurs to me that I've also kept the same pictures. Emily may think she's a full-grown woman now, but at least here, she'll always be a curly-haired four-year-old with a freckled nose.

A stack of memos spills out of my in-box and my assistant has dutifully left a log of phone messages that goes on for pages. A smart young associate named Chandler, who doesn't trust e-mail, has stuck four Post-its around my computer, each marked "Urgent." Today quite literally won't be a day at the beach, but surprisingly I feel energized.

Despite what the cabbie thinks, this is one place where I always know what I'm doing.

I throw myself into two pending lawsuits, and by noon I've impressively negotiated a settlement in one of them. Or at least I'm impressed. I smugly hang up the phone. The legal eagle is back on the case.

When Arthur summons me to his office, I stride down the hall, ready to report on my morning triumph and happy to see him again.

But he doesn't seem all that happy to see me. He barely looks up when I walk in, then ignoring me, he takes a phone call while I stand in the doorway, shifting my weight from foot to foot.

He hangs up and, busily jotting notes on a yellow legal pad, says, "Sit down."

So much for small talk. I perch on the edge of a small hard chair across from Arthur's mammoth desk. Every so often, I realize how brilliantly his space is designed for maximum power impact. If the Oval Office were this intimidating, the North Koreans would have caved long ago.

"Good to see you," I say cheerfully to Arthur. "How are you doing?"

"Not well," he says, putting down his pen and frowning in my direction. "I'll get straight to the point, Hallie. I've tried to be understanding, but you're pushing my good nature. I can't work with you if you're never here."

"*Never* here?" I ask incredulously. "It's just been a few weeks." And that week when Bill first left. And those weeks after when I was totally unfocused.

"You ran off at Thanksgiving and never came back—even though you had a court appearance scheduled in that slander suit."

Shit. I forgot all about that case.

"I'm lucky Chandler was here. You're lucky too. He took over the case and saved your ass."

"I'm so sorry, Arthur," I say contritely, the glow of my morning's success quickly fading. "You know that's not like me."

"I do. And that's why I'm giving you one more chance."

I stare at him incredulously.

"I like you personally, Hallie, but I can't run a firm this way. Our next big problem is Tyler."

"I've been working on it. You know I ran into him on Virgin Gorda."

"Yes, you told me. Very cute story, et cetera, et cetera, but it doesn't solve anything. Save it for your memoirs," he says brusquely.

I look at him, startled. If he keeps talking to me this way, he's not going to want to read those memoirs unless he's had a few shots of scotch first.

"I'm supposed to meet Mr. Tyler and take Melina Marks's deposition in a few days," I say calmly. "I'll do everything I can, but I can't guarantee a perfect outcome."

"Well, then, I can't guarantee you'll still have a job."

On Thursday, Mr. Tyler shows up at my office as promised, but marriage hasn't made him any more talkative. He asks if he can pay his way out of the lawsuit. He's still adamant that he's not in the wrong, but he's willing to offer the plaintiff, Beth, a chunk of change to go away.

Except Beth won't bite.

"She doesn't want money, she wants vindication," her lawyer tells me.

"A big check can be big vindication," I say, trying to negotiate a settlement and save my job at any cost.

"I wish I could, Hallie, but I know Beth will tell me no. A big fat no. So all I can tell you is no deal."

I hang up the phone, frustrated. Plaintiffs always say it's not about the money—and just my luck to hit the one who really means it.

Screw it all. If Arthur's not happy, I can walk out of here tomorrow and fly back to Kevin. Isn't that what I really want to do, anyway?

I get up and pace around my office. Yes, Kevin. I miss him desperately. I miss his body rubbing against mine and his crinkly-eyed smile. What I wouldn't give to be in his strong arms right this minute. But that's exactly the question, isn't it? What would I give up to be with Kevin?

When I was in Virgin Gorda and dreaming of staying forever, little details like my law practice didn't seem very important. I convinced myself that I could do my work over the Internet and fly to New York for meetings. But apparently Arthur doesn't see that as a possibility. If I move to Virgin Gorda, I'm going unemployed. Maybe I'll open my own little island practice. Should be plenty of work. Some local lawyer has to write those risk waiver forms that scuba-diving tourists sign, promising not to sue no matter how negligent the scuba company and how dead they end up.

I have too many decisions, but I'm going to be the one who makes them, not Arthur. I sit back down at my desk. If I quit my job to go to Virgin Gorda, I quit. But I'll be damned if I'm going to let myself get fired.

For the next several days, I work tirelessly, and when Adam and Emily call, all I can talk about is the Tyler case. Bellini thinks I need an evening away, and she urges me to join her at a play.

"Maybe. I haven't been to Broadway in ages," I say, trying not to think of the three dead ends I've hit on Tyler and how I need a new approach.

"This show's not exactly Broadway," Bellini admits. "More Off-Broadway. Off-off-Broadway. Off Manhattan, in fact."

"How far off?"

"Brooklyn. We'll take a subway."

At seven o'clock, we squash ourselves into a packed subway car, something I haven't done in years. The crowd seems better-behaved than I remember—fewer panhandlers and more slick-haired salesmen carrying briefcases. At the end of the day, they're both trying to get you to part with a buck, but at least the panhandlers have a talent: they play the harmonica.

In the crowd, I can't even reach a strap to hang on, and as the train sways, I almost fall over. A young man sporting dreadlocks and a baggy Sean John sweatshirt gets up and elbows the buddy next to him to do the same.

"Why don't you sit down, ma'am," he says considerately.

I look at him in surprise. When did New Yorkers become so polite?

And even more startling, when did I get so old that I'm offered a seat by someone who calls me "ma'am"?

"I'm fine," I say, deciding that I'd rather collapse on the dirty subway floor than admit I'm ancient enough to have earned someone's spot.

"No, really," he says. "I think it's terrible when young people don't give their seats to older women."

I point to another woman standing nearby, wearing a long skirt and a parka. "Well, then, let her sit. She's older than I am."

"No, I'm not," she shoots back, planting her Easy Stride crepe soles firmly in place.

"How about her?" I ask pointing to a woman with white hair and skin pruned from at least eighty summers without sunscreen.

"I'm good, I'm good," she says with a tap of her cane.

But not everybody feels they have to prove they're young. Some people just are. As we're haggling over who's the right vintage to sit, two Beaujolais Nouveaux pour themselves into the abandoned seats. The young men smile at the miniskirted teenagers, who cheerfully put down their bags and get comfortable.

Forty-five minutes later when we arrive at our stop, my pride is intact, but my back isn't. We rush down the narrow Brooklyn street, and I'm looking forward to sinking into a cushy velvet theater seat. But Bellini's neglected to mention that we're going avant-garde. Finally at the theater, I see the stage is an open bare black box and the audience is perched on backless benches.

"I didn't know we were coming to a Quaker prayer meeting," I say, trying to find a tenable position on the wooden slats. "How'd you pick this show?"

"Free tickets. My Starbucks friend gave them to me."

"You're dating the barista?" I ask, remembering the guy she picked up at lunch.

"Actually, he's an actor. And anyway, he's not the barista, he's the assistant manager."

"Excuse me. All the difference in the world."

"Probably a difference of about two bucks an hour," she admits.

"He's a sweetie. I stop in at lunchtime and he gives me samples, no charge."

"You should go by Costco at dinner. They give out free tastes of generic mac-and-cheese in little paper cups. And the nice ladies in hairnets who are serving it always let you take seconds."

"My Starbucks guy doesn't wear a hairnet, and in this show, I don't think he wears anything. He said there's a whole scene with full-frontal nudity."

"Convenient. You can check him out before you decide whether to get serious," I suggest.

"Don't be gross," she says with a giggle. "I think your time with that scuba diver has coarsened you."

"That scuba diver happens to be . . ."

"I'm not interested," she interrupts.

"I wasn't going to tell you about his full-frontal nudity," I say defensively. But to be fair, she's already had to hear ad nauseam how wonderful it felt being with Kevin and how great he was in bed.

"It's okay," says Bellini. "I don't mind talking about Kevin. And I hope it works out for you two even though he's G.U."

"Gee you?" I ask.

"G.U.," she repeats. "Geographically undesirable. I once had a man tell me we couldn't date because he lived in the Village and I was on the Upper East Side. Too many subway stops. And it's even harder for you and Kevin. You guys have to go through customs."

"This gives a whole new meaning to the question of how far a girl will go," I say, shifting my knees to make room for two black-clad theater lovers who slide onto our bench.

"As long as we're talking about men, there's Bill," says Bellini.

"Ouch," I say, as one of the new arrivals steps on my toe.

"Bill. Ouch. Natural reaction," Bellini says. "And try to remember it. Now that he's on a break from Ashlee, he's going to want to come back to you. An ex-wife is like a comfy old shoe. But, darling, old shoes get pushed to the back of the closet again. You deserve to be somebody's new Manolos."

"Thank you, I guess," I say, realizing that Bellini thinks she's just paid me the ultimate compliment. But my goal isn't to be anybody's costly accessory.

"I mean it," she warns. "You can't settle."

"Bellini, I'm not taking Bill back. Done is done. Now could we just watch the play? I think the curtain's about to rise."

"There's no curtain," says Bellini, and I realize she's right. A no-frills production—no chairs, no curtain, no clothes.

Mercifully, we don't have to talk anymore because the lights in the theater fade to black. When they come back up, there he is, Bellini's barista, with nothing on him except a spotlight. I thought that would be the finale. Aren't you supposed to save the best for last?

"Talk about generous," I whisper to Bellini, our eyes clearly focused on the same place.

"I'd say he's a Venti," says Bellini, using the Starbucks slang for extra large.

"Aren't you embarrassed that a man you're dating is naked?" I ask.

"I like it when the men I date get naked."

"In public?"

"If you've got it, flaunt it," says the black-clad theater-lover on my left, who's obviously overheard our conversation.

"You'd go out with him, wouldn't you?" Bellini asks, leaning over me to talk to the Venti admirer.

"I'd have to see him in a Pinter play before I decide," she says. "How is he with pauses?"

"He never pauses," says Bellini. And with a satisfied cat-that-ate-the-canary grin, she settles back to enjoy the rest of the show.

Even though it's after midnight when I get home, I call Kevin for our nightly good-night kiss. I'm always eager to hear his voice, but no matter how good the connection, phones can't substitute for wrapping our arms around each other. We struggle with awkward pauses that we can't fill with a hug.

"My bed feels awfully empty without you," Kevin says.

"I'm glad," I joke. But then I quickly add, "I think about you all the time."

"When are you coming back?" Kevin asks.

"Maybe a little later than I'd planned," I say hesitantly. "I have to settle this Tyler case."

"Since when's Tyler more important than me?" asks Kevin. "I've seen the guy. I'm sexier than he is in a wet suit."

"Much sexier," I say. I know Kevin's joking, but every man needs his manhood stroked. I decide not to mention I've spent the evening gawking at a naked man who must have once worked at McDonald's—he'd clearly been supersized.

"Too bad your work's so important that you can't·be with me for Christmas," Kevin says with a slight edge.

I'm briefly taken aback. "It's not just my work. My kids will be home for the school break." Kevin's silent for a moment, getting my message that maybe he's not my number one after all. But I need to let him know that he's still wanted.

"You could come up here," I suggest.

"I can't; it's our busy season," he says. I don't point out that I'm not the only one whose priorities get in the way of our being together.

"I'll miss you," I tell him.

"I'll miss you, too."

We hang up and I think how easy it is for misunderstandings to brew long distance. I close my eyes and try to picture what the holiday is like on Virgin Gorda. I imagine palm trees strung with lights, mangoes roasting on an open fire, and Santa arriving on a speedboat. Our own white Christmas at home is always more conventional, though this year, even I'll be bending tradition a bit.

Adam and Emily arrive home for winter break, but I can't possibly take any more time off from work to be with them during the day. They're busy seeing friends, so they don't mind. But I feel terrible. What nobody tells you is that as your kids get older, they need you less and you need them more.

Late one night, we bring down the carefully packed boxes of ornaments from the attic and merrily decorate the seven-foot fir tree that I had delivered from Fresh Direct. They'll deliver anything. On another night I duck into my study to go shopping for the bountiful presents I'll put under the tree, picked lovingly from Amazon.com, the working mother's real savior.

The kids each invite friends from college to join us—four exchange students who can't make it to their own families in Brazil, Italy, Spain, and Indonesia for the holidays. Christmas dinner turns into a giant smorgasbord, with each of the students contributing a dish. It may be the only time that the South American black bean and pork stew *feijoada* is on the same table with the Indonesian *lampung* banana chips. Bellini brings the accessories—bejeweled bangle bracelets from Bendel's that we use as napkin rings and a beautiful woven metallic-thread Missoni scarf that she puts down as a table runner. I'm reluctant to plop a sticky plate of yams on top of it, but Bellini assures me she knows the city's best dry cleaner.

Instead of Christmas songs, the stunning Brazilian student Evahi puts on Latin music, and I immediately remember Kevin teaching me to dance.

"Great beat," says Adam, grabbing Evahi and swaying her spiritedly around the dining room. She laughs, her full skirt swinging in a colorful blur and her thick hair falling across her face.

The two of them look flushed when they sit down again, and beautiful Evahi moves a little closer to Adam than before. Every woman says she wants a man with a sense of humor, but what she really wants is a man with a sense of rhythm. And where did Adam get his, anyway? Clearly not a gene he inherited from his parents. I've always had two left feet and Bill has three.

With the sexy music, the inventively designed table, and the U.N.-inspired cuisine, it's not a Norman Rockwell holiday. But happily, instead of a silent night, we're having a raucously good time. I've bought little presents for all our guests, and after dessert, the table is quickly covered with discarded ribbons and ripped-open wrapping paper.

"Ooh, this is perfect," says Evahi, flipping through the book I found of black-and-white movie stills from the thirties. "How'd you know I love old films?"

"Adam told me," I say.

She looks at him with a huge grin and then slips her arm into his. So Adam dances—and pays attention to what Evahi says. I don't know how he's doing in quantum physics, but as boyfriend material, Adam's scoring an A+.

And he just gets better.

"Evahi, such a pretty name. How'd you get it?" asks Bellini, who might be ready to trade in her current moniker for a trendier model.

"My parents named me after a South American goddess," she says.

"That's because you *are* a South American goddess," Adam says. The kid will graduate summa cum laude, with a degree in girls.

"Are you majoring in film studies?" Bellini asks, continuing her interest in the pretty girl she's decided is about to become my daughter-in-law.

"She's majoring in astrophysics so she can study black holes and jets from active galactic nuclei," Adam says proudly. "Minoring in film."

"So I can have something to talk to people about," Evahi says with a laugh.

"Good idea," says Bellini. Then to prove that everyone connects with movies, she adds, "Hallie has a client in the film business."

"Not exactly holiday conversation."

"You talk about it every other day," says Bellini.

"Who's the client?" asks Evahi.

"Alladin Films," I say, not eager to spoil my mood by telling the whole story.

"Wow," says Evahi. "Do you happen to know a publicist there named Melina Marks?"

I put down my cup of eggnog a little too abruptly, and it sloshes treacherously, but I manage to save it before it spills on the Missoni runner.

"How do you know her?" I ask, bracing the cup with two hands.

"She's the next guest speaker in my film class. It's really cool. We get to meet directors, casting agents, producers—all of these people who work in the industry."

"Should be interesting," I say. And possibly interesting for me as well. Could the college's inviting Melina to speak be evidence that she deserved her promotion? Or maybe it's just evidence that she slept with a dean at Dartmouth, too.

I notice that Emily and her friends have drifted into the living room, bored with the film talk. Maybe we should have stuck with astrophysics. I go in to join them, and a few minutes later, the time-honored sounds of caroling cuts through the sitar music, which one of the kids has now put on.

"It must be Rosalie and her crowd," says Emily, who knows the Chaddick Christmas drill. "We listen for a while and then Mom goes to the kitchen to get the plate of homemade oatmeal-raisin cookies."

"Pepperidge Farm homemade oatmeal-raisin cookies," corrects Adam.

"Don't destroy my illusions," groans Emily. "Next thing you know, you'll tell me there's no Santa Claus."

Adam opens the door to the carolers and then turns to Emily with a smile. "Nope. Santa Claus is right here," he says.

We all gather at the door, and sure enough, a Santa with a big white beard and a red velvet suit is robustly singing with five other neighbors. Santa is impeccably costumed, but he hasn't bothered to put a pillow in for his belly. I'm not surprised. Because I know immediately that this is a vain, unworthy, cheating Santa, not deserving of the red pom-pommed hat. And certainly not one who should be singing "Come All Ye Faithful."

"Bill, have a cookie," I say to my unfaithful husband when the song is over.

"Daddy, is that you?" Emily asks, delighted, rushing onto the snowy porch to throw her arms around her dad. "Come on in."

"If your mom doesn't mind."

Bill casts me a sidelong glance, but he knows he has me over a barrel. Even the little town of Bethlehem made room for visitors. How can I cast out my children's father on Christmas?

"Sure, you can all come in," I say, flinging open the door.

Rosalie, who's been leading the caroling, now leads the singers into the living room.

"Didn't I bring you the best Christmas present?" she asks, gesturing toward Bill, who's ladling himself a cup of hot spiced wine.

"Your song was very nice," I say, commenting on the only thing she's brought to the house that I'm sure I like.

Santa Bill, the singers, and the kids are all talking animatedly, and instead of joining them, I escape into the kitchen. Everyone else seems happy, but Bill's arrival has abruptly ended the party for me, so I start stacking dishes and filling the sink with warm, soapy water.

"Nice to be eating meat again," Bill says, coming up behind me, his fork poised over a plate of food. "You make all this? I love the *nasi goring*. And these lamb-skewer things. What do you call them? *Sate?* They're the best."

I step away from the sink, dry my hands on a towel, and slowly turn toward Bill.

"What are you doing here?" I ask, my voice harsher than I mean it to be.

"It's Christmas," he says jovially. "Ho, ho, ho, and all that."

I don't answer, because what am I supposed to say? "You have a 'ho. Go back to her?" No, I can't put this on Ashlee. It's Bill's fault.

"I guess you and your girlfriend are still on a 'break,'" I say, making quotation marks in the air with my fingers to emphasize the word.

Bill puts his plate on the counter. "Actually, we're not on a break. We're broken. It's over."

"Gee, too bad," I say, since that's all the sympathy I can muster.

"It is, but it's good, too," he says. "Because now you and I can get back together."

I'm dumbfounded. "You must be joking," I say. "It might be Christmas, but there's not that much good cheer in the world."

"Think about it. There's no reason not to. I'll take you out on New Year's. We'll have a good time, drink champagne. And you can see if you want to kiss me at midnight."

Chapter FIFTEEN

WHO NEEDS BILL? Once Christmas comes and goes, I have plenty of options for New Year's and his invitation isn't even in my top ten. My kids want me to join them at the revelries in Times Square. Amanda's throwing a party at her house with champagne for the adults and a clown for the children. She's calling it "Bubbles and Bozo." Bellini can get me into the Swarovski crystal black-tie bash at a downtown club featuring champagne and great gift bags: The invitation reads "Bubbles and Baubles." I've said no to all of them, and instead I'll take a bottle of Moet & Chandon into my Jacuzzi. I'll toast the New Year with Bubbles and Bubbles.

But by eleven P.M., I'm lonely. Even Dick Clark's not around this year to keep me company, and Ryan Seacrest is just a little too young for my taste. I pick up my cell phone to call Kevin, but then I snap it shut. We've already talked for an hour tonight and I probably can't reach him now anyway. He must be on the boat, taking a group of tourists on a midnight dive. At least that's where he told me he'd be, and why he wouldn't be able to call later.

I hang up the two coats Emily tried on, rejected, and tossed on the front-hall chair before going out tonight. How could she have said no to Grandma Rickie's hand-me-down mink jacket or my vintage Persian lamb? She settled on her own wispy pashmina shrug. Well, I guess she'll have cozy shoulders. And there'll be plenty of warm bodies packed together in Times Square.

I straighten out the front-hall closet and look up at the dusty chandelier. Rosalie's pointed out more than once that it could use a good cleaning. Maybe she's home from Amanda's party by now and would like to come over and help. I could use the company. I rifle through the pantry and find a half-full bottle of Windex. At least I have the right attitude; I don't see it as half-empty. But by the time I find a clean rag, I decide to abandon the project. Polishing the chandelier on New Year's Eve would be just too depressing. Besides, so much has changed this year something in my life should stay the same, even if it's just the dust.

Restless, I pad around the house in my chenille bathrobe and bare feet. It's been an interesting year. Certainly not the one I'd expected last January first when I thought about what might be in store. As Ravi might say, change happens. I can't even begin to imagine where I'll be twelve months from now.

Through the living room window, I notice headlights coming up our very quiet suburban street. Strange that someone's coming home now. Amanda's family-clown shindig ended at ten, and everybody else should just be getting ready for the ball to drop.

Even stranger, the headlights stop in front of my house.

Whoever's driving doesn't even turn off the engine. I see him dash to the front door, leave a package, and turn back to his car. When he's gone, I go to the foyer and open the door. A blast of freezing air whips my face.

A big, brightly wrapped box is sitting on the top step. I bring it inside and read the card, even though I already know it's from Bill.

> *You didn't want to have champagne with me tonight,*
> *but I hope we can break open one of these another time.*

I rip off the paper and unveil Bill's romantic gift. A six-pack of Dr Pepper. I shake my head. This is supposed to seduce me? What's the matter with that man? But then I pick up one of the bottles and laugh.

How Bill. He was probably very pleased with himself when he figured out how he could give me a sweetly clever New Year's present without springing for Dom Perignon because, in a funny way, this is just as good.

I probably married Bill in the first place because he knew how to make a perfect New Year's night with just the two of us. I've never liked big parties, which is why no combination of Bubbles, Bozo, and Baubles could get me out of my robe tonight. Bill understood, and for our first holiday together, he bought two pair of snowshoes and took me to Central Park. It was a perfectly clear, crisp evening, and the ground already had a thick white cover. We clomped across the Great Lawn—or, that night, the Great Snowfield—and as if on cue, soft, gentle flakes of snow began to fall. At the stroke of midnight, we toasted our future with two bottles of Dr Pepper, just like those he brought me tonight. "I don't need anything but you to feel intoxicated," he'd said, kissing me.

Remembering all that, I get misty-eyed, but then I sigh. Don't get too nostalgic, Hallie. Sure, two days later you were engaged. But twenty-odd years later, he walked out.

My phone rings, and as I walk over to pick it up, I know it's going to be Bill. And what the heck, if he wants to come over and have a Dr Pepper, I'll let him.

But instead it's Kevin. I can barely make out his voice over the staticky connection. It takes me a moment to shift gears. But then I'm thrilled to hear from him.

"Where are you?" I ask, not able to hear the first few things he's said.

It sounds like he replies "gggmmmegmmme . . ." then a long whine that ends in a "t," which, I'm guessing, means "I'm in the middle of the ocean, on the diving boat."

"I can hardly hear you," I say.

"I mmmmmmm . . ." he replies. Loosely translated as "I miss you my beautiful woman."

"I miss you, too. I love you."

"MM lllv ggmgmgemem," he says.

That one's even easier to interpret. "I've never loved anyone as much as I love you right this very minute." These one-sided conversations actually aren't so bad.

"We should talk later," I say, as the signal seems to be fading away.

But even if Caribbean wireless isn't cooperating, Kevin seems determined to tell me something. He keeps talking, and just before we lose the connection totally, I make out six real words: "New York . . . day after tomorrow . . . coming."

The kids stay out late partying, but they're still up before me on New Year's Day. How did I raise the only teenagers in America who don't sleep until noon? After I groggily join them for coffee and doughnuts, they head to the garage and load the old Volvo with ski equipment. Adam's going back to Dartmouth early to get in some skiing before classes start again and he's taking Emily with him. I'm glad my kids are buddies. On the other hand . . .

"Keep your football-player friends away from your sister," I warn Adam.

"Are you kidding, Mom? I'm trading Emily for free lift tickets."

Emily grins. "How many passes am I worth to you?"

"Depends how much you put out," he says.

I know they're joking, but I'm finding this conversation decidedly not funny. I reach into my wallet and pull out five twenty-dollar bills. "Here, Adam. Buy your own lift tickets."

"What about cash for me?" asks Emily. "Or am I supposed to find out my value on the free market?"

"Great values," I mumble as I shell out another hundred bucks for her. Whatever she has or hasn't learned about feminism, she must be doing okay in macroeconomics.

When the kids are gone, the minutes on the clock refuse to move forward. I speak to Kevin three times and confirm that I got it right. He's coming to visit. I can't believe how eager I am to see him. Tomorrow, and tomorrow, and tomorrow. Talk about creeping in a petty pace from day to day. How did Shakespeare know just how slowly the time goes when you're waiting for your Virgin Gorda lover to come to New York?

I change the sheets—even though I'm the only one who's slept on them—and put candles around the bedroom. In the interests of making Kevin feel at home, I move the goldfish bowl from the family room and put it on my dresser.

Knowing Kevin's grabbing a taxi to my office the moment he gets to New York, I take forever getting dressed the next morning. I unearth a lacy pink La Perla bra from the bottom of my lingerie drawer, but I can't find the matching undies. I hold two different panties in my hands. Which would a man prefer—the sensible, high-waisted Wacoals in almost the same color as the bra, or the blue that definitely doesn't match, but is, after all, a tiny bikini? I put away the Wacoals. Anybody who can't answer that question doesn't deserve a boyfriend.

I grab a blow-dryer and a tube of Frederic Fekkai Smooth Hair crème to tame my curls. Forty-five minutes and two aching arms later, my hair is miraculously straight. So what if it's sticking a little flat against my head? I'm smart enough not to dab concealer under my eyes because I don't care what anybody says, unless you're Bobbi Brown, it always makes your bags stand out more, not less. And Bobbi didn't offer to come over and help me this morning. I tuck myself into my favorite little black dress—or LBD as Bellini and *InStyle* call it—and change my earrings only twice because I'm running way late.

I remember how much I dislike commuting as I miss one train by ten seconds and wait impatiently for the next. Finally in the city, I try to slip quietly into my office, but as I rush down the hall with coffee cup in hand, Arthur is turning the corner. By the time I notice him, I've managed to dump half my decaf light with two Splendas onto his blue suit.

"I'm so sorry," I say, trying to mop it up with a paper napkin—and leaving behind a lapel full of lint.

"This is what happens when you're late," Arthur says curtly. He takes a monogrammed hankie out of his back pocket and, clearly annoyed, dabs at the mess.

"Can I take that to the cleaners for you?" I ask.

"I hope you have something better to do today," he says reproachfully.

I fumble for the keys to open my office, balancing my purse, my briefcase, a sheaf of paper that my assistant handed me, and the half-cup of coffee that's left. Arthur stays at my elbow, and then follows me in.

I drop everything unceremoniously on the desk.

"Did you have a nice New Year's?" I ask Arthur.

"No," he says gruffly.

Well, that's promising.

"I looked at your update memo on the Tyler case," he says. "A lot of fancy legalese, Hallie, but I don't see that you're getting anywhere."

"I'm still trying to negotiate a settlement."

"They said flat-out no. What do you think you're negotiating?"

"I have some good leads," I bluff.

"Tell me one."

"Melina Marks is speaking at Dartmouth," I blurt out, going for the first thing I think of, even if it's irrelevant.

Arthur glares at me. "What does that mean? More of your personal life interfering? Let me guess. You want a day off to go listen to her—and see your son while you're there."

I feel like I've been slapped, and it takes me a moment to regain my composure. "Arthur, I've worked hard to get where I am in this firm, and I won't have it undermined. You can question anything you like, except my professionalism."

"It's exactly your professionalism that I've been questioning."

And he may have a point. Because just then I hear my assistant giggling at her desk and a moment later there's a flurry at my door.

"Surprise, babe. I got here early," says Kevin.

I look up, stunned. Kevin, my wonderful Kevin. He's wearing a maroon Polarfleece jacket with khaki shorts, and he's holding a bouquet of flowers from the same deli where I got my coffee. He strides in past Arthur and gives me a big kiss.

Flustered, I pull back and catch Arthur's eye. If this is how I'm making my case for being a professional, it had better be as a professional playgirl.

"Kevin this is my boss, Arthur," I say. "Arthur, my friend Kevin."

"The infamous Arthur," says Kevin jocularly. "I hope you haven't been giving my Hallie too hard a time."

Arthur looks Kevin up and down, his eyes moving from his thick-soled Merrill boots to the bare legs to the gold Neptune medallion at his neck. In Virgin Gorda, I loved Kevin's laid-back sexy style, but right now I'm wishing he'd stopped at Brooks Brothers. Arthur is smart enough not to judge a book by its cover, but this is one dust jacket screaming for attention.

"What are you doing here?" Arthur asks. "This is a workplace, not the set of *Survivor*."

"Hey, chill out. Be cool," says Kevin.

Arthur crosses his arms in front of his chest. "I'm as cool as I need to be."

"Yeah, man, in fact, you're stone cold." He shakes his head. "I've been back in New York an hour, and I suddenly remember how harsh this city is. The weather. The people. Brrr."

"If you're cold, may I suggest long pants?" says Arthur.

Oh, wonderful. My boyfriend and my boss in a pissing match. No matter which of them wins, I come out the loser.

But Kevin isn't here to embarrass me, and seeing what's happening, he changes his tone.

"Listen, I'm sorry. I know Hallie's busy and you have a law firm to run."

Arthur just stares, so Kevin adds politely, "Really, sir, my apologies for bursting in."

Arthur seems mollified, and I'm so proud of Kevin that I give a big grin. Realizing he's on a roll, Kevin continues graciously, "I didn't mean to barge in, Arthur. I'll get out of your hair." It's just a figure of speech, but my boss is mostly bald and pretty sensitive about it. Trying to back-track, Kevin quickly amends, "I mean, I'll get out of Hallie's hair."

"You have no idea how much trouble hair is," I say, trying to help but only making matters worse. "The washing, the conditioning, the blow-drying. Then the mousse and the gel."

"I can never figure out the difference between those two," says Kevin.

"Mousse is a little lighter," I start to explain, but Arthur has already turned on his heel and is storming out of my office.

"Really, there's nothing good about hair," I call out after him. "Did I ever tell you about the time in 1996 that Emily had lice?"

There's silence in the office for a moment and Kevin and I look at each other, not sure how much damage has been done. But then, despite myself, I start to giggle.

"No lice in Virgin Gorda," Kevin says with a laugh. He comes over and embraces me. "Now how about a proper kiss hello."

Our lips meet eagerly, and I can tell that Kevin's idea of a proper kiss involves jumping out of our clothes and onto the couch. As much as I'd like to, I think we've drawn enough attention to ourselves today. I give Kevin an unsatisfying peck and he gets the message.

"I guess I can't tempt you to get out of here early?"

"Early, but not this early," I say.

"Lunch? My favorite Chinese place, Ping Tong Palace, is around the corner."

"Hasn't been there in about fifteen years," I say.

"You're probably the La Côte Basque type, anyway," he says.

"Not anymore. That closed too."

"Then where do people eat around here?"

"At their desks," I say.

"Okay, okay, I can take a hint," he says, grabbing his beat-up L.L. Bean backpack. "I can play tourist for a while. I'll come back at the end of the day. Five?"

"Six. Six-thirty."

"Fine." He kisses me on the top of my head. "By the way, you look good."

"I do?" I ask happily.

Kevin makes a face and reconsiders. "Not really. I mean, it's good to see you. You're beautiful. But what's with the straight hair and black dress? It's just not you."

"It's the New York me," I say.

* * *

By six-thirty, I'm feeling more guilty working while Kevin's here than I ever did being at the office when my kids were home. At least they had playdates. The best I can do is make sure Kevin has a good playdate with me tonight. Since he's come to New York, this is my chance to show him how fabulous the town really is. Bellini's gotten my name on the list for a hot opening-night party.

"Ready to go home?" Kevin asks when I meet him outside my office building. He's decided he doesn't want to come in—probably ever again.

"Better than that. I've planned a big time in the Big Apple." Excited about our evening together, I give him an enthusiastic kiss. "For starters, I got us into a major opening of Himalayan art."

Kevin looks at me dubiously. "Why would we want to do that?"

"It should be fun. One of those only-in-New York kind of nights."

"The only kind of night I want is in your bed."

"Later," I say, giving him a little kiss on the nose. "I mean, have you ever seen Himalayan art?"

"I've never even seen a Himalayan goat," he says. "But if you have your heart set on it, let's go. Just like in high school. I can tell you're trying to teach me things again."

We head downtown to the Rubin Museum of Art on Seventh Avenue and Seventeenth Street. The building used to be a Barney's store, and shoppers who worshipped at the shrine of Prada were horrified when low-rent retailer Loehmann's took over half the space. But the Rubins bought the other half of the store, and now there are more Prada shoes on display than ever before—on the feet of the patrons visiting the rarefied art museum.

A big crowd is gathered outside and Kevin and I join the line under a large orange banner heralding the exhibition: *Handprints: Twenty-First Century*.

"Be a lot easier to make our own handprints," Kevin says petulantly, pushing his palm against the museum's glass front.

We move slowly forward, Kevin continuing to make greasy prints all the way to the entrance. When we're finally in front of the broad-shouldered, earphone-wearing, clipboard-carrying bouncer, I confidently give my name. He checks the list and passes us on through.

"I guess we're the Chosen People," I say proudly, taking Kevin's hand. "And we didn't even have to give up pork."

He shakes his head. "Why do you New Yorkers only like places where you can't get in?"

"But they did let us in," I say.

"Great, and we probably could have gotten into Burger King, too."

I squeeze his arm. "Better food here," I promise, spotting tuxedoed waiters circulating with silver trays. One of them comes over to us immediately, probably because in this neighborhood—unlike my office's—the pairing of Polarfleece and shorts in wintertime make Kevin look like an MTV star.

"Hors d'oeuvre?" asks the waiter. "It's porcini mushroom with minced crabmeat and a dab of crème fraîche."

"My favorite," says Kevin, scooping up five of them, since he obviously hasn't had dinner.

We edge our way toward the special exhibit.

"Handprints. I'd recognize those anywhere," Kevin confirms staring at the long wall of framed pictures. He wiggles his own fingers. "This little piggy went to market, this little piggy stayed home, this little piggy had roast beef, this little piggy had—"

"—none," says a man next to us, completing the rhyme. He's dressed in all black with rimless glasses. He has a pointed goatee and an intense look in his eyes. I'm sure he's dripping with disdain for Kevin's childishness, but instead, he turns to him with a rapt smile.

"You've hit perfectly on what this exhibit is about," he says. "The hand as the fundamental underpinning of human myth and meaning. As the basis for both common folklore and high culture."

"Right," says Kevin. To continue proving his intellectual prowess, Kevin makes two fists and raises the thumb of each hand. "Where is thumbkin? Where is thumbkin?" he sings.

"Here I am! Here I am!" chimes in the man, animatedly waving his own thumbs at Kevin.

I'm suddenly afraid that this is a gay mating call, and Kevin doesn't know it.

But the man is simply thrilled to think he's found a fellow aficionado of the finger. "What you've so innocently pointed out is that the thumb is the engine of the hand, and far more important than pinky or pointer. But it has different significance in Mongolian culture and Tibetan. Come let me show you what I mean."

I'm intrigued now, so I start to trail after him. But Kevin isn't impressed. "Pretentious asshole," he whispers in my ear. "I'm going to get some more hors d'oeuvres."

In front of another wall of prints, the man starts making cultural comparisons and gesturing wildly—I guess proving that the hand is also the fundamental basis of language. From across the room, Kevin waves to us. With his hands. I'm starting to think this really is an important exhibit.

"Sweetheart, look at this," I say, when Kevin finally ambles over. "I've just been learning from my new friend Digger that the extended middle finger in that painting is a sign of royal lineage, denoting the high status not of the artist, but of the patron who commissioned the work."

Kevin gazes at the picture skeptically, then extends his own middle finger in the air. "Hasn't anybody ever told you two what this really means? I think it's a pretty universal symbol."

"Stop that," I say, trying to cover his hand before anybody else sees. Digger may be a little offbeat but he's also smart, and he's attracted a small crowd of art lovers who are milling around us, wanting to hear what he has to say about the importance of hands. I look down at my own. Maybe I should have gotten a manicure.

A photographer from the *New York Post* pushes through the throng.

"Digger? I need a shot of you for the society page. With your friend."

Digger puts his arm around me.

"The other friend," says the photographer, pointing to Kevin. "She's a nobody. I can't have a nobody in the picture"

"I'm a nobody, too," Kevin objects.

"Then you're a nobody with great style," says the *Post* man. "I love the look. So faux downscale."

"Genuinely downscale," Kevin says disdainfully. "And why would I want to be on the society page, anyway?"

The group around him titters, knowing that everybody wants to be on the society page. And despite his protests, they still think Kevin's somebody. In Manhattan, you have to be very rich or very famous to dress with such nonchalance.

Suddenly, the photographer turns away, obviously noticing a celebrity even more worthy of his attention. Or maybe somebody just dressed worse than Kevin.

"Sorry, pal, catch you later," he says, dashing after bigger prey.

Kevin looks at me and shakes his head. "I don't understand these people. Your people. Your New York people," he says. "Your boss thinks I'm dressed bad and that's bad. The *Post* thinks I'm dressed bad and that's good."

"Badly," I say.

"What?" he asks.

"You're dressed badly."

"You think so, too?"

"No, darling. You're gorgeous," I say, realizing I'd better not explain that I had automatically corrected his grammar. That would make me sound like the teenage girl who was always smarter than him.

"Let's see the rest of the exhibit," I suggest.

"I'd rather just eat some more of those crabmeat-mushroom things," he says, practically tackling a waiter walking by. But after he stuffs a few in his mouth, he doesn't mind when I take his hand to wander through the rest of the museum.

We slip away from the crowd and walk upstairs, past textiles embroidered with Mongolian goddesses and silver Shiva sculptures.

"Look, a female Buddha," I say, admiring a bronze statue. I read from the card next to it. "Gender identity is a powerful tool for exploration of the divine."

"My feelings exactly," says Kevin, putting his arms around my waist and nibbling my ear. "It would be divine to explore your gender. All I want is to make love to you."

I giggle. "Don't tell me you've seen enough Himalayan art already."

"I've seen enough of everything except you," he says.

He leads me toward a dark alcove, where it's just us and a painting from Bhutan of naked gods.

He slips his hand down the front of my dress and caresses my breast. "Ever have sex in a gallery of Himalayan art?" he asks, kissing me.

"Just once or twice," I tease.

"Then let's do it again." He starts to unzip the back of my dress, but I spin away.

"Not here," I say.

"Why not?" he asks. He lowers his lips, kissing my neck. "Trust me, all these gods and goddesses will give their blessing."

"But the people downstairs won't," I say, squirming away and tugging my dress closed. "Come on, honey. We can't do this in public."

"We never worried about that on the beach in Virgin Gorda," he says.

"Manhattan's a different island," I say.

The mood slightly altered, we drift back down the widely elegant, circular staircase, out of the museum, and into the frigid night. We take a cab to Grand Central, and while we're waiting for the train to Chaddick, I point out the twinkling constellations that cover the station's vaulted ceiling. Not quite the big open sky of a Caribbean island, but the New York version of Nature.

"The funny story is that the city spent a fortune renovating the ceiling, and after all that, whoever did the map drew it backwards. It's like you're looking down at the sky instead of up."

"Yeah, funny," says Kevin, who doesn't seem entertained. In fact, he doesn't seem like he wants to be here at all. His eyes are downcast and his shoulders slumped, and his arms are crossed in front of him.

I rub his arm. "Are you mad at me because I wouldn't make love in front of Buddha?"

"No, I'm just—" He clutches his stomach and lurches away from me, rushing down a staircase toward a sign that says RESTROOMS.

I scramble after him and wait outside for what seems like a very long time. I check my watch. We're about to miss the train to Chaddick, but I feel as helpless as I used to when Adam was in grade school and I had to let him go into a men's room by himself.

So I do what I did then, and standing at the doorway, shout into the vast tiled room.

"Kevin? Kevin? Are you okay? I'm right here. I'm waiting for you." My voice bounces off the walls, but nobody answers.

"Kevin? Kevin, do you need any help?"

A businessman in a blue pinstriped suit, carrying a briefcase, comes out of the men's room and gives me a smile.

"Is your little boy in there?" he asks. "I know how you feel. My wife always panics when our son uses a public bathroom by himself. Want me to check on him?"

"That's very nice of you," I say, but I hesitate, since trying to explain why my six-year-old is six feet tall might be a little tricky.

Just then, Kevin stumbles out of a stall and staggers toward us. He's pale, his eyes are bloodshot, his mouth is hanging open, and there's a little drool on his chin. The businessman grunts disapprovingly at what he assumes is my drunken companion and hurries off.

"My god, you're sick," I say to Kevin, taking his elbow and trying to steady him. "What happened? All you had tonight was seltzer."

"And crabmeat," he croaks. "I've been poisoned."

"Food poisoning," I say, trying to be consoling. "It's awful, but it goes away. Let's get you home."

We make our way up to the trains, and Kevin leans heavily into me. I hold his elbow more tightly and feel his body swaying out of my grasp. "We're almost there," I say encouragingly.

But maybe not encouragingly enough.

Thud.

Kevin collapses on the floor of Grand Central, his half-closed eyes staring upward at the constellation-filled ceiling. One way or another, he's seeing stars.

I kneel down next to him. "Are you okay?" I ask stupidly, because obviously he's not. He's breathing raggedly and out cold.

Two policemen rush over to us, their nightsticks swinging against their legs and their guns sticking noticeably from their holsters. They're each leading a sleek, bomb-sniffing dog.

"No grenades, just bad crabmeat," I explain as they circle around us.

The policemen are quickly satisfied that we're not an international threat, but the dogs aren't sure yet. One of them sniffs at Kevin's neck, and I want to explain that he usually smells a lot better than he does right now. But the dog and I obviously have different tastes in men because he gives Kevin a little lick.

"That's nice," says Kevin, just starting to come to. But in a moment he realizes he's on the floor with a dog and sits up, startled.

The policeman leans over. "Would you like us to call an ambulance, sir? Get you checked out at the hospital?"

"Yes," I say, worried about him.

"No," says Kevin.

"Come on, maybe a doctor can give you something," I say.

He shakes his head. "It's okay. A couple of hours of vomiting and I'll be fine."

If only. Kevin's right about the vomiting, but instead of a couple of hours, we're at day two and counting. Yesterday I played Clara Barton, bringing him ice chips, then ginger ale, and finally by dinnertime, clear chicken broth with saltines. He was cranky the whole time, but no match for Arthur, who practically fired me on the phone when I called in to say I was staying home with my sick Kevin.

I can't possibly miss more work, and I'm dressed for the office when Kevin finally wakes up, obviously feeling a little better.

"You're leaving?" he asks, looking at me in disbelief.

"Just for one shift," I say. "There's no relief nurse, but I think you'll be okay."

"Can we make love first?" he asks. "I've been here three days and we still haven't made love."

Instead of snapping, "That's because you were too busy throwing up," I go over and give him a long kiss.

"Stay in bed," I tell him. "I'll join you there as soon as I can."

"It won't be soon enough," he says, kissing me and stroking my cheek. But then he sits up. "Anyway, I'm finally hungry. Mind getting me some breakfast before you go?"

"Sure. What would you like?" I ask, looking anxiously at the clock and hoping he's hankering for a Pop Tart, not a pile of pancakes.

"I don't know. What do you think? Maybe a couple of hard-boiled eggs, or an omelette."

"Either," I say, trying to be agreeable.

"Hmm. I could eat oatmeal or eggs benedict. French toast with maple syrup. Or a bagel with cream cheese," he says, thoughtfully going through every breakfast food available anywhere. "I love Belgian waffles. Do you have a Belgian waffle maker?"

"Sure," I say slightly exasperated and finally losing patience. "I always keep a Belgian cook who specializes in waffles tucked away in the pantry. For God's sake, it's only breakfast. Just tell me what you want."

Kevin crosses his arms in front of his chest, insulted. "I don't mean to be a burden," he says. "But I did rearrange my entire schedule to come up here and see you, and you can't even rearrange a day to be with me."

"I'd have to rearrange a lot more than a day to be with you," I say, blurting out what's been in the back of my mind for weeks now.

"What's that supposed to mean?"

"If we're going to be together, I'd have to change my whole life. Move to Virgin Gorda and give up everything."

"So much to give up," he says snidely. "New York's just a fabulous place, isn't it? A thankless job. A bunch of pompous jerks at a party. People fawning over stupid art any three-year-old could make. Poison food. Yeah, so much to give up."

"You forgot a couple of things," I say, my voice trembling. "My kids. My friends. I thought that museum was interesting. At least it was different. And I happen to like my job and I want to keep it."

"Then that's it," says Kevin, angrily getting out of bed. "I don't want to keep you from anything. I'll just leave."

We stand across the room from each other, glaring, neither of us taking a step or giving an inch. Same old Kevin. Hurt him, and he's done. But this time I'm not letting go of him that easily.

I walk over and put my arms around him.

"Don't go. Not like this. I love you, Kevin. And if you love me at all, please be here when I get home."

He strokes my hair but doesn't answer. I feel my heart pounding. I couldn't bear to come back later and find Kevin gone.

"You can't go now; your plane ticket's not until tomorrow. It's got to be worth a night with me not to have to pay the penalty fare," I say, making a weak joke.

Kevin sighs. "I'll stay. Of course I'll stay. The real penalty would be leaving before we had one more night together."

Chapter SIXTEEN

INSTEAD OF OPENING *The New York Times* when I get on the train, I stare out the window, thinking about Kevin and what we'll say when we see each other later.

"Mind if I join you?" asks Steff, taking the seat next to me. Then, knowing commuter-train etiquette, she adds, "We don't have to talk. You can read the paper."

"I'm not reading, as you may have noticed." And it wouldn't matter if I were. A man can get away with parking himself next to a friend, burying his head in the headlines, and not exchanging a word beyond "Morning." No sense wasting a syllable on whether it's a "Good" morning or not. But working women sharing a seat are compelled by the laws of sisterhood to chat. On our way into the city to run corporations and make high-powered decisions, we spend thirty-five minutes swapping stories about the new nail salon in town, the cheating butcher (he's having an affair, and, worse, he overcharges for the ground round), and how the kindergarten art teacher gives too much homework.

But one look at Steff, and I realize she's worried about something other than ground round or her new self-ear-piercing business. Her eyes are puffy and she looks like she hasn't slept. She reaches into her bag and some silver Hershey's kisses tumble out. She unwraps three and heedlessly pops them into her mouth. Uh-oh. Eating chocolate in the morning can only mean one thing.

"Richard says he's leaving," Steff sobs. "It's not me. We've had a great run, but he's ready for his second act."

I look at her in disbelief. Bill's exact words. Did he feed Richard the lines or do men come preprogrammed with a midlife escape clause printed on their DNA? Maybe behind those *Wall Street Journal*s they do talk on the train, after all.

"Oh, Steff, I'm so sorry," I say, reaching for her hand. "I wish I could do something for you."

"You already have. I've been thinking about you every day. You give me hope," she says, fumbling for a tissue.

I straighten my shoulders, feeling a tinge of pride. When you come right down to it, I've handled this pretty well. People always say that divorce is like death and you go through the same five stages—denial, anger, bargaining, depression, and acceptance. I'm glad to be a role model for Steff on making your way through, but I should clue her in on the real phases: fuck him, fuck him, fuck him, fuck him, and what the hell I don't care anymore.

"There is hope. Life goes on. After you get over the initial shock, it's actually kind of exciting to go back into the world," I say in my best encouraging tone. "We can make a future for ourselves, whatever it is."

"Easy for you to say," says Steff. "Bill told Richard that he and Ashlee broke up."

"What does that have to do with me?" I ask.

"That's what's giving me hope," she says, apparently not as inspired by my fortitude as by the latest rumor. "With Ashlee out of the picture, you two could get back together."

"No, we couldn't," I say flatly. "I'm not that stupid. He ran around once; he'll do it again. If it's not Ashlee, it will be Candi or Randi or Mandi. With an 'i' instead of two 'es.' "

"At least you wouldn't be alone. You'd have a husband."

"Not the kind of husband I want," I say. "Besides, I have a boyfriend."

Steff drops her tissue in astonishment.

"A boyfriend?" she asks, taking in the new information. And then, giggling at the word, adds, "That sounds so sixth grade."

"Trust me, it's not," I say smugly.

"Do you sleep with him?" asks Steff, somewhere between shocked and interested.

"Of course," I say airily. Though between the distance and the dysentery, Kevin and I haven't made love in way too long. At least that's one thing I know I can fix tonight.

When I get home, Kevin's the one doing the fixing. A chicken is roasting in the oven, the table is set with candles—and despite the twenty-degree weather, Kevin greets me wearing a skimpy bathing suit.

"Nice look," I say, untying my scarf and playfully draping it around his neck.

"I would have come to the door naked, but this is my concession to the conservative suburbs."

"Speaking for myself and the entire block association, naked would have been good."

"Not a problem." He pulls off the bathing suit and flashes in front of the window.

"Kevin!" I shout, quickly closing the blinds. I told Steff I had a boyfriend, but she doesn't really need this much proof.

"I'm sorry about this morning," he says.

"Me, too. My fault."

And that's it. We both know there's more to say—a lot more—but there's something we have to do first.

"Hungry?" Kevin asks, kissing me.

"For you."

"That's what I was hoping you'd say."

We make love—hungrily—right there on the living room floor. Maybe I should have left the shades open, if not for Steff, at least for Darlie. She probably hasn't seen it done right in a long time.

Dinner isn't quite as formal as Kevin had planned, but it's a lot more romantic. We take the whole chicken (perfectly roasted, but a little too much garlic) up to bed on a tray, and tear it apart with our fingers. I hold out a piece for Kevin, and he takes it in his mouth, then licks my fingers, one by one. We kiss, greasily, and I giggle as our lips slide apart.

"Breast or thigh?" I ask, offering him another piece of chicken.

"Mmm, both," he says, kissing my breast and making his way slowly to my thigh.

We forget about dinner, and make love again. As the bed bounces, our leftovers topple off the tray and onto the sheets, but I'm too transported to care.

We're lying in each other's arms when the phone rings, and noticing it's Adam's number, I pick up, as I always do. "Hi, Adam. How are you sweetheart!" I say.

Adam launches into an enthusiastic description of his day skiing, and as I sit up to talk to him, I mouth "Sorry" to Kevin, who shrugs.

Mogul by mogul, Adam tells me about his run down one of the black-diamond slopes. While I'm busy talking, Kevin rolls over so his back's to me, and I reach across to rub his shoulders.

"Sounds like a great day," I tell Adam, willing for once to cut the conversation a little short. "Say 'Hi' to Emily for me. And when you head back to school tomorrow, drive carefully."

"Thanks, Mom. I'd never think to drive carefully if you didn't remind me."

"Don't worry. I'll always remind you," I laugh, knowing that no matter how old they get—and how self-aware I think I am—I'll continue to offer every cliché known to motherhood.

I hang up and kiss the back of Kevin's neck, but before he even has the chance to turn around, the phone rings again. Emily.

"Mom, you told Adam to say 'Hi' to me," she says in mock indignation. "You couldn't even say 'Hi' to me yourself? I didn't know you were so busy."

I look over at Kevin, thinking I'm not telling Emily just what a busy girl I've been.

Emily's as full of stories as Adam was, but she has a different slant on the slopes. Notably, a handsome ski instructor bought her hot chocolate and she thinks she's briefly fallen in love. First scuba, now skiing. I've got to keep my daughter away from sports. Who said you should get a girl involved with athletics so she doesn't spend all her time thinking about boys?

"My kids are such a kick," I say happily to Kevin when I finally slide back under the covers.

"You've got good kids," agrees Kevin, but instead of expressing any deeper interest in family life, he takes the remote and flips on the TV. We nestle against the pillows, and he scans the channels—hockey game, news, bad sit-com, rerun of *TV Guide's Twenty Greatest TV Moments* (the original was fifty, but who has time?), weather channel, bad sit-com. If we stop at QVC, maybe I'll buy some more jewelry.

I gently take the remote from him and click off the set.

"Is something wrong?" I ask.

"No," he says, unconvincingly.

"I'm sorry we got interrupted," I say, trying to snuggle closer. "But I'm always going to pick up the phone when my kids call."

"You should," he says.

"There's a 'but' in there."

He sighs and gets up from the bed, pacing in front of me. "I'm just starting to understand what you meant this morning about rearranging your life. It's not that easy, is it? I haven't had that much fun this trip, trying to fit myself into your world."

"That's just the food poisoning speaking," I say.

"No, it's reality."

"I'm sorry you didn't enjoy yourself," I say feeling defensive. "I did the best I could."

Kevin stops pacing for a moment and looks steadily at me. "I know that. We've both tried. I dropped everything to come up and see you during my busiest season."

"And now you're mad because I didn't drop everything to be with you every minute."

"I'm not mad." Kevin stands square-shouldered at the edge of the bed. "I care about you, Hallie, I really do. But your world is here, mine is in Virgin Gorda. I've always been honest that I could never move back. But now that I'm here, I can see what your life is really like. It would be lousy for you to have to sacrifice everything for me."

"Being with you could never be lousy," I say. I walk over and put my arms around him, laying my head against his bare chest. Then softly I add, "But it might be hard. Too hard."

We hold each other, not saying a word. Kevin strokes my hair and I feel my tears spilling against his chest.

"What do you think?" he asks.

I take a deep breath and bury my head deeper against him. "I think I can't move to Virgin Gorda," I say, my voice breaking, "even for you. I guess I've known that in my heart for a while now, but I couldn't face it."

"I've known it, too," he says. "I'm not good at commitments. You figured that out the first day we were together. But I thought, maybe this time. Go for it, go to New York. But what can I say? The place made me sick."

"Not fair. Our future being determined by a rotten crab cocktail."

"Who would have thought." He hugs me and we're quiet for a long time.

"Are you sorry I tracked you down? Should I have just left you alone after all these years?" I finally ask in a small voice.

"Never," he says ardently. "It's been wonderful. It was a vision to see you that first day on the island. High school Hallie come to my own paradise."

"For me now it's going to be paradise lost," I say.

At least he catches my literary allusion. "I think we were supposed to read that senior year," he says. "Dickens, wasn't it?"

"Milton, but close enough."

"Did they write at the same time?"

"No, a couple of centuries apart. But Dickens and Milton were both English."

"At least I got that right," he says.

"You got a lot of things right," I tell him. "In fact, I can't think of anything you do wrong except live in a place I can't."

We hold each other tightly, Kevin running his strong hand up and down my back.

"Do you think it would have worked if we'd stayed together after high school?" I ask finally.

"No, our worlds were too different even then." Kevin lifts up my chin and gives me a plaintive smile. "I guess that's one thing that hasn't changed."

"Can I still visit you in paradise?" I ask.

"Anytime," he promises.

"And can we fall in love with each other once every twenty years?"

"You bet," he says. He gives me a long, tender kiss. "Something to look forward to. And the best reason I can imagine to get older."

Kevin and I manage to do now what we couldn't after high school—stay friends. After he leaves, we speak almost every day, and by our second week apart, our conversations are easygoing, actually a lot more comfortable than they were in the will-we-or-won't-we phase of our relationship after I left Virgin Gorda. Sitting in my office late one night, I call him just to chat. He's cheerful and full of stories because the movie shoot with Angelina Jolie has started. Everything is going—in his words—swimmingly. I laugh and tease him about how many times he thinks he can use that joke.

I hang up, feeling comforted and knowing we made the right decision. In those years with Bill, I'd sometimes get exasperated with my marriage and imagine what my life would have been like if I'd stayed with one of my other boyfriends. Now I got a chance to go back and make my decisions again. And I still said "no" instead of "yes"—to Kevin, to Eric. To Ravi? Well, I didn't really get to say "no" to Ravi. I didn't get to say much of anything to him.

Thoughtfully, I open my desk drawer to retrieve the napkin I'd tucked away after my brave solo-night dinner at the Brasserie—where

I'd written down the names of the men I didn't marry. I take out the list and stare at it, looking at the fourth name, Dick Benedict. Ravi made me realize that you have to live in the present, but that doesn't change the endless regret I'll always feel about name number four. I fold the napkin up again and hold it in my hand for a minute. No, not every choice you make in your life was the right one. I still have to confront that.

I go back to work and make myself focus on the papers in front of me. Frankly, there's nothing else to focus on right now. No husband, no boyfriend—no way I'm going to blow this job. Looking for clues in the Tyler case, I go over every deposition we've taken. I reread Melina Marks's but there's nothing. Just like Mr. Tyler, she stonewalled neatly, saying only that she deserved her promotion. Going to hear her speak at Dartmouth may be grasping at straws, but right now I'm following any lead. I send a late-night e-mail to Arthur explaining why I'll be out of the office tomorrow. All I can hope is that when I get back, nobody else will be sitting at my desk.

I leave at five A.M. the next morning to drive up to Dartmouth and, in honor of Kevin, I speed along the highway with my windows down and Bon Jovi blaring from the speakers. Icicles form on my eyelashes and I finally give in and turn on the heat. Easier to be a free spirit in the tropics.

When I get up to Dartmouth, I walk through the campus, envious of the kids who get to spend their days listening to great professors and pondering life's important issues. I yearn to be back at college. Going to classes and writing papers always sound so appealing when you don't have to do it anymore. But why do I think it's any better than going to meetings and filing briefs?

I get lost three times wandering around looking for the building, but helpful students cheerfully point me in the right direction. Finally, I see Adam and his friend Evahi outside the lecture hall waiting for me, and they both come over and kiss me on the cheek. Evahi on both cheeks. When I'd called Adam to tell him I'd be coming up today, I told him all about the case, Melinda's role, and the threat to my job. My loyal son promised that both he and Evahi would help.

"Thanks for letting me come to your class," I say.

"No problem, I think what you're doing is cool," says Evahi, who's dressed in jeans and a baggy sweater. She's not wearing any makeup, but with a nineteen-year-old's natural glow, she looks even prettier than she did at Christmas.

"Maybe we'll help you crack the case and we'll all end up on Court TV," says Adam.

"Or make a movie of it," says Evahi excitedly. "So many sexy actresses in movies about sex discrimination. Demi Moore in *Disclosure*. Meryl Streep in *Silkwood*. Charlize Theron in *North Country*."

"Melina Marks in *How Mom Lost Her Job*," adds Adam.

"Thanks, darling," I say, patting my son on his shoulder.

The classroom is crowded and while the kids take their seats, I'm happy to slip into a spot near the back, out of the guest speaker's line of sight. From my experience, I expect the professor will be white-haired, stoop-shouldered, and wearing a tattered tweed jacket with frayed elbow patches. But this one, who the kids call Joe, is in his early thirties and tall and handsome enough to be in movies instead of teaching about them. Another incentive to be back at college. He gives a gracious introduction to Melina, who smiles and thanks him for inviting her. Stepping to the podium in her navy pantsuit and flat shoes, Melina doesn't exactly look like the femme fatale of the case. She flips through some note cards, then launches into a smart, thoughtful lecture on the ins and outs of film marketing, explaining that publicists are more important than anyone knows in creating a star's image.

The students in the class are riveted, and even I'm learning a thing or two. Alas, not about the case. But now I know that Tom Cruise flipped out on Oprah's couch only after he ditched his longtime handler and hired his inexperienced sister—who found keeping him in line a mission impossible. And I learn that to get celebrities on the cover, women's magazines sometimes let the publicist pick the photos and the writer and control what gets asked. So much for the ethics taught at journalism school.

After about half an hour, Melina starts winding down from her pre-pared speech. "I'd be delighted to take questions," she says pleasantly.

A few hands shoot up enthusiastically and Melina points to a young woman sitting near Evahi.

"First of all, thank you for all this wonderful information. You're such an inspiration—a woman in a high position," says the student who's obviously about to shove her résumé into Melina's hands. "Can you tell us the best way to land a job?"

"Get A's in Dartmouth and then suck up to somebody in the film business," jokes Melina. The class laughs, and I look around to make sure there's no spy for the other side writing down that line to use it against Mr. Tyler in court. But no, I seem to be the only mole.

"Seriously, contacts are important," Melina continues, "but I've al-ways found it's really hard work that pays off."

Well, that's better. Now she's quotable for the defense.

Melina calls on another student.

"Is the film business really as viciously competitive as we've heard?"

"Yes, cutthroat," she says, taking a finger and drawing it dramati-cally across her neck. "I have so many scars that I have to wear turtle-necks." She tugs at the cowl on her sweater for proof while the kids laugh again.

"Hermes scarves would also work," suggests a hopeful girl in the second row, who's probably already bought her ticket to L.A. Maybe after class I'll tell her about Echo scarves—lovely and an eighth of the price.

"Other questions?" asks Melina.

More hands pop up, and the next three questions are all about get-ting jobs in film publicity. Melina is relaxed and easygoing with the kids, telling them everything they need to know short of her cell phone number and e-mail address.

"What's the one most important thing you can tell us about mov-ing up in the business?" asks a young man in the front row.

Melina pauses and adjusts an earring as she thinks about her an-swer.

"Keep your ego in check," she says finally. "If you're the idea person you have to try not to get upset if someone else takes the credit. What's important is that your boss knows what you've done, not that the whole world does."

I sit forward. That's interesting. I'm dying to ask a question myself. But I'm obviously better off as spectator than interrogator. Melina's a lot more unguarded with the class than she's ever been with me.

Evahi's madly waving her hand, and Melina looks encouragingly at her.

"Did that ever happen with you?" Evahi asks. "A time you didn't take credit?"

"Sure," says Melina.

Now she's really piqued my interest. Could that uncredited work be why Melina got the promotion over Beth? If so, Mr. Tyler knew about it and had some reason for keeping it a secret.

"Can you tell us about it?" Evahi persists.

Just what I wanted to ask. If Evahi doesn't become my daughter-in-law, I may just adopt her.

"I can give you a theoretical example," says Melina, trying to be helpful to her eager young audience. "Let's say you came up with an idea that brought a lot of attention to a big star, completely changed her image and her career. She's really grateful, but the head of the company takes the credit. He makes it very clear that he has to stay numero uno with the star. All ideas are his ideas. If you go around bragging that this genius plan was yours, he's going to get pissed off and fire you."

"Did you get anything at all for what you did?" asks the girl who recommended the Hermes scarf, not convinced that it's worth being a team player.

"A promotion," Melina says. But then realizing she's said too much, even to a group of college kids, she quickly amends. "I didn't say this was me. Just theoretical."

"But it is you, right?" asks Evahi eagerly.

Melina shakes her head no, and then says, "No, no. Not at all."

"Who was the star?" shoots Evahi, not letting up.

A shadow crosses Melina's face. "Look, forget about that example," she says nervously neatening her note cards and pulling at her turtleneck, as if the room has unexpectedly become too hot. She looks plead-ingly over to Professor Joe and cuts the session short. "I guess that's all I have to say. Thank you for the opportunity."

The students give Melina a generous round of applause and she smiles shakily. Class over, the would-be movie moguls gather around Melina. I lurk in the back of the room, trying to put the pieces of the puzzle together. And suddenly I think I get it. A few minutes later, as the crowd thins, Melina notices me. She looks briefly startled, but then she excuses herself from the remaining students and comes over to me.

"My son's girlfriend mentioned you were lecturing today," I say, be-fore she has a chance to ask what I'm doing here. "You were excellent."

"Thank you. I hope the students enjoyed it. But maybe I said too much."

"No, you said exactly what you should," I tell her.

She looks at me worriedly.

"Look, I finally understand what happened. Your husband, Charles Tyler, didn't promote you out of favoritism. You earned the position over Beth because of some idea that your boss, Alan Alladin, claimed was his."

"I didn't say that," says Melina.

"No, I'm saying it. And am I right?"

Melina hesitates a long time. And then in a voice so soft I can hardly hear her, she says, "Yes."

We look at each other and she gives a big sigh, as if relieved to fi-nally be free of her secret.

"Why haven't you or Charles told me about it?" I ask gently.

Melina sinks down into one of the old-fashioned chairs in the lec-ture hall and leans her elbows on the attached desk. "Look, Hallie, I begged Charles to tell you," she says. "But he knew if the story got out, Alan Alladin would fire both of us and blackball us in the whole com-munity. He's powerful, and nobody would hire us if Alan said not to. Charles wanted you to pull off some miracle and settle the case some other way."

"Oh, come on. You two have to be exaggerating. Mr. Alladin couldn't possibly demand you stay quiet about it in the middle of a lawsuit."

Melina shakes her head. "Yes, he can. The man's ego is limitless. company's logo is everywhere and all his shirts are monogrammed . He's thinking of suing Alcoholics Anonymous for using his ini- als."

"Well, right now, Beth Lewis is suing your husband."

"It's not really Beth's fault," says Melina. "All she knew was that Charles and I were close. We fell in love at work, and I guess everybody sensed it. But that had nothing to do with the promotion. Beth had no idea that I was pulling all the strings for Angelina Jolie."

"An-ge-li-na Jo-lie?" I ask drawing out the name.

"You might as well know everything," says Melina with another sigh. "Angelina's been Alan's client for years. Everyone thought she was a wild woman kissing her brother and wearing vials of blood around her neck, and I had the idea to turn her into Audrey Hepburn. That whole U.N. ambassador position she has? I thought of it; I arranged it. Then those trips to Africa about AIDS? Arranged those, too."

"But Alan was the front man?"

"Right. Now it's the only way anybody thinks of her. And the funny thing is that under all those tattoos, I think Angelina really is a great hu- manitarian."

"You've got to let me use this to settle the case," I entreat.

Melina shrugs. "Won't do any good. Alan will just say it's a lie and that he did all the arranging. Who could prove otherwise? Then it's my word against his. Charles will look even worse, and we'll both be out of work."

"Make that we'll all be out of work, including me. My job's on the line with this case, too."

"Sorry to hear it," says Melina. "But I've been around and around on this. I just don't see any way out."

"I might be able to come up with something," I say, thinking about Kevin. "I have a friend who knows Angelina. You might say she relies on him for every breath."

Chapter SEVENTEEN

THE OPENING DAY OF THE TRIAL, I take a car service with Arthur down to the courthouse at 60 Center Street in Foley Square. Ever since the building became the backdrop for *Law and Order*, I always feel like I'm going to a TV set rather than my job when I come down here. Today I'm definitely hoping for a good plot twist. But Arthur isn't in the mood for anything unscripted.

"I don't like surprises," Arthur grumbles to me. "We can't be going into a courtroom not knowing every single thing that's going to happen. That's rule number one of being a lawyer."

"Yes, be prepared. Also rule number one of being a Boy Scout." I don't stop to tell him that I've often wondered what rule number one is of being a Girl Scout. Sell cookies?

"Anyway, I'm prepared, Arthur," I continue. "But sometimes you just have to go with the flow."

"You did good work at Dartmouth, getting the information about Melina doing Alan Alladin's job. But as she told you, he's just going to deny it. We're going to end up with he says-she says."

"At least a different kind of he says-she says than you usually get in sexual harassment," I suggest. "Isn't that worth something? Keeps our jobs interesting."

Arthur just grunts and looks out the window. Despite my bravado, I'm hoping that after today, I'll still have a job to keep interesting. Kevin's promised to deliver our secret witness, but like Arthur, I don't really trust surprises. Sometimes they blow up in your face.

When court convenes, Judge Ruth Warren, an elegant, gray-haired woman, walks quickly to the bench in black pumps and her black robe. Unlike me, she doesn't have to worry about what to wear to work every morning. Since both sides have agreed to waive a jury, the judge makes a few comments, then calls for opening statements. Plaintiff Beth Lewis's lawyer goes first, explaining the grave injustice done to his client.

"Talented, hard-working, Beth Lewis deserved a promotion. But it was denied because her boss, Charles Tyler, unfairly gave that promotion to Melina Marks. And why?" He pauses to look at Beth, who is sitting demurely at the table next to him. "Because Mr. Tyler, the defendant, was having an affair with Ms. Marks, whom he later married." He pauses again and then takes off his glasses to face the judge. "Your honor, the law says the workplace must provide a level playing field. But how can the playing field be level when there's a bed in the middle of it?"

He sits down as we all mull the image of a king-size mattress at the fifty-yard line of Giants Stadium. At least it would make things more convenient for the football players and all their groupies.

But I shake off the thought and stand up to make my own opening comments. I carefully lay out our position, explaining that the defense will not be challenging the fact that Mr. Tyler and Ms. Marks have a connection outside of the workplace. (Come to think of it, they have a lovely two-bedroom apartment on Sutton Place. Irrelevant to the case, though it's an impressive victory in the New York real estate market.)

"The defense will show that Mr. Tyler gave the promotion to Ms. Marks based strictly on merit, and we will offer irrefutable testimony to that effect."

I see Beth's lawyer shuffling through the thick stack of papers in front of him, preparing to call his first witness. Mr. Tyler looks nervously at me, knowing that he's about to be sworn in. "We're going to be fine," I whisper to him, hoping that I sound more certain than I am.

Just then there's a flurry in the back of the courtroom, and a woman enters, immediately recognizable despite the dark sunglasses, voluminous brown coat, and Grace Kelly head scarf hiding her long thick hair. Eschewing courtroom protocol, she strides forcefully down the aisle, directly toward the bench.

"Judge, I just have a few minutes and I need to talk to you," says the mysterious interloper. A court officer steps forward to intercept her. He touches the Glock automatic in its holster but then, deciding she doesn't look all that threatening, puts a firm hand on her arm to make sure she doesn't get any closer to the judge.

"Who is this person?" asks Judge Warren, looking from Beth's attorney to me.

"It's Angelina Jolie," whispers the stenographer, looking up from her transcription machine, mouth agape.

"I'm touching Angelina Jolie?" asks the court officer. He immediately lets go of her arm, figuring that in a mano a mano with the star who played superhero Lara Croft, he's going to lose. Besides, he has more pressing issues. "Can I get your autograph for my son?"

"Officer!" calls out Judge Warren. "We need some order!"

Angelina walks over to the witness stand. "Could you just swear me in or something so I can testify?"

Beth's attorney jumps up to object. "This is completely out of order. She's not on my witness list. She can't appear."

"I have appeared," says Angelina, whisking off her coat and handing it to the officer. She folds her sunglasses and tucks them into the V of her already low-cut sweater, which pulls the material down so much farther that the astonished officer drops the coat on the floor. They both bend down at the same moment to pick it up and knock heads on the way.

"Wow," he says, rubbing his forehead as he stands up. "Now I can truthfully say I've banged Angelina Jolie."

The star gives a deep, throaty laugh, and everyone else in the courtroom joins in—except Judge Warren, who takes the opportunity to bang her gavel. "Ma'am, may I ask you to please take a seat?"

"I would, thanks, but I can't stay," Angelina says graciously, as if she's just been invited to tea. "Look, all I want to tell you is that this poor man, Charles Tyler, is innocent. You know me. I have a reputation for correcting injustices wherever I go. And that reputation is thanks to this wonderful woman right here, Melina Marks."

"Your honor, if this is a new defense witness, she needs to be properly deposed," says Beth's lawyer, hopping to his feet again, red-faced and flustered. "This is completely inappropriate."

"Yes, it is," agrees Judge Warren. "Completely inappropriate. But kind of interesting. And I've just figured out who you are, Ms. Jolie. I loved *Mr. & Mrs. Smith*. Please go on."

Angelina nods. "Thank you. I'm sorry I didn't know about this lawsuit earlier, but my cameraman, Kevin, just told me what was going on. So I did some investigating and I found out that he"—Angelina points to Alan Alladin, who is sitting in the audience—"is taking credit for everything that she"—now pointing to Melina—"did for me. Nobody else knows it, but Melina was the one responsible for changing my career."

Angelina gives a dramatic pause while we take in her information. Then the star continues. "And he"—her long, slim finger is now indicating Charles Tyler—"did exactly what was right in rewarding Melina with a promotion, and shouldn't be sued by her." Angelina swivels around to aim at Beth.

"I had no idea," says Beth.

"You were duped, too. We all were," says Angelina.

"Hold on a second. I'm the head of this company, and I say none of this is true," proclaims Alan Alladin, now standing tall—or as tall as a man about five foot five can stand—and waving his hand to reveal the AA monogram on his shirt cuff and his diamond AA cufflinks. This man has a serious identity issue.

"The head of the company, but not the brains," says Angelina. "I've spoken to all my friends at the U.N. Everyone says they worked with Melina, not you. She was there talking and convincing and making everything happen for me. You tricked me, Alan. I hate people who pretend to be something they're not."

Pretending to be something you're not is exactly what the whole acting profession is about, but I don't point that out since Angelina is my new hero. I may even watch the DVD of *Girl, Interrupted* and try to figure out why she won the Oscar.

By now Beth's lawyer is practically apoplectic, but there's not much he can do. Angelina looks at her watch.

"I have to go, but I hope that settles everything," says Angelina, taking her coat from the bailiff and finding an autographed picture to hand him.

"Are you absolutely sure that everything you're saying is right?" Beth asks as Angelina walks past her.

"Absolutely," she replies confidently.

"Well, then, it does settle it for me," Beth announces before her lawyer can stop her. "If Angelina's correct, I'd like to drop the case."

Thoroughly satisfied with her morning's performance, Angelina waves good-bye and strides to the exit. We look after her in silent astonishment, but then suddenly the courtroom erupts as Arthur congratulates me, Charles and Melina embrace, and Beth calls out, "I'm sorry." But one person isn't so thrilled with the outcome.

"You're FIRED!" Alan Alladin screams furiously in the direction of Melina and Charles. "In fact, you're both fired!"

Angelina pauses on her way out and flashes the same smile that must have won over Brad Pitt. "Oh, good!" she says. "That makes it easier. Because now I can leave the Alladin Agency and hire the both of you."

Arthur calls me into his conference room later that afternoon for an impromptu celebration in my honor. A few of the partners and associates, and all of the paralegals, are gathered to toast me with apple cider. But I've been around long enough to know that they didn't come for me, they've really come for the free cake. And what a cake it is—a colorful Elmo-shaped ice cream confection that says "Happy 3rd Birthday, Petey."

"I never dreamed you'd win that case today," says Arthur's assistant apologetically. "So I didn't order ahead of time. This is all Carvel had left."

"Why didn't poor Petey get his cake?" I ask her.

"He threw a tantrum and told his mother Elmo was passé. She had to spring for Shrek."

I take off the three candles that nobody bothered to light. Oh, well. "Happy Birthday, Petey" isn't such a bad message. The cake could have said "Bon Voyage," since I came darn close to this being my farewell party.

Arthur gives me an awkward hug and makes a brief speech about how wonderful it is to work with me. Apparently all is forgiven.

"Why don't you head home early tonight," Arthur says five minutes later, as everyone leaves the room to get back to work, plates of cake in hand. Parties in our law firm are more concept than occasion.

"I don't mind staying," I say.

"Go. You did a good job. Sorry I've given you such a hard time," Arthur says graciously.

I leave and catch the early train, but once I'm back in Chaddick, I don't know what to do with myself. The house is silent and feels emptier than ever. I change out of my clothes and slouch around in sweatpants, turning the TV on and off, then doing the same with the radio, the DVD player, my computer, and Adam's old video game player. It was never clear to me why they called it an Xbox when only people with Y chromosomes use it.

Given my amazing morning, I should feel triumphant, but instead I'm dragging. I've already spoken to Kevin today, but I call him again to marvel at what a miraculous feat he pulled off.

"You're right, I did," he says smugly. Then more modestly, he adds, "But you don't have to thank me. That's what friends are for, babe."

"At least friends who know Angelina Jolie," I laugh.

Of all the outcomes I considered when I first went down to see Kevin in Virgin Gorda, his helping me save my job and win a high-profile lawsuit weren't on the list. But as I've discovered, life takes unexpected turns.

When we hang up, I feel even lonelier. It would be nice to have someone to celebrate with tonight. I wander into the kitchen, open one of the Dr Peppers that Bill left on New Year's, and take a swig. Cheers.

I thoughtfully turn the bottle around and around in my hands. What would it be like to have Bill in the house again? I'm not sure I can imagine it. All the joyful memories of years past are confused in my head with the stunts he's been pulling lately. Bill used to be the first one I'd want to tell when something good or bad happened because I always knew he'd be on my side. But then he had something else on the side—Ashlee. And I wonder whether she was the first, or could possibly be the last.

My gut tells me that Bill's wanting to come back was just a passing fancy on his part. He and Ashlee broke up, so as Bellini warned, he thought about slipping back into his comfort zone of familiar chain saw, familiar garage, familiar backyard, and familiar wife. What was it she said about my being like an old shoe?

Still, old shoe or not, I could do with some familiarity now, too. I quickly dial Bill's cell phone before I can think about it too much. When he answers, I tell him about my big win today, and sure enough, he guffaws and gives a big cheer of approval.

"Wish I could have been there to see that," he says.

"It was pretty neat," I admit. Then I pause for a moment. "If you're not doing anything tomorrow, I'm going shopping for Emily's birthday gifts. Want to come?"

"Sure," he says. "Why not? I'm not very good at picking presents on my own."

By the next morning, I'm annoyed at myself for making the plan. What was I thinking? I keep busy with errands—dry cleaners, CVS, and the fruit store. Then I stop at the fancy French bakery in town. As I drive down to the South Street Seaport to see Bill, I munch on a chocolate cupcake for courage. I used to complain about the raisins strewn across the backseat of the car when the kids were little. Now that they're gone, how can I explain all the crumbs?

"You have frosting on your lip," Bill says when I meet him outside the Abercrombie & Fitch store. He wipes it off and kisses me on the cheek, eyeing the bakery bag I'm carrying. "Is that for me?"

"As a matter of fact, it is," I say, handing him the jumbo black-and-white cookie I'd bought, knowing it's his favorite. After I stood in line for ten minutes at Le Pain au Francais (or as we call it, the French Pain), I was embarrassed to buy one lonely cupcake. But now I'm even more embarrassed to be bringing something for Bill.

"This means a lot to me, Hallie," Bill says looking at the cookie as if it's the Nobel Peace Prize.

"Don't read too much into some flour and sugar," I say.

"I won't. But it's good." He takes a bite of the topping. "And having you here is the real icing on the cake."

I smile despite myself. "It's okay. You don't have to be charming."

"It comes naturally."

We push into the store and are immediately greeted by a blast of loud music and a male model wearing low-slung jeans and a big grin. His bare chest is bronzed and buff and his perfect pecs glisten.

"Welcome to Abercrombie!" he says. "What can I show you?"

"A shirt," I say, half-joking. I look around and there are stacks of them everywhere, but apparently none were good enough for this guy. How smart is it for a retailer selling tops to send the message that you're sexier without one?

Bill and I head onto the crowded main floor and immediately raise the average customer age by about ten years. Or maybe twenty. Throngs of teenagers storm past us, searching for the perfect pair of jeans with an intensity they should be saving for applying to college. But the qualifying exam here is much harder.

"What's the difference between stonewashed, whiskered, and antique finish?" Bill asks, looking at the tags.

"The bigger question is where you want the rips," I say, pointing to a display. "A hole at the knee? A rip at the thigh? Or some shredding at the butt?"

"All of the above," he says. "Nothing's too good for Emily. In fact, let's forget the jeans and just buy the holes."

"Genius. It worked for Dunkin' Donuts," I tell him.

Bill laughs. "Too complicated to buy Emily jeans, right?"

"Right," I say. "How about a sweater? That's safe."

"What?" he asks, trying to hear me over the music, which seems to have gotten louder now that 50 Cent is playing.

"A sweater," I say, practically screaming as I compete with the beat of the heavy bass. It occurs to me that neither Abercrombie nor Fitch really wants me shopping in their store. If they did, they'd be piping in Carly Simon, about thirty decibels lower.

But since we've come all the way down here, I grab a hot-pink argyle sweater and a corduroy blazer, both of which Bill immediately approves. Of course, I could get him to approve anything right now. For anybody over twenty-five, shopping at this store is practically torture. Now that the government has closed down Guantánamo, Homeland Security might want to conduct their interrogations at Abercrombie. After an hour facing a wall of cargo pants available in seven different shades of khaki, any terrorist would break down and confess.

After we've paid, Bill picks up a navy blue T-shirt with a moose insignia—the last remnants of the days when Abercrombie was a hunting store. Not that I think an alligator is more elegant, but why do teens suddenly want to run around with antlers on their chests? Give me the Ralph Lauren polo player any day.

"Do you really want that shirt?" I ask Bill.

"I really do," he says, going back to the register.

But when we get to the front of the store, he hands the package to the bare-chested male model.

"It's January. Put something on. You could catch a cold," Bill tells him.

The model looks stunned and I burst out laughing. Bill takes my hand and pulls me out of the store.

"A cold's the least of what he could catch," I say.

Since Abercrombie was my idea, Bill gets the next choice. He walks by J. Crew, Guess, and Coach and leads me over the cobblestone street toward Brookstone, the fancy gadget store selling everything from rotating shower heads to radar detectors. Bill is in male shopping heaven, immediately captivated by four different versions of a digital travel clock.

"Look at this one. You can get the time in seven zones, the local humidity, and the barometric pressure."

I pick up the square black object with its blinking electronic dial. "Ah, yes, the perfect choice for a young woman," I tell him.

He puts it back down. "That's a no, huh?"

"Huh," I confirm.

"So I don't always know what women want," Bill says with a shrug. "What man does?"

I sit down on one of the black leather chairs on the selling floor and glance at the price tag: four thousand bucks. For that much money, this chair better sing and dance. I play around with some buttons on the side, and suddenly the chair is murmuring sweet nothings and gently caressing my hips.

"What a woman wants is a man as good as this chair," I tell Bill as I lean my head back into the headrest with its hidden speakers and feel the lumbar support getting toasty warm, its vibrations soothingly massaging my back.

"Is that what your boyfriend does?" Bill asks.

"What? I don't have a boyfriend. Where'd you hear that?"

"I ran into your friend Steff's husband in the city. Richard and Steff aren't talking but at least they're gossiping. He told me that you told Steff about some young stud you've been shacking up with."

"I didn't say anything like that," I protest, impressed at how my one little mention snowballed. If I let the rumor mill keep grinding, maybe by tomorrow everyone will know that I'm marrying Jake Gyllenhaal, if only they could pronounce his name.

"So what's the real story?" asks Bill.

I squirm in the chair. A little hard to have a serious conversation with your ex-husband about your ex-boyfriend when you're nestled into a chair that's fighting for your attention.

"I visited an old boyfriend and then he visited me, but now we're just friends."

"You slept with him?" asks Bill, sounding a little like Steff.

"Why do you want to know?"

"I'm trying to figure out if this makes us even."

Annoyed, I turn the massage dial to "high" and the chair gets as agitated as I am. It's worth every penny to find an inanimate object that can express your innermost feelings.

"We're not even," I say. "You're the one who walked out, ran off with some girl, behaved like a jerk."

"I suppose that's one way to look at it," Bill says cavalierly.

"That's the only way to look at it. We'll never be even."

Bill gets up and wanders over to the "Auto Care" section. I watch him from across the store, not sure what I'm feeling. If I could give second chances to all my former boyfriends, doesn't my almost-former husband deserve one, too?

"Come here," he calls to me, motioning me to join him. "I don't think you should be driving around alone without a Talking Tire Gauge. I'll buy it for you."

I look at the tool. A typically sweet Bill present—and only fifteen bucks. High-end for him.

"It displays and speaks the tire pressure up to 150 pounds per square inch," he says. "Underinflation is a tire's number-one enemy."

"Then we have to fight it," I laugh. For a moment, I let myself feel close to Bill, and my spirits begin rising.

But not too high. Bill's cell phone rings and he glances at the number and grins. Flipping open the phone, he doesn't even turn his back to me as he gushes into the receiver.

"Hi, gorgeous. Great night, wasn't it?" he says lustily, obviously to some woman. He pauses as she says something, then replies, "Of course you're not interrupting anything, doll face. I'm just here all by myself. Nobody I'd rather talk to than you." He winks at me then struts away to continue his conversation.

I stare after him. How could I have allowed myself even forty-five seconds of feeling good about my deceiving ex-husband? I was right when I told Steff I could never trust him. Bill's a jackass, but it's really myself I'm annoyed with. By the time he comes back, I'm fuming.

"Who was that?" I ask.

"Nobody special. Just some woman I'm dating," he says dismissively.

"Bill, let me ask you something. What was that whole little game of yours on New Year's Eve? Asking me to go out on a date, bringing me Dr Pepper. The whole bullshit about your wanting to move back."

"It was a definite possibility, but you didn't seem too interested."

"I've got good judgment, don't I?"

"I don't understand it, Hallie. We were married for years. I like you a lot. Why do you get so threatened just because I'm going out with other women?"

Maybe if I weren't so angry, I could laugh at what a self-serving moron he is. But at the moment, all I can think to do is toss down the present he wanted to buy and head out of the store. I don't need his stupid tire gauge. My number-one enemy isn't underinflation—it's overexpectations.

The next afternoon, it's my turn to entertain the Chaddick pack and I'm glad for the diversion. They start to arrive promptly at four, and Bellini, more used to being fashionably late in Manhattan than anally on time in the suburbs, strolls in twenty minutes later.

"This is such a great idea," says Amanda. "A Sunday afternoon get-together. So decadent."

Bellini looks around, trying to figure out what could be decadent in a room of six properly dressed women. If she's expecting a male stripper, I better warn her that the most shocking thing she'll see today is a burnt quiche.

"I never leave the twins on a Sunday. It's always family day," says Amanda, explaining why this gathering seems so illicit. "But I'm glad to get a break from the noise."

"And I'm glad to get a break from the quiet," the recently separated Steff says mournfully.

"Poor you," says Rosalie sympathetically. "I can't believe Richard left."

"Or that Bill left," adds Amanda.

"Every time we get together there's one less husband to worry about," says Darlie cheerfully. "It's like an Agatha Christie novel—*And Then There Were None*."

Rosalie looks at me hopefully. "Any chance . . . ?"

"No," I say resolutely. "You can try and try to hold on to old things but at some point you have to clean the closets."

I stop there, not wanting to get into a lengthy explanation of what happened yesterday—how I wanted to see Bill, knew it was a bad idea, thought I owed it to both of us to try, and then discovered all over again why it wouldn't work. I can't let Bill trample my heart again. The world doesn't have an unlimited supply of double-stuff Oreos.

"Clean the closets," I say, getting myself back on track. "Get rid of what doesn't work anymore and try not to regret it."

"You always regret it a little," says Bellini, jumping in to help me out. "But whether it's a polyester wrap dress or a cheating man, you have to move on. And that's what we're doing today, right? At least with the wrap dresses."

"And I'm so excited!" says Rosalie clapping her hands, completely missing any of the poignant overtones of the conversation. "Wasn't it clever of Hallie to invite us?"

We all troop into the dining room, where the women had deposited their shopping bags on the way in. I'd invited them each to bring over at least one item of clothing they'd bought and never worn.

"Here are the rules," I say. "Everybody has that Big Mistake hanging in her closet with the price tag still attached. With luck, somebody else here will think it's a Big Find. If not, we send it off to charity, and you never have to think about it again."

"I love this idea of Swap & Talk," says Amanda.

Bellini gives a little laugh. "When I told Hallie about this I said it was called a Switch & Bitch."

"This is the suburbs," I chide her. "We don't bitch."

"I bitch, and under the right circumstances, I might be available to switch," says Darlie provocatively.

"That's a different kind of party, dear," says Bellini, patting Darlie's shoulder. "And it went out of style in the seventies."

Jennifer titters. "Well, speaking of going out of style, let me show you what I found."

She pulls out an orange velvet blazer with a sequined floppy flower sewn onto the lapel, and we're off. The Big Mistakes—most of the women have brought several—spill out of the bags. Bellini takes Jennifer's blazer, saying she could wear it to a club in the East Village. My boxy pleated suit finds no takers, even though it still has the tags on, because it makes everybody's hips look big. We vote to send it to Teri Hatcher along with a chocolate triple layer cake. One way or another, Teri'd look better with a few pounds on her.

The problem with the slinky cocktail dress Bellini's brought isn't that it makes her look too big. Rather, she bought the dress too small.

"I found it at Roberto Cavalli right after I'd been on a grapefruit and cucumber diet for two weeks," Bellini says, holding up the skinny mini. "Even then it barely fit, but I always figured it would someday. I've held on to it for two years for inspiration. But I had my real inspiration this morning when I realized screw this. Who needs to be that thin, anyway?"

We all laugh in agreement and decide to put it in the Teri Hatcher care package.

Amanda then shows us her big bargain, which was irresistible at the time. "It's Moschino, marked down to thirty dollars from six hundred," she says, displaying a white vinyl miniskirt with metal grommets at the hem. "But who'd ever wear something like this?"

"Heather Locklear. Anna Nicole Smith. A well-dressed hooker on Forty-second Street. The patrons at Lucky Changs," suggests Bellini.

"And me," says Darlie, snatching it from Amanda's hand and obviously thinking she's putting herself in good sartorial company. I don't tell her that Lucky Changs is a famous downtown transvestite club.

"How about you, Steff? What's your Big Mistake?" I ask.

"Buying this teddy and thinking Richard would care," she says tossing a beautiful creamy silk Natori onto the table. Her eyes glisten with tears and she stares at the lacy confection. "Nobody will ever get to see it now. One of you might as well take it."

"I will," says Darlie, grabbing again. She's like a vacuum cleaner, sucking up everything she can find.

"No, you won't," says Amanda snapping it out of her hand. A cat-fight over Natori? I start to step in and explain you can get them on sale at Bloomingdale's, but Amanda has a different agenda.

"You keep the teddy, Steff," Amanda says firmly, giving it back to her. "Somebody will get to see it. There'll be another guy. And then you'll thank me."

Steff runs her fingers over the soft material. "I can't imagine there'll ever be someone else. Would you believe I've only slept with one man other than Richard? Just one other man."

"Where is he now?" I ask.

"I have no idea," says Steff, "but I'll never forget him. Peter. Tall, broad-shouldered, and the sweetest person on earth. We'd stay up all night talking and we planned to have six children together."

"Thank God you didn't marry him," says Darlie. "Six children. Even if you stopped at five, think of the stretch marks."

"StriVectin for the stretch marks," advises Jennifer.

"I had a Peter, too," says Amanda dreamily. "Didn't we all?"

"It's a common name," says Rosalie, as usual missing the point.

Amanda laughs. "My Peter was named Jean-Paul. Very sexy, very French, very rich. I could be living in Paris right now. I mean, I'm happy right here in Chaddick, but think what my life could have been." She trails off, obviously lost in reveries of being Madame Jean-Paul, eating croissants and Valrhona chocolate, one of those French women who never gets fat.

"Even my mother had a Peter," says Bellini. "I was looking through some old photo albums in her house a couple of months ago and found a faded black-and-white picture of some handsome blond guy on a beach in a tight bathing suit with his arm around her. I asked my mom who the guy was and she stared at the picture and got really flushed. 'That's the man I dated before your father. The man I didn't marry.'"

"How old's your mother?" I ask curiously.

"Sixty-five. Can you imagine? She knew this man more than forty years ago and she's been happily married ever since. I asked her why she still keeps the picture and she said, 'I like to think about him some-times.'"

We're all quiet for a moment.

"It freaked me out a little," says Bellini. "What if my mother had married her light-haired hunk instead of my dad? The path not taken. I wouldn't even exist."

"Or else you'd be a blonde," suggests Darlie. "I mean, a *natural* blonde."

I laugh. "The thing about the path not taken is that you can sometimes stroll down it again. I did."

"Really?" asks Steff.

"Really," I say, and I begin slowly sharing the story of my post-Bill quest. Eric, Ravi, Kevin. The women look at me wide-eyed. Suddenly, I'm no longer Hallie the mother, Hallie the lawyer, Hallie the down-to-earth next-door neighbor. I'm Hallie the adventuress. From the stunned looks on their faces, I might as well be telling my friends that I went bungee jumping off the Empire State Building. And in a way, I did. I took a risk and bounced back.

"Wow, what fun that must have been," says Amanda, and from the glint in her eye, I have a feeling that she's going to be Googling the French phone directory.

"It was," I say happily.

"It would take me a lifetime to look up all the men I didn't marry," says Darlie.

"Are there men you didn't marry?" asks Steff sweetly, reflecting on Darlie's four trips down the aisle.

"Never mind that," says Amanda. She picks up a crocheted vest that Rosalie has contributed and plays with the fringe of pom-poms. "There's something appealing about looking at old things from a new perspective. I think it's lovely you reconnected with your past boyfriends."

"You know what's even lovelier?" I say thoughtfully. "I didn't just see the men again—I got to remember who I was all those years ago. I'd been attracted to so many different kinds of men: the sensitive guy, the go-getter, and the bad boy. I guess it was part of figuring out who I am and trying on different selves."

"Which self wore that Laura Ashley blouse?" asks Steff, making fun of the primly bow-tied flower-print shirt I brought to the swap.

"The one who wanted to get a job. But don't forget I also wore this tight, fire-engine red knit dress," I say, holding it up to my shoulders and wiggling.

"Three men," says Steff shaking her head, as if she can't imagine such a thing. She rubs her hand over the silk teddy that Amanda insisted she keep. "Anybody else on your list?"

I hesitate and bite a hangnail on my thumb. Anybody else?

"No," I say. "That's it."

After all the other women have left, Bellini and I get busy bagging the extra clothes for charity. Just before I tie the package shut, Bellini decides to toss in the orange blazer she'd claimed, convinced there's an eighteen-year-old somewhere who needs it more than she does.

When we're done, I make a fresh pot of tea and we flop on the sofa.

"So," says Bellini, taking a sip. "Now that it's just us, I can say it. You weren't quite honest when you said nobody else was on the list."

"What makes you say that?"

"I know you, darling. You give yourself away when you bite a hangnail."

"Safer than using a scissors, you know. Cutting your cuticles can lead to infection or weaken the nail bed."

"Thank you, Sally Hansen."

In case my beauty advice hasn't been enough to divert Bellini from asking about my list, I check the tea tray and notice that I've brought out lemon but not milk.

"Whoops, what kind of hostess am I? Let me get the creamer," I say, starting to head to the kitchen.

Bellini grabs my arm. "I don't like cream. I don't like milk. I don't even like cows. Sit down."

I sit. "Who doesn't like cows? The Hindus revere them. But I have some powdered soy, if you prefer."

"Yummy. But stop trying to change the subject."

I sigh. "Bellini, I tell you everything. But this one's just too painful."

"You have to face your pain to move on," says Bellini, sounding like she swallowed one too many self-help books.

"That's the old-school therapy. New school believes in denial."

"When did it change?" asks Bellini.

"Probably when health insurance stopped covering months of visits to your therapist."

"So how's denial working for you?" asks Bellini.

"Not that well," I say with a shrug.

"Who was it? Someone you really loved?" asks Bellini.

"Someone who mesmerized me." I stare off for a moment as the memory swirls back of my whirlwind three months with Dick. I was swept off my feet by his Southern gentility and sophisticated charm, not to mention his parents' extravagant Nashville mansion and swanky parties. Nothing felt more worldly than standing on their veranda, drinking mint juleps. He declared he wanted me to be his wife a week after we met.

"His name was Dick. I thought we were going to get married," I tell Bellini.

Bellini nods. "I know what you mean. I've had nine or ten men I thought I was going to marry."

"Yes, but for you, those were all first dates."

Bellini makes a face at me. "You've been so daring since Bill left. What could keep you from looking up this last guy?"

I look out the window at the cold gray day. "He's tied in with Amy."

"Your little sister who . . ."

"Right," I say.

"Maybe it would help if you saw him again."

"I just don't know. I'm not sure I can handle it. Sometimes when you fall in love you get hurt. But until the earth crumbles under your feet, you never really realize just how much hurt love can cause."

Chapter EIGHTEEN

THE NIGHTMARES START AGAIN. For years after we broke up, Dick would float in and out of my dreams, and I'd wake up screaming. Now that I've said his name out loud to Bellini, it's like I've raised the devil again. Night after night now, Dick haunts me, morphing from Don Juan to Satan, taking on lurid shapes, chasing me down alleys. One morning, I wake up disoriented, drenched in sweat. I stumble over to my bureau and take out the article I'd clipped from *Time* magazine mentioning Dick, who's running in a special congressional race in Tennessee.

Running for office? He should be ashamed to show his face in public, never mind plastering that face on campaign buttons. I study again the few sentences about the race. It's a hotly contested seat and Dick Benedict is catching up to his opponent. If there were any justice in the world, instead of gaining ground, Dick would be under the ground. I can understand why nobody calls him Richard. His longtime nickname has always been more fitting: Tricky Dick, Dirty Dick, Dirty Trick Dick. I should write his election slogans and let the voters know who he really is.

I make arrangements to fly down to Tennessee. I'm practically on automatic when I take the Delta flight, go to the Hertz counter, and drive to a vaguely familiar part of town. A few minutes later, I'm standing in a small office surrounded by four-foot-high posters of the man I've tried to erase from every corner of my mind. Why did I venture down here? My hands feel clammy and my heart is pounding.

An enthusiastic young woman manning the front desk at Dick Benedict's campaign headquarters jumps up when she sees me. "Hi, are you here to volunteer?" she asks excitedly.

"Not exactly," I say, wiping my sweaty palms on the edge of my cotton sweater. "I've come down from New York to see Mr. Benedict."

"New York money!" says the woman. "We've been trying to get donors from out of state. Do you know Donald Trump?"

"Yes," I say confidently, remembering that my friend Amanda's mother-in-law's cousin lives in one of his buildings. Less than six degrees of separation counts as a personal friend and I got there in five.

"Will you call Mr. Trump for us?"

"Only if you buzz Mr. Benedict immediately and tell him Hallie Lawrence is here."

The woman turns her back as she makes a call, but I clearly hear her saying, "Okay, I'll tell her."

When she faces me again, her smile is a little less welcoming. "Mr. Benedict is tied up. He apologizes and suggests you leave a phone number."

"I'll just wait," I say.

"He'll be a long while."

"I have time."

"A very long time. Maybe even tomorrow."

"Tomorrow's good," I say, taking a bottle of Poland Spring water from my bag to prove that I could survive here for as long as necessary. I snag a chocolate cookie from a plate on the table set out for volunteers and settle down into a folding chair.

"You really have to leave, please," says the young woman, nervously circling over to me.

"Let me guess," I say, "Icky Dicky Benedict told you he doesn't want to see me."

"He said to get rid of you, whatever it takes," she whispers.

"Well, try this," I say. "If he doesn't see me, every newspaper in Tennessee is going to know about a story that he buried twenty years ago."

She seems uncertain what to do.

"Go tell him that," I say. "Use those exact words: A story he buried twenty years ago."

The young woman looks stunned. Her freshly minted degree in poli-sci didn't prepare her for scandal. Although probably it should have. But sympathizing, I decide to take her out of the middle of the situation. I stride past her desk and boldly open the door to Dick Benedict's office.

"Don't . . ." calls the young woman rushing after me. But we both see immediately that the room is empty. A half-eaten sandwich is sitting on the desk and a TV tuned to a local news station is still on. The volunteer looks around, baffled, but I notice a back door, still ajar, and rushing through it, find myself outside in a parking lot. Someone is just turning the ignition on a Mercedes, and I race over and plant my hands angrily on the hood.

Through the windshield, I stare at the silver-haired man behind the wheel, but he refuses to return my gaze. He looks behind him as if ready to back up, and revs the engine.

I pound my fist against the hood, and without thinking scream out, "Go ahead, Dick. Run me over! Why not kill me, too!"

He leans out the window, his face frozen. "Please get out of the way. I don't want to have to call the Secret Service."

"You don't get Secret Service when you're running for Congress," I snap. "And anybody who knows you wouldn't even think you rate help from a crossing guard."

"Please just get out of the way," he says tersely.

"I got out of your way once, and I'm not doing it again," I scream.

Dick turns off the engine and gets out of the car, closing the door behind him. I'm almost surprised to realize that he doesn't look at all like the monster who's loomed so large in my nightmares. He's maybe five nine and ordinary looking, not six foot six with bulging eyes and veins popping out of his forehead. Instead of a malevolent gleam, his eyes just reflect the average weariness of middle age.

"If you want to talk to me, this isn't the way to do it," he says.

"What would you suggest? The moment you heard I was here you ran out."

"I had someplace to go."

"Where? Your daddy's office, to see if he could protect you again?"

Dick takes a long moment before answering, and I can see him trying to hide his uneasiness. "What do you want Hallie? What are you doing here?"

I glare at him scornfully. "I hadn't been to Tennessee in a long time, Dickie," I say, practically spitting. "Thought I'd check out Dollywood. Or maybe the Grand Ole Opry."

The Grand Ole Opry. I try to stay cool as I say that, but I have to steady myself against the car as I remember that evening with my little sister Amy sitting on one side of me, Dick sitting on the other. All of us are in high spirits, celebrating Amy's Sweet Sixteen.

"Been to any good concerts lately?" I ask Dick bitterly.

"Hallie, don't do this," he says, a tinge of anguish in his voice.

My birthday gift to Amy had been a trip to Nashville to meet my boyfriend Dick. I couldn't believe how fast I'd fallen in love and how wonderful Dick seemed, and I wanted Amy to get to know him. Dick arranged a special surprise—tickets for all of us to hear Amy's idol, Reba McEntire. Amy kept telling me I was the best big sister in the whole wide world. Dick's family controlled half the state, so our seats were front row, center. Midconcert, Reba sang "Happy Birthday" and stepped off the stage to give Amy a hug. My sister squealed in delight, kissed me and Dick, and said we'd given her the most fabulously amazing night of her life.

How could I have imagined that it would also be her last?

"Why shouldn't I talk about this?" I ask Dick now. "Somebody has to tell the truth. Do the voters know about that part of your life? Do they know that you killed an innocent sixteen-year-old?"

Dick takes a deep breath. "Hallie, I'm not going to have this conversation with you."

"I bet it's nice to be able to forget all about it," I say venomously.

"I haven't forgotten. That was the worst thing that ever happened to me."

"Not as bad as it was for me," I say, and in my overwrought state, I suddenly burst into tears. My sobs echo through the parking lot, and I clench my fists against my eyes to stop the flood of tears. Dick steps uncertainly forward and reaches a hand to my shoulder as if to comfort me. I flinch and pull away.

"Get away from me," I say, my whole body shaking so hard now that I'm afraid my knees will give way and I'll collapse in a heap on the asphalt.

It must look that way to Dick, too, because he says, "At least sit down," and opens his car door. Without thinking, I slide onto the smooth leather backseat and he joins me. When I realize where I am, I turn even more hysterical.

"I want to get out! I can't be in a car with you. Nobody should ever get in a car with you."

Dick turns ashen as he realizes what it means to be in a car with Amy's sister. His head drops down and his own shoulders start to shake.

"Hallie, it was just a horrible, horrible time," he says.

I hear his voice break and I'm momentarily stopped. I'm the one who's been tortured by this, not him.

"I've re-lived that night a million times, with every 'if only' you could imagine," he says. "If only I didn't get so stoned. If only I hadn't gotten so mad at you after the concert. If only I hadn't driven off in a rage with Amy and hit that tree. If only I'd been the one to die."

"Die? You never suffered for a moment. My sister was killed but your parents pulled every string to get you off. Two months probation and a suspended license. Barely a slap on the wrist."

Everyone in town knew Dick used cocaine but laughed it off as the drug choice of the rich. I'd been too innocent to understand that he had a serious problem. Dick was older than me—smart, rich, and handsome. I naïvely believed my beloved when he said the drug was harmless. Then at the concert, he got high and for the first time turned mean and raucous. Dick sneered when I confronted him and told me to grow up. Why was I such a little priss, he taunted. I got scared, and we had a nasty fight.

"It was my sister," I say now. "I should have known. I should have protected her."

"You tried," Dick says. "You'd insisted you were going to drive us home, but the coke made me feel invincible. I whisked Amy off and told her you'd meet us later."

"You wouldn't listen to anything. I didn't know how to stop you."

"Nobody could stop me. After the accident, I spent six months in rehab before I could even admit it to myself. There was nothing you could have done."

"I could have stayed away from someone like you."

Dick grimaces. "Could have, would have, should have. Isn't that how we all destroy ourselves?"

"Pat little answer to make yourself feel better," I say angrily. "I can't let myself off the hook that easily. How can you?"

"What other choice do I have? I've come to believe that you change the things you can and accept the things you can't. Here's what I could change. I got straight and now I have a wife and three good kids."

"Bully for you. But how do you have the gall to run for Congress?"

"Whether you believe it or not, I think I can do some good. Maybe improve people's lives."

I get out of the car and Dick follows me. I know why he bolted when I showed up—he realizes I can ruin his plans. I turn around and face him squarely. "I came down here to make sure that you drop out of the race. I could cause such a nasty scandal that even your daddy's money won't buy you out of it."

Dick takes a deep breath. "Yes, you could. But is there a way I can convince you that I'm doing my best to make up for a bad past?"

"You can never make up for someone being dead," I tell him. "No matter how clean you are now, or how many bills you sponsor, you can't give me another sister."

* * *

When I leave Dick, I'm too shaky to get into my own car, so I wander through the neighborhood near his headquarters. Nashville has changed since I was last here. The street scene is even more crowded with camera-clicking tourists and every block has a couple of good restaurants and at least one bad trinket shop.

I gaze into a store window that's full of vintage guitars, and I think of Amy sitting in her room when she was growing up, strumming and dreaming of being a big star. Seeing a poster advertising upcoming concerts now at the Grand Ole Opry—Clint Black, Garth Brooks, Vince Gill—I think how much Amy would have liked to hear them. She'd laugh to know that the whole country has gone country. Back when she was a teenager, her taste for twangy tunes was considered offbeat for a New York girl. Now stars like Clint and Garth are national heartthrobs.

On a whim, I go into the store and pick up a Gibson guitar.

"That's a nice one," says a young salesman coming over to me, tugging at his jeans to keep them from falling off his skinny hips. "Is it for you or someone else?"

"I guess I'm just looking," I say, putting it back carefully. When Adam and Emily were little, I sometimes imagined that they'd grow up like Amy, playing guitars and loving country music. But neither showed the slightest interest in cowboys with broken hearts or standing by their man. Emily perked up when I sang a few bars of "Don't It Make My Brown Eyes Blue" only because she thought I might buy her colored contact lenses.

The salesman strokes the finely polished wood at the neck of the guitar. "I've been saving for one of these for years," he says.

"Expensive?" I ask, looking for the price tag.

"Not bad. But every penny I have goes to tuition. I'm working my way through college."

I look at him sympathetically, knowing all about tuition woes. Across the store, two other young musicians are looking at an amplifier and the salesman excuses himself to help them. I overhear one of them say that he has a club date coming up, and the others slap him a high five.

"Are you still studying with that cool guitar teacher?" asks the salesman.

"Couldn't afford it," says the kid with the gig.

"Know what you mean. But you gotta keep playing," says the other.

Thoughtfully, I walk around the store, trying to imagine what it would be like to have Amy with me right now. Would she still be writing songs? Maybe she'd be playing duets with Reba McEntire at the Grand Ole Opry. Or maybe music would be a hobby and she'd be working as a doctor in a free clinic in Costa Rica. Or she'd be living in Rochester, contentedly raising two sons. All the possibilities that will never be because that bastard Dick Benedict slammed the brakes on her future.

Thinking about Dick makes me so angry again that I grab for a guitar and swing it in the air. I suddenly understand how good Pete Townshend must have felt, smashing an instrument at the end of every Who concert.

"You okay?" asks the salesman, coming back as he sees me recklessly dangling one of his two-thousand-dollar babies.

I abashedly put the guitar back down. "Sorry, just thinking about The Who," I say.

"The what?" he asks.

"The Who."

"From where?"

"You've never heard of The Who?" I ask, wondering if being in Tennessee is the same as being trapped in an Abbott and Costello movie.

He grins. "Just playing with you, ma'am. I knew exactly what you meant. I love The Who. In fact, if I ever have my own band, I'm thinking of calling them The Whom."

"Crossover band," I say with a laugh. "For fans of rock, country, and grammar."

He grins. "I might lose the rap audience. They're not big on grammar."

"Well, you keep at it. I hope you finish school and get that band one day."

"Thank you."

I leave the store, grateful to the young salesman for cheering me up with his little joke. I walk for a while and go into Centennial Park, where I spot a bench and sit down. This section of the park is mostly empty and the shrubbery is barren, though I notice a few brave flowers trying to bloom in the dim winter sun. I sit back on the bench and close my eyes. I've built up two decades worth of rage at Dick, and what good has it been? Nothing grows from the seeds of resentment. Anger is destructive—whether it makes you want to smash guitars or smash someone's political career.

I came down to Nashville with half a thought of ruining Dick. But now that I'm here, I'm not sure what that would accomplish. His dropping out of the race won't improve my life, won't bring back Amy, won't even help the kid in the guitar store become a musician. I don't ever have to forgive Dick, but it would certainly feel better not to keep hating him. Adam and his professors might not be able to prove it in their physics labs, but negative energy saps the strength right out of you. I'm tired of holding on to the fury.

Thoughtfully, I take out my cell phone and play with the buttons for a while. Finally, I dial Dick's office and after a long wait on hold, I'm finally put through.

"Yes, Hallie," says Dick hesitantly.

"I'm in Centennial Park. I need you to meet me here."

Now the pause is so long that I'm thinking it will be spring by the time he answers.

"Don't worry, it's a public place. I'm not going to shoot you," I say, trying to hurry things up.

"That's something of a relief," he says.

I describe exactly where I am, and Dick reluctantly agrees to come find me. "Can you tell me what you want, Hallie?" And then nervously, "Are you looking for a payoff?"

"All you have to pay is penance," I say.

Dick arrives sooner than I would have expected, and I catch sight of him walking with his head down, a plaid Burberry scarf wound around his neck. He shoves his hands into his pockets and moves toward me. It's odd that for all these years I've thought of Dick as the powerful one who rammed into my life and did whatever he wanted. Now I'm the one in the proverbial driver's seat, but my goal is no longer to smash Dick's world.

"I've spent a lot of years thinking how much I hate you," I tell him when he stops in front of me.

Dick shuffles uncomfortably and digs his hands deeper into his pockets. "I don't hate you."

"Why would you?"

He gives a faint smile. "I have a feeling you're about to show me."

"No, I'm not." I shake my head. "But I've always thought you don't deserve to have anything good happen. Tell me the truth. Have you been happy?"

Now Dick looks even more uncomfortable, obviously not wanting to say that except for my being here, life has really been pretty okay. He pulls a picture out of his wallet and shows me three tousle-haired little girls.

"Whether I deserve it or not, I've been blessed. I'd be pretty ungrateful not to be happy every time I look at my children."

Despite myself, I smile at the photo of his sweet, eager-faced daughters in their matching blue-and-gold soccer uniforms. "Maybe one of them will be the next Mia Hamm," I say, handing it back to him.

"The little one's pretty uncoordinated, but I haven't told her that yet," Dick says, tucking the photo away. "My wife says I'm an overprotective father. But it's because I know how quickly bad things can happen." He looks at me meaningfully, then sighs and sits down next to me.

We both stare off into the distance, and I try to think of reckless Dick as a doting dad. "Your kids are lucky. My kids are lucky. Amy wasn't," I say.

Dick looks down. "If I could bring her back for you, I would."

"You can't, I know that. I heard what you said before. All you can try to do is change what can still be changed."

"It's a hard lesson to learn." He rubs his hands together, warming them against the chill. "So given where we are, what can we try to do now?"

Good question. Vague ideas have been whirling in my head all afternoon, and now they start to take shape.

"I met a kid today in a music store who's trying to put himself through college and start a band," I say slowly. "Why not do something for him?"

"We can hire his band to play at my campaign rallies," Dick suggests.

"Not enough. I was thinking you could pay for his college—in Amy's memory. And not just him. Take some of that family money of yours and fund ten music scholarships in Amy's name."

He thinks about it for a minute. "I'd be glad to do that. Very glad."

"And an endowed chair at Vanderbilt," I say, my plan building steam. "I want there to be an Amy Lawrence Professor of Country Music."

"I should have done something like that years ago, I guess."

"Do it now," I say.

"I will. We can think of it as my way of telling you I'm sorry."

"Sorry. Something you never bothered to say."

Dick puts his head in his hands. "My parents wouldn't let me talk to you after the accident and then they hauled me out of town to a rehab center in Arizona. Eventually, I woke up and realized what I was doing to myself and everybody I cared about. When I got out and finally tried to call, you never answered."

"By then there was nothing for us to say to each other."

"Both of our lives were turned upside down. And there was nothing either of us could do. We'd been in love and then we couldn't even talk. It's awful to feel so helpless."

"I had plenty of ideas about what I could do. Pulling you apart limb by limb was high on my list."

"And there were plenty of days back then when I wished you would." He looks at me plaintively. "What else can I do now to make amends?"

I clasp my hands so tightly in my lap that my knuckles are almost white. Am I really ready to let go of my anger? I was always able to displace some of my sorrow about Amy into hate for Dick. It almost seemed that forgiving him would be letting myself forget my sister. But now I'm hoping for better ways to keep Amy's spirit alive.

"One more thing you can do," I say slowly. "Get yourself elected to Congress. And when you're there, do something that matters."

Dick looks at me, his eyes filled with relief and appreciation. "Thank you. Maybe this sounds naïve, but I really do think I can make a difference."

"I hope you can," I say. I look out across the park and in the distance I can make out the columns of Nashville's very own Parthenon, an exact replica of the one in Greece.

"Only thing I ask is that once you're in Congress, you don't ask the American people to build the great state of Tennessee a fake Roman Colosseum to go with the fake Greek Parthenon," I say, trying to make a little joke to relieve the tension.

Dick smiles and reaches across the bench to seal the deal by shaking my hand, but instead I give him a hug. When we pull back, both of us wipe the corners of our eyes, embarrassed.

"I mean it about no Colosseums," I say sidestepping any more deep feelings. "I've never understood why you southerners copy other countries' landmarks. You don't see the Greeks building statues of Robert E. Lee."

"A Colosseum down here wouldn't be such a bad idea," Dick says, pretending to look around for the best place to build it. "And we don't copy, we improve. Ever hear of Foamhenge in Virginia? It's a full-sized replica of Stonehenge but lighter. Made entirely of Styrofoam instead of rocks."

"One of the great landmarks of the world, minus the heavy lifting. At least nobody got a hernia building it this time."

We smile at each other. "You would have made it as a southern belle after all," Dick says.

Tears spring to my eyes as I realize that for many reasons, I'm sorry I never got the chance. Dick squeezes my hand and then stands up. "Hallie, thank you again. More than I can ever say."

"It's okay," I tell him, and for once, it really is. I lean back against

the bench. After thinking about Amy for a tumultuous day and two tumultuous decades, I'm grateful to feel a moment of peace.

Visiting Amy's grave usually makes me sad, but when I get back from
Nashville, the cemetery is the first place I go. For once, I don't feel like
crying as I walk through the wrought iron gates, and the slight dusting
of snow gives a peaceful glow to the bucolic grounds.

The cemetery is old, and making my way through the well-kept
paths, I notice a pair of elaborately carved headstones commemorating
"a loving husband and father" who died in 1897, and his "devoted wife
and companion," Mary Alice, who lived until 1917. Twenty years without him. I try to imagine how she felt to be alone for those final years.
Was she scared to be by herself or did she make a new life? I wonder if
she ever again had someone to cuddle with at night. So long ago, there
couldn't have been many options for a woman on her own.

Wandering along, I glance at other headstones and I'm struck, as I
always am at a cemetery, by how fleeting life really is. The time you have
is never enough. My meeting with Dick was surprisingly freeing and I
feel now like I can celebrate the moments I had with Amy rather than
regretting the ones I've lost.

I step hesitantly toward Amy's plot, and brush my hand gingerly
across the headstone.

"For you," I say, as I place the yellow roses I brought.

I sit down on the damp ground and pull my knees up to my chest.
I think Amy would like to know about Dick, so I tell her the story of my
last two days. I imagine her smiling when she learns about the Amy
Lawrence Professorship of Country Music. Amy was always modest
and funny, and I can almost hear her teasing me for being so sanctimonious. "That's cool," she'd say, "but what's it mean? Does someone get
to major in Loretta Lynn?"

Without thinking, I give a little laugh, and a security guard nearby
looks at me sternly. I want to tell him that you can't be sad forever. All
you can do is try your best and go on.

Moving on is what I've been attempting to do since the day Bill left.

And I have to believe that the journey to the men of my past has put me on the right course for my future. Did I really think that Eric or Ravi or Kevin would provide me with a fairy-tale ending? It would have been nice, and people do marry their first crush later in life. Even if it didn't work out for me, there is a romance to reconnecting.

I was even half willing to reconnect with Bill, but that pretty clearly won't work out, either. Bill and Ashlee. Bill and dandy Candi. Bill and whoever's next, which won't be me. I was a good wife, always support-ive. I picked up the dry cleaning, made that stupid lasagna, and—how many points is this worth?—trimmed his ear hairs once a month. I didn't deserve to be so dismally dumped.

I reach over and touch Amy's headstone again. Alas, who says you always get the good life you deserve? All you can do is take the hand that's dealt and play it the best way you know how. Flying home from Nashville, I napped easily on the plane, knowing that I'd faced Dick and forgiven him. I'd be justified in waiting another two decades to for-give Bill, since he hasn't earned anything better. But for my sake, I'm ready to forgive him now.

Standing up, I look at the dates under Amy's name and think of the people just like me who'll be walking by a generation from now, think-ing how sad it was that a girl died so young. But maybe they'll be wise enough to understand the real lesson of her short life—that there's nothing any of us can do but make the most of the time we have.

Chapter NINETEEN

DESPITE THE INTENSITY of the previous few days, life goes on as always. I speak to the kids, take on two new cases at work, and make myself hot oatmeal in the mornings. That's something of a change, and a definite nutritional improvement over my usual chewy bars for breakfast. At the office, I get a bouquet of flowers from Charles and Melina, telling me they've just opened their own publicity agency. If I ever star in a movie, they promise to represent me for free.

Bellini has news of her own—or, more accurately, a complete and utter surprise. "The barista asked me to marry him!" she squeals as she hops out of a cab on the street corner where I'm waiting to meet her after work.

I'm so stunned that I drop the Pottery Barn bag I'm holding and don't even care when I hear my fourteen-dollar gold-leaf Venetian vase shatter.

I know Emily Post advises that you don't say "congratulations" to a bride, but she probably wouldn't approve of my response either.

"You said 'No,' didn't you?" I ask.

"Why would I?" Bellini asks jubilantly. "You saw him in that nude play. He's the handsome, um, Venti guy."

I'm sure there are worse reasons to get married, but I can't come up with any right now.

"I didn't realize you two were that close," I say, thinking that I don't even know the barista-slash-Venti guy's real name. And I'm not completely convinced Bellini does, either.

"I didn't know we were that close, myself," she says, which makes me a tad concerned that he's just become the eleventh of those nine or ten guys she thought she'd marry after the first date.

"How exactly did he propose?" I ask.

"We'd just had a night of unbelievable sex, and he put his hand on my thigh and said, 'What do you say you and I get married?' That's definitely a proposal," she says defensively.

"Never believe what a man says when he has his hand on your thigh," I counsel, offering the same advice that I'd give Emily.

"For your information, he asked me again in the morning, when we were brushing our teeth," Bellini says.

Now I'm getting a little anxious. A proposal made while flossing under fluorescent lights is about as serious as it gets. Maybe I need to be more supportive.

"If you want an underwater wedding, I can get you a good photographer," I say helpfully.

Finally Bellini laughs. "Don't buy the waterproof rice just yet. I was flattered, but of course I finally said 'No.' He's fun to be with, but I don't think he's my soulmate. Plus, I don't want my babies to be weaned on moccachinos."

I grin and give her a little hug. "You'll find the right guy eventually."

"I know," she says optimistically. "If the young, sexy barista wanted to make it official, one day I'll be able to marry someone I really love."

As we've been talking, Bellini and I have walked halfway down the block, and now she leads me upstairs to a small, softly lit showroom with beds of every shape and height lined up along each wall.

"You remembered I wanted to get a new mattress!" I say. "I'm tired of sleeping with the memory of Bill. His imprint's still in the foam."

"And a new bed for me, too," she says. "I realized one of the perks of marrying the barista would be the bridal registry. I'd finally get a matching set of china and have an excuse to buy a luxurious king-size bed. But it suddenly seems so old-fashioned not to get it for myself."

"I guess if you can jump into bed before marriage, you can buy yourself a bed before marriage, too," I say.

Bellini laughs and looks at the display of expensive mattresses. "These styles are sold only in London, and now they're being introduced to the U.S. market. You happen to be at an exclusive showing. For the trade only."

It never ceases to amaze me that you have to be an insider to do anything—including getting a good night's sleep. I enthusiastically bounce on one mattress, then notice the price tag and bounce right off.

"Twelve thousand dollars?" I gasp. "Is it spun out of gold?"

"Silk, lamb's wool, and cashmere," says Bellini, who's obviously done her research.

"Nicer than my sweater," I say, tugging at my merino wool blend.

"There's something about the way the seams and rivets are encased that you never wake up with lines on your face, which is important at our age," says Bellini. "Queen Elizabeth sleeps on one."

"Queen Elizabeth?" I ask skeptically. "She's not exactly an advertisement for dewy-faced youth. What does Nicole Kidman sleep on?"

"Botox," says Bellini with a grin.

I tentatively sit back down on the royal mattress. "Is this a Duxiana?" I ask, having heard the radio commercials for what's allegedly the world's most comfortable bed.

Bellini plops down beside me, and miraculously, my side of the bed doesn't move. "It's a Hypnos. That Duxiana is yesterday's news," she says, her scornful tone making it clear that the once-vaunted brand is now the Hilton Hotel of beds—a nice place to sleep, but certainly not the Ritz. "Luciano Pavarotti sleeps on a Hypnos. So does Vladimir Putin."

"The new Russia," I say, shaking my head. "A twelve thousand-dollar bed kind of makes you mourn the fall of Communism."

Bellini laughs, but then she says, "Really, a good mattress is worth any price. You spend a third of your life in bed."

"Or in your case a half," I tease.

"In a good week," she winks.

I roll onto my back trying to decide if this highfalutin mishmash of stuffing and springs would really help anybody sleep better. Someone once told me that sampling a mattress for five minutes in a store won't tell you what it's going to be like to spend every night with it for the rest of your life. Same could be said about men.

"You could save yourself some money and buy a Sealy Posturpedic and a box of Sleepytime chamomile tea," I suggest to Bellini.

"Or Ambien and a vibrator," says Bellini, more practical than I would have expected.

I snuggle against a pillow, thinking of imparting to Bellini my new-found wisdom about making the most of what you have. But on the other hand, a little yearning isn't a bad thing. Especially if it's for a nice bed and someone great to share it with.

Bellini props herself up on her own pillow. "What do you think, Hallie? After all you've been through, do you still think marriage is a good idea?"

"You mean just because I'm getting divorced?" I realize I haven't said that word aloud yet, and it feels strange coming out of my mouth. "I never really thought my marriage would end. When I said 'I do,' I meant it to be forever. I do, I did, I would, I will. But life takes funny turns. No matter how hard you try, you can never predict what will happen."

"All the unknowns make it tough," Bellini says. "If the barista turns out to be Matt Damon, do you think I'll be sorry I didn't marry him?"

"You've always wanted to go to the Academy Awards. But what if all he wins is Starbucks' Barista of the Week?"

"I'd still be proud of him," she says loyally. "But I guess in either case, I wouldn't be in love. I mean, you don't wish you'd married Eric even though he turned out to be so rich."

"No, but I wish I had his New York apartment."

"Prime real estate has always been a reason to get married. Leave it to you to let integrity get in the way."

"You're right. How could I pick love over four bedrooms with a Central Park view?"

"Because you're you." She smiles. "Maybe I shouldn't be saying this when we're lying next to each other on a mattress, but having you as a good friend is better than settling for a mediocre man."

"Thanks," I say. "But I should warn you that I don't chop wood or kill spiders."

"That's okay. At least you don't leave the toilet seat up."

Emily calls to tell me the classes she's picked for her second semester. I listen carefully and realize there's a decided lack of art, literature, feminism, or history.

"Let me get this right. Game theory, macroeconomics, financial markets, and a special college seminar on selling rice to China?" I say, looking at the notes I've scribbled as she talked. "Don't the Chinese already eat rice three times a day?"

"Exactly. The challenge is to expand the market."

"What happened to your interest in Susan B. Anthony and the Brontë sisters?"

"This is the new feminism, Mom. It's not about theory anymore. It's about how to take care of yourself and feather your own nest. Most women end up alone. Look at you."

"Yes, look at me," I say. "I'm not exactly sitting here eating cans of cat food."

"I know, Mom. You always have Bumble Bee tuna in the cabinet." She sighs dramatically. "I figure if I major in econ, I'll be ready for whatever life brings."

"Your life will bring a lot of wonderful things. Mine did," I tell her, quickly adding, "and I'm expecting many more wonderful things."

Emily's silent for a moment. "Mom, I have to tell you the truth. Adam's friend Evahi was in New York and she happened to run into Daddy. He was on a date with some girl."

I feel only the tiniest twinge. Emily's not exactly delivering a news bulletin.

"Honey, that's okay. Daddy and I aren't together anymore." Ever since that day I went shopping with Bill and heard him on the phone with yet another conquest, I've understood that over is over.

"Mom, Daddy's turned out to be so shallow. It drives me crazy that he keeps hurting you."

"He doesn't. I'm over being hurt by things I can't change." Apparently I've learned something even from Dick.

"Don't you just hate him?"

I think about it briefly. "I don't. And you shouldn't either. Daddy loves you. Remember what he always said?"

"He loves me more than all the stars in the Milky Way."

I smile, remembering how Bill would read Emily bedtime stories when she was little. Then, hugging her tightly, he'd talk about the vastness of the universe and how his love for her filled every corner of it. How could I hate a man like that, even now?

"Families might get screwed up, but we're still a family," I tell Emily.

"Yeah, I get that."

"Have a little faith in your prospects. This is the time in your life to study what you love and assume that everything will turn out the way you want."

Emily seems to think about it. "Okay, I hear you. But I'm still taking the econ classes. One of the teaching assistants is really cute."

After my conversation with Emily, I decide it's only fair to everybody to make the end of my relationship with Bill official. I mull it over to get used to the idea and finally call Bill to suggest we go to a mediator instead of wasting our money on divorce lawyers. He hesitates.

"I'm not sure I even want to get divorced."

"Bill, our marriage is done. We both know that."

"I'd really rather stay married," he says.

I know enough not to be flattered. "Give me two reasons."

"That's easy. Number one: If I'm married, I can still come to the house and chop down the occasional tree. And number two: None of the women I date can expect me to become her husband."

Despite myself, I laugh. "Bill, I can't help you with your women. But if you want to stick around as my now-and-then gardener, you're welcome."

"You're being really understanding."

"I'm trying."

There's a long pause. "We should get together to talk about this, right? I guess we have some things to settle. Like custody of those Knicks tickets."

I snicker. Who would have thought that would be my great leverage? He'd probably swap me the Knicks tickets for a Picasso drawing, if only we had one.

"We do need to talk."

"Come on over. I just bought a twenty-five-year-old Highlander Scotch that I can open."

"I don't drink scotch," I remind him.

"Then how about we watch the Super Bowl? I got a new flat-screen LCD television."

Fancy scotch that's older than his girlfriends, expensive flat-screen TV? Bill's like the Merck Diagnostic Manual's description of a man at midlife. Easy to understand why we don't fit together anymore, though if I'm coming to terms with all the men from my past, I guess Bill counts as one of them.

I get to Bill's apartment on Sunday afternoon and am greeted by sixty inches of Terry Bradshaw screaming in SurroundSound.

"Great place, huh?" Bill asks, ushering me in. "One of the partners in my office has had this pied-à-terre for years. Told me to use it as long as I want."

"And you bought a new TV?"

"A man's got to live," he says expansively.

I look around, wondering if a man can really live on scotch, beer, a store-bought container of guacamole and a ripped open bag of Tostitos, which seem to be the only edibles in the apartment. Oh, no, I underestimated him. Bill proudly brings out a plastic grocery platter of greasy spicy chicken wings, blue cheese dressing, and a few anemic stalks of

266 — Janice Kaplan and Lynn Schnurnberger

carrots and celery thrown in for decoration. So this is who buys the $24.99 Superbowl Special. If Bill can't eat every meal at a diner, he's going to turn his apartment into one.

Bill sits down and motions for me to join him on the leather sofa. We're both mesmerized by the almost life-size football players crashing around on his big-screen TV. I know we're nowhere near kickoff, but there are forty years of Super Bowl highlights to catch up on, not to mention the really interesting part of the games, the commercials. I understand why advertisers use half-naked women to hawk products to men, but what's with the Budweiser frogs, the Clydesdale horses, and the Monster.com monkeys? Talk about appealing to animal instincts.

"Adam called a little while ago," Bill says, dipping a Tostito into the blue cheese. "We reminisced about those father-son Super Bowl parties we used to have."

"You miss him, don't you," I say, realizing how close Bill has always been to the kids.

"Yeah," he says wistfully. "Those were great times we used to have."

"We were a great family," I agree.

"Sounds like Adam and that new girlfriend, Evahi, are having fun," says Bill.

"She's a very sweet girl," I say.

"No, I mean *fun*," says Bill with a sly grin.

"That's your child you're talking about!"

"Fun's what college is all about," says Bill cheerfully, the casual father of a son.

"Emily would agree with you on that. Did she tell you about the ski instructor?"

"I'm sure they're just friends," says Bill, suddenly the protective father of a daughter. "Emily's still my sweet little girl. I'm sure she spends every second studying."

I just laugh. "Yes, that's what we women do."

Bill looks at me. "Right. You already told me about that old boyfriend. Which one was it?"

"Nobody you'd know," I say. "A guy named Kevin."

Bill lowers the sound, more interested in my commentary than Terry Bradshaw's. "Kevin from high school?" he asks curiously.

"Yes," I say, but I'm momentarily taken aback, realizing just how much Bill knows about me. Over the years, we've shared all of our stories with each other.

"Wasn't that the slimeball with the leather jacket who made you skip class?" Bill asks.

"He wasn't a slimeball," I say, trying not to smile.

"If you were going to look for an old boyfriend, I would have thought it would be that rich Eric guy," Bill says, shaking his head.

"I saw him, too," I say.

"So you slept with two people?" Bill asks, raising two fingers in the air and inadvertently making the victory sign.

"I didn't sleep with Eric," I say, grabbing the victory right back. "All I did was go to his apartment and eat caviar."

"Anyone else I should know about?" asks Bill.

"Not that it's any of your business, but Barry Stern."

"The romantic intellectual you met in Europe who took you to museums," says Bill, proving that he had been listening to me for twenty years. "Whatever became of him?"

"Long story."

"Sex, yes or no?"

"No. Not with his boyfriend around."

Bill raises an eyebrow. "Your old boyfriend has a boyfriend?"

"Life gets complicated."

"Tell me about it," says Bill.

We're both silent and after our banter, a slight melancholy sets in. I look distractedly at the television, where barely clad cheerleaders are enthusiastically shaking their pom-poms at the team's slack-stomached, fiftysomething coach. The nubile girls adoringly drape themselves over him and cameras snap. No wonder middle-aged men are confused. If they don't want to grow up, nobody ever makes them.

I reach into my bag and hand Bill a manila envelope.

"Separation papers," I say, shakily handing them over to him. "Makes things easier down the road. It'll get everything started."

"Not started. It'll get everything ended." Bill opens the envelope and takes out a pen, then puts it back down. "I'm going to be sorry about this after a while, aren't I?"

"Probably," I say, thinking that someday he'll realize what a good life he walked away from. And it's even nice that he vaguely understands that now.

"A lot to be sorry about." But because he's Bill and would always prefer not to dwell on anything that makes him uncomfortable, he just shakes his head, grabs for the remote, and turns the sound back up just in time for the opening kickoff.

"Game's going to be a blowout," he says. "We don't have to watch if you don't want to. Everybody already knows how it's going to end."

I take a carrot stick and dip it into the blue cheese dressing. "You never know how it'll end. That's why you keep playing."

Chapter TWENTY

BILL AND I are both determined to keep things civil, and Emily and Adam seem relieved that there's not going to be a War of the Roses. We have no problems splitting our assets—until it comes to dividing the old records we'd stashed in the attic. We agree that we'll each just keep whatever we brought to the marriage, since they all have sentimental value. I take a whole afternoon putting my records in two big white crates and Bill's in two blue ones. When he comes to pick them up, his eyes brighten when he sees an old Bob Dylan album.

"Wow, I'm glad to get that one back," he says. "It'll always be a favorite. Track two was playing the first time a girl gave me a blow job."

I clear my throat. What can an ex-wife-to-be say? "I only hope the record brings you much more listening . . . um, pleasure."

"Thanks," Bill says heartily. He eagerly pulls Cream from the crate. "And this one. I'll never forget. Track five was . . ."

"That story I remember," I say, holding up my hands. In fact, that particular tale of high school groping I heard at least five or six times. And now that we're not married, I'm not obligated to listen again.

Bill glances over at my crate and a shadow of suspicion crosses his face. "Why's the White Album on your side?"

"Because it's mine," I say.

He picks it up and holds it tightly. "No, the White Album was mine. Black Sabbath was yours."

"You're confused. Black Sabbath was yours and Purple Rain was mine."

"I bought Purple Rain. You were Pink Floyd."

Maybe we're not having a War of the Roses, but we're definitely having a color war. Before Bill starts frantically thumbing through the crate looking for Yellow Submarine, Green Day, or Maroon 5, I decide to use the White Album as a white flag.

"Take it. Take whatever you want. I don't want to fight," I say.

In the karmic category of getting back what you give, Bill adopts my generous spirit. He looks longingly at the record in his hands, then offers it to me.

"Nah, it's okay. Keep the White Album. These days, I prefer the White Stripes anyway."

"With lead singer Jack White, as opposed to comedian Jack Black," I say, and at the silliness of it all, we both laugh.

Bill looks relieved that this final separation is going so smoothly.

"It's good to laugh with you again," he says.

"It is," I say. "We can get divorced without making each other miserable."

"We can get divorced and still make each other happy," Bill says. He comes over and puts his hands on my shoulders. "How about a little sex to prove we're still friends?"

"You can't be serious."

"Why not? One last roll in the hay for old time's sake. Come on. It won't take very long."

"I remember." I pat his cheek. "Little lesson to improve your social life. It's supposed to take a long time."

Bill looks at me uncertainly, and I take his hands off my shoulder. I'm grateful for the proposition because for one thing, it's always nice to be asked. And for another, getting divorced is easier when Bill keeps reminding me what a fool he is.

* * *

But I'm no fool. I'm planning to go to the best party in town. Bendel's is throwing a bash to celebrate its exclusive new jewelry line featuring the creations of Inka, a hip new designer who works with a rare red stone found only in Peru. His wildly expensive heart-shaped pendants are the hit of the season.

"Whole hearts, chipped hearts, broken hearts—and half hearts for people who could use a little more enthusiasm," says Bellini, who, as the store's accessories guru, inked the contract with Inka.

"Sounds like the man's a genius. He takes the cracked stones anyone else would throw out and charges extra for them."

"People are even snapping up the broken-heart pendants as wedding gifts. *Women's Wear Daily* calls them brilliantly post-ironic."

I'd guess that most women would still prefer an un-ironic perfectly cut five-carat diamond, but what do I know.

"Wait until you hear what we're doing for the launch party at Chelsea Piers," Bellini says excitedly. "We have a light show, acrobats from Cirque du Soleil, the coolest d.j. in New York, and two dozen celebrities who've already said they're coming. Plus the best part: it's going to be BYOB."

"Bring your own bottle? Given what Inka charges, Bendel's should be able to spring for a few cases of Cabernet."

"This BYOB is bring your old boyfriend. Isn't that fabulous? You show up with an ex—and then we can all trade. I got the idea from the clothes swap party at your house."

"Come on, 'fess up," I tease. "You got the idea because I've been visiting all my old boyfriends."

"Well, both," admits Bellini. "But think about it. If someone could want that cast-off red dress of yours, just imagine what they could do with a cast-off old flame."

"Toast marshmallows?"

Bellini laughs. "I was figuring those old flames might light some fires, ignite some new romances. Think of the possibilities. A roomful of men who've already been vetted."

"And just which one of my old boyfriends am I supposed to bring?" I ask.

"Any one you want," she says.

Bellini's being a little optimistic. I could show up with Barry, the gay swami, as easily as with Eric, the unmarried billionaire. But I have to admire her: Bellini's always cooking up creative ways to meet men. And this time she's getting Bendel's to foot the bill.

I think about it for a couple of days and decide that if I'm going to the party, my only possible date is Eric. Kevin's working on his movie, Barry's busy being a guru, Dick's out of the question. I hesitate because I don't want Eric to get the wrong idea. After that night I spent at his apartment, he predicted I'd come back, but now I'm trying to recycle him, not rekindle anything romantic. Finally, I go to my computer to e-mail Eric, asking if he'd like to come to a party as my old beau.

Not that you're old! I write, then quickly delete it because that sounds too fawning. *I had many choices!* disappears because I don't want to appear vain, and even the innocuous *It should be fun!* gets cut because what if Eric misunderstands the kind of fun I want? Twenty minutes later I'm still battling to compose the two-line message that should have taken two minutes. I revise every sentence more often than Hemingway. Who said e-mail would make our lives easier?

Apparently, it's made Eric's life easier, because barely a minute after I hit "Send," I get the message back from his BlackBerry: "*Sure. Hot.*"

Okay, that requires another twenty minutes on my side for interpretation. Am I hot or has he read Page Six and knows that Bellini's party is already the hottest invitation in New York? Possibly he's just reporting on the heat wave in Arizona.

The party starts generating so much buzz that all my Chaddick pals ask me to snag them invitations, and I do. Men around town stop boasting about the size of their bonuses and start bragging about how many different women have invited them to appear as their official Old Boyfriend.

"I've heard Jude Law got four invitations but two of them were from nannies," Bellini tells me in one of our many conversations.

"And let me guess. Charlie Sheen got six calls, but four were hookers," I suggest.

"I hadn't heard that," says Bellini, making a note. "But I'll see if Cindy Adams would like to run with it."

The gossip columnists are also excited that Inka's fans include the Jennifers—Aniston, Lopez, and Garner. It's not surprising that the actresses have the same taste in jewelry since at least two of them have the same taste in men.

"We told Ben Affleck he can't come with his wife, Jennifer Garner. But if he wants to come as the man J. Lo didn't marry, that's another story," Bellini reports. "It's going to be some night."

The day of the night isn't bad either. I arrive at Bellini's East Side apartment at about noon to be fussed over by the hair and makeup artists who arrive courtesy of Bendel's beauty department and to get dressed in the elaborate gowns Bellini arranged for us to borrow, calling in favors from her favorite designers. I twirl in front of the mirror, admiring myself in the Badgley Mischka satin-and-chiffon gown with embellished hem.

"Don't you dare sweat tonight," Bellini warns me as I preen. "These dresses go back tomorrow."

"Maybe I should have had my underarms Botoxed," I say, having read about the miracle drug's latest use as an antiperspirant.

"If you're going for Botox, I'd do that line on your forehead first," Bellini says, and when I look worriedly in the mirror, she chirps, "Gotcha. No lines yet. Just joking."

"Very funny. Scare me like that again and I'll need an emergency face-lift."

Our jewelry, of course, is by Inka. I fasten the clasp on a pendant heart that's chipped, not broken, since I seem to be on the mend. The heart on Bellini's necklace is whole, but has gold barbed wire wrapped around it. Way too post-ironic for me to understand, but maybe she and Jon Stewart could start dating.

We're almost ready to leave when Eric calls my cell phone.

"What'd he say?" Bellini asks, when I hang up.

"He's jetting back from Moldova, and he'll be a little late for the party. He'll meet me there."

Bellini nods. "The barista is auditioning for a show in which he actually gets to wear clothes, so he's not even going to make it."

We head, unescorted, to a cab. "I know it's hard to get a boyfriend, but who knew it would be this hard to get an old boyfriend," laughs Bellini, as we slip into the backseat. The driver notices us in our glamorous getups and tosses us appreciative glances in the rearview mirror.

"I bet you're not going to shoot hoops tonight," he says, as he pulls off the West Side Highway and wends his way through Chelsea Piers, the massive complex strung along the Hudson River that includes ballrooms and TV production studios, not to mention climbing walls, bowling alleys, putting greens, skating rinks, and basketball courts. There's space for every sport a New Yorker could ever want to play—at least the legal ones.

"The party's at Pier 60. Just follow the limousines," directs Bellini.

The cabbie falls in line behind two black limos with tinted windows. A white stretch Hummer comes up next to us with a lone woman lounging in the backseat. Maybe she needs an armored tank big enough for a battalion to make her entrance, but I think she should repaint the damn thing and send it to the U.S. Army.

When we pull up to the entrance, I reach for my jeweled evening purse. I spent a half-hour this afternoon performing pocketbook triage, choosing what to bring along in this teeny-tiny bag. I managed to squish in a lip gloss, three Listerine breath strips, half of a folding hairbrush (I had to break it in two), and my house key—just the one for the front door, not the back. I was sure I'd put in two twenty-dollar bills, but now I can't find them.

"Do you have any cash?" I ask Bellini.

"Are you kidding? I didn't even have room for a spare false eyelash," she replies, holding out her borrowed minaudière, which being half the size of mine cost twice as much. In the world of fashion, less is definitely more.

I ponder our predicament for a moment and then explain it to the driver, asking him for his address.

"I'm so sorry, but I'll send you cash the minute I get home to-night," I promise apologetically.

"Yeah, sure. I'm not falling for that line." He turns off the motor and as we get out of the cab, he does, too. He's about two hundred and fifty pounds with a scraggly black beard and torn sneakers.

"What are you doing?" I ask.

"I'm going in with you. If you don't have money, someone around this snazzy place should be good for my twelve-fifty plus tip."

"Stay here. I'll find someone myself," I say, panicked that the driver might actually go in and create a commotion.

"No way. You're trying to stiff me. You'll never come back," he roars as he storms toward the door.

"Wait a minute!" I call out, but he barrels forward. Clearly he's a man who's been left before, but now's not the time to deal with his abandonment issues.

The cab driver steps inside where the party is already under way. The music blares and waiters pass by with glasses of Dom Perignon. Three hundred of New York's choicest and perhaps choosiest women circulate through the room, talking and flirting as they flaunt their expensive dresses and desirable exes.

Before I can stop him, the cabbie plants himself at the edge of the crowd. "Who's got fifteen bucks to lend these rich ladies?" he hollers.

I hear assorted gasps. A few people look up nervously from their fluted glasses, and several others pointedly walk away. There's probably enough capital in this room to finance the next seventy-million-mile mission to Mars, but nobody's coughing up cash for our three-mile cab ride.

"Come on, people. Fifteen bucks. One of you can handle it," the cabbie yells.

Somebody better handle it soon, or I'm going to die of embarrassment. Either that, or I'll put a price on these priceless Inka earrings I'm wearing—fifteen bucks. Maybe I can make it thirty, and score enough for a cab ride home.

While everyone else is skittering away from our ruckus, one tall, tuxedoed man heads in our direction.

"Problem?" he asks, looking straight at the cabbie.

"These women got in my taxi and couldn't pay me," he says accusingly.

"Small pocketbook," explains Bellini, shrugging and holding up her minipurse.

The tall man smiles, obviously amused and ready to help. He takes out his wallet and peels off a twenty-dollar bill.

"Here you go," he says, giving it to the cabbie. Then he adds graciously, "Can I offer you something to eat before you leave?"

"Sure," says the driver, pocketing the twenty and waiting for his big bonus.

Mr. Handsome-in-His-Tuxedo goes to an overflowing buffet table, comes back with two large skewers of seafood and hands them to the driver, who brandishes them like matching swords and quickly heads out the door.

"How about you?" says our dimpled do-gooder, now smiling at me. "Can I get you some shrimp, too? Or something from the oyster bar?"

"No," I say, avoiding his eye. I mumble a quick thanks for his gallantry and hastily turn to get a drink. Bellini shoots me a surprised look then, to make up for my lack of manners, she gushes her gratitude.

"What's wrong with you?" she asks when she joins me a few minutes later. "That guy was cute. I think he liked you."

"I know him," I say through gritted teeth. "I'm mortified. That was Tom Shepard."

"Who?"

"Eric's friend. The one who rescued me when I took a hike one day right after Bill left. Remember? He found me crying on the side of the road in Cold Spring and gave me a ride to my car. That's how I got back in touch with Eric."

"So now he's rescuing you again. He's practically your own personal Clark Kent. That's good, isn't it?"

"Yeah, fabulous. Last time, I was muddy, swollen from bug bites, and couldn't find my car. This time I'm the idiot who can't find her money. Can you imagine what he'll say about me to Eric? And what's he doing here, anyway?"

"Who cares? Hallie, dear, you're a single woman now. When a handsome man offers oysters, you bite."

I grimace. "Oysters are slimy. And didn't you notice? He's wearing a wedding ring." I glance across the room at Tom Shepard, even better looking in his tux than his Timberlands. But when he returns my gaze, I quickly turn away.

Bellini shakes her head at my awkwardness. "You're hopeless. But if you're not going to talk to Tom, let's cruise."

"Did you really just say 'Tom' and 'cruise' in the same sentence?"

"Not on purpose," Bellini grins. "But Tom Cruise. That could be our secret code when we're meeting men. Girlfriend talk for 'Let's go find someone else.' "

Laughing, I take my white wine and stroll with Bellini around the Chelsea Piers ballroom. Looking out of the enormous windows, I'm awed by the stunning view of the majestic Hudson River. But the party offers plenty of distractions from the view. At one end of the room, leotard-clad acrobats from Cirque du Soleil are dangling from three high ropes, and effortlessly twisting themselves into impossible positions. A trapeze artist swings back and forth overhead, and apparently, we're her only net. As I watch, a slightly tipsy older man with a big belly and even bigger diamond cuff links comes over and throws an arm around Bellini.

"Hey, beautiful, can I buy you a drink?" he asks, looking lasciviously at Bellini. Then eyeing me, he says, "Buy you both a drink. Two for the price of one."

"Tom Cruise," I say to Bellini.

"Tom Cruise," Bellini agrees, and we both break into giggles. As we turn to walk away, we bump directly into Darlie.

"Darlings," Darlie says, double air-kissing each of our cheeks, and smoothing her hands across her skintight Harve Leger dress. "Fabulous party. I see you've met my old boyfriend Hiram. What do you think?"

"He's exactly the type of man I'd expect you to be with," says Bellini, managing an honest reply. Personally, I can see why it didn't work out. Darlie would never have stayed with a man who wears bigger diamonds than she does.

"It was nice of you to bring such an eligible ex," I say, trying to be gracious.

"He's not eligible," Darlie snaps. "Once in love with Darlie, always in love with Darlie."

I'm not sure how long "always" lasts for my much-married Chaddick neighbor, but she does make a lasting impression.

One look around the exuberant crowd confirms that Bellini's Bring Your Old Boyfriend party is a big success. Couples who haven't seen each other in years are flirting again or helping their exes meet new propects. My happily married neighbor Amanda introduces her old boyfriend to just-divorced Steff, and the new twosome immediately fall into animated conversation.

"You have to meet the guest of honor. That's Inka," says Bellini, leading me over to a studly blond man who's interpreted "formal attire" to mean cowboy boots, red pants, and a thin black bolo tie. A throng of admirers is gathered around the famous jewelry designer, who's glowing and holding hands with an equally hunky blond standing next to him. When Inka spots Bellini, he turns on a thousand-watt smile.

"What an idea. Thank you for this party," gushes Inka. "Meet my old boyfriend, Aztek."

As best I can remember, the Incas and Aztecs were separated by a continent, but tonight seems to have brought them closer together.

But it doesn't seem to be bringing me any closer to Eric. I look at my watch again.

"Think that old boyfriend of yours is going to show up anytime soon?" asks a man coming up behind me.

Startled, I turn around and am suddenly face-to-face with Tom Shepard, who smiles at me and takes a sip of his scotch on the rocks.

"His plane's late," I say.

"I can never figure out why Eric keeps that private jet. His on-time arrival record is worse than United's." He puts down his scotch. "By the way, in case you don't remember, I'm Tom Shepard."

"Of course I remember you. My roadside hero."

"Eric invited me to come along tonight. He thought I needed to get out of my house and meet some new people."

"I was wondering what you were doing here," I say.

"He's definitely not a Tom Cruise," murmurs Bellini in my ear as she walks away, obviously to leave the two of us alone.

Tom puts his hand out to shake mine. Despite myself, I feel a little tingle.

"I was a lot muddier last time we met," I say.

"You clean up nicely. That's a beautiful dress. Very lovely."

"Borrowed," I admit.

"Not at all. That loveliness is all your own."

I stare at the gold band on his hand. "Thanks for the compliment. But I have to tell you, I'm a little sensitive. I don't really think married men should flirt."

Tom looks taken aback, but before he can answer, the net worth in the room rises as Eric arrives, his assistant Hamilton trailing behind him in a flurry of cell phone-ringing, BlackBerry-beeping activity. Eric pulls himself away long enough to give me a kiss on the cheek and grab Tom for a hearty back-patting hug.

"I'm glad you're here," I say to Eric.

"Me too," he says. But Hamilton interrupts our barely started conversation with an urgent question, making me wonder if Eric is really ever "here" when he's here. Still, Eric looks with satisfaction from Tom to me.

"So you two met up with each other already. Good. My work is done," he says, as if approving a business merger.

"Your work is never done," jokes Tom.

"Sure it is. Now you have to do your part," says Eric. He snatches a mini-hot dog from a passing waiter, dips it in the mustard sauce, and pops it in his mouth. "Mmm, good. I've got to have my assistant find out what those are. Maybe we can get some for the plane."

Tom and I exchange a knowing look and start to laugh.

"Pigs-in-a-blanket, Mr. Billionaire," says Tom. "You may know them as *petit boeuf en croute*."

"Don't give me a hard time," says Eric with a grin. "I found you a new girlfriend, didn't I?"

I'm confused. Does Eric regularly find new girlfriends for wedding ring-wearing Tom?

"Not my girlfriend yet. Anyway, I found her myself. Grubby, but with potential," Tom says, smiling at me.

"And you've been talking about her ever since. Thought she was an astute judge of character when she wouldn't fly off with me to Bermuda. Or was it London?" Eric shakes his head in mock despair. "Great support I get from my best friend."

Now I'm distinctly uncomfortable. I want to take Eric aside and ask what the deal is with Tom. But, as usual, Hamilton reappears, as annoying as a mosquito you can never quite swat away.

"Mr. Richmond, the president's on the phone," Hamilton says importantly.

Eric stands a little taller as he strides away.

"Don't be too impressed," says Tom. "It's probably just the president of Eric's country club wanting to set up a golf game."

"Or the president of Moldova," I suggest. "Asking help from Eric in getting the country on the map."

We laugh again. Damn, I don't care what Eric had in mind. I'm not going to start liking this man.

Tom puts a hand on my elbow. "As much as fun as this is, want to get out for a little while? Take a walk and get some air?"

I hesitate. Maybe I'm being overly prudish. Tom doesn't have to be single for me to join him for a walk. On the other hand, there's the problem of where that walk could lead.

"Look, I'm a lawyer. I like to get my facts up front. Does that ring mean anything?"

Tom looks at the smooth band and self-consciously twists it around on his finger. "Yes, it means a lot. But if you're asking whether I'm married, the answer is not anymore. I'm a widower."

I'm suddenly embarrassed at having been so blunt. "I'm so sorry," I sputter, apologizing both for my question and his loss in the same meager sentence.

"Thanks. It hasn't been easy. Eric's been a good friend. He makes time for our fly-fishing trips and checks in a lot. Harasses me, I might say," he adds with a little smile.

"Did you lose your wife recently?"

"Five years ago. That's when I moved upstate to focus on raising our children, get all of us away from the city and all the memories."

"How are the kids doing?"

"Amazingly well. They're happy and I love being with them. Unfortunately, they grow up. My second child went off to college this year."

"Mine, too," I say.

"A big change, isn't it? I can't spend every weekend going to soccer games and swim meets anymore. I guess it's time to get back into the real world."

"If you call dating the real world," I laugh.

"And I'm not very good at it. For example, I'm standing here with a beautiful woman, and all I can think to offer her is some fresh air."

"Well, you already gave me fifteen dollars," I say, thinking of the cabbie.

"You're a lawyer. Fifteen dollars only buys me a minute and a half of your time."

"Let's make the most of it," I say.

As we step outside, I give a little shiver, and Tom takes off his tuxedo jacket and drapes it over my shoulders. Rescuing me again— which, as Bellini pointed out, is kind of nice.

We stroll along the pier, talking animatedly about our children. In short order, I find out that Tom is an internist and has spent the last few years working quietly in a small practice as a country doctor. Now he's thinking about moving back to the city and accepting a teaching job he's been offered at Columbia Medical Center.

"I'm finally ready for a fresh start," he says.

"It's funny, our kids are supposed to be the ones with their whole lives in front of them, but I'm feeling ready for anything."

"Me, too. It's a good way to feel," says Tom, steering me up some steps.

We go inside, but I haven't been paying attention, and instead of returning to the party, we seem to be in a different part of Chelsea Piers.

"Do you like bowling?" Tom asks with a mischievous grin.

"I haven't tried since I was about twelve," I say, wondering how my eight thousand-dollar dress will look with bowling shoes.

A few minutes later, I find out.

"I think the silver and green shoes are very becoming," says Tom, smiling as I stand up in my rented size eights. It feels good to be out of my high heels, no matter what I'm wearing.

"Bowling's a lot different than I remember," I say, looking around the alley, which seems more like a disco than a sports center. Rap music is playing and a fog machine is pumping out atmospheric clouds of wispy smoke. Instead of unflattering fluorescents, the alley has black lights and Day-Glo-painted pins.

Tom takes my ball off the rack and I go to the line, trying to mimic the classic bowler's one-handed form. But the ball's a little too heavy and my dress a little too tight for any fancy maneuvers. So holding the fifteen pounds of solid ceramic in both hands, I bend over, drop it on the lane, and give it a little shove. The ball ambles slowly down the center of the smooth alley.

"Strike!" calls Tom delightedly, as the pins all drop and the scoreboard starts flashing.

"Beginner's luck," I say, strutting back to him.

On Tom's turn, he releases the ball with great style, and it starts promisingly down the middle, then careens precariously over to the edge of the gutter. One pin down. Second try produces the same result.

"Not your fault. It's hard to bowl in a bow tie," I say encouragingly, when Tom comes back.

"Don't patronize me, ye ballgown-clad woman who got the strike."

"A strike," I say with a shrug. "Nobody wants to get a strike in baseball. Nobody wants a labor union to go on strike. Who decided a strike was the best in bowling, anyway?"

"I have no idea. Maybe the same person who decided we should strike a deal or strike up the band."

In the next frame, our fortunes reverse. Tom manages a spare but the best I can do is throw two gutter balls.

"I guess I'm the all-or-nothing type," I say, looking at my score on the overhead electronic board.

"You definitely deserve to have it all," Tom says, putting his arm around me.

"I do," I say, and then going for it all, I lean in and give him a light kiss.

Tom looks delighted. "If you like a woman, take her bowling. That's what I'm going to teach my son," he says, flashing me his dimpled smile.

"Not standard advice, but it's working for me," I admit.

We look at each other, wondering what will happen next. And, sure enough, something does. Tom's cell phone rings. He looks at the number.

"I wonder what Hamilton wants," he says as he takes the call. Tom listens for a moment then snaps his phone shut and grabs my hand.

"Hamilton's in a panic. Emergency. They need a doctor. Eric's choking on something."

"Probably a hot dog," I say, figuring that Eric probably doesn't know how to chew anything but caviar.

We dash out of the bowling alley and we're halfway down the pier before I realize that I'm not having any trouble running.

"I'm still in my bowling shoes," I say in surprise.

"Shoot, you're right," says Tom, who's also in his. He looks down briefly. "We'll have to exchange them later. We don't have time right now."

Holding hands, we run back to Pier 60 in what must be record time. When we get there, Eric is lying on the floor, with a crowd gathered and a beautiful woman practically lying on top of him. Bellini.

Tom rushes over and kneels beside his best friend Eric, whose eyes are wide open. He looks fine and happy. I kneel next to my best friend, who looks even happier.

"Everything's under control," Bellini says looking up from her position hovered over Eric. She turns back to her patient and presses her lips against his, then turns away, presses, turns away, presses.

"What are you doing?" asks Dr. Tom.

"Eric was choking, so first I did the Heimlich," explains Bellini calmly. "And once he was okay, I laid him down to do some mouth-to-mouth resuscitation."

"Good work on the Heimlich, but I'm not sure you need to do mouth-to-mouth," says Tom, gently pulling Bellini back.

Grinning, Eric half sits up and reaches for Bellini—his new medical practitioner of choice. "She definitely needs to do that. I've never felt better in my life."

Tom laughs and we all stand up. "Come on, Eric, give me five minutes to check you out. Then you and Bellini can get back to playing doctor."

The two men walk away and Bellini and I look cheerfully after them.

"You better watch out. Eric's a pain in the neck," I say fondly. "Demanding and self-centered."

"Also good-looking, rich, and a great kisser."

"True, but he's arrogant."

"Boldly confident," parries Bellini.

"Never available."

"Not the clingy type who gets on your nerves."

I laugh. "I give up. You two are a perfect match."

Bellini gives me a hug. "You don't mind if I take your old boyfriend?"

"Of course not. I'm ready for a new one."

I look up and see Tom Shepard, warm-hearted, supportive, and sexy, walking toward me. His head is slightly down, and I notice him slide off his old wedding ring, hold it in his palm for a moment, and then discreetly tuck it into his pocket.

"Any lingering regrets about all the men you didn't marry?" Bellini asks me, watching Eric as he heads her way.

I shake my head. "I've finally realized you can't go back. All you can do is move forward."

Tom comes up next to me. I think for a moment about how much fun we've had tonight and all we still have to discover about each other.

I can't begin to guess what the future will be. Maybe twenty years from now, I'll look back and remember him affectionately as a man I didn't marry. Maybe I won't think of him at all. Or maybe I'll be waking up next to him in bed every morning, blissfully content.

Tom holds out a hand to me. "May I have the first dance?" he asks.

"Of course," I say. I smile to myself, realizing that if you let yourself, you really do learn from the past. A few short months ago, I would have hemmed and hawed and made excuses about how I have two left feet. But now I just add, "Though maybe we should get our real shoes back first."

"Absolutely not," says Bellini, the arbiter of the au courant, as Eric reaches for her hand. "Ballgowns and bowling shoes. I love it. You two could be starting a whole new trend."

We all laugh and I slip into Tom's arms to glide across the dance floor. A trend? Probably not. But with any luck, we'll start something a little longer lasting.

Between them, JANICE KAPLAN and LYNN SCHNURNBERGER have lived in three countries, raised three children, and published nine books—including the bestselling novels *Mine Are Spectacular!* and *The Botox Diaries*. They've produced hundreds of hours of network television shows and written articles for just about every women's magazine in America. Both have appeared regularly on television shows including *The Oprah Winfrey Show, Good Morning America,* and *Today*. Each is happily married and living in New York. Visit their website: www.janiceandlynn.com

ITC Berkeley Oldstyle, designed in 1983 by Tony Stan, is a variation of the University of California Old Style, which was created by Frederick Goudy. While capturing the feel and traits of its predecessor, ITC Berkeley Old Style shows influences from Kennerly, Goudy Old Style, Deepdene, and Booklet Oldstyle, all of which were also designed by Goudy. It is characterized by its calligraphic weight stress, and its x-height, now described as classic, is smaller than most other ITC designs of the day. The generous ascenders and descenders provide variations in text color, easy legibility, and an overall inviting appearance.